The Light
at the End of the World

A story of spiritual transformation
in a time of catastrophic change

Dear June,
Good luck on your move.
Happy reading! Thanks,

Lorraine Dopson

Lorraine Dopson

To June,
Best Wishes!
love,
Jennifer Wood

ANGEL FIRE PRESS

Published by Angel Fire Press
P.O. Box 7374
Bismarck, ND 58501-7374

Story Illustrations by Lorraine Dopson
Map Illustration by Julia O'Reilly
Cave Drawings by Mike Bruner
Book Design by Eva Long
Book Cover Design by Ferguson Design

Library of Congress Cataloging-in-Publication Data

Dopson, Lorraine,
The Light at the End of the World:
a novel / by Lorraine Dopson
LCCN 2002102059
ISBN 0-9712123-0-9

This work is dedicated to the Sophia Foundation of North America, whose home is in Eugene, Oregon. I'm happy to have found you.

ACKNOWLEDGMENTS

One is helped by many people over the course of five years. Correne, the massage therapist who kept my carpal tunnel problems manageable. Carol, the cleaning woman who dug out the house once a week. My dear friend Wanda, who tenderly read my manuscript in its early stage. And wonderful Ann, with her sustained faith in me. Thanks to my husband, neurologist Richard Arazi, for his generous support. Richard was able to find typos long after I insisted that all were gone. How he relished that job! My appreciation also to Alex, our teenage son and resident computer expert. I'm grateful as well for Comet, Aurora, and Gingerbread, the brown dogs who took turns sitting by my feet for hours at a time.

My sincere thanks goes as well to the handful of scholars whom I will never know, but whose vision inspired this work. Each is mentioned in the Epilog.

And finally, thanks to Eva Long, my editor and book designer. Eva took my naked manuscript, shaped and nurtured it, and prepared it for its birth. Her expertise, generosity, and friendship have been vital to the success of this endeavor.

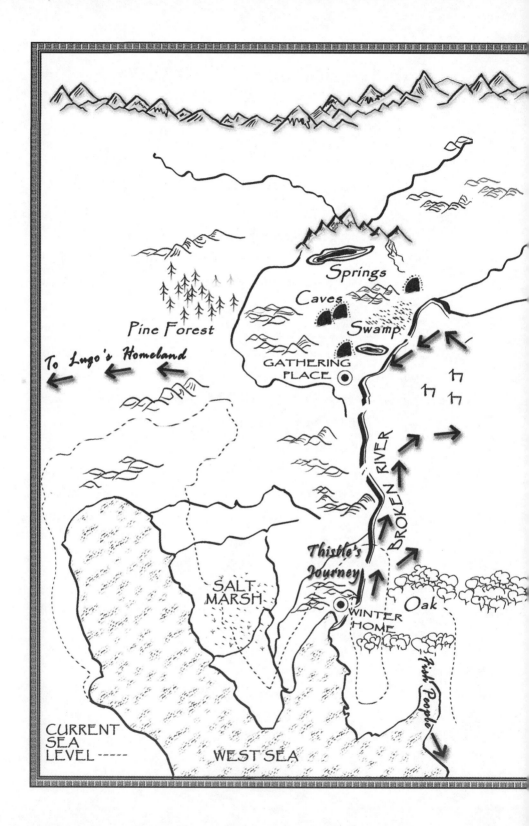

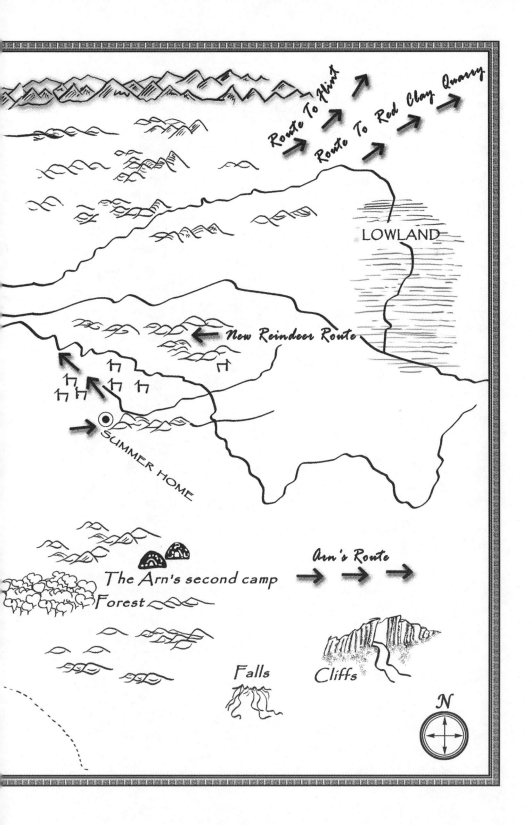

Route To Flint

Route To Red Clay Quarry

LOWLAND

New Reindeer Route

SUMMER HOME

The Arn's second camp

Forest

Arn's Route

Falls

Cliffs

N

Characters

Name	Sex, Age	Archetype
Thistle	female, 11	Changer (Idealist)
Silka	female, 12	Golden Child
Birch	female, 8	Nourishing Mother
Reen	male, 11	Communicator
Berry	male, 9	Soul Father
Leu	male, 10	Artist-Priest
Rube	male, 12	Warrior
Fire	male, 3	Warrior and Golden Child
Zale	male infant	Warrior
Tenja	female, 24	Warrior and Mystic
Ephus	male, 30	Teacher-Traveler
Magla	female, 28	(Thistle's mother) Elder Leader
Ochre	male, 26	Warrior and Nourishing Father
Litva	female, 32	(Reen's mother) Nourishing Mother
Bakar	male, 34	(Reen's father) Warrior
Frightened Eyes	female, 23	Mystic
Yarrow	female, 25	Elder Leader and Warrior
Zalec	male, 24	(Yarrow's partner) Warrior
Idra	female, 40	Teacher-Traveler
Zlatar	male, 45	Idealist and Warrior

Sela	female, 44	(Thistle's grandmother) Elder Leader
Otok	male, 46	Warrior
Thought Holder	male, 48	Warrior and Mystic
Lida	female, 42	Nourishing Mother & Artist
Ivy	female, 38	Artist-Priestess
Gokihar	male infant	Warrior & Idealist
Narta	female infant	Golden Child & Mystic

~Children who would have been ages five to seven died in infancy.~

The Arn (principals)
| Andor | male, 28 | Artist-Priest |
| Anish | male, 14 | Lover |

The Fish People
| Ziva | female, 35 | Mystic |
| Belov | male, 13 | Golden Child |

The West People
Eda	female, 46	Elder Leader
Lugo	male, 26	Artist-Priest
Vasto	male, 24	Warrior

The Bull People
| Konya | female, 28 | Teacher-Traveler |

Earthmaker's Symbols

Term	Symbol	Related meanings
Earthmaker	Y	tree, roots, support
Male	Λ	rise, reach, outward
Female	V	contain, protect, inward
Wisdom	◇	outward and inward together
Dream	◈	power, Earthmaker's Eye
Mountains	M	MMMMMM = range
Water	W	WWWWW = sea
Bowl or cup	U	food, feed
Reindeer, grazer	h	hhhhhh = herd
Path	<<< or >>>	travel, leave
Day	O	OOOOOO = six days
Night	●	●●●●●● = six nights
Person	I	IIIIII = many people
Death	X	XXXXXX = many deaths

Moon Months

Time of the Great Tree ~ Summer Solstice

The Ripening of Fruit

Month of the Fat Deer

The Storing of Food

Return to the Sea

The Gathering of Fish

The Great Darkness ~ Winter Solstice

When the Babies Cry from Hunger

The Waiting

The Melting

Time of the Reindeer Calves

Journey to the High Meadow

The Gathering of Medicine

Contents

Part 1
The People of the Mother

Part 2
She Who Walks Alone

Part 3
Children of the Twilight

Introduction

"We are ourselves plus our environment," wrote Spanish philosopher Ortega ý Gasset. This is a book about a woman and her people, about consciousness and catastrophe and the relationship between the two. Though the story could have unfolded in many places, I chose to set it in Eastern Europe, the longest continuous site of human habitation on the European continent.

Who were the people living in Eastern Europe around 10,000 B.C.? They were most likely descendants of African immigrants who had crossed a land bridge between the two continents more than 35,000 years ago. Dark-haired, dark-eyed Caucasoids, they were modern humans in brain size and general appearance. Like their relatives for hundreds of generations, they were tribal people, gatherers and hunters whose distinguishing characteristic was not brute force, but emerging mind. Adaptive and creative, they followed the reindeer, nurtured their children and Old Ones, and expressed the ancient archetypes that remain the bedrock of consciousness. Unfortunately for them, they lived during a time of rapid, even violent, climatic change. Geological, botanical, zoological, and mythological records point to a major earth disturbance around 9600 B.C. As people of the Late Paleolithic went out to explore their icy Eden, perhaps a few of them sensed that their world was about to change—that the mountains, seas, and shores which cradled them would be transformed, that coastal communities would disappear like sand towers at high tide, and that a remembrance of terror would again be planted in the human soul.

That disturbance and its devastating impact is the subject of this work.

Part 1

The People of the Mother

The Mother of Songs, the mother of our whole seed, bore us in the beginning. She is the mother of all races of men and the mother of all tribes. She is the mother of the thunder, the mother of the rivers, the mother of trees and of all kinds of things. She is the mother of songs and dances. She is the mother of the older brother stones. She is the mother of the grain and the mother of all things. She is the mother of the younger brother Frenchmen and of all the temples, and the only mother we have. She is the mother of the animals, the only one, and the mother of the Milky Way. It was the mother herself who began to baptize. She gave us the limestone coca dish. She is the mother of the rain, the only one we have. She alone is the mother of things, she alone. And the mother has left a memory in all the temples. With her sons, the saviors, she left songs and dances as a reminder. Thus the priests, the fathers, and the older brothers have reported.

Song of the Kagaba Indians, Colombia
from *The Great Mother*, Erich Neumann, 1991

Winter's End

Spirit, come to me. Answer the prayer of a woman now old, but one who remembers what it was like to be a girl, when all of life unfolded before me like a ripple on an endless sea. One who remembers the laughter of friends, high rivers of blue ice, stars slowly turning, the quivering flanks of the grazers, the blood scream of the big cats, the clear, cold howl of wolves, and the world before the Change.

As it once was for me, change is now upon you. Not the same as ours. Change, all the same. I tell my story through one of your people —this woman who makes words with her hands. I will tell you what I recall. Perhaps some good will come of that.

My eyes see little now of the outside world, but I remember that it was beautiful. I am the one they called She Who Walks Alone. My people left little that you can remember us by, but this you should remember: My blood runs in your veins.

I begin my story with the melting of snow, the time I loved the best. Each year at our winter camp came a morning when we awakened to a slow, steady dripping outside. Once again, Sun had set the ice free and we were free as well, stretching, running, breathing deeply, no longer prisoners of the cold. Soon we'd wrap our bundles and hike to the high country, to the place where long ago, in the time before remembering, Earthmaker had once told us: *This mountain is your home.*

In my twelfth year they called me by my child name, Thistle. I was born in the summer, when those rough, purple-headed plants bloomed. Thistle was a proud name and the name of a healer. From the plant's veins came a milky tonic. If children ate bad mushrooms or Old Ones held poisons in their bodies, they drank the juice of the thistle. Each summer, I picked the round, purple heads and strung them on a loop to wear around my neck. There were white thistles, too, but I only picked the purple ones. Silka, who was close in age to me, though shorter, and sometimes my friend, said I was given my name because I was rough and scratched other children. But Silka was often mistaken.

Like all who walk on two legs, we needed the animals and went where they led. Each autumn, we followed the reindeer down from the high mountain meadows and back to our winter home, a small cave close to the sea. The cave was made of the same rough, white stone that formed all the hills nearby. The People scraped their heads when they stood quickly and the Old Ones were cranky as winter dragged on, but the cave kept us dry. During the long winters, Silka and I hollowed out holes in the soft walls to store things. Someone had dug a basin for drinking water long ago. On winter nights, I sat with the others just inside the entryway, sheltered by a wall of hides and an overhanging rock that kept back the wind and protected the fire. And there we waited, long after Sun had left us and Wind reclaimed the shore, listening to the smash of waves on rocks, the rough breathing of Old Ones, the whimper of babies, the hiss of rain on the flickering fire, the yelp of a distant coyote, and the wind itself, welcoming us to something immense.

"THISTLE, STOP DREAMING!" Magla's voice found me and brought me back.

"What?" I looked up at my mother, her black hair pulled back from her stern face. The day of the melting had come. Tiny streams of melted snow snaked outside the cave. By midmorning the once-frozen ground had turned to mud. I'd gone outside with Silka, feeling as light as the shine on the running water. The Mothers had been clearing out the cave since dawn. Those Who Serve the Mother, that being the name we called the men once hair grew on their faces, had left to find their traps and pull in the fishing lines. My brother dug holes in the mud and floated sticks in the puddles, while Silka and I admired our reflections in a silver pool, this being a day I liked her.

My mother had swooped over to us like a bird of prey, as was her habit. Of all the People, Magla was the best at breaking camp, strong and quick, never resting until the work was done. She wore her new tunic, just like the one she'd sewn for me, made from two soft reindeer hides held together by antler pins. Her sleeves were pushed back, freeing her short, strong arms. I glanced up at her narrow nose and sharp eyes, imagining she was a hawk. She crossed her arms as she spoke. "You girls find Birch. Then come help me. Earthmaker commands our journey. This is no time for games."

"Beak nose," Silka whispered, covering her mouth with a delicate hand. The hairs on the back of my neck prickled.

Magla glared. "What did you say?"

Silka's voice when she answered was like ripe fruit. She looked up at my mother with wide, dark eyes, speaking gently. " 'Because.' I said 'because.' I was explaining to Thistle that we have to help, because we're leaving."

"Thank you, Silka," Magla replied. Just then, shy Birch emerged from the shadows. She sat down quickly, as if it hurt to be seen. Birch was younger than Silka and me, but we played with her because she did what we said. Nodding at the newcomer, Magla continued, "Go get the hides and the ties I cut. Take the old hides off the babies' feet and wrap new coverings. Don't tie them too tight."

Magla scanned the beach, looking for idle hands. Silka jumped to her feet. The only time the girl moved quickly was under Magla's watchful eye. She turned to me, a slender hand on her hip. "Thistle," she asked, "aren't you coming?"

Birch picked up the hides and we walked toward the little ones. There were three babies now: Zale, born that winter to Yarrow; and the older two, already big enough to walk. One of them we called Fire, our best baby and also my brother. No babies had died this winter. Silka and I fetched the two older ones from the mud and Birch lifted Zale from the pouch on his mother's back. Fire squirmed and kicked, but when I finally wrapped the new hide around his feet, he ran about waving his arms and laughing. We'd made new boots for ourselves already, cutting the soles from elk hide, stitching fur to the heavy sides, and binding them with leather strips. I went back to Magla, who was with the other Mothers, shaking out our bedding.

"We're done," I said.

"All right. Pack the salt fish. See if Fire's hungry." I turned to go. "Don't forget the fire stones!" she called after me.

My mother became excited whenever it was time to move our camp. I didn't mind the work. The melting came quickly and we had to be fast as well. Between us and the mountains was a wide expanse of flatland. Frozen like stone all winter, it became a giant marsh each spring. If we started late, we'd have to wade across it surrounded by clouds of biting insects. I called to Birch and we went to feed the two older babies, giving them bits of salted fish, dried apples, and water. I was sick of fish. Birch sat with the children while I headed back to the cave for the fire stones. Silka had disappeared, probably slipping away the moment Magla's back was turned. Silka could carry the fire stones this year, I thought. I'd always done it before.

The sky was bright. The Mothers were already rolling up our bundles, a sign we were almost ready. I stepped into the empty cave and let my eyes adjust to the darkness. Then I stopped and patted the ground, looking for any of the heavy iron stones we might have left behind. We'd need them for our fires during the damp nights ahead.

"Watch out!" someone snapped. I lurched and almost fell. "Be careful! You're stepping on them," Silka said. She  sat far in the back of the cave, surrounded by the pile of conch shells she'd been gathering all winter. Usually she stored them in a tunnel she'd burrowed into the soft stone. Now they lay around her, glowing faintly in the soft half light.

"What are you doing here?" I asked. "Everyone else is working."

"Counting my shells."

"Come on then. We're ready to go. You can't take them with you."

"I'm not done," she said, turning her back.

I glanced around once more for the fire rocks and left. Most of the Mothers had hoisted their bundles and were ambling to the shore. Those Who Serve paced along the beach, loaded with their tools and nets, eager to leave. Magla stooped over two bulging food bags, checking the ties on the salted fish and the remains of last autumn's nuts and dried fruit. She lashed the final one and rose slowly. "Have you seen Silka?" she asked.

It would serve the foolish girl right to be left behind, I thought. "She's coming," I replied. "She said I should take Fire and she'd take the food pack and the fire stones, since she carried nothing last year." My mother would put an end to Silka's foolishness. No one else would try to bring along a bag of shells and make someone else carry all the food. I grabbed my brother's hand and ran to catch up with the others. Like bears we were, I thought, looking at the group that stood on the shore. Our heads shaggy, our bodies stiff, our bellies hungry for berries and fresh meat. Spring!

The journey would take eight days. We'd follow the coast a short way south then turn east at the river and go inland, walking fast the first day, not stopping until we cleared the lowland. It wasn't only the insects that would make us hurry. We were eager for the deer. They wintered to the south of us, eating the sparse grass beyond the frost line, then heading north once their babies were born. The men had seen fresh hoof prints in the meadow, telling us the deer were on their way.

Fire tried to pull away from me, wanting to follow the older boys as they scrambled across the rocks at the shoreline and jumped back from the surf. What was keeping Magla and Silka? To pass the time, I sat on the ground and pulled Fire into my lap, telling him all I could remember of the reindeer and their young.

Sometimes, in warm years, the deer left their winter home early and gathered near the sea, feeding on seaweed and escaping the insects as the mother animals waited for their time, finally giving birth along our rocky beach. Silka and I had seen them once, the babies. We'd hidden in the dry grass and watched as the newborn deer dropped wet and weak to the ground. They'd struggled to their feet to nurse, tails wagging and eyes open wide. Tawny white they were, with dark markings, strong enough to travel in a few days. The newborns' legs could take them far, though we knew many would never finish the trip, dragged down by wolves with babies of their own.

Like us, the deer would hurry through the marshes. Some years we were close enough to watch them as they moved along in a great brown sea, warm breath rising like mist in the morning, the herds surging upward toward tender meadows rimmed by familiar peaks. There they'd join the other grazers: elk, ibex, bison, and the red aurochs with the curving horns. We'd soon find them in the high country, just south of the Ice Mountains. No traveler, whether grazer, cat, or human, could ever go beyond that ridge of fog-hidden, jagged peaks.

I glanced back again at the cave. Finally, Silka was making her way down to us, plodding behind Magla. My mother seemed unencumbered by her large food pouch, but Silka bent low under her load. The fire stone pouch dragged at her feet as if she carried a boulder, while two misshapen bags bounced at her hips. I was glad to see she carried a food bag. I'd be free this year.

Magla looked around to see if everyone was finally there. Satisfied, she nodded to Yarrow. Yarrow gave a signal and with a great heave and sigh we were off. I skipped along with Fire, telling him tales of the wonders we'd see, the country, the creatures, the memories. Not until we reached the river did I remember Silka. I glanced back to see her staggering along the beach at the back of the group, the food pack lurching from side to side. "Fire," I said, "slow down. Let's wait."

We stepped aside to let the others pass, while Silka plodded toward us. Silka had belonged to the Grandmothers ever since her parents died in a rockslide. But we all kept an eye on her. She made me angry, but never for long. Whenever I tried to be mean to her, I ended up pitying her instead. She stopped a man-length away and stared at the ground. I looked at the two odd pouches at her sides. "Silka, what's in those bags?"

She looked up, tears streaming down her dusty face. Her upper lip quivered. "You know," she replied.

I hadn't planned to take the food pack, but I loaded it on my back. "Go on," I said, waving her by. "Catch up with the others." I trudged behind, holding Fire's hand, watching Silka's delicate feet pick their way over the stones, the two bulky pouches bouncing on her hips and the fire stones dragging behind. Everyone was waiting for us when we reached the river.

We took our usual places, toward the middle, with the Old Ones and the children. Those Who Serve and the Mothers were both in front and behind, Yarrow and her man Zalec in the lead. Then we headed out, as many people as the fingers on six hands, from the great sea, along the swollen river, across a low meadow on a thin path made by deer, toward the greening slopes and the glint of mountain snow. Our winter legs loosened. Small clusters of aspens, brightening buttercups, and ponds jumping with fish welcomed us on our way. Later that day we began to climb, scrambling over rough ground made of the same white stone as the beach. Sponge stone we called it, full of holes and coarse like sponge from the sea.

By midmorning of the third day, we'd left the foothills and our path as well. My feet were blistering, having grown soft in the winter. My calf muscles burned and my ankles wobbled. Magla must have looked back to check on us and noticed I was limping.

"Thistle, stop!" she called, then came weaving through the group.

Everyone else halted as well, dropping their packs. No one was ever left behind. The countryside was hungry. "Let me see your feet," she demanded, as if I'd stolen them. I pulled off my pack, sat on the ground, and removed my boots. She shook her head, made a clicking sound with her tongue, and pulled a long strip of hide from her bag, wrapping an extra layer around my feet. "Stay off the rocks. I mean it," she said. "I'll put ointment on them tonight." She turned to go, then added, "Silka, you carry the pack." We began our climb.

We'd come upon the roughest part of the trip. Gentle slopes gave way to deep ravines. Swift streams, fed by melted snow, cut through the hillsides. Fire began to whine and I sent him to the front with Magla, who hoisted him onto her hip. But if the country was hard, it was also familiar. I remembered the lake at the top of the next rise and the range of mountains beyond it. Notched in those peaks was the narrow pass that would take us home. I forgot all about my sore feet and looked back for Silka. She'd fallen behind and Ochre had stopped to wait for her. I dropped back and grabbed her arm.

"Silka, hurry up, come on. Everyone will start looking at you," I said, pulling her along. Silka was both lazy and proud. Sometimes I found just the right words to make her do what I wanted. She grimaced, but quickened her pace. Up we traveled, along a milky green stream that burst into foam at the boulders in its way, past huge rocks strewn over the hillside like moss-headed giants. Hoarse crows called, surprised by humans after a winter alone. Still we climbed, the cool air misty, a distant waterfall thundering up ahead. Finally, weary and hungry, we made it to a level place part way up the hill and stopped for the night.

Silka dropped the pack and I plopped down next to her, then unwrapped my burning feet and stuck them in the stream. The skin was worn away in three places, one red circle half the size of my heel. Magla would come looking for me soon, I knew, and I wouldn't have to do any work that night. In a little while, I heard the crunch of feet on stones. Magla crouched beside me.

"Here, give me your feet," she said, shaking the water from my right one and looking at the blisters. She lathered on a cool paste made of bear fat and crushed willow. "Stay off your feet for tonight. Silka, you can take care of Fire and make Thistle's bed," Magla ordered. Then she went to see about supper. Silka glared at me. I sat back and surveyed the country below.

Sparse pines covered the rough stone hills we'd just crossed. Further down, in the sheltered places, larch and alder leaves were beginning to unfold in the lengthening sunlight, while white and yellow flowers dotted the slope. The little alpine plant we called star flower would be opening soon. I smiled and listened to the sounds of other people working.

The sky was clear, so no one put up a lean-to. We just stretched out on our sleeping hides and gnawed the rest of the burbot, a long river fish we dried each summer and ate all year. Tomorrow we'd cross the high mountain pass and clamber down to the valley on the other side, the hardest part of the journey behind us. We were almost home.

On our seventh day of walking, we came to the forest I remembered well. We were close now. All that separated us from home was the wide meadow before us. Across the open country, wedged between two high peaks, was our home. Even from a distance, we knew the place easily, the caves on the mountainside standing forth like the sockets of two huge, black eyes. My own eyes burned when I saw them.

The young children ran ahead, as I'd once done, crying, "It's there! I see it! It's there!"

"Wait!" cried Yarrow. The grass eaters weren't the only ones who ran here. "Quiet."

Yarrow was sister to Magla and our leader for journeys. A strong, quiet woman, she told us things without speaking, for she was *Acha*, one to whom Earthmaker spoke. Her baby asleep on her back, she studied the silence and the wind. Tilting her head, she closed her eyes and sniffed. Black hair curled on her sweaty forehead, which was lined from years in the sun. Yarrow had been taught the ways of animals by Thought Holder, an old man once given to us by Earthmaker to keep us safe. It made me happy to watch her.

The People stood together, faces toward the wind, the eyes of the small children huge. Yarrow sniffed again and turned to Zalec, her man and our best hunter. "Aurochs?" she asked. He nodded. The dank odor of the grazers hovered on the breeze. Great herds of the red creatures lumbered through this valley, their flesh tender, but their curving horns lethal. They weren't our concern today.

"Lions?" she questioned him again. Zalec shook his head. He was a listener and rarely talked, his thoughts always on the ways of animals. He spoke mostly with his kind brown eyes. Since their baby had come to them this year in the winter cave, Zalec watched even more closely.

No scent of cats, it seemed. Maybe they'd followed the grazers farther up the meadow. The lions didn't surprise us often. We traveled in the bright sun, when the cats dozed and licked the bones of their prey. But we knew never to be by ourselves in the cool of the morning or at night. Once a cat saw a human alone, that human was gone. Glancing around one more time, we stepped into the open country.

Yarrow was still alert, sniffing the air for another smell. After lions, I most feared the boars. They hid in the tall grass, the male digging, snorting, waiting. If a boar heard us, it charged, gouging with its tusks, cutting and throwing and cutting again. Not because it was hungry, just angry we were there. It was a boar that took my sister Narta four years ago, took her and trampled her before the hunters came. Sometimes when I slept, I smelled that boar, saw his short, stiff hair and his small black eyes. Sometimes when I was awake, I watched for him, my belly like ice. I followed Yarrow's glance to the freshly torn ground and the dig marks of a boar's sharp feet.

Yarrow motioned the young ones to move to the middle of the group. Those Who Serve moved to the outside, their spears ready. The Mothers clenched their knives. I hated the boars and rarely ate them. Yarrow said they belonged here, but I hated them anyway.

We moved quietly into the tall grass. It was last winter's dead brown grass, noisy beneath our feet. The swish of our legs blended with the breeze, soft as a breath on our faces. The sun was bright. Small gnats followed us, their buzz louder than the rustle of our feet. We moved like a small wind through the meadow, ruffling the stiff grass. It closed behind us and hid our passage. As we walked, I repeated with my footsteps, "It cannot find us, it cannot find us, it cannot find us." Someday I would like to kill a boar. We didn't see any that day.

By the time we crossed the open grassland, the sun was at our backs. We'd spend the night at the foot of our mountain and tomorrow climb over the boulders and go home. I sat down to unwrap my feet and knead my sore legs. My body was small enough that I could still be a child, but my thoughts told me I should work. I lay down to listen to these two voices inside me. When I awoke, Magla was telling us the food was ready.

I smelled rabbits roasting. Looking around, I noticed Silka smashing walnuts on a stone in the middle of camp, her face framed by graceful braids and lit by the afternoon sun. Silka did no good thing unless someone was watching. Sometimes I liked to leave my own work undone, to give her a chance to show her goodness to others.

I stood up and limped over to her. "So you found the pouches we hid last fall," I said, reaching for a few.

Her slender hands covered the bowl. "These are for the People," she said. "You'll have to wait."

"But I'm the one who picked them, while you slept under a tree."

"No one likes you when you're cranky, Thistle," she murmured.

Next spring I'd be the one to find the stashed walnuts. I'd crack them outside of camp, not under everyone's feet. Tonight I wouldn't even eat any, not until everyone else had some first.

"Come and eat," Magla called.

I was too happy to let Silka bother me for long. This was the night we celebrated our journey's end. We'd stay awake and watch the stars, laugh and talk, feed the fire and hear stories. "Silka," I called, as she laid the pouch of shelled nuts by the meat, "sit by me." I huddled between Birch and Silka, pulling my tunic close about me in the cool night, and laughing at the boys when the wind blew smoke in their faces.

Those Who Serve threw more wood on the fire. The damp logs smoked for a while, then crackled and burned. We talked about the journey, the sky lit by flecks of starlight and a little strip of moon. The faces of the People shone around the soft, dancing flames and the fire warmed me. This was the time I loved best of all, the time the Grand-mothers spoke.

There were four Grandmothers now, though last year there had been six. The Mothers could become Grandmothers after they'd loved children for a very long time and knew all the stories of the People. Idra winked at me. She was the best of the Grandmothers. I hoped she'd tell my favorite story. She smiled at me and began:

There have always been the Grandmothers. We were with the animals for a very long time. We followed and ate the meat when the cats were done. We did not know the Mystery but we watched. At night we lay awake. We saw the Light in a Circle, the Light that grows and disappears. We saw it and we saw it, the light we call the Moon. We saw that it took as long to grow large as to become small again. We saw it when there was no baby in us. We saw it when the baby grew inside us. We saw it when the baby came out. We saw the pattern. We told Those Who Serve. We made the marks on the bones.

We made one mark for each darkness and called the darkness Night. We made one mark for each time our bodies bled. We saw that our bodies bled once each time the moon grew large. We saw that if we did not bleed when the moon changed, we had a baby inside us. We made the mark on the bone each time the moon grew large. When we made nine marks, we knew it was time for the baby to be born.

We made these marks many times. We did it many times. Then we knew the Mystery. We knew the mystery of numbers and of change. We knew the pattern and the flow. We knew it not just in our bodies, but in our thinking. We knew not just what had come before, but what was to come in the future. Our knowing changed us. For then we were separate from the animals. No longer did we just live in fullness and die. We had become separate from the animals. We had become The Ones Who Watch. We had become The Ones Who Watch and Earthmaker looked upon us in a new way.

The story was over for tonight. We sat quietly, leaning against each other. Wolf was calling to her friends in the distance. Earth was so huge, I thought. I loved Her, but sometimes She frightened me. It was good to have the People. The fire burned down to red coals and we were too sleepy to stare at it longer. Those Who Serve moved to the outside of the circle, protecting us. Some would lie awake and listen in the darkness. Some would join with the Mothers. Some would pull their robes around themselves and sleep. The Mothers smoothed out a place for the babies and laid them close to each other, like pups in a den. The darkness covered us like a robe full of stars. The People sighed and stretched and pulled their robes tight. Our bellies were full and we slept.

The People

"WAKE UP!" MAGLA SHOOK MY SHOULDER and daylight greeted me too soon. The camp had come awake. Those Who Serve had left already, climbing the steep hill to clear out any other creatures before we arrived. Bears stayed in our caves some winters, digging shallow holes and curling up in them while the ledge filled with snow and the wind raged. The bears were usually gone when we returned, though the men had found a dead one four years ago. The stench lasted all summer. I ate some dried apples and rolled up my pack.

"You're slow today." It was Reen. I jumped at the sound of his voice. Reen, the best of all the boys, the fastest runner, the one who made me things. The one who'd carved the shells for my necklace, shiny purple discs with holes in the center. I was happy when he was near, glad I wouldn't have to find a man from outside. The morning was warm and he wore a short summer tunic, freeing his long, brown legs. A line of black hairs had appeared beneath his nose.

"Race you to the top," I called, forgetting about my blisters.

He just smiled and shook his head. Then, catching me unaware,

18

he said, "Go!" and ran ahead. We clambered over the rocks and I grabbed his ankle long enough to slow him down.

I lurched ahead and would have won, but a voice behind me called, "Sissle, Sissle!" I stopped and looked back. My brother, Fire, had made it part way up the hill. Now he stood on the grassy slope, wobbling on his short, fat legs and crying. Reen raced past me. I headed back down. Fire was as plump as a badger. The fat babies hardly ever died, so I'd given him part of my food all winter. He grinned as I came closer. Tears had washed lines through the dirt on his face. I stopped beside him. This would be his third year at the summer cave.

"Get on my back," I said, feeling his small hands on my neck all the way up the hill. "Fire, we're home!" I announced as we cleared the slope and reclaimed the ledge, to be greeted by crows and long-tailed jays.

Our home. Yes. Earthmaker had told us this long ago, in the time before remembering. Here we returned each time the snow melted. I held Fire high and looked around. To the south rose a range of low mountains smooth as the flanks of fine, tan horses. Below us ran a jagged path to a meadow. Beyond the meadow flowed a river. From our height we saw the animals grazing, the animals we often watched with joy: giant deer as tall as the People's shoulders, ibex, the lumbering ox, the reindeer.

A wide ledge ran along the side of the hill. Off to one side stood a rough pine woods, to the other a brushy patch of juniper. The ledge had been cleared of brush and loose rocks long ago, probably at the same time our ancestors rolled stones around the fire circle. Two caves were set back about four man-lengths from where we stood. The smaller shelter was where we lived, its walls smooth and hard, not like the rough winter place. The large cave was cold, a foreboding place used only for storage and celebrations. I let Fire slide off my back and dropped the pack.

The men were already sharpening their spears and talking of the hunt, the women bringing order. Magla was hard at work. "Boys, get the wood," she called. "Birch, help me sweep. Thistle and Silka, bring up grass for the bedding." Home.

Back down I went to cut the fresh grass, with Silka right behind me. We'd put the grass under the sleeping hides for comfort and to keep the cave smelling fresh. Ochre had sharpened my blade before we left the sea, so the work went fast. I piled up several bundles and hauled them up the hill, stacking them outside the cave. By the fourth trip, sweat poured from my face and my heart pounded.

"Thistle, where's Silka?" Magla asked as I dropped another bundle. "You didn't leave her down there alone, did you?" Where indeed was Silka? I hadn't seen her since my first trip. I stared at my feet, waiting for a good lie. "Find her," Magla ordered.

I walked slowly down the hillside, looking back and forth. Nothing moved but the tall grass in the wind. I studied the stones that had lodged in level places. Everything was as it should be. And then I saw it, a foot protruding from behind a boulder. I crept over and slid behind the rock. "Silka, what are you doing?"

The startled girl sat up. "Hush. Don't be so rough. I'm resting."

Perhaps I'd rest, too, I decided, looking for a private spot far away from Silka. I sprawled out near a little juniper, awash in sunlight and alone with my thoughts, my eyes sweeping the valley. I doubted I'd ever have a desire to go beyond this place.

We were the People of the Mother. Earthmaker called us forth long ago and guided our ways. We were only one small group, though there were many like us. Some of them we saw at celebrations. I knew, from the stories of the Grandmothers, that the People had lived in these mountains for a time beyond measuring. This was the way it should be. The Grandmothers had told us of restless People who had no home. Sometimes travelers from distant places brought special things for trading, like the red iron stones we used for fire. Or the hunters would walk for days and bring back flint for axes and scrapers. Or they'd hike to the pits to dig the red clay for celebrations. They'd have to go east, then north, around the jagged Ice Mountains which marked the end of our home, but never farther than that. The way was passable only in the summer. Beyond those mountains lived monsters, screaming creatures with giant horns that jutted from their heads and snouts as long as legs. Ephus the Traveler told us these things.

Perhaps, to some people, the land around the summer cave was not so fine as our winter home. All that grew amid the granite and loose gravel were ragged shrubs and a few hardy pines. But Earthmaker had made places for all the People and She'd led us here. In the forest below, home to foxes and red deer, we'd pick walnuts and berries. Since the lower land was soggy in the summer and swarming with bugs, it was better to be up here, where we could watch  the grazers going about their days. We could have stayed by the sea all year, gathering shells, hauling in nets, and sleeping with the murmur of the waves. But then we'd have only eaten fish.

We even had a special place, a deep pit not too far away where we stored fresh meat and unworked hides. A treacherous place, hidden under slippery rocks, forbidden to children, always cold. The men went down into it with ropes around their bellies. Animals stayed away, though one summer Ochre found a lion in the pit, frozen where it fell. Magla had made him a beautiful coat, the mane bunched handsomely around his neck. Magla! I jumped up and hurried back up the hill.

I strode across the ledge toward the cave, trying to look as though

I'd just done a good thing. I peered inside. Silka was on her hands and knees, spreading fresh grass over the floor. Then the voice of the hawk behind me. "Thistle, you left all your work for Silka. You're not to make her do everything."

Silka smiled and brushed the hair from her face with a delicate sweep of her hand.

"I'm going with Reen to get wood," I replied, turning quickly.

I found Reen at the stand of pines, dragging out dead logs. He grinned when he saw me coming. "How's it going with you and your helper?" he asked.

"Send Rube to help Silka," I said. "I'll work with you."

Rube was a little older than Reen, but not as smart. He strutted like a young stallion and Silka laughed at everything he said. There were two other boys as well, Berry and Leu. The seven of us almost grown and the three babies were the only young ones now, the middle children having died two years ago from coughing. Everyone had been sick that winter except the babies still getting milk. All the older children recovered. The younger ones we buried by the winter camp, wrapping them in furs and covering them with stones on the frozen ground.

"Fine with me," Reen replied. So we worked side by side late into the day, piling the firewood along the wall of the big cave until it was as tall as a man and three times as long. It never seemed like work.

Three of the men returned at dusk with a red deer. The Mothers tossed more logs on the fire. I sat with Reen, needing nothing. Waiting for the meat to cook, I watched the Old One's faces. They were all with us that year, as it should be, four Grandmothers and three Grandfathers.

Some years, when the Grandparents were sick, they remained at the cave near the sea. One of us would have to stay with them, to fish and fetch water. If they got sick here, we'd have to carry them out in the fall. No one survived the mountains in winter.

I studied the lined faces of the old men sitting across from me. Thought Holder was the only Grandfather who still hunted. Stooped and thin he was, with piercing eyes. And very powerful, for he saw both worlds. He seemed warmed by some inner fire. All he ever wore, even in the winter, was a thin cloak. Thought Holder had no woman, but two of the women whose partners were gone took care of him.

Then there was Zlatar. White-eyed Zlatar was the partner of Idra, my favorite Grandmother and our best teacher. Idra had chosen Zlatar when they were young and she a woman from another group. We'd needed him to hunt, so Idra had come to live with us. Zlatar was a friendly man. Though almost blind, he still helped Idra with her teaching.

And finally Otok, my mother's father, crippled in his arms and hands. His fingers curled and he couldn't feed himself, so I usually helped him eat. The Grandfathers sometimes told stories, but they never talked as much as the Grandmothers.

"Thistle, wake up and take this to Otok." Grandma Sela, the meanest Grandmother, handed me a hot rib bone from which the meat hung loosely. Otok was her man and she tried to get him the fattest pieces, since he had only seven teeth.

"Yes, Grandmother." The hot bone stung my hand, but didn't seem to bother Sela. I brought the meat to Otok and pulled off strips for him. I'd have to wait until he was done to get my own food. I watched him chew for a while, then looked away. Maybe I could count how many of us there were, like Tenja did. Tenja was our star watcher. She and Frightened Eyes were the only women who hadn't taken men. Tenja knew more numbers than anyone.

Four Grandmothers. Idra, the best Grandmother; Sela, my mother's mother; Lida, the Singer; and her sister Ivy, whom we sometimes called Bulging Eyes. Tending the fire and cutting up meat were the seven Mothers. There were six men besides the Old Ones, three born to our band and three from other places.

Magla, Yarrow, Frightened Eyes, and Tenja were sisters. Yarrow, more than anyone, was our leader when we traveled, but Magla knew the most about home. Magla's man was called Ochre, for the color of his hair. He was not one of us. He was Magla's man, but he wasn't my father. My father was taken by a wave years ago, at the winter camp, bringing up nets before a storm. Ochre laughed often and was good to me, though it was strange to see a man whose hair wasn't black. And now one baby, my brother Fire, had red hair as well. Enough of names.

Otok finished chewing and I brought him a horn of water. Then Fire crawled onto my lap and I pulled the venison into small pieces for him. Everything was as it should be, except that I was getting hungry. Our lives were taking back their summer ways, when nothing seemed to change but the sky.

SEVERAL DAYS AFTER OUR RETURN, I awoke when the sky was still grey and the birds not yet singing. I rested, nestled among the sleeping People, our breathing like that of a tired bear, Fire warm as a cub beside me. Then I got up quietly to go outside. In the night, we peed close to the cave, and farther out in the daytime to keep the flies away. The air was damp. A low mist covered the ground.

When I returned, I noticed Grandma Sela sitting on a rock near the mouth of the cave. Sela, mother of my mother, the one who watched me when she didn't think I was looking. Had she been there earlier? Her body seemed small on this shadowy morning, her grey hair pulled into thin, wispy braids. "Grandmother! Are you ill?"

"No, my child." She patted the ground beside her. "Sit here."

Sorry I'd said anything, I tried to find a comfortable place by her feet. Sela scared me. My mother said Sela was stern because she worried and she worried because she loved us. Dawn's soft light smoothed her wrinkles. I could see the black holes where her teeth had been.

"I'm troubled," she said, "and can't sleep." Then she told me her dream:

The Voice that Comes When We Are Sleeping came to me last night. It said that sometime, in the time that is not yet, we would separate out. We will not be just The People. Each of us will separate out. This is because we are The Ones Who Watch. We will stand together in the light and lie next to each other in the dark, but we will not be together. What I will do, I will do. What you will do, you will do. Those Who Serve may go away alone and forget. The children will say, 'Your ways are not my ways.' We will see only into our own minds and forget our stories. I wanted to cry with the same crying I have when a baby turns cold and hard. The Voice That Comes said it must be this way because we are not like the animals. We are The Ones Who Watch and we will separate out.

Her dream made me uneasy. I didn't understand her words, though I was sorry she was sad. Why had she told me? Her words were like weapons. I crept back to the cave and lay down, but I was no longer tired. A restlessness had come upon me. Silka made little pig noises in her sleep. I knew I wouldn't be kind to her that day. I wished for the peacefulness of the early morning, not the puzzlement of an Old One's dream. A crack of thunder woke everyone. It began to rain.

Teachings

"I'VE NEVER SEEN SUCH RAIN!" Grandma Idra shook her head as we looked out upon a shifting wall of water. The weather had changed several days ago, angry clouds rolling like breakers over the valley. For three days we'd listened to the downpour, gnawed the last of the salt fish, set out shells to catch fresh water, and waited for Sun's return. The cave was beginning to stink but the path to the meadow was too slippery to climb. It was a good time for stories. That was Idra's job.

"I'll tell you about Spirit," she'd said soon after the rain began. The Mothers and the men knew the stories by heart. Mostly she spoke for Silka, Birch and me, and the four boys. We learned from all the Mothers and from Those Who Serve, but Idra was our main teacher. Zlatar helped with the man's part. "I'll tell you about Bear and Wolf. All the animals, the plants, the stones, all things that have Spirit, and how Earthmaker breathed Spirit into all of us," she'd said, looking right at me. She knew how much I loved the stories.

I didn't know what this Spirit was, but I saw it once as it left a bird that had smashed against the rocks. I heard it alone by the river when

I went there in secret. It sounded like the wind but sang words like the songs of the People. I loved to walk by myself, hoping Spirit would talk to me. But I was also afraid. Idra's stories these last few days had made my wonder grow. I fell asleep each night listening to her voice above the rain.

The storm broke on the fourth day, sunlight bursting through the entrance at midmorning. Magla's frown had grown deeper each day as the food bags emptied. Now she stood and stretched, picked up her knife and gathering bag, and nodded to the women. They grabbed their baskets and followed her across the ledge, disappearing down the hillside. Ochre pulled himself up as well, rubbed his hand across his red beard, and waited for the men to join him. Rube and Reen looked up, but Ochre shook his head. The two of them went out with the men sometimes, but there were hunters enough without them. Ochre liked to leave them behind to watch the Old Ones and the babies. The men took up their spears and shuffled out. We'd eat tonight.

"Get your knives and bladder bags," Idra said to the seven of us who were almost grown. "We're going to the river." The Old Ones and the babies would stay behind.

The world smelled fresh, the valley a shining green that stretched unbroken below us. The fierce sunshine and our restless legs quickened us and we slid noisily toward the slope. Silka slipped on the muddy ground and everyone laughed but her.

"Wait!" Idra ordered. "The cats are hungry, too." We froze and looked around. They didn't usually come close when there were so many of us. And now that the reindeer had returned with their babies, the cats had plenty to eat. But the rain could change their habits. "Slow down. Listen," she whispered, shaking her head and drawing her lips into a line. We picked our way down the wet hillside, moving at an angle, then crept around a pile of boulders, watching the rocks for yellow fur.

A sudden frenzied yelp halted us. "Get back!" Idra shouted. We crouched behind the stones and peered around. Beyond the rocks, in the damp meadow below, a herd of musk oxen circled, the large males  drawing around the females and the young. A pack of wolves had come upon them, growling and snarling at the slow red beasts. As if to some silent signal, the attack began. Jowls drawn back and teeth bared, the canines lunged at the oxen's legs, leaped for their bellies and nipped their hooves, looking for an opening. The oxen stood fast, their bent heads, broad horns and massive shoulders making a protective ring. When a wolf tried to break through that wall of flesh, the oxen moved against her, kicking and butting and closing the gap.

But the wolves were relentless. They charged and retreated, then came at the oxen again, snarling fiercely, wearying them. I held my breath and watched as the front legs of one old bull buckled. The animal struggled to regain his balance, stomping and snorting when he stood again.

And then came a piercing howl. A large wolf was suddenly hurled away from the pack, flung through the air by a gouging horn. Her grey body dropped and lay motionless beyond the fray. The others renewed their attack, rushing at the oxen again, but the fight had gone out of them. One by one, the wolves withdrew to pace at the edge of the circle, sniff the wind, and circle the body in the grass. Then, looking to the horizon as if something better awaited them there, they bounded off for the open country. The oxen broke their circle and rambled away. Idra followed them with her eyes. At her signal, we stood and moved downhill in silence, walking to the river in a roundabout way.

We stopped where the stream flowed gently, the stream we called Black River. Its course meandered through a long valley between two mountain ranges, ours and the foothills of the Ice Mountains. Here it rested from its mountain journey, the secrets of the north country held in its dark, liquid silence. Along the banks, as far as we could see, grew the grass we cut for weaving. We'd bundle it here and work it at home, making mats and baskets.

Weaving was the first task we learned, soon after we could walk. The young ones were better at it than the old ones since their fingers weren't stiff. Once, long before my life, the Mothers had made a stone floor outside the summer cave, laying hot rocks in mud. The first thing the young ones wove were the mats for sitting there.

I worked contentedly under the cloudless sky, sawing at the grass, swatting at large flies, staying close to Idra so I wouldn't miss anything she said. Idra sat on the riverbank, catching her breath and wiping the sweat from her forehead. Then she folded her hands over her belly, sighed, and continued her story. Everyone was listening except Silka and Rube.

> *Earthmaker has always been. We call her Mother, for She is the source of all, but She has many names. She is Earthmaker and Spirit Taker, for she warms us with morning and enfolds us in night. Earth is Her body, through which we are born. Earth is Her tomb, in which we are buried. Our Spirit is Hers. The Spirits of the animals are Hers and She lives through them. She lives through all of us and we are like Her fingers, bringing Her*

pleasure through our lives as one brings honey to one's lips. When we look at the animals, we see Her Spirit and come to know that Spirit in ourselves.

Today I will tell you about Horse. His Spirit is that of the Teacher and I am your Teacher. He is tall and wide, with very strong legs. Horse loves the bright blue sky and is happiest when he runs far and travels fast. Then he returns to tell the others what he has learned. Horse is restless when he has to stay in one place. He loves the world and would see it all. Horse loves adventure and this makes him exciting. But sometimes Horse goes too fast and travels too far. Wanting the next adventure, he leaves the present one behind. And sometimes he loses them both.

When we had all the grass we could carry and had filled the bladder bags, we headed back. I walked slowly, thinking. First I thought about Idra. Each time she spoke, she answered some questions and left more behind. It was easy to see how the Spirit of Horse ran in her. She brought us all together with her teachings. She herself had come to us from a distant group, wanting Zlatar when she first met him, so the story went. He'd been young then, our finest hunter. He couldn't leave, so Idra came to us. Since then, she'd had her adventures, but had given up her own people, having seen them only twice in all those years.

I hoped I'd never have to leave what I loved for something else I longed for. I wondered about old people and their adventures. Then I wondered why, if Earthmaker was so powerful, She'd let Horse run too far and too fast. I'd make animals who would behave.

Rube, the most annoying of the boys, interrupted my musing, knocking into me while chasing Silka. "Sorry," he said, and was off. Silka was squealing like a young pig before its neck is cut. The last few months, she'd become foolish around Rube, finding a reason to bump against him even if she had to cross the entire camp to do it. And Rube, proud of his muscles, had taken to wearing the shortest of garments. It wasn't his fault that he'd grown quickly, but surely he knew he needed new clothes. Now the two of them wove back and forth in front of me. Then he grabbed the laughing girl and pinned her to the ground, his tunic riding high on his butt.

"Oh, strong Rube," I called, "have you butchered a squirrel for your new clothes?"

Silka stood and brushed herself off. "Thistle, you're no fun. Just stay and walk with the Old One and leave us alone." She darted off with the boys and I waited for Idra.

Over the past year, Idra had been getting slower. Sometimes her heart raced and she had to sit until it was calm. Now she made her way carefully. Birch, quiet as a deer, walked behind her. I could hear Silka's laughter ahead of us as she and the others hiked up the slope. I could see her in my thoughts, hear her shriek and pretend to struggle as Rube chased her. But I knew if she'd wanted to, she could have easily knocked him down the side of the hill.

I smelled meat roasting soon after we began our climb and walked faster, soon catching up with Silka and the boys. Magla and Frightened Eyes were waiting on the ledge, the carcass of a red deer close by, his antlers longer than my arm. The others had eaten, but Magla had kept food for us. We took our places. Frightened Eyes, looking down, shuffled over to us with a wooden tray. She laid the plate of meat on the ground, clasped her cloak around her thin body, and hurried away. Was she cold? "Thanks," I called out to her back.

Frightened Eyes was the sister of Magla and Tenja. That had been her name for as long as I remembered, the only name I knew for her.

She'd twist her thin fingers through her hair and start to cry if we spoke to her, so we usually left her alone. Whenever I asked Magla why they called her sister by that name, she'd answer sharply. All she'd say was that once, when they were children, Frightened Eyes had been left behind. Grandmother Sela had thought the girl was up ahead with the others. It took them several days to find her once they realized their mistake. When they did, Frightened Eyes had forgotten how to talk. She hadn't spoken since. But she watched and always knew what was needed. In a moment, she returned with a bowl of dried currants and a bladder bag of water.

Grandma Idra and Birch finally made it up the hill and sat with us, nibbling berries. Once the food was gone, the boys slipped away, giving Silka a chance to be less annoying. She knew better than to giggle and yelp under Magla's watchful eyes. Instead, she showed us a different face. Perhaps this one was the real Silka. Or maybe she was many people.

"Teacher," she said to Idra, "let Thistle and me comb your hair." The old woman nodded and smiled and settled back against a stone, her faced still flushed. Her bare arms lay loosely in her lap, white flesh crossed by blue veins. Idra's black hair was going grey.

Silka and I had made new combs last winter, carving them from scallop shells. The curved discs fit our hands and the strong teeth smoothed the thickest curls. I worked a comb through Idra's tangles until her hair tumbled smoothly down her back, noticing how her chest rose and fell with the movement of my hands. Then Silka pulled the long mane back, wrapped it with a leather strip and tied it. We admired our work, listening to the old woman's soft snores. "Our Teacher has the Spirit of the Horse," I whispered. "And now she has Horse's tail as well."

Silka looked confused. "Why are you talking about horses?"

I stared at her. She'd heard nothing Idra had said that day. I crept into the cave where it was cool to rest and think. A sharp tap on my leg awakened me. "Ouch!" I jerked up and looked around. Berry and Reen stood over me, laughing. Skinny Berry, toothless in the front, held a hollow bird bone and a fistful of gravel. I would have yelled at him, but I was happy to see Reen.

"Get up," Reen said. "It's time to build the fire."

Had I forgotten something? "What fire?"

"I heard Idra tell Magla. This is the night we thank the animals."

Reen didn't care for ceremonies, except this one. He looked like a lynx ready to pounce.

"Tonight?" I jumped up, knocking my head on the ceiling. I'd grown since last year. So this was the night! The night our spirits joined the spirits of the animals and we made pledges. The night of the ceremony cave, when we followed the narrow path into Earth's great belly, through dripping pools and dark tunnels and the twisted roots of long-dead trees. Down to the passage where the floor fell away, leaving a dark pit. To the place of the Dancing Animals.

I ran out with Reen and Berry. The ledge was busy, the Mothers cleaning the butcher site and smoothing the ground. The Grandfathers sat off by themselves, their grey heads bent low, preparing their hearts for the night. The three of us went to the ceremony cave to drag out logs for the fire. No one had ever found the end of that cave, at least none of us. I liked to think it ran under the Ice Mountains, though no one else believed that. The cave's mouth was wide, three man-lengths across, and tall as a giant's shoulder, though it quickly narrowed inside. We'd stacked the firewood along the walls to keep it dry. Now, as always before the journey to the animals, we'd make a fire and Idra would tell stories to capture our minds.

Reen and I raced ahead of Berry and entered the cave together, met by a blast of cold air. "Thanks for coming to get me," I said, reaching to pick up a branch. Reen reached out just as I did, grabbing the same limb, his hand on top of mine. I caught my breath, startled by the heat of him, feeling like I'd jumped into a warm river. He tightened his grip. I heard Berry's footsteps behind us and jerked my hand away. We dragged the branch to the fire circle.

As darkness fell, we took our places. I dropped down next to Silka. Reen squeezed in beside me, his leg pressing against mine. The Grandfathers had entered the ceremony cave well before sunset, lit their torches, and gathered the things they'd need to honor the animals. They were gone now, trudging down the long passageway alone. They'd reach the dancing animals first and prepare a place for us. The Mothers sat quietly at last, hushing the children. My eyes followed the Grandmothers, lined up at the other side of the circle like owls on a branch.

The old women wore necklaces of clacking shells and held sand-filled rattles made of gourds. I gazed at Idra, admiring her hair. She seemed to look through me, her eyes focusing on nothing nearby. Perhaps she already glimpsed the other world, her ears hearing the call of a deeper home. The rattle quivered in her hand and the other Grandmothers followed her lead, the slow rustle of sand against surface soothing my thoughts. I reached for Reen's hand. Idra's voice, rough with years, readied us for the journey:

> We go into the Earth, for this is a time of Deepening. Our Mother, Earthmaker, who is Mother of the animals, calls us into Her. Into the darkness, into Her deep roundness, Those Who Serve the Mother enter the Earth. Into the darkness, into Her deep roundness, the People enter the Earth.

The Grandmothers spoke about our ancestors and about the time to come, a time unfolding like the present. Then we were ready. The hunters, Zalec, Ochre, and the others, walked into the ceremony cave, joined by the somber boys. Each of them picked up a hand lantern, a hollowed-out stone filled with moss and fat which Idra ignited with her torch. Carrying their dim lights, the men began walking. All except Zalec. He'd go last, making sure no one was left behind.

stone lamp

The Mothers, the Grandmothers, and the children lined up behind the men, moving close together. Silka was beside me. Gone was the laughing girl and the dutiful helper, replaced by a frightened child. She reached for my hand before we even started, digging her nails into my flesh. The lanterns threw strange shapes on the stone walls and we stepped into the quivering blackness.

Tunnels snaked out from the central shaft like spider legs. Some were dead ends, others endless. Only one went to the dancing animals. If any of us were left behind, we knew to sit and wait. To take a wrong tunnel would be death. No one had ever died this way, though one year Zalec pulled a wolf carcass from a passage, its bones picked clean by creatures who loved the darkness. I grabbed Magla's sleeve, while Silka gripped my other hand. If I became lost, I wouldn't be alone.

We moved on, our old selves beginning to flicker like our shadows. There was no sound but the clicking shells of the Grandmothers' necklaces and the muffled rub of feet on stone. Deeper we went. I felt myself change in the darkness and part of me became as large as the cave. We moved on. I felt myself change in the darkness and part of me became as deep as the earth. We went into the Mystery and then we knew ourselves. And we were not alone.

The lights ahead had stopped moving. Those Who Serve stood

in a circle, their faces lit by a flickering glow. We'd come upon the pit. We moved closer, bunching around the others so that we rimmed the opening several bodies deep. Two logs protruded from the hole in the floor, placed there long ago by our ancestors. I knew from years past that the Grandfathers had already climbed down those beams and extinguished their torches. They stood in the dark at the bottom, waiting.

Zalec set a lantern on the ground for those who'd stay behind, the babies and the Grandmothers too stiff to climb. Anyone strong enough could go. To me, it was more frightening to stay above, alone, in the black dome lit by one small flame. This was my sixth climb. Each time I loved it more.

"Thistle," a quivering voice whispered, "I don't want to go. Stay with me."

"You'll be all right. Remember last year. You liked it," I said, squeezing Silka's hand.

"I hated it. You just said I liked it."

Reen's father, Bakar, edged down first, moving steadily along the log even with a lantern in one hand. We peered down after him as his flame lit the darkness. The walls jumped in small surprises. One by one the People lined up for their descent.

Silka's hold tightened. "We'll go together," I said. "I'll go first, then I can catch you if you slip." That was the same thing I'd said last year.

"All right," she sobbed, seeing that everyone but Grandmother Sela and the babies planned to make the journey.

We waited until the end. Then, putting my bare feet on the rough wood and clinging to it with both arms, I moved downward.

"Wait!" cried Silka, coming so soon after me she almost stepped on my hands. The logs wobbled.

"Go slow," I hissed, lurching to the side. I clasped my whole body to the wood, held tight, and slid the rest of the way, jumping to the floor when I was level with Ochre's head. Silka must have let go at that moment. She tumbled to the ground with a thud. No one noticed.

Now that everyone was there, the Grandfathers moved to relight their torches. A sudden glow burst forth in that small place. Sudden life burst forth on those cold walls. For the walls of the pit were rimmed with animals, sleeping animals who'd lived there almost forever. In that moment they awakened. All the animals which are tender for humans were there. Bison, elk, and re- indeer. Oxen, too. Around and around they walked, legs intertwined, backs arching over backs, proud heads lifted.

The Old Men who waited for us were not the same as the men we'd known above. The Grandfathers, Otok, Thought Holder, and Zlatar, had become the animals. On their backs rode the hides of rein- deer, on their heads the antlers, in their hearts the Spirit. Black stripes slashed their faces. White-eyed Zlatar, whose vision now looked in- ward, raised his arms, closed his eyes, and spoke:

> *Our Mother, You who are Maker of Life and Taker of Life, You from whose body we are born and who gently covers our dead bones, You who feed us with all manner of food, You who give us dreams for our hearts that we may have hope, beauty for our eyes that we may have joy, and touch for our bodies that we may know You, come into us this night. Those who walk on two legs need food for the summer and our time of fullness on Earth. We ask that the animals run near us and be many. We ask that some of*

the many give themselves to us. We honor them. We honor You. As
our breath is their breath, we honor them.

Zlatar knelt on the ground. Before him lay three small worn
pouches, one for crushed sandstone, one for ochre, one for coal. I
knew those little bags well. He reached for one, pulled out a lump of
coal, stepped to the wall and, in a single bold stroke from his memory,
drew the head and back of a reindeer cow. On her flank, he made two
lines, the sign of union and birth. Thought Holder joined him, reaching above his head with his lean arms to rub crushed sandstone into
the wall. The damp surface took the color and the reindeer's yellow-
gold belly emerged. Then Otok took up a hollow bird bone, secured it
between his gnarled fingers, and sucked the ground ochre through it.
The Old Ones began to sing their high and urgent song as Otok blew
his red breath into the animal. In that moment, in the shifting light,
the reindeer took Otok's breathing and began to dance.

Then the old men began their drumming, the thud of their hand
drums pounding like the hearts of animals, coming faster and faster,
the animals themselves swirling around us. The Grandmothers joined
them with drums of their own and rattles. Silka had forgotten her fear.
Like the others, she swayed and clapped, her bare feet pounding the
earth. The animals' power moved upwards, through the ground and
into our legs. Then we were moving, bending, growing, breathing faster.
The Spirit of the animals filled us, their tender longing, their lean
journey, their rough dying part of our sinew and blood. The drums
grew louder and still we danced, at one with Earthmaker and Her
creation. Then Zlatar's voice resounded above the drums:

Pah pah pah pah, pah pah pah pah, pah pah pah pah.

You will find me in the valley, say the deer; you will find me by the river, say the bison. I will come to you in your hunger, I will come to you in your need, from my shank you will feed The People, from my skin you will keep them warm. Pah pah pah pah, pah pah pah pah.

The men were happy with the animals and we danced on. When the little lanterns sputtered, the Mothers added more moss. Then the flanks of the grazers pulsed with new life. I noticed Idra leaning against the wall, breathing hard, the head of a bison looming above her. Finally, the last of the moss burnt down to dark smoke, stinging our eyes. The Mothers relit the long torches. We said goodbye to the flickering animals, climbed the creaking logs, and waited. Zlatar's was the last head to appear. The wiry old hunter crawled out of the earth and greeted us with a smile. "Our Mother will feed us," he said.

Back through the tunnel we went, to be met at the end by the grey of morning and the scolding of crows. Thought Holder had seen a large herd in his mind. They'd find it one fast day's walk to the east, he told the hunters. We had red deer and small game nearby, but we'd need more than a few random creatures to feed and clothe us for the year. This would be the first big hunt. But before they left, the men stretched out to rest, sprawling near the fire pit like wolves. The Mothers threw some cloaks over them and nudged the babies into the cave, shushing them. Thought Holder, the only Grandfather who still hunted, would be staying behind. His legs weren't up to the journey.

The Mothers had to pack the men's things, but the rest of us could sleep. I limped to my sleeping place, pulled Ochre's lion robe about my shoulders, and closed my eyes. The night still danced behind my eyes. The fullness of life was within me and my mind felt as huge as the sky.

Silka's Story

SILKA AND I HAD BEEN GATHERING GOOSE EGGS in the marshland all morning, ambling through the warm mud under a bright sky, our bare legs brushing against the new grass. Startled curlews flitted away from us. A falcon followed overhead. Compared to Silka, the ways of creatures seemed simple. Her moodiness confused me. That day she carried a long stick and swept the grass before her as if commanding it to part, her feet as light as larks. She ignored me, except to glance my way from time to time and make sure I was watching.

We'd had no Teachings for three days. Idra had needed to rest since the night of the cave ceremony. Instead we wandered the countryside contentedly and helped gather food. The Mothers were in the lowland with us that day. The women knew the ways of plants and were filling their baskets with leaves and berries and tubers. My brother had followed Magla with a digging stick of his own, poking at the ground when she did. The sounds of their laughter rose above the cry of birds. By midday they'd filled their baskets. I watched from a distance as they sauntered toward our hill, the meadow silent again.

Silka and I stayed behind, each trying to find more eggs than the other. Unlike Fox, who ate all the eggs he found, we took only one from each nest. Once I took two. We carried them in baskets made of sticks and lined with dry grass.

"I have a great secret," Silka whispered at last, breaking the silence as she grabbed a large brown egg. "I'll tell you soon."

"Can you tell me now?" I asked each time we came upon a nest.

"Later," she whispered.

Five times I asked. Each time she grinned and told me "later." So I stopped asking. She raised her eyebrows and waited for my question until she grew tired of my silence. Then she blurted out her secret. "My bleeding started."

I was bewildered. Silka was a child, a little older than me. But now she was like a Mother. "Does it hurt?" was all I could think to say.

Silka looked at me smugly, her chin high, as if Earthmaker Herself spoke through her. She sighed and answered, "One day you'll know." Then she walked away, sweeping the grass before her.

I stared after her. A swarm of gnats lit on my sweating face and I slapped them. I was sick of Silka and her specialness. "Silka," I called to the figure gliding into the distance, "I release you from the burden of being my friend." I turned and marched off in the direction of the cave, my long strides soon leaving her behind. I'd be scolded for deserting her, but I didn't care.

Now the tall grass clawed at my legs, scratching me in my haste. The faster I thrashed, the worse I felt. I'd find better friends than this — snakes and foxes, squirrels, Rube. From behind me came a frantic sound, like the cry of a rabbit when he sees the shadow of a hawk. "Thistle, wait!" I walked faster. "Wait, I'm coming. Don't leave me here!" Silka sounded afraid. I started to run, enjoying her suffering.

Silka had always been slow. Once I was far enough ahead, I turned around and watched her staggering toward me through the mud.

"Maybe the lions will be your friends!" I yelled. "Maybe the jackals will like your special ways!"

Silka scuttled closer, a solitary shape in a sea of green. "Thistle, don't leave me," she sobbed.

"What do you want with a friend like me, you who are so wise, so old, so precious, Silka the Fine One, Silka the Adored?"

She came closer, her face crooked with fear. "No, no, I'm not," she whimpered. "Don't go. Please don't leave me. You're the one who has everything. You have a mother. You have a father. You have a brother. I have no one. I have no place. Today I am nothing. You have everything, Thistle. You know where you belong. When I'm a Mother, I'll belong too. Now I have no place. I belong nowhere. I have only my future." She turned away, her thin shoulders shaking.

I had never seen this person before. I knew she didn't want me to see her now, as she shuddered, choked, and sobbed. So this was Silka the Special, Loved by All, the most brilliant flower in our rough field? A new feeling rose up through me like a fast-growing plant; its roots were pity, then a stem of understanding, and a small blossom of love. Silka had never spoken of her parents' deaths, but the memory of the landslide hadn't left her. I forgot for the moment how much she angered me and Earthmaker gave me a plan. I ran back to her.

"Silka, I know! You'll be my sister! Come with me."

She stared at me, mumbled something, then hurried after me, crossing the meadow and climbing the hill close behind me, too surprised for questions. We were panting when we reached the ledge. "Wait here," I said. She stood quietly, still baffled, while I ran to find Magla.

My mother looked up from her cooking. "Thistle, you're late. It's almost dark." It wouldn't do to have her angry. I set my basket at her feet.

"Look how many I got!" She glanced at the seven large eggs and nodded. "Mother," I continued, choosing each word, "Silka is lonesome. She is really sad. We didn't know. She feels she has no one. I want her to be my sister." Now it was Magla's turn to look confused.

"Silka has everyone. And she belongs with the Grandmothers."

"No, she's lonesome. She's too proud to say it to anyone else, but it's true. That's why she tries so hard. That's why she's so annoying." I saw a rare sight, Magla smiling.

"Bring Silka to me tonight after you've eaten. I'll speak to Ochre and the Grandmothers," she replied.

I hurried back to the ledge. It was the old Silka I saw there, the lonesome one already hidden away. She was shaking dirt from the mats, her head held high as if she'd come bringing gifts. "Magla wants to see you after we eat," I said. "She will ask a favor."

Stew simmered in the skin-lined pit. The Mothers had heated cobbles and dropped them in to cook the food. We each scooped out a shellfull. I burnt my mouth on a turnip and spit it out in my hand. But Silka ate unhurriedly, dabbing the corners of her lips with a fingertip, honoring us with her presence. When she saw that Magla had finished eating, she glided over to her. I followed close behind.

"Silka, sit down," my mother invited, as she sat rubbing a smudge from Fire's face. I lurked beside her, only another shadow at dusk. "The Grandmothers, Lida and Ivy, have spoken with me," Magla began. "They love you, but now they worry. They're old and fear for you when they're gone. This worry is not good for them. You are grown and can make your own way, but I fear their worry will make their last years unhappy. I have a plan." I glanced sideways, noticing Silka's narrowed eyes and creased forehead. Not even she was quicker than Magla.

"Ochre and I would like you to be our daughter. You will still care for your Grandmothers, but you can help me, too. You can help Thistle look after Fire. And you can find Thistle for me when she wanders off."

My first humiliation in front of my new sister. Silka turned to look at me, her eyes shining strangely. "I could help you with Thistle," she said kindly. "Fire, too."

"Good. Then you are my daughter and you can bring me my cloak. Tomorrow we will tell the People and prepare a celebration."

My plan for Silka's adoption had worked! I hurried to the fire and nestled down by Reen, hoping I could keep the news a secret for one night. But the People were pensive, their thoughts on a different concern. The hunters had been gone for four days. When would they be back and what would they bring? If they were successful, we'd have meat and hides enough to store. There'd be a feast and a journey. My excitement went unnoticed. We fell asleep watching the coals.

Their questions were answered the next morning. Reen and Berry, watching from a hilltop to the east, were the first to see the men. "They got three reindeer!" Berry yelled as he dashed into camp. Everyone dropped their work and ran to see.

Those Who Serve staggered up the hill with the carcasses, the legs of the animals lashed to long sticks. Reen had already gone down to give a hand. Once the men cleared the ledge, they hauled the animals to the butcher area, while the women clapped their hands and cheered. "Good hunt, good hunt," said Thought Holder. The younger men smiled.

Zalec stepped forward. Zalec, Yarrow's man, the leader of the hunt, small but strong. A man who rarely spoke except to tell of the hunt. Black hair coiled over his head and face, spreading like dark moss across his chest. He rubbed a lean arm across his body. I wondered if all that hair scratched him. His brown eyes shone as he told their tale. "Never have I seen so many," he said. "An ocean of reindeer."

The men threw off their packs and sprawled on the ground, while Magla ladled out cold stew and Frightened Eyes and I hurried over with water. I felt a pressure on my knee and looked down. My brother hid behind me, staring at his father, waiting. Ochre saw him. "Come here, boy!" he bellowed, holding out his arms. Fire bounded over him and tugged at Ochre's beard, squealing as the big man lifted him into the air.

"The deer came through there," Zalec continued, pointing northeast at a pass in the mountains. "We got above them and waited. Ochre took the first one." He nodded to the red-haired man. "I got the next. Then Bakar." Our eyes moved to each hunter. Bakar shrugged.

Bakar, father to Reen, was a patient, steady man. Reen was his only son, though he'd looked after Rube and his brother, Leu, for years. Rube's mother had died when Leu was born and their father disappeared soon after, probably taken by a lion. Now the three boys glanced at each other and grinned. The men soon drifted off to sleep, a few going to the cave, the others snoring in the sun. Everyone was home. Safe. With food enough for days. This was the best time.

"Thistle, Silka, come help us," Magla called. The Mothers were carrying out the second attack on the deer, going at them with their knives, removing the hides, gutting and butchering the carcasses, setting aside the shanks for roasting, slicing, or freezing. When the butchering was done, the boys raked the bloody ground with an antler and covered the area with dirt, while Silka and I shilled the beans the women had picked earlier.

Reen's mother, Litva, ambled through the campsite, keeping order and bringing whatever Magla requested. A slow-moving woman with large, gentle eyes, Litva left beauty wherever she walked. She painted red circles on her tunic, using crushed stones for paint and outlining the circles with coal. In her hair she wore feathers and tiny, dangling shells. She'd come to us from the Fish People, which was why she did these things.

Meanwhile, Silka and I pulled the stems from the long, skinny finger beans, popped open the pods, and pulled out the round seeds, working faster when Magla looked our way. This would be a fine feast.

Bakar was the first to awaken, staggering from the cave and splashing water on his face. He sat on a mat and looked around. Litva, his woman, sauntered over with a shell full of warm deer fat and began rubbing his shoulders and arms. Bakar growled and stretched, rolled his head and shrugged under Litva's fluid strokes. Pleasure spread like sunrise across his lined face. Then Ochre took his place, clenching his teeth and grimacing when Magla went to work on him. She dug her hands into his flesh, scolding the pain and pushing it back to where it started. Soon he'd had enough. It was time to eat. And to hear Magla's announcement.

I dropped down by Reen again, keeping my gaze on his lean arms, afraid if I opened my mouth I'd give away the secret. At last, the eating was finished and the talking could begin. All eyes were on Magla as she stepped to the center of the group.

"*Aeii*. I speak," she said. Magla's body was slender but sturdy, carrying a strength beyond her size. She wore the lion-tooth necklace Ochre had made for her. "This day is good," she stated. "Those Who Serve the Mother have brought us meat. We'll leave soon for a journey. But there is still more news for the People." She scanned the group, studying each of us, demanding that we bear the weight of her message. "Lida and Ivy have spoken to me. Someday Earthmaker will call them from us. To ease their minds before that day, Silka will become a daughter to Ochre and me, as well as a granddaughter to Lida and Ivy. We will celebrate our new daughter."

A soft murmur arose, with smiles and questions all around. Silka stood, her eyes down but her face beaming, nodding as the People called out to her. Plump Lida, her round face glowing in a toothless grin, dragged herself from her mat, teetering on her tiny legs like a shorebird with a good fish. She was joined by Ivy, a tall, gaunt woman who rarely spoke. The two Old Ones smiled at their wisdom, nodded happily to everyone, and beckoned to Silka. Then Magla embraced all three. Our family was now very large. I leaned against Reen's shoulder, tired and happy, thinking about my sister and tomorrow's trip.

The Place of the Warm Mist

I AWOKE TO THE NOISE OF THE MOTHERS DRAGGING out the sleeping hides, shaking them in the sun. And then the sound of a low, cranky voice. "Go. Go on now, woman. I need some quiet." Otok. I crawled to the mouth of the cave and looked out, rubbing my eyes in the bright sun. Otok sat by the fire circle, a pile of unworked flint before him. Zlatar hunched nearby, carving a bird head from an antler. Zlatar's eyes were white as moons, but the memory of animals was within him.

Grandma Sela stood near Otok, trying to drape a sheepskin over his bony legs. I saw that she'd set out turnips and deer ribs. It looked like the old men weren't going with us.

"It's chilly. At least cover your knees," she demanded.

Otok threw it off. "Leave us, woman. I have work to do." He reached for one of the sharp stones, uncurling his fingers with his free hand long enough to grasp the rock. A wolf-tooth necklace hung on his chest. Sela threw down the hide and stomped away.

I reached for the hanging water bag and splashed my face. Then I went to make tea for the old men, helping Otok hold the drinking horn to his mouth. Otok had Sela and four daughters, but he liked it best when I brought him his food and drink.

"Granda, aren't you going?"

"Ah, it's too far. Too much bother. Leave it for the young ones."

"And Thought Holder? Is he staying behind?"

"Probably."

This was the first year the old men hadn't come along, but he was right; it was a long way. The path was rough and we always had to run to get back by dark.

Everyone else was leaving already. I glanced at their backs just before they disappeared down the hillside. Then I rushed to the cave, dug into the bags until I found the willow bark, and hurried outside. "Here, Granda, chew this if your hands get sore. I'll bring you something from the lowland. I promise."

"Bring me straight fingers."

I gathered up my things and ran after the others, scrambling down the slope and toward the morning sun. It wouldn't take long to catch them.

I loved this journey almost as much as the destination. Picking my way over the rocks and downward, I soon reached level ground. Then I came upon a deer path. It crossed a narrow forest that nestled against the hills. Here the sunlight glinted through trembling aspens. Tiny snow flowers peeked from the grass. Clumps of blueberries lined the trail.

Idra was last, as usual. I heard her shuffling through the brush before I saw her. "Oh, it's you, girl," she said when I grabbed her shoulder. "I wondered what was thrashing behind me."

"Grandma Idra, why is it you're always behind?"

"Because I wait for the slow ones, those even slower than me."

Just ahead, I saw Magla and Fire. Fire was squealing as the ground squirrels fled before him. We passed a clump of tall thin plants with little yellow flowers. Yarrow. We'd be stopping here tonight for the flowers, I was sure. We used them for a salve. Spring was the time to pick healing plants. Idra had taught me that. Plants were most powerful then.

Ochre and some of the men were walking ahead of Magla. I could see their bouncing spears. They always brought their weapons, though few meat eaters came to the forest. Boars hid under the trees. But they couldn't charge through the brush, so they left us alone. I wondered where Silka was. Probably at the front of the line with the boys.

"Slow down, girl," Idra growled from behind. "I waited for you. Now you wait for me."

"Yes, Grandma." I picked berries while Idra caught her breath, the voices of the others soon falling away. The sun climbed high as we made our way through the quiet woods. It was midday when I noticed that the foliage up ahead had thinned. The sky was a brilliant blue. "We're almost there!" I cried.

Once we left the trees, we entered a strange and barren world. A rough mountain face rose up on one side, its stone surface shining black from the snowmelt above. The ground on the other side dropped away quickly. Great slabs of wet stone sloped downward, crushing all vegetation except for a few twisted shrubs. Like the mountain, the stones were bathed by the steady wash of melted snow. We stepped out onto the slippery rock, staying close to the hillside.

"Idra, take my hand." The old woman moved carefully. Years ago, this probably had been a simple journey for her, as it was for me. But I knew her legs no longer obeyed her. I heard the bubbling of hot water up ahead and a waterfall crashing from a high stream. Mist swirled like low clouds and warm air rose to meet us. "Idra, grab these roots."

"Go on now, girl. Catch up with the others," she said. "I'll take my time."

"I'll wait."

"I'll just watch from here."

"You can't see anything. Come on, you can make it." I pulled her further out onto the slippery rocks, while she shook her head and resisted. "Come on, Idra! Sit down." I tossed our bundles, heard them tumbling down the stones.

"No! Thistle, I mean it!"

She flopped about like a fish on the shore, while I tried to drag her down beside me. At last, I got a good hold. "Ready?" I asked. I pushed off before she could answer. We slid like otters down the slick stones and through the swirling haze, crashing into a shallow pool.

Idra pulled herself up on shaking legs. "Thistle," she hissed, "never again!" There was another route we could have taken, the same gradual incline we'd be climbing that night. But it was much slower.

I heard laughter up ahead. "Come on, Idra, I'll race you!" I threw off my tunic and ran to join the others in the steaming pools.

It was strange to see the People without their clothes. Their bodies were white as clouds, their hands and faces brown. Even the Mothers behaved like children, jumping, splashing, laughing. We always swam at the closest pool first, although it was deep and we had to hold the babies. I jumped in next to Reen, screaming when he splashed me, swirling with a liquid life.

After a while, we left the Mothers and their men behind and headed for a shallow pool. Silka and I helped the Grandmothers with the babies, while the boys ran ahead. We stopped at a place where several small pools bubbled and a gnarled oak spread its branches in the mist. There we swam and basked like turtles, remembering the sun. When the young ones tired, they fell asleep by the tree. The Old Ones soaked the stiffness from their bones and washed each others' hair. I stretched out next to Silka, leaving the pool to the Old Ones. Rube and Reen sat on the rocks, tossing pebbles at our feet. Berry and Leu kept their eyes on the two older boys, following them like goslings.

"Look at Rube," Silka whispered, laying on her belly and peering at him through shaded eyes. "Have you ever seen such a man?"

I did as she instructed. He was shorter and more solid than Reen. Otherwise he looked pretty much like the others. "Idra found some yarrow. We'll probably pick it tonight."

"Look how his arms curve. Is he looking this way?" she asked.

I glanced over. Rube and Reen were both staring at us, heads together, laughing. I looked away. "I'm going back in."

"Me too!" Silka slipped into the water with me and we swam, splashing up little liquid stars. We climbed back out, dived, and jumped, Silka flying from the water like a fish longing for land, her tiny breasts pointing upward and disappearing under the foam. Then we sat underwater on the smooth stones, our heads just breaking the surface. I watched the sky, dreaming animal shape into the clouds, my hair floating around me like river grass. Berry and Leu pushed each other in, wrestled up the rocky sides, and rolled back down. Rube and Reen jumped in as well, laughing as they dunked the younger two.

I watched Reen as he sidled from the pool to the rocks. His legs were sure on the slippery stones, his arms fuller than I remembered, his wet body shining. He turned around and I was startled by the patch of black hair above his legs. Dropping down lazily, he sprawled on the rock. Surely he was much finer than Rube. He lifted an arm to shield his eyes from the sun. Slowly, before my sleepy gaze, like a plant arcing toward the light, his penis began to rise. A creature moved within me, crawling through my stomach, pushing out against my breasts, catching at my throat.

Rube had pressed in next to Silka, jostling me aside. Now he noticed Reen and pointed, laughing loudly. Reen jerked up and glanced our way, his face suddenly red. Then he rolled into the water. I lunged toward Rube, grabbing his head as his mouth fell open in surprise. "Here, Bear Turd, can you laugh underwater?" I asked, pushing hard. He thrashed until I let him go. Then he sputtered and slunk off with Silka, saying words I was glad not to hear.

I swam over to Reen, who sat staring at the water. "The Old Ones are asleep," I whispered. "Let's go up the hill." He got up to follow, keeping his eyes down. "Birch, Leu, Berry, come on." I gestured to the others and we crept away.

Every year we made this secret trip, sneaking away while the old people rested, crawling back up the slope to the deeper spring. Large boulders encircled this pool like beads on a giant necklace. We'd wedge between two of them, hidden from the Mothers and the men, any sound we made muffled by the bubbling water. There we'd wait.

At last, like tired seals, the Mothers and Those Who Serve left the water and beached themselves on that strange shore, white flesh glowing on the dark stone. We watched as two of their hungry bodies joined together, crawling as one large creature, writhing across the wet rock. At first their cries were like those of famished wolf pups when the food is near. Then like the screams of gulls as they reach the sea. I felt Reen's breath hot on my shoulder. Finally, we turned and made our silent way back down. I was sure some babies had been made that day.

Idra and Sela were feeding the little ones when we returned. Silka and Rube were gone. We filled up on yesterday's deer fat and went to join the others. Once again, like other years, the People lingered at the pools until dusk, hurrying homeward only when the last orange fingers of light embraced the sky. We were too late for the yarrow. And when I stopped to fill my pouch with plums for Otok, Idra and I again fell behind. But even in the dark we saw the path, lit by the moon like a hazy white line.

Idra was limping. "When my Zlatar was young," she said, "he'd never leave the old people alone and hurry ahead. Now the young men forget their duties."

"We'll be fine," I replied, glancing into the darkness between the trees. I wished it wasn't so far home.

"No, it's no good getting old. Can't watch the young ones like I used to, make sure they don't sneak up the hill and bother the Mothers," Idra said. I said nothing. "Run ahead, girl. Tell Ochre to come back here."

I looked into the trees again, off to the side of the path. A pair of orange eyes was following us. The eyes of a tall animal, its head almost the height of my belly. "That's all right, I'll stay here."

"Well, I need to sit for a while."

"We'll walk slowly." I took a few more steps. The eyes followed, unblinking.

"I need to sit," Idra repeated, stopping to lean against a slender birch.

"I'll yell. Ochre will hear me. He'll come for us." I threw back my head and screamed.

"Hush, girl!" Idra said.

I screamed again and heard the welcome sound of feet on the path ahead. Ochre suddenly stood before us, clutching his spear. "Thistle, shut up!" he commanded. "The cats will find you!"

"A wolf followed us."

"There was no wolf," Idra scoffed.

"Go up with the others," Ochre ordered. "I'll stay with Idra."

I ran to the front of the group, jostling past Magla and Fire, sliding between Zalec and the hunters, keeping my eyes straight ahead as I rejoiced in the shuffle of feet around me. Then up the hill, over the ledge, and toward the fire. I was the first one home.

"Granda," I called, "I got you plums." Otok took the hard red fruit and patted my hand. "A wolf followed me!"

"A wolf? Where is your mother, girl?" Magla stumbled over the ledge soon after and trudged toward us. "Magla," he said, as if speaking to a disobedient child, "it's foolish to come back so late." It was strange to hear my mother scolded. Not unpleasant. She dropped her bundle and frowned. "What's this about a wolf following Thistle?" he demanded. Then she turned to glare at me.

"What wolf? She was afraid of the dark, that's all. No one else saw it." Still Otok scowled. Magla threw up her hands. "Why would a wolf come near us? They have the reindeer calves."

Otok looked away, one hand clasping the wolf tooth pendant on his chest. "There is another reason," he said.

"Father, no one believes that. It's just a story." He looked back at her, his face like a storm. Maybe Magla would be punished. "Thistle, go to bed," she said.

"Not yet!"

"Go."

I shuffled to the cave, planning to stay awake to hear what was said. But exhaustion overtook me and I was soon asleep. My dream was about a bird in the distance. I didn't know what kind.

Tenja and the World Tree

THE OLD MEN SCOWLED AT THE SKY and shook their heads, declaring they'd never seen such weather. It had rained every day since our return. Still there was work to be done. Sometimes I stayed with Fire and the babies. When it wasn't raining, I wandered through the marshland with Silka. The geese had hatched out long ago. While the large goslings swam with their mothers, we pulled the down from their nests, stuffed it into our carrying pouches, and took it home to dry. We'd use it in the winter to line our boots. On clear days, Zalec and the men took the boys to the valley to hunt. Idra was still tired, so Yarrow had taken over the women's teaching.

Silka, Birch and I sat at the bottom of the hill with Yarrow one humid afternoon. A line of sweat had formed above my lip. I was having trouble staying awake, though I tried to listen to Yarrow's words. "Earthmaker put power in plants," she was explaining. "So a plant's spirit works with our spirit to heal us. I'll show you. Thistle, wake up."

"What . . . ?"

Once again we walked into the forest, this time to see where the different plants grew, some hidden in dark places, others thrown open to the sun. We studied their roots, some like the hairs of a baby, others like Otok's gnarled hands. We smelled them, tasted them, and sat silently, waiting for their story. "Each plant has a different tone," Yarrow said, brushing the dirt from her fingers. "Listen." I lay on my side, head on my hands, waiting, unsure of what I was to hear.

"Thistle, wake up."

"I'm listening."

"Come with me."

So I followed her to the deer path, the other two staying behind. The trail turned sharply and I looked up as golden light broke through the treetops. Ahead of us a little stream rushed over white stones. "Sit here," Yarrow said. "I'll be back."

"But what . . . ?"

"Wait. Listen."

I crouched down in the leaves, hearing only the skimming water and the hoarse call of a jay. All else was silent. The warmth made me sleepier. How long did I have to do this? Talk, plants! I stretched out my legs and lay back, hands under my head, smelling the dirt beneath the foliage, happy for the tall plant on the bank that shaded my face. My eyes followed the plant's slender stems to its pointed leaves and the round seed clusters growing at the top. I waited. My ears heard nothing. I waited some more. A soft language was coming through my skin.

My eyes followed the stalk again, from the wide bottom, along the narrow middle, up to the plump seed balls at the top. As I lay in the dappled light, a calmness seeped into me. The sun perhaps. But when I glanced at a small shrub nearby, the feeling lifted. If

wild celery

I looked back at the tall plant, it returned. And so it was that my skin began to listen to the forest's small language, my senses floating in a quietness beyond my heartbeat. Bees swarmed, carrying on, in their own small world. I sunk deeper into this other place. Perhaps that world was always there, beyond my noise. Long before she returned, I felt the ground quiver. Yarrow's footsteps. My eyes shifted and she stood above me.

She nodded. "Sweet Stem, we call it. See. It's all along the stream. It likes the shade of a north-facing slope."

I stood up and touched the reed-like stem that towered over my head. I'd noticed these plants before, wondered how the thin stalks could support the large clusters of seeds. "What do we use it for?"

"Sweet Stem shows us the strength that comes from balance. We make a medicine from the seeds when women have trouble with their bleeding. The roots are for infections. Some carry the stalk when they pray."

Like Thought Holder, I thought, remembering the tall shaft he sometimes held.

"Now you hear a new language, Thistle, the speaking of the rooted world. As we are healers for the People, so plants are healers for the Earth." We walked back to find the others and headed home.

As Yarrow was my teacher for plants, so Tenja was our teacher for stars. By midsummer, the rain had almost stopped. The sun burned high overhead. Once again, we were waiting for the year's longest day, the time when people from all over returned to the center of the world and Sun made His promise. Tenja was the one who prepared us for this day.

Tenja was my mother's sister, the youngest one, Yarrow being in between. She was different from the others, which made her interesting. She had little meat on her bones and wore an amber pendant shaped like a new moon. And she had no babies. Magla said she was supposed to be different because we needed her that way. Tenja watched the stars while the rest of us slept, then the Mothers hushed the babies while she rested in the day. Sometimes I'd fall asleep in the afternoon to see what it was like to be Tenja. No one hushed the babies for me.

Silka and I liked to talk about her, wondering why she stayed by herself and never spoke about people, only stars. Tenja liked teaching me, probably because Silka often seemed stupid. Silka cared most about men and women and had little time for stars. Stars were interesting to me, but I still wondered about the other things in Tenja's life. Silka insisted there was more to the Star Watcher's story.

One day, when I was alone with Tenja, I asked her, "Tenja, do you not love babies?"

She looked surprised, as if she'd never considered this question. Her dark eyes passed over me and I wondered if she ever really saw anything close to her. "Earthmaker is good," she said after a while. "She gives us many things to love. I love you and all the children. But someone must watch the stars." She smiled, as if that were a good answer.

After the lesson, I hurried to find Silka. She hadn't moved from where I'd left her, sitting on the ledge, combing her hair. "She loves children, but someone has to watch the stars," I said.

"I don't believe that," Silka said.

"Thistle, Silka, get over here," Magla called. "Have you girls done anything this morning?"

"I was helping Thistle with her lesson," Silka explained.

"Well, join us. Tenja has something to say." Magla hurried back to the circle.

"Anyway," Silka continued, "Tenja's fooling you. Ask her about Ephus the Traveler. Does she not love him?"

"Ask her yourself," I replied, running toward the others. Silka followed.

Each summer, before we went to hear Sun's promise, Tenja told us the same story. Before Tenja, Thought Holder had told the story, and before him, his father. Now we gathered around her again, slipping into the circle behind the boys. I always listened closely. Some day one of us would be chosen to speak those words. Silka drew on Rube's bare back with a stick until I pinched her. She stared at him the rest of the time. I doubted that she'd be the one the People chose.

Tenja began, her soft eyes flashing when she spoke of stars:

Long ago our Mother created all things. She once lived in the wind, as Spirit only. Around Her was nothing that was formed, only Chaos. But it was Her nature to make things and She lived Her nature. From the dust that spun in the wind, She created Her body and called it Earth. Earth spun in the wind, dry and hard and cold. She created fiery Sun to warm Her body. When Sun's hot rays came into Her, She gave birth to stars and flung them to the heavens.

Stars are the children of Earth and Sun is their Father. At first the stars were afraid, because they saw only Chaos. But She defeated Chaos and brought forth Order. Long before Earth created the People, stars were her only children. They loved Her so much that they circled Her forever. When all the sky was in Order, Earth said, 'I will now bring forth water to cool me.' In the cool of night, She turned Her face away from Sun and brought forth mist. Great clouds formed. Rain fell, covering Her hot face and flowing over Her warm belly.

'I would create more,' Earth said. 'Come into me again, Sun,

that I may create.' Sun entered Her again with a ray of golden light. Where Sun pierced Her, there grew a great tree. Its roots plunged deep into the Earth and drew up Her moisture and Her richness. Its branches flung themselves into the sky and drew down Sun's warmth and light. Together the moisture and the warmth made seeds. Wind blew the seeds over the Earth. They took root upon Her fertile belly, becoming all manner of plants and animals. They flourished and Order was brought to the land. And from only these four things, wind, water, fire, and dirt, all else was made.

Tenja's words lingered as we prepared for the trip. On the day of our departure, I awoke even before the Mothers. I shook Silka by the shoulder and we stumbled through the dark cave and outside, going to find Tenja. It was our job to help her, since we were now her students. Once again, Tenja had spent the night outside in her round stone enclosure, a structure Thought Holder had built years ago, when he was a young man and the Star Watcher for our people. He'd crossed sticks and lashed them together to make an open roof, keeping out the animals, but letting in the sky.

I pushed back the entry stone and stuck my head inside. The walls were lit by dawn's soft light. "Tenja, Tenja, wake up. It's time!"

Tenja turned toward me and met my gaze. Her eyes always seemed large in her thin face, but they were even wider now, like those of a rabbit before a blow.

"I am awake," she muttered, and turned away.

Soon the others were stirring. This year, all of the Old Ones planned to stay behind with the babies. The rest of us would be walking fast for four days to reach the gathering at the Great Tree. The Tree was straight west of here, near the sea, but far north of our winter cave, in the rocky foothills of the Ice Mountains. There we'd meet the others, the Fish People, the Reindeer People, our relatives. Once again Yarrow would lead us, with Zalec at her side to warn of cats.

I grabbed my bag, hugged Fire, and brought him to Grandma Sela. He didn't cry until he saw that Ochre and Magla were also shouldering their bags. Then he wailed, his tears washing dusty paths down his face. "Here, little squirrel, keep this for me," I said, placing my purple shell necklace over his head. "Guard this until I come back. It's magic." He stared at the necklace and back at me, wanting to believe.

Tenja was quiet. I'd noticed her earlier, sitting on her haunches next to Thought Holder, their heads bent low. Now she hovered near the ledge with her small bundle. Yarrow gave baby Zale to Idra and strode to the front of the group. That was our sign to go. Where was Silka? We were the Star Watcher's helpers. People would be watching us. At that moment, Silka strolled from the cave, a bulging pack over one thin shoulder. Then she stared off into the distance as if a vision unfolded there.

"Silka, what's in there?" I asked.

"Where?"

"Your bag."

"Just things."

"What things."

"Special things—my rocks, my shells, the prettiest ones."

"Put them back now or I'll tell Magla."

"They're my best ones," she wailed.

"Choose one and leave the rest." She skulked back to the cave. Once again I was at the end of the line. But Silka wouldn't spoil this day for me.

Silka and I fought less than we once did, at least when Rube wasn't around. I liked to talk about what we were learning. Silka wasn't really interested in the teachings, but she seemed to sense that power came from knowledge. Sometimes she listened. We prattled on in the cool, bright morning, me talking of plants and creatures and stars, Silka commenting on Rube. He walked in front of us, his dark eyes seeking her out from time to time. Birch, three years younger than I, followed along, while I repeated the names of the thirteen journeys Moon took every year.

"Moon's journey is now called The Time of the Great Tree," I recited, loving an audience. "Then comes The Time of the Ripening Fruit, then The Month of the Fat Deer, and then The Storing of Food. Silka, do you remember the month when the leaves turn gold?"

"Ah . . . Return to the Sea?" she said.

"Good. Then the Gathering of Fish, and The Great Darkness," I continued. The worst time came just after that. We skipped over its name, When the Babies Cry from Hunger. Then came The Waiting, The Melting, and finally The Time of the Reindeer Calves.

"Birch, do you remember my favorite month?" I asked, giving her an easy question.

"Journey to the High Meadows!" she said.

The month just passed was called The Gathering of Medicine. I liked holding all the names in my mind, but Birch soon tired of us and dashed ahead to join the boys. At the bottom of the hill, we turned west. Our path would take us in a straight line through a high narrow valley.

"Tenja was strange this morning," said Silka after Birch left. "Do you think she misses Ephus?"

That seemed unlikely, since Ephus the Traveler had been gone for three years. "No. Something else. Maybe a big cat awakened her."

"Or she had a bad dream," Silka guessed. "Maybe the Voice That

Comes in the Night warned her of an illness."

Tenja was well and strong. "I don't think it was that. Maybe the Voice told her something about this journey, something she didn't know before." If it were a dream that had bothered her, it wouldn't be right to ask. The Voice in the Night came from Spirit and only Tenja could decide what to do.

The days were long now and we walked until the blinking of the first stars. "We'll stay here," Yarrow said at last, dropping her pack by a stream that ran through a clump of aspen. The Mothers hung hides on three young trees, giving us some shelter at our backs. Then they built a small fire on the bank. We watched as Ochre showed us how to fish with sticks. We'd stopped only briefly that afternoon and my belly had been growling half the day. Birch speared the first one, a fat trout almost as long as her braids. She squealed when Ochre helped her toss it on shore. Once we had a pile of them, we slit their stomachs and roasted them on green sticks. I sat on the bank, satisfied, licking the grease from my fingers.

"What did you and Silka talk about all day?" said a voice behind me. Reen. I turned and noticed again the little line of black hair that now grew beneath his nose. Ever since I'd dunked Rube, Reen had sought me out to tell me little things. He never stayed long, just popped up like a marmot, then disappeared.

I shrugged. "We talked about which of the boys was most pleasing to look at."

"Who did you choose?"

"We couldn't decide," I said. "They were just too handsome to choose between."

Reen was about to reply when Tenja stepped to the center of the group. She wore a cloak made of deer hide, a small fox pelt at her neck.

We turned around to listen. Everyone was silent. When Tenja spoke, she talked not just of the things that all of us could see, but of the pictures in her own mind, and even things that had no picture yet. She'd said little all day, which seemed odd, since it was so close to the time of Sun's promise. "Tonight," she began, "I'll tell you about the duties of The People." Her voice trembled at first, then grew stronger:

The Great Tree the Mother created, the tree that reaches toward Father Sun, grew higher and higher. It became a pillar linking Earth to Heaven. Around that pillar the Sun and stars turn forever. Around that pillar, Order rules and Chaos is pushed back.

Of all the creatures the Mother created, the People were the strangest. They were the ones who watched Her closely and learned Her ways. To them She said, 'You who have counted the days, you who know the mystery of time, you who would yourselves be Creators, watch Me. Dance at my pillar, as my stars dance around Me. Keep watch each year and know Order, if you would know Me. See how the stars come back to you. Know that you are part of that circle.'

And so each year we gather. We dance around the pillar tying Earth to Sky, the pillar where all things turn. Summer to winter, want to plenty, going in to going out, longing to celebration. We see the Order. We see the day Sun reaches the far point of its journey and turns back. We thank Sun for returning. We thank Earth for our lives and give our bodies as an offering to the Mother, She who holds back Chaos, uniting Earth and Sky.

As the wind sighed through the junipers in the cave-black night, Tenja stood silently, waiting for our questions. No one spoke, so I waved my hand. "Have the People ever known Chaos?"

Silence. And then Magla's glare.

"It's late," Tenja replied. "We need to sleep."

I had asked a bad question. Zalec added more logs to the fire. He and Ochre would take turns watching. Smoothing out my sleeping hide, I pulled it around me and lay down, my back to the others. Tenja's story wasn't all that good, I decided, and soon fell asleep.

The second night we spent in a high meadow, bedding down in a clump of young aspens. Our rest was broken by the crash of thunder. I bolted awake as streaks of lightning tore open the sky and lit the valley. Ragged treetops jerked in the gathering wind. There was no rain yet, but the air was cold. Yarrow staggered to her feet and brushed the hair from her face.

"Let's go!" she yelled. We quickly rolled up our robes.

The eastern sky was tinged with grey, but we were moving west, toward the black clouds and away from the dawn. "Let's get as far as we can before the rain," Yarrow called back to us, her hair swirling behind her. We set out, thrashing through the brush and into a bare, high meadow where we were met by a howling blast. Our cloaks whipped around us like angry wings. On we moved, as fast as we could with the wind in our faces, following a path made by mountain sheep, keeping an eye on the swelling clouds. The rain caught us at midday. We covered our heads with our sleeping robes and trudged on, no shelter in sight.

By evening the sky had cleared. We stopped for the night, huddling together on a rocky outcropping under a canopy of ash trees. It was too wet for a fire, so we gnawed salt meat and shivered. I couldn't believe Earthmaker had led us to this.

Yarrow tried to lift our spirits. Tenja spoke little, letting her sister say the brave words. "Earthmaker has made you strong," Yarrow said, her hair hanging about her shoulders as if she'd come from the sea. "Earthmaker has made us all strong. Remember the cave at the world's center, and the hot springs, better than the little springs at home. We'll be there in just one day."

Earthmaker hadn't made me that strong, I was sure. By the time Yarrow finished talking, I'd begun to cough. By nightfall my throat burned as if I'd swallowed hot coals. All night I shivered, watching my breath in the chilled air.

On the fourth day, rain gave way to fog. We were close to the sea, though farther north than our winter home. I could smell the salt. And the earth was made of the same white rock of our beach. Like giant honeycombs, pockets of sponge stone opened into jagged caves and deep pits. In this strange, stone land, entire rivers disappeared underground and rumbled through water-carved crevasses for great distances before surging to the surface again. One misstep in the fog and we could plunge into that hollow ground as well.

By midday our food was gone. We'd seen nothing to hunt in the rain or fog. My stomach was raw. I shivered and burned at the same time as I picked my way over the sharp stone, each footstep deliberate. Soon I was watching only the feet ahead of me, Silka's perhaps, no longer hearing my thoughts, just stepping as she did. When dusk at last gave way to darkness, I'd forgotten we even had a destination. And then Yarrow called out, "Look, look there!"

In the distance, through the lifting fog, I saw a light. Fire surely. The People! We'd made it to the Great Tree. A new strength lifted me. We called out and began to run, mindless of the rough land. As if in a dream, I stumbled through the cave entrance and onto dry ground, remembering nothing else of that day.

Sun's Promise

I AWOKE TO THE NOISE OF PEOPLE LAUGHING, talking, moving. My head felt light, the voices far away. Had I come upon a dream world? Someone had pulled me to a corner of the Gathering Cave and covered me with a second tunic. The now-dry hides were stiff and smelled of smoke. Forms loomed and swirled around me and I watched their dance, too stunned to move.

A rhythmic clacking told me the Fish People were near, the most colorful of humans. Three groups of them lived to the south, beyond our winter cave, dwelling by the sea all year, living off the creatures who swam and scuttled there. Bracelets of fish bones hung on their arms and ankles and clicked when they walked. I lay limp as sea grass as their words washed over me. Suddenly it seemed the space inside and outside of me was too full, leaving no room for air. I gasped and coughed, trying to fill my lungs. Then I started to choke, my body shaking, hot tears flooding my eyes. Like a seabird, Magla swooped down. "Thistle, don't move. I'll get Yarrow."

Then Yarrow's cold hand on my face. "She's burning. Let's get her to a quiet place." They lifted me, the Fish People backing away. A short woman as round as a plover led us to a small room in the back of the cave.

"Put her here," said the little Fish Woman as she tossed a fox pelt on the ground. I lay down.

"I'll get my pouch," said Yarrow. "Heat some water."

Magla rose slowly, still watching me. The Fish Woman spoke, using our words in a different way. "I am Ziva. I will stay." I watched the backs of the other two becoming smaller. Were they leaving me? Or was I going away? Ziva murmured and smoothed my hair. She smelled of mint. "Rest awhile, rest awhile," she said. I wanted to obey, but when I glanced into her stranger eyes, I saw another world reflected back, felt myself enter an unlit tunnel. Ziva's face dissolved like footprints near the sea.

I closed my eyes. The cave fell away and I was flying low over a dark land. Shadows lived there and leaned out around corners to watch me. They were the spirits of the Dead Ones, their eyes as round as shells. I eluded their outstretched arms. And then I was no longer flying, but floating, bobbing under the sea. "I want to go home," I whimpered. My throat filled with cold water. There was no one to hear me. I swam upward toward a faint skylight. Ice! My hands hit ice. I pushed against it and screamed, water pouring down my throat. I coughed to clear my lungs, choking in the freezing liquid. The part of me that never slept began to wonder, was this the place I'd die?

Yarrow and Magla returned. I heard them, but I couldn't reach them. "Earthmaker, I want to come back," I begged. I wanted to be with the People, away from this strange place. I wanted to tell them I saw the dead babies, I saw all the babies who died in the winter. I saw the Old Ones, some I didn't know. I saw my own father. He was floating underwater, his hair streaming about him, his arm held fast by a log. The faces of the dead ones drifted about me, their mouths moving in the waves. They wanted to talk. They wanted me to tell them about the living world.

"What have you learned? What have you learned?" they demanded.

"I know nothing! Don't take me. I know nothing!" I cried, as Yarrow lifted my head.

"Thistle, Thistle," she whispered. "Drink this, just a little, just a little."

Now the liquid in my throat was hot. I coughed out the coldness, felt a tingling warmth. Yarrow's eyes were big as shells, Yarrow, teacher, healer . . . . Then she was floating around me, floating away. I slept deeply, dropping below the first place to a new world, dark but dry, like an old riverbed. What was this place? Had anyone been there before?

In front of me was a man carrying a large fish. The man smiled gently. The fish was alive. The man's voice filled with love as he spoke. "Those without fathers push on the farthest. Their quest fills them with a longing they can't explain. The time will come when there are many without fathers. Your People will grow restless. Even when they become fathers, they will not rest. They can never rest without a father's blessing."

The man with the fish disappeared. My chest tightened. I wondered if the air could still get in. Then I heard my breathing and knew I was alive. Two other figures emerged in the grey light. One of them said in a raspy voice, "The girl is here."

They were Bird People, with the heads of vultures and long, dark robes. I wasn't afraid. They stood before a black passageway. One of the Bird People spoke again.

"If you go here, you will find your own bones."

I entered the passageway and saw that it was filled with animals, including many sheep. The sheep spoke to me.

"If you tame us, you must protect us."

At the end of the passageway, I saw the smiling man again. This time, instead of a fish, he cradled a human. Then I slept with no dreaming.

I awoke famished and exhausted to the voices of Yarrow and Ziva. "I gave her yarrow tea to break her fever," Yarrow said. "See how she sweats. And a tonic from dried rose pods."

"We use that," Ziva chirped. "You should boil pine bark for her lungs."

I opened my eyes and saw the heads of two vultures becoming Ziva and Yarrow.

"Thistle!" It was Magla, sitting in the shadows. "You're here!"

I smiled weakly. "Did I miss Sun's promise?"

"You missed three days of sunlight," Magla said. "Sun's Promise is not until tomorrow."

All I could think of then was food. Magla brought me a broth made from sea bass. I scooted up onto my elbows and gulped it down. A sweet aroma wafted into the cave. I recognized the smell of the pudding the Mothers made each year, mashed white beans mixed with honey and baked in covered shells. I'd wait for that.

Magla returned, stepping lightly as a girl and carrying a piece of honeycomb. "Thistle, Thistle, Thistle," was all she said, shaking her head as she handed me the dripping wax. She flitted back once more with warm water and a piece of soft hide. "Thistle, Thistle, Thistle." I sat up to wash my face and noticed three clusters of wilted flowers by the fox pelt. Pink thistle heads, purple clover, and tiny bluebells. Reen.

At last I crawled out of the den and into the larger cavern, its orange and white walls like streams of animal fat. Earthmaker Herself had poured those liquid walls long ago, hardened them, and opened up her body to amaze us. Like the cord that attaches a baby to its mother and forever leaves its mark, this place was Earthmaker's navel, the entrance to the center of the world. I dragged myself to the entryway, not yet ready to walk.

A circle of cleared earth lay before me, already crowded with people. A short distance to my left stood the Great Tree, its red branches outstretched. So broad was its trunk that four men could barely embrace it, so wide its boughs it shaded all the People. I leaned against the cave wall, the scent of cedar mingling with the smell of cooking, and watched the comings and goings.

Most years travelers came here from eight different places. No one lived to the North, of course, the land of Ice Mountains. I recognized two groups of reindeer hunters who came from the east, though not as far as we had. Grandma Idra's first family was from one of these groups. They'd ask after her and Magla would tell them she'd been sick.

Another band lived in a cove on the West Sea, where they hunted and fished all year. They didn't seem as rough as my People. Perhaps their lives were easier. Even their Old Ones still had teeth. Every year they brought carved wooden beads and strings of fox teeth to trade. We brought loops of sinew, taken from reindeer spines, important but not so interesting.

Then there were the southern tribes, the Fish People. From their hair dangled bird plumes and tiny strings of shells. Their men wore tufts of osprey wings on their heads, while the women wove caps from orange turnstone feathers and the dusty blue plumage of loons. Even their clothing was different. They hated the cold and stayed away from snowy places, so they never wore the heavy elk and reindeer tunics that we made. The Fish Men trapped fox and lynx, while their women draped themselves and their babies in fur. For trade, they brought tusks and shells and plumes.

The stories of the Fish People amazed me. It was said they moved over the water on floors made of wood. Those floors couldn't travel on the fast rivers, but floated easily on the calm West Sea. They said the sea was as clear as air and animals walked about on the water's ground. The Fish People told the best old stories of all.

When we came together, our differences disappeared and we were just the People. I couldn't count how many we were. I just knew when all of us ate together, we ate four reindeer in one day. At home, one reindeer fed our little group for three days. Keeping a hand on the cave wall, I pulled myself up. Then I took a step to test my legs, walking into the circular area where the earth had been raked smooth. It was here Sun would once again make the promise. My legs wobbled, but I kept walking.

"It's Thistle, she's here! She's well!" Silka's voice rose up from the crowd. She and Birch ran toward me, a group of new friends trailing behind. Silka always knew everyone's names soon after we arrived, especially the boys. This time only girls followed her, four from the Fish People and three from other reindeer bands. The seven of them stopped and stared at me.

"My mother said you saw Spirits!" cried one of the Fish girls. "Did you? What did they say?"

I smiled and shrugged. "Can't remember just now." My eyes swept the circle of people. A cluster of boys threw stones at a target just beyond the ceremony ground. One of them was Reen. He looked our way, rubbed his hands on his knees, and ambled to the edge of the circle.

"Come with us," Silka said. "Come see the Fish People's things."

"In a little while."

I watched them run off and turned when I heard a voice behind me. "So, I see you chose to do no work on this trip," Reen said.

"That's right. I left my chores for you. Don't forget to pick the flowers." Suddenly the world seemed to lurch and I grabbed Reen's arm. But it was only me that had moved. Holding on to his elbow, I sat down, not yet as strong as I once was.

"Are you all right?" Reen asked, the smile leaving his face.

"Just weak. Maybe you can come back when the ceremony begins?" He nodded. I waved him away and dropped my head between my knees. I'd just sit and think.

Though I'd missed three nights of stories, I remembered all I'd ever heard about Sun and the Promise, how Earthmaker created Sun to warm Her and bring forth life, how Sun promised to shine forever, how Sun traveled to the limits of His journey twice each year and returned. If Sun kept His promise, we'd have Order. If not, Chaos would return and we'd die. Sun had never disappointed us. The People remembered Change, but not Chaos. We had struggled and our bodies had died. But the People went on forever.

I lay on the ground, hands under my head, readying my mind for the ceremony. We watched Sun's turning twice each year, on the longest day and the shortest, though we came here only in summer. In the winter the wind raged and heaped up snow. No one came here then. Instead, my people huddled in the dark at the winter cave, Tenja marking her moon calendar, counting, and announcing the day the year would be reborn.

The Gathering was the only time we were all together, shy and bold, afraid and happy, angry and kind all at once. Some years Earthmaker entered into the bodies of those without mates, sending them home to new families. I would never do that, leave my home for a stranger. It was enough to make the journey, to see the Great Tree quiver, and to know Sun's Promise.

I was feeling a little stronger. Once again I gazed around the circle. Silka and her band were returning, Silka striding like a lion with her cubs, leading a younger girl by the hand. "Thistle, come with us," she called. "Come see the Fish People's things with Luba and me. They have shells that look like stars and stones like moons. She's making me a necklace!" So the girl's name was Luba. A smile lit up her tan face. Someone had woven tiny shells through her braids. I'd never seen such a lovely creature.

"Not just yet. Maybe later." Silka loved the beauty of every moment, but sometimes I liked to think about the future. I wanted to be ready for tomorrow's ceremony.

Each summer when we gathered, Sun was rising far to the northeast. Sunlight poured into the mouth of the cave each day until midday. But only on the longest day did Sun show us a great wonder. The ground had been arranged to prepare us for that miracle.

Long ago, the People had made a circle of twenty-eight stones, each stone half the length of one's arm. They'd placed a flat stone in the center of the circle and set a tall post five steps to the east of that stone. Some said the post was a branch that fell from the Great Tree in a storm. Beyond the rim of the circle, to the northeast, they'd stood another taller post. Beyond the circle there rose a range of jagged mountains. If we looked from the center of the circle and past the outside pole toward the horizon, we'd see a little notch where two peaks came together. That notch was the portal for Sun's Promise.

I noticed that the Star Watchers from each group had already scattered the crushed ochre around the outside of the circle, the blood-red stone of the Mother. Someone had lashed three sticks to the middle post, making steps. We'd gather inside the circle after dark that night.

Then, before sunrise, Tenja would climb those steps. For years, she'd been the one to announce Sun's decision, a great honor for her and our small group. Everyone knew she watched the sky closely and understood most about the movement of stars. Everyone knew that Thought Holder had been her teacher.

My strength was returning, my thoughts clearing. As the sun dropped beneath the purple sky, people began gathering at their cooking fires, which glowed like small stars beyond the circle. Magla appeared with water and pudding and my robe. "Here," she said. "See that you stay warm." Soon everyone was ambling back in the gathering darkness. I heard Silka before I saw her. She plopped down with her little group, Reen and Rube edging in between us. We whispered, waited and dozed as the moon crept high. Tenja would soon tell the final story.

Once the night turned black, I saw Tenja at the edge of the group, not far from where I huddled with my friends. She slowly walked into the circle and raised her arms to the People and the Great Tree. The murmuring crowd grew silent. Her pale tunic stood out against the black sky. She seemed thinner than I remembered. Had she also been ill? Perhaps the darkness just made her look that way. But then why did her voice sound strained? She began to speak:

Like a pillar joining Earth to Sun, the Great Tree grows. It points forever upward and marks the Sun's journey and the center of Earth's womb. Here life was born, when the seeds of its mighty branches fell to Earth to be warmed by Sun. Here order is revealed and shown again and again. Here Chaos is pushed back.

The Great Tree guides Sun's turning and points to the six directions: upwards to Sun, downwards to Earth, East to the land

76

of Rebirth, West to the land of Dying, North to the land of Ice, and South to the land of Heat.

Sun has now traveled far to the North, warming us, lighting our days. Sun has traveled as far north as He will ever go, following the same path He will always take. On this night, Sun stops His northward journey and promises to return. In the morning, we will have proof of that promise. Order will be strong and the People will live. Order will be strong and the People will live.

Her words drifted off into the black silence. My mother came back to touch my shoulder and tell me to sleep. The world was still dark when I awakened to the sound of drums and the men's deep voices:

Your People await you, Sun. Come back.
Your animals await you, Sun. Come back.
Your stones await you, Sun. Come back.
Your trees await you, Sun. Come back.

I joined the others, shuffling through the dark to take our places. Tenja was at her post, perched on the top step, glowing as soft as the moon. All our voices merged to hasten the day:

Your People await you, Sun. Come back.
Your animals await you, Sun. Come back.

Beyond our songs, I heard at times the high, clear call of a bird. My spirit went out into the People and we were one voice, rising on the wind, smoke from the fire of our longing.

Now the first hint of light tinged the eastern sky. We stared at the mountains, where we remembered the notch to be, waiting for the Promise. On this day, and this day only, Sun would peek through that cleft and throw a single ray of light to the outer and inner posts, a straight golden line between the People and the Sun. Then, because we were at an angle, Sun would briefly disappear behind a mountain. It was that golden ray, that fleeting moment we awaited.

The drums fell silent. The singing ceased. Even our breathing became quiet. As if startled by the silence, the bird no longer called. The air was damp, cool and still. A hint of gold appeared. Our eyes never left the cleft in the ridge. Suddenly, as in the Beginning, a bright ray shot perfectly from the notch to the outer then inner poles, bathing them in gold. "Sun comes back! Order lives! The People live!" Tenja cried out. All around me the People cheered and sighed. Earthmaker had not forgotten us. Our gratitude poured from us as the drums again pounded out our heartbeats and we danced in the dark around the pole.

Wolf's Story

ALL THAT DAY AND THE NEXT, WE LAUGHED and talked and feasted. The lake near the cave was too cold for swimming, but close by, under an overhanging cliff, were four steaming pools fed by springs. That was where we spent our days. When Earthmaker created those pools, She gave them the power to heal all kinds of pain. So we hurried to the water each morning, the young ones splashing and running, the Old Ones soaking their bones, me talking to Silka and Luba and Reen.

We gnawed the last of the reindeer bones three days after the ceremony. It was time to gather our things, say goodbye, and to give the last of our gifts. Ever since the night of Sun's Promise, the Fish Women had been watching Ochre, perhaps with a special gift in mind. He was the only red-headed man they'd ever seen and now they surrounded him again, each of them as colorful and round-eyed as a trout, darting near him each chance they got. "For you," they twittered, laying bird plumes and shells at his feet. "A bracelet, a cap, something for your hair?" The freckled man just smiled and blushed and picked up the trinkets. Zalec and the other hunters laughed. And Magla, like a falcon, once again swooped in, laid a wing across his shoulder, and watched the women scatter.

The sky was a bright, vaulting blue when we departed, the country no longer the dark land we'd recently crossed. We moved quickly, striding over open, treeless ground for four days. Our pace was slowed only once, by a strange event our second day. Tenja and Yarrow were leading us, the sound of their voices rising over the shuffle of feet. Silka and I hurried behind them, trying to make out what they said. Suddenly Tenja stopped short and gasped. Everyone else halted as well. On the path before us stood a grey wolf, his yellow eyes fixed on our Star Watcher. My gaze moved from his bold stare to Tenja's rigid back. How strange in the daylight for a wolf to stop so close. No one moved. In a moment the creature bolted and ran into the grass. Tenja glanced back at us, white-faced. She said little the rest of the day.

My brother must have been waiting for us on the ledge. "Ma!" he yelled as soon as we began our climb, tumbling down the hill to meet us. I wondered how many days he'd waited. At the top of the slope stood the Old Ones, waving and smiling their toothless grins.

"Did you see my People?" asked Idra as we cleared the ledge. "How are they?"

Grandmother Sela joined in. "The Fish People, how many came? What did they bring? How is Ziva?"

"There's nothing to eat," Otok grumbled. "What took you so long? What did you bring?" We dropped our bags. "Show them your bracelets, Ochre," Magla said, nudging him toward the Old Ones. "Come on. Show them your fine cap." He opened his pack, dug around for it, then set the feathered hat sideways on his head, his face as red as his hair.

Earth was at Her fullness, the grass in the meadow taking on the gold of the sun. The girls went with Yarrow to the low country to learn the medicine of plants, while Rube and Reen followed Zalec to the grasslands to hunt. Idra's ankles were swollen, so she rested most days. Some nights, when she felt strong enough, she told us stories of the animals and how their spirits mingled with ours.

"Idra's heart is tired," Yarrow said one day as Silka and I returned from gathering black walnuts. "The walnuts may strengthen her and keep her with us for a while."

I'd do anything Yarrow asked to keep Idra with us, I thought that evening, cracking the nuts and feeding them to her. It was the quiet time, after we'd eaten, while we waited for the sun to set. Silka and I had plumped up the hide under Idra's ankles and pushed the hair from her damp forehead. I knew we couldn't keep her with us forever. Idra was like a star at dawn.

But she did seem stronger that night. I decided to ask her a question. "Idra, what do you know of Wolf?" Reen put down the stick he was straightening and slid closer.

"Ah, Wolf," she sighed, as if recalling an old friend. "Wolf is different. Of all the animals, Wolf is the most separate. He watches from a distance and that makes him like us. Wolf sometimes crosses over into our world and tells us things. But not often. I'll tell you how Wolf's spirit is most likely to come into ours. Come here, girl." She patted the ground beside her. "Help me sit up." I rolled up my sleeping hide and propped it behind her. She began:

Wolf gives the People courage and strength, not the slow, plodding strength of the ox, but fierce strength.
His is the power that makes us push on when we're tired or

afraid. Wolf is like Hawk or Ram in his solitary force. His power brings a restlessness to humans. He is restless like Horse, but Horse is excited where Wolf is fierce. What Wolf is often restless for is the next challenge. He seeks comfort only long enough to decide what that challenge will be.

Wolf's is the spirit of a warrior, the spirit that goes with the hunters when they take an animal. But Wolf doesn't need to hunt to be a warrior. He challenges our cowardice and our comfort, asks more of us, dares us with what is difficult or new. Wolf would have us speak our thoughts even when they anger others or make them afraid. His courage has saved us many times.

But Wolf's courage has killed us, too. His restlessness causes him to dare when he should be cautious, fight when he should plan. Others fear his impatience. If he tries to force his way, they may not follow. Then Wolf goes away alone. Two People together, who know only Wolf, may fight until one is destroyed. When the spirit of Wolf is too strong, a person may die from a great rushing of blood to the head.

"Do any of us carry Wolf's spirit?" Reen asked.

"Some. Otok. He was a great warrior, a leader. He learned patience when he was still young." She glanced around to see who might be listening and whispered, "Sometimes he forgets it now." Then she gestured toward the muscular boy polishing a spearhead by the fire. "And Rube over there, Wolf runs in him."

She leaned back, picking her teeth with a piece of straw before she continued. "An animal's spirit comes to us not just so we can have its power, but so we can tame that power in ourselves. That's why Zalec teaches men not only how to attack an animal, but how to deserve an animal, and how to wait."

Then she nodded toward Tenja. The Star Watcher sat alone, studying the slab of stone she notched each night, her way of counting the days. "Tenja is a warrior, a sky warrior, fighting the Mystery. She hates Not Knowing. Wolf isn't the only spirit that moves in her, but Wolf is the one that keeps her alone and makes her love her quest more than anything."

Her answers were interesting, but not the ones I wanted. "I understand about Wolf being a warrior," I said, trying to hide my own impatience. "But why does Wolf cross over into our world to tell us things?"

"Wolf sometimes crosses over to tell us something that will happen in the future. But only when what is about to happen to humans is also about to happen to him, and Wolf has grown lonely with the waiting." Idra yawned and patted her belly, ready to sleep. Her answer didn't fill the hole in my thinking. I was wide awake.

The Fall

IT WAS THE TIME OF RIPENING FRUIT. I walked to the forest with Silka and Birch most days, filling our bags with apples and plums. We'd already dug the carrots, beets, and parsnips that grew in sunny places and picked the white bean pods. The boys came later in the day to haul the bags to the drying racks. Some of the food we ate fresh, but we needed enough to last all winter.

The birds seemed happiest now, chirping brightly, diving at clusters of red currants. Jays perched on pine branches and pecked the cones for the seeds inside. Sometimes we ate the seeds too, but getting them was tedious. Usually we left them for the lemmings and voles, private creatures of the forest floor, their little tooth marks all that told us they were near. Winter seemed far away.

We listened and watched, those days in the woods, knives at our belts and sticks at hand. Sometimes we came upon badgers, plump as bear cubs and ready to tear at the flesh of unwary humans. They hissed if we surprised them, but when there was more than one of us, they left us alone. The curled-tooth cats never came to the forest. They stayed in the meadow, hiding in tall grass, waiting to drag down the grazers. But lynx stalked the woodlands, spotted creatures with tufted ears come to hunt for hares. We stayed close to each other and away from the low branches if we saw their scat or fur. Lynx pounced on their prey from above. Two of us together could kill a lynx, or so I'd heard.

On this day we were looking for mushrooms near a stand of dead trees. The skeleton trees, probably stripped by hungry elk, reminded me of the months to come, when moss and bark would be the only food the forest offered. A raven regarded me silently from a bare branch. Yarrow had told us how to find safe mushrooms, the ones with plump, round tops, tan flesh, and purple gills. We stayed away from any that were red or green or yellow, or those that lived under oak trees. That was where the death caps grew, their yellow-green tops and sheathed bases rising innocently from the loamy ground.

"Come here, I found them!" Silka called. I followed the sound of her voice and found her sitting on the damp ground, beaming, surrounded by a cluster of small, white plants.

"Let's see." I pulled one up and looked at the underside, its mauve ribs rising to the flesh-colored top. "That's it." I knelt to pick them. Birch joined me, her small hands working quickly. Silka leaned against a tree and sighed, her work complete. It didn't take us long to fill the bags. They were light enough that we could carry them ourselves. I hoisted mine over my shoulder. "Come on Silka, let's go home."

"No," Silka replied, sliding down the tree and reclining on the ground. "I'm sleepy. Wait until the boys come." She closed her eyes and stretched her arms like a butterfly opening its wings. This was the fifth summer I'd gathered food with Silka. She'd never been in a hurry to work if no one was watching. But she wouldn't have wanted Magla to think she was lazy either. This year something was different. She had become stupid. Some days she roamed off and left Birch and me behind, saying she wanted to look for berries. Later Reen and Leu would wander by, asking if we'd seen Rube. We'd shake our heads and wait, knowing we couldn't go home without them, hoping we'd get back before dark.

Whenever Rube wasn't around, Silka spoke of nothing else. "Rube is so strong," she'd say. "Zalec says he'll be a great hunter." Then she'd sigh, run her fingers through her hair, and think of some other marvel. "Yesterday he brought me a rabbit skin. One day he'll bring me a lynx fur, just like the Fish People wear. Don't you think he's fine to look upon?" I'd say nothing, thinking only that Rube had at last discovered one other person who found him as beautiful as he found himself.

Even when they were both with us, Silka and Rube got little work done. He'd stare at Silka as if he had never seen brown skin and white teeth. She'd look at him as if he were a fine, tall horse and not a haughty fool. Now I was the serious one and Silka the one the Grandmothers watched with sideways glances. It was clear on this day that Silka had no intention of leaving. Birch and I wandered a short distance, picking up any good apples we found on the ground. I was hungry, sick of fruit, and ready to leave.

"Thistle, Birch, over here!" I turned to see Reen leaning against a walnut tree, his long, brown arms folded across his chest. Leu sat on the ground nearby. The younger of the two, Leu was a plodding boy whose eyes followed Reen hopefully whenever he wasn't sure what to do. Brother to Rube, Leu seemed closer to Reen. He was shoving walnuts into his mouth as fast as he could crack them.

"Where have you been?" I asked. "It's almost dark."

"We just got here," Reen replied. I looked from his face to the broken shells by his legs. "Just a little while ago."

86

"Silka," I yelled. "Reen's here." The woods were silent. "Where's Rube?"
Reen shrugged. "He said to wait here until he got back."

Birch and I dropped down next to Leu and started cracking walnuts between two stones. Dusk came early to the forest, the shadows of the trees already lengthening. Magla would be angry. I'd tell her it was Silka's fault. I ate my fill and sprawled on the grass, the red-gold world of late summer spread about me like a feast. After a while, Silka and Rube sauntered back.

"I was lost," she said. "Rube found me." She gazed at him, all sense washed from her face.

"Tell that to Magla," I replied, standing and brushing the grass from my hair.

We hauled the bags up the hill and emptied them near the other piles of mushrooms and nuts. The ledge was dotted with drying racks. The Mothers made two kinds of racks, flat stones tilted at an angle to the sun, for small things like fruit, or webs made from thin strips of hide and stretched between posts, for meat. I was in no hurry to see Magla so I wandered around the racks, noting that the fruit was almost dry. We'd probably be refilling them tomorrow. I took a deep breath and walked toward the cooking fire. Magla was waiting.

"Silka was lost," I said, talking fast. "She decided to stay lost until Rube could find her." I bolted to the cave and left Silka to face my mother.

In a little while, I crept back out and away from camp. We wouldn't be eating until later. This was a busy time for the Mothers, who'd try to get in the last bit of work before dark. Silka wasn't speaking to me, which was good. I liked to sit alone on the ledge where no one could see me and watch the sun go down. Once again I dangled my legs over a familiar rock and waited, ready for sunset to flame the sky. The sound of footsteps surprised me. Reen. He slipped down next to me. I glanced sideways, amazed at how the gold of the sky lit his face. How strange to be here with him when no one else was around. A thudding sound came from my chest.

He smiled. I watched his mouth, noticing again the line of dark hair above his lips. "Your friend seems to think little about her work," he said. "She sighs like the wind and clucks like a hen."

"And your friend struts and preens like a grouse."

"Does he bother you?"

"No. I don't think about him." I turned to watch the huge, orange sun, dropping of its own weight behind the mountains.

"So what do you think about?"

My right foot was going to sleep. I twitched, feeling the close warmth of his thigh. "I think about snow . . . I think I'm tired of hauling and picking. I wish we could curl up in the cave and sleep all winter, fat as bears, and not walk back to the sea."

"Do you think about anything else?"

I shrugged. The sky was as purple as a ripe plum and streaked with gold. "I think about, ah, the teachings, Tenja . . ." My face was hot. I was glad the dusk would hide its redness. I stared at my hands, surprised to see that the second finger on my right hand was jerking. My thoughts were dry leaves in the wind.

"Anything else?" he whispered, his leg pressing against mine.

"Well, I thought about you once."

"Thistle!" It was Magla, calling from the shadows. "Bring Otok his supper, then come get your brother."

"I have to go." I jumped up.

"What did you think?" he asked. "What about me?" He grabbed my arm.

"I can't remember. I'll tell you later," I mumbled.

"When? When will you tell me?"

"Soon. Really soon. I have to go." I pulled my arm away and ran back to camp, filling a shell with meat for Otok. I hurried over to him.

"Supper must be better than usual tonight, girl," he growled, reaching out his hand.

"Why's that, Grandfather?"

"You've never been this happy to bring me my food."

SILKA AND I WERE BACK IN THE FOREST the next day. She'd forgiven me for telling Magla why we were late. Or she'd forgotten it even happened. My hands were busy picking plums but my thoughts were on Reen. Would he ask again tonight what I thought of him? What would I say?

"Thistle! Don't you hear me?" Silka stood before me, hands on her hips.

"What?"

"I said I'm going to look for berries."

"Forget it, Silka. They're not coming today."

"Who?"

"They went with the men to the river, to work with their spears." Reen and Rube had practiced for years, throwing stones from the time they could walk, hurling the flat throwing axes once they were strong enough to hold them. Then they'd moved on to spears. Silka and I threw with them sometimes. My aim was good, but I couldn't throw that far.

"Oh." Silka dropped to the ground like a leaf.

I sat down with her. "Remember when we were young? Rube and Reen and those sticks? They'd chase each other and Rube could never catch him?"

"He was only pretending."

"They'd run on the rocks. Rube would dare him to jump to the next one and he would?" Silka looked bored. I bit into a plum. Reen was the most handsome by far, faster and smarter than Rube. But I decided to keep my thoughts to myself.

I tried to imagine Reen in the meadow with the men. For years, he'd had to stay in camp, chipping small points for bird spears, listening to their stories. Last winter he'd cut the flint for his own spear blade. I could see his dark hair falling over his face in the firelight, his hands on the stone quick and sure. I'd gone with him when he'd cut the branch for the spear shaft. And I'd watched as he'd bound the blade to the shaft and wrapped it with wet sinew. The sinew shrank and held fast when it dried.

This year the men had started taking the two boys along. A man wasn't safe in the grassland until he could handle a spear, the only protection from cats. Even then, cats had little fear of humans. Reen's own father, Bakar, had been jumped by a lion last summer. Ochre had been close by and speared the animal, but not until its claws ripped through Bakar's flesh. His scarred arm still hung weakly at his side.

I myself preferred throwing axes to spears. They were easy to carry, not much bigger than my hand. And unlike spear points, which could disappear with the wounded animal, throwing axes were rarely lost. We only used them to stun the game, so the same one could be thrown many times. Even by herself, a strong hunter with a good aim could fell a grazer. It was Ochre who'd shown me how to make them. First he'd shaped a point on a flat stone, not for cutting but to keep the aim true. Then he'd sharpened every edge but the bottom. "Find where the herd comes for water and wait," he'd instructed. "Then you'll never have to go hungry, even if you're alone."

Once the animals were milling around the water hole, the hunter would hurl the stone into the center of the herd. The creature that was hit would flex its legs at the impact, stagger, and fall. Sensing danger, the others would run blindly and trample the fallen one. Their sharp hooves might kill the animal. If not, the mangled creature would be easy to pick off and you'd eat again that day. Even if the stone didn't hit, the sound of it might be enough to panic the herd. I myself had brought down a young ibex last summer when I went to the river with Ochre.

"Maybe I'll go with them next time," Silka said. I glanced her way. She'd emptied her pouch and picked up a plum, raising her arm to toss the fruit at a tree.

"Silka, stop that! Pick those up. You and Rube are fools enough when you're here. If you went together to the meadow and both had spears, neither of you would return."

"Rube told me what you did. None of them like you."

"What I did when?"

"That time when the men were gone and he was with Reen and Leu, practicing with the spears."

"Oh, that." The boys were somber around the men, who were likely to laugh at anyone who boasted. Their mothers they avoided all together. But around the little ones and the girls, the three of them, Reen and Rube and Leu, strutted like lions. Sometimes when I saw them swaggering about, I'd yell, "The Warriors!" then scream and run. "I stopped doing that."

"He told me you did it last month."

"Well, that's when I stopped."

"Ochre took you hunting. He'd take me," she said.

"That's because I know how to throw." I stopped myself before I said more. The only way to win an argument with Silka was to ignore her. "Let's go home." I was tired of Silka, tired of the woods and the plums. We picked up our bags, found Birch, and headed back, almost empty-handed.

The hunters were back already. They'd done well, I could see. The Mothers had started to butcher three deer, while the men rested outside the cave, recounting the day to the old men. I didn't see the boys.

"Thistle, I need you over here." It was Magla, hoping to finish one more task before nightfall. "Start on this one." She gestured to a butchered carcass. I handed her the plums, got out a knife and a bone needle, and went to work.

It was my job to get the sinew from the backbone. First I cut away the flesh, sawing at the tough membrane covering the spine. Then I pulled out the long strands of sinew that ran the length of the back. The work was tedious, but I was good at it. Whether they were sewing or binding weapons, people came to me when they wanted sinew. Magla was the one who made our heavy rope, twisting together strips of hide.

I'd seen Silka walk by Magla, heard her say sweetly, "I wonder where the boys are."

"At the top of the hill," Magla had answered. "They'd better get back before dark."

Just as I thought. They'd gone to their private place, the ridge above the cave, beyond a cliff so steep the younger children couldn't follow them. Silka and I sneaked up there behind them sometimes. We'd hide in the rocks and watch them until our laughter gave us away.

The late afternoon sun bathed me in orange light, warming the blood on the ground. The smell of death rose around me. Fat flies droned by my head. When the Mothers weren't talking, I could hear the distant shouts of the boys. They still dared each other on, as they had when they were children, Rube's deep voice taunting the other two.

My thoughts drifted back to Reen. What would I tell him? I remembered a day along the creek. He'd come with Fire and me to search for bilberries. But the sky had grown dark. Thunder had cracked across the sky and the first of the raindrops were tapping on the leaves. We'd run for shelter and found a hollow place, along the bank and under a tree, a nest woven of roots and vines. And there we'd hidden, waiting out the storm in the damp earth.

And then there were the flowers he'd left when I was sick. The strange stone he'd given me once, as yellow as a little sun. My necklace of purple shells. His long fingers as they'd polished and drilled and strung each disc. My hands worked by themselves, tugging at the bloody spine, not needing the rest of me to do their job. The voices of the Mothers were soothing as they visited over their work. I watched my own fingers working, pulling, scraping, pulling, scraping, the rhythm pulling me toward sleep. I would tell Reen that what I thought about most were his hands.

Suddenly I heard a scream. I dropped my blade, pushed the carcass aside and jumped up. From the hill above came male voices calling, "Reen, Reen!" There was no answer. I looked at the faces around me, each looking to another, perplexed. Something was wrong. Everyone knew it. Ochre and Bakar pulled themselves up and stood motionless, as if waiting for an order. Then we heard the yells again. "Help!" The two men moved fast across the flat ground and lunged up the hill. Two voices kept calling. Was it Rube and Leu? "Hurry, hurry!" they were yelling. Ochre and Bakar disappeared over the top of the slope.

Reen's mother, Litva, had dropped her tools and was standing in front of the cave, her hands over her mouth. I began to shake, the sweat of the day chilling my flesh. My thoughts were jumbled. Where was Reen? I stood with the others, watching the hill. A hawk circled, looking for rabbits. I must have bitten my lip. I tasted salt. Then Ochre again stood at the top, yelling, "Get a rope! Reen fell!" Litva dashed into the cave, grabbing the rolled cord, and starting for the hill. Magla ran to help her, but Litva pushed her aside. Both women scrambled up the hill. Yarrow grabbed her medicine pouch and started after them.

Again we waited. My feet didn't move. Only my mind worked, showing me the same thing over and over again, jagged cliffs and a falling body. "Don't worry, Reen. Ochre's coming." The words repeated themselves silently inside of me. The next sound I heard was a scream. Litva. The drone of the flies grew louder, as if they too wailed for Reen. The noise was too much and I lurched to the side to vomit. Ochre and Bakar were coming down, carrying an animal between them, its legs falling loosely at its sides. No, not an animal. Litva followed, looking like a deer with no place to hide.

The People gathered round the broken body. Motionless, I watched. Their cries pierced the sky as if the valley itself was screaming. Still I couldn't move. My eyes caught sight of Reen, who looked like a deer himself, the hunt over. Litva collapsed on the ground and Bakar, with Ochre's help, placed their son's body in her arms. On legs like sticks, I walked toward her and dropped down beside her, watching as she rocked her boy back and forth. And there I stayed, staring at Litva's round, black eyes and her body swaying.

Into the night she held him, talking to him between her sobs. The rest of us sat without speaking. Rube and Leu hovered at the edge of camp with bowed heads until Magla went over and nudged them toward the group. Sometime that night Ochre lit a torch and entered the ceremony cave. I saw the other men join him one by one. Then I heard the scratch of scrapers against the packed dirt. They'd probably put

Reen next to the baby who'd never lived and the Mother who'd died with her.

Litva was no longer crying, but whispering as she rocked, telling Reen secrets. The breeze was cool. The Mothers built another fire, this one near the entrance of the large cave. Then they went to get their things. Bakar took Reen from Litva's arms and placed him on a hide near her feet. Magla handed her a doeskin and a bladder bag filled with water, so she could wash her son's face and wipe away the dried blood. When the moon was high, we shuffled into the cave and sat around the open grave, the children in the back by the wall. Magla lit a lantern. So many People, I thought. Where is Reen? Tears ran down other faces, but I was quiet, for someone else was now in my body.

Ochre laid a hide in the bottom of the grave. Thought Holder stood over the pit. "It's ready," he said. "The hunter will be warm." Ochre and Bakar lifted Reen and laid him in the ground, on his side, knees bent, head resting on his hands. They placed his things near by. The pouch that held his magic. I knew what was in it: two stone beads he'd carved himself; an elk tooth, a gift from Bakar after they made his bow; the spine bones from a sturgeon he'd caught last winter. His spear. His cup. Then Litva crouched down, giving him meat and the red berries he loved. A great longing went out and the People's tears fell on their arms.

I watched the faces of the children as the shadows flickered, their eyes reflecting the light of the torch. Thought Holder and Grandfather Zlatar drummed. Otok, his hands too crippled to join them, offered his deep voice. All through that long night, the People swayed and wept. The creature who'd come to live inside me only watched.

The voices faded and the weeping ceased with morning's grey light. Outside the cave the birds had begun their day. Thought Holder crawled to his feet and Idra handed him a pouch filled with powdered ochre. He reached inside, sprinkled a handful on Reen's body, and spoke:

Blood of the Mother, we return this child.

Then Idra placed twelve cowrie shells into the pit, saying,

Womb of the Mother, we return this child.

Those Who Serve covered him with dirt and laid flat stones over the mound to protect him from winter animals. The People stood and sang in low voices:

Come from woman, go to earth, come from earth, go to woman, our child, our child, our child. Come from light, go to dark, come from dark, go to light, our child, our child, our child. Come from joy, go to sorrow, come from sorrow, go to joy, our child, our child, our child.

It was a new day. Some of the People slept. Once again I sat on the rock ledge, watching the grazers kick up dust as they gathered at the river far below. I remembered nothing of the rest of that season, except that I was no longer a child.

Return to the Sea

THE MOON CONTINUED HER ROUND JOURNEY, through the time of The Fat Deer, The Storing of Food, Return to the Sea, and finally The Gathering of Fish. I was glad to leave the mountain. Reen's voice still called when I slept, though I no longer looked up each time I heard shuffling feet. Idra had told me it would be wrong to hold Reen's spirit here. I'd tried to let him go and return to who I'd been. But I wasn't the same. There was a layer, like a cloud, between me and the world. The world used to shine more. I was sure it did. The part of me that saw its brightness was gone.

I'd never seen as much grey as I saw now, here by the sea: the cold, churning grey of the winter sea meeting the heavy sky; the silver-grey fishes we sliced each day; the grey stone beaches; our grey stone faces. In the mornings I watched the men fish. Each day, Ochre and Zalec clambered over the slippery boulders and threw their nets into the water where the river met the sea. Sprayed by the waves, their bare feet gripping the stones, they'd watch and wait, hoisting in the net when it was full. They brought in large letnica and fleshy sea bass.

The little ones they let go.

In the afternoons, I'd watch Ochre carve fish gorges from fragments of bone. Sometimes he and Zalec tied the bone hooks onto lines made of sinew and dangled them in the river. The fish just looked at them and swam away, bubbling the water with bitter fish laughter.

I was learning to use the fish spears, along with Silka and Rube. I was good at it. We'd climb across a path of wet stones, find a foot-hold above a pool, and wait. Silka and Rube worked together, arms on the same spear, laughing at some secret fish game. My partner was the sea. First I made my thoughts as still as ice. Then I waited for the moment, never hurrying, letting the fish feel safe, watching as it circled and shimmered, my body part of the spear, waiting, and then my arm flying up and jamming down hard. I'd pull the spear from the red water and toss another fish into my basket. Sometimes I'd get a sterlet and we'd slit her open and eat the eggs. Or one of the salmon circling the frigid bay, restless to spawn.

When my basket was full I'd take it to the women at the drying racks, where the beach was littered with bones and shells of previous years. That's where I'd spend my days, cutting the jack fish and bass into strips. When Idra was well, she worked with me. Sometimes Silka helped. First I lined up the bodies of my victims. My hands were cracked from the cold. They burned where the salt water touched them. I worked quickly, at war with the dead, stinking fish, knowing the grey bodies would soon shrink in the light, commanded by a new voice inside me. "Slash them, throw them, slash them," it urged.

If Magla said we had enough dead fish, I'd pry oysters from the rocks at low tide. We roasted the plump-fleshed creatures in their shells. Most people loved them. To me they tasted like warm mud. I just picked the oysters and speared the fish to make the night come sooner.

98

When I tired of fish and oysters, I'd walk up and down the sponge-stone beach, sometimes with Silka, sometimes alone. I hated everything I did. Even more, I hated doing nothing. I wanted the voice inside me to go away.

"Idra," I said, slicing a bass one drizzling day on the beach, "when someone dies, can they take another's spirit?"

Her voice was like warm salve. "When someone dies or we have great sorrow, our soul is wounded. We don't die. But part of our soul goes away. Earthmaker keeps that wounded part and lets us live with less awareness. She protects us until we're strong enough to take back our broken parts."

Her words knocked against me like a wave. Was that what had happened? I'd lost part of my soul? The drizzle turned to rain and Idra and Silka ran for shelter as the first hard drops hit. I stood thinking until lightning flashed nearby. Then I rushed to join them, huddling on the floor of the cave with the others, watching as the men dashed across the beach with their nets. The fire in the entryway sputtered. For a while I thought about my broken soul. Then I stared outside.

This was no small shower, but a howling storm that lasted several days. We waited, watching as the rain slashed against the beach at an angle and brown streams gurgled down the hills. "Such rain, such rain," Idra said several times, rocking back and forth and hugging her knees. "We've never known such rain." We were stuck in that hole like snarling bears.

I reminded myself that the storm would soon be over, that I'd wander again along the shore, maybe learn more from Tenja about the stars. She told us stories as we waited and showed me how she marked a stone to count the days. But a great clawing restlessness was rising up in me. All my learnings brought me no peace. "Earthmaker," I prayed, "let me know you in a new way."

Finally, on the fifth day, Earthmaker answered, awaking me early on a foggy morning with no rain and the clear call of birds before dawn. Everyone else was sleeping. Out of the cave alone I crept, and onto the shore. Before me lay a strange beach strewn with seaweed and branches tossed up by the storm. With the breeze in my face and the mountains looming beyond the bay, my stiff legs stretching and my animal heart crying, let me out! let me out! I walked into this ragged new world.

I headed north, toward the mountains, stepping over fish flung out by the sea and trees from foreign places. The fog was lifting, the sea spent, yellow fingers of foam retreating to the dark water. Wet stones, the smell of salt, the distant cry of a gull. I saw no other sign of life. This was the world Earthmaker wanted to show me? And then a sudden movement caught my eye.

On the ground ahead was a young snow goose, not full grown, lurching over the rocks with a broken wing. Along the shore she ran, ran and stumbled, ran again, her wing dragging like a heavy bag. Sensing me behind her, the goose turned, arched her long neck, and made a rough cry. Then she ran again, desperate to fly, falling back on the rocks flightless and afraid. I felt a cold knot in my belly. Left behind by her flock, she would die.

"Earthmaker, help her!" I pleaded. Then Earthmaker gave me a plan. Earthmaker quickly gave me a plan. *Run back to camp, grab a fish net, return.* I turned and ran home, stumbling over the rocks. When I returned, the goose lay on the shore, the sea lapping near her, her good wing thumping weakly like shuffling feet, her soft chest rising and falling. I stepped closer. Her wing beat faster. Fear could kill her, I knew. Perhaps she'd die if I came too near. I sat a man's length away, unsure what to do. "Let her live, Earthmaker. Take her fear. Let her live. Please let her live!"

I clutched the net, my eyes burning, my shoulders rising and falling with the goose's thumping wing. Dawn's light was thin and watery, as if Sun itself was unsure of this day. Through the pale morning I waited, hating my helplessness, my eyes hot with unshed tears. The goose no longer moved. Exhaustion? Thirst? Was she dead? And then another weak shudder of her wing. She was alive! A great, wrenching sob came from my chest. I froze, afraid the sound would terrify her. But I couldn't stop my tears. Held back too long, my weeping began. Grasping my knees, I cried and rocked, cried and rocked, bitterness like poison coursing through my body. And then the tears were no longer mine. They were the tears of all broken creatures. I cried the tears of creatures who had no tears of their own. As I sobbed, I wondered, Did Earthmaker give people tears for animals, too? At last, too tired to think, I slumped to the ground, my hot cheek against the cold stone. The bird was watching me. Her black eyes glistened. Her head bobbed slightly. A breeze lifted the soft, white feathers on her back.

Still I couldn't move. I was planted to that place as though roots had grown from me and fixed me there, a crooked, windswept tree that must grow or die. And then my roots took hold, my roots were feeding me a deeper blood and the rocks were nourishing me, they were praising me and feeding me and the wind was singing, We know you and you are ours.

A golden light gathered as the sun at last burned off the fog and the world awoke. The day was so much brighter than any day that I remembered, clear and glowing as if the mountains were aflame. And then I knew what had happened. Earthmaker had given me back my soul, the part that she'd protected until I was ready to care for another.

I looked at the quiet creature before me. No part of her moved but her eyes. "Little goose," I said, crawling to my knees, "it's time to go." I placed the net snugly over her body and lifted her, her heart beating under my hand. "Come home with me," I whispered. "You'll never be hungry. I know how to fish." We headed for the cave.

She was thirsty when we got back and I brought her water in a shell. The People looked at us strangely. All that first night, I kept her close, the net still holding her broken wing. Little, chortling sounds rose from her chest. Eventually she slept. When the sun came up, Yarrow followed me outside, carrying her healing pouch. We loosened the net, so that only the bird's head and the broken wing protruded.

"Look here," said Yarrow, lifting the feathers on the upper wing, "see where it's broken?" The slender bone was cracked, though the sharp bone ends were still attached to each other. "She must have caught herself in the rocks and been pushed by the wind."

"Or maybe the waves," I said.

Yarrow held the bird's wing, working the bone ends back together, matching the rough edges, wrapping the bone with sinew, weaving the sinew through the feathers. The goose made a soft questioning sound, but hardly moved. When the bone was secure, we wrapped the net around both wings to hold her while she healed.

I named her Shine and kept her with me. All that winter, I gathered the feathers she dropped, stringing the largest ones into a necklace. When the snow in the mountains melted, Yarrow said it was time to unwrap the wing. The bone had grown together, but Yarrow rebound it with a single strand of sinew for extra strength. By then, Shine had found her voice again. She made a squawking sound to let me know her needs. She'd grown plump on oysters and little fishes. "No more food for you, Fat One," I told her as the days grew longer, "or you will never fly."

Throughout that winter, as their bellies growled and they grew tired of fish, the People had come to look at the stout bird in a bad way. I made sure I kept her with me whenever I left the camp. "You must be strong enough to leave us when your brothers and sisters return," I told her, "not so fat we eat you first."

"*Wraack?*" she'd ask, waddling over the rough beach by my side, and I'd explain it all again. Shine grew restless in the spring. She'd flap her wings and jump, trying to get off the ground, skimming over the rocks for short distances before she crashed. She'd have to do better than that to join her kind. When the ice in the river started breaking up, I knew we didn't have much time. I needed a plan. Silka began holding Shine on the beach while I climbed the hill above the cave with a pouch full of herring. Then I called for the bird, refusing to feed her until she flew.

And then came the morning when the loud cries of snow geese filled the sky. All that day and into the night the birds passed over, clouds of them darkening the beach with rushing shadows, stopping by the river to drink and feed. The honking and the flapping of thousands of wings told us that winter was over. Shine called out to them. In the morning she was gone.

Soon we'd be going as well. Magla had started the packing, hauling our belongings out of the cave, shaking out the sleeping hides, giving directions. I was to stay with Fire, keeping him away from her and out of trouble. My brother had become rough and loud in the past months, running through the camp on his fat, little legs. "You Who Chase Shine," I'd called him all winter. But now, with the bird gone, I liked him again. I watched Yarrow's son as well. Baby Zale was only in his second year, but I was sure he'd be even wilder than Fire. On this day, the boys were floating sticks in a pool left by the melting ice. Yarrow and Zalec sat nearby, talking about the trip. Would the rivers be too high? What path would be best? I wasn't that interested in the route, but I hovered around them hoping to catch Yarrow alone. I wanted to tell her of a picture I'd seen in my head, but I was afraid Zalec would laugh. Finally, Zalec stood and headed for the shore to check his nets. I had my chance. I jumped up and took a step closer. No one could hear us but Fire and Zale. "Yarrow," I said, "can I tell you something?" The picture seemed so clear to me. I hoped she'd understand.

"What?" She bent to wipe Zale's nose with the back of her finger.

"If we had many geese, maybe as many as the fingers on six hands, and we clipped their wings, they could stay with us for a long time. We could feed them and eat their eggs. Clip the wings of the babies and eat the old ones. Travel only when we wanted."

Yarrow looked at me with narrowed eyes. "We follow reindeer. There are no People who follow geese."

"Some day there could be. Maybe some day there'll be no reindeer and we'll tend geese."

"There will always be reindeer, foolish one." She went to help Zalec pull up the nets.

The Changers

SHINE WAS GONE, BUT THE WORLD STILL HELD ITS BRIGHTNESS. It was time to return to the mountains. We followed our old path, through the lowlands where marsh marigolds bloomed, beautiful but poisonous to reindeer. Then across three sweeping valleys, and upward. The round-headed rampions and primroses were opening, the buttercups ready to bloom. In the distance we heard the roar of water. Fed by melting snow, green glacial rivers tumbled over cliffs, surged through gorges darkened by mountain shadows, and swept across bright meadows.

Our path was rocky once we left the marshes, the white sponge-stone giving way to granite. The rocks would hold the memory of our passing. To tell other humans we'd traveled there, we left small mounds of cobbles. I drew a picture of Shine on a flat, dark stone, making my lines with a soft rock. I left the picture stone behind. The marks would wash away, but the stone would keep my thoughts. I'd make a carving of her one day.

I walked with Idra and thought about geese. Idra, my favorite

Grandmother and Teller of Tales, Idra of the Racing Heart. She could no longer keep up with the others, so we stayed at the back of the group, followed by Zalec, Protector of Stragglers. Sometimes her breathing was fast and loud. On the fourth day, she grabbed my hand. "Thistle, rest here." She pulled me to a tree and lowered herself to the ground, panting. I waited for her to catch her breath. Zalec was leaning against a rock a few man-lengths behind us. At last she said, "Listen well this year. I won't make this journey again. When my time comes, I want to die by the sea."

"Grandmother," I said, seeing an opening, "if you had geese with clipped wings, you could stay by the sea all year." There. Perhaps Idra would understand the importance of my idea. She said nothing. I watched her lined face, her eyes narrowed from years of squinting in the sun, her breathing easier now. A jay cried sharply to warn us this was not our tree. Idra's voice sounded weary when she replied. "Earthmaker gave us reindeer. It is not ours to change."

"But, Grandma, there is change. Earthmaker Herself makes change."

"So," she mused, nodding slowly, "so, you're one of them."

"One of whom?"

"Some call them the Bird People. I call them Changers. Like your father, my Zlatar, too. They soar on the wings of their great ideas while someone else carries the wood. It's not good to have too many in one place."

A shiver of familiarity ran through me, as if I had just come upon myself in a forest. "Tell me about the Changers!" She sighed and glanced around. Zalec was scanning the brush, his spear at his side. Maybe he was hoping for a rabbit. He seemed to be in no hurry. Happy to rest and talk, Idra collected her thoughts:

Like birds, the Changers fly above everything, their vision ranging widely. They see the past and the future. And what they can't see, they invent. They look to the horizon rather than directly below. Their thoughts are far away even when their bodies are beside you.

Sometimes they fly by themselves. Sometimes they fly together, if there's another Changer close by. When they return, they jabber like gackles to any one who will listen. They talk about what might be, for they care little about what is. By the time you begin to understand them, they've flown away again.

Changers are too quick for many of us. The People do better with many habits and few dreams. Changers like many dreams and few habits. They want all of us to share their far-reaching vision. But, for most of us, our task may be what's right before our eyes.

"But surely a Changer has much to give the People, if ever the old ways don't work?"

"Perhaps." Idra frowned. "But a Changer can lead the People only when she loves them as much as she loves her dreams."

"Your words seem harsh, Grandmother."

"Not harsh. Familiar. I've had this talk many times. All my grown years I've spent teaching the People their traditions, so they can know what is and what has been. But my man only questions the old ways and tells us of new ideas. It confuses the People. What is must be as important as what is possible, or we are only the stuff of dreams, vanishing in the light of day. Be sure you know the old, Thistle, before you embrace the new."

So Zlatar was like me! I thought about the lanky old man with the moon-white eyes, saw him by the fire. I liked to sit with him and cranky old Otok in the evenings. "What do you want, girl?" Otok would growl. Zlatar answered all my questions. He liked to smile. Some nights I'd glance around to see what was making him so happy, but it was never anything in the outside world. I'd watch his scarred hands as they carved, giving birth to birds and snakes and fish, never the same thing twice. He wanted new visions, new wood, new stones. What had already been done held no interest for him. And meant everything to Idra. What would it be like, I wondered, to spend your life with someone who saw the world differently, especially if you thought they were wrong? It was good to know who I was. But so much thinking confused me. I left Idra by herself and stepped off the path to pick buttercups.

The season passed peacefully, only the violent rainstorms surprising us. Idra taught me many things that summer and the next winter, making me repeat her words until they were part of me. I listened and tried to remember. I might be a Changer, but I didn't want her to think I was flighty. She told us again of Wolf the Warrior, Horse the Teacher, and Bird the Changer. My thoughts and memories joined, like the roots of plants. I was glad to be one of the People.

As Idra had predicted, that was her last trip to the mountain. When Spring rolled around again and we left for the mountains, Idra and Zlatar, the Teacher and the Changer, stayed behind. When we returned to the sea for yet another winter, Zlatar told us of Idra's passing, of how one morning she'd never awakened. He'd buried her with the others in the back of the cave, near the sea she loved so much. We marveled when we heard of it, how Zlatar, almost blind, dug her grave in the dark and covered her with dirt and stones.

The others were amazed that Zlatar had lived on alone so long, feeding himself when he was barely able to see, no food in the cave but stacks of dried fish. I knew his secret as soon as we reached the shelter. There, marking the sandy entrance, were the three-pronged tracks of geese. I followed their low sound to the shoreline, passing their nests in the tall grass, their down and poop dotting the beach. Then I saw the fat birds. They didn't try to fly, but ran to me instead, clamoring wildly to be fed.

Strangers

I SAT BY THE FIRE WITH THE MOTHERS, weaving rushes, on a chilly morning in early summer. We'd just returned to the mountain. The women's voices rose and fell like the calls of geese, summoning memories of Idra and Zlatar and the three-pronged tracks by the cave. What if . . . ?

"Thistle! Your mat. It's in the fire!"

At the sound of Sela's voices, I glanced down as my rushes burst into flame. Sela grabbed the mat from my hands and slapped it against the ground. The fire went out, but my own face burned with shame. The old woman glared at me, hard as a wasp.

"I'm sorry," I said.

"Girl, you wander even as you sit here. I'll speak with you later." She shook her head and returned to work. I gathered my rushes and moved outside the circle to finish my weaving alone.

It was my fifteenth summer. Reen's memory was fading, like a bruise almost healed. Other pictures now appeared in my mind, pictures of places I'd never seen. The images came whether I was sitting with the People or walking alone, as if I were dreaming while awake, as if I lived in two places. One place was the world of my People, close and warm and rough. The other, the world behind my eyes, was steeper and harsher, a wind-swept vista with seven distant mountains and a glimpse of sea. Did such a land exist?

I hadn't told anyone of this other place. Nor would I. Maybe everyone had other worlds inside them. Maybe not. I didn't want them to know if I was the only one. I glanced sideways at Sela. Perhaps the old woman would forget my carelessness. That seemed unlikely. Sela missed nothing about me. I'd heard her talking to Magla just last night, when they thought I was sleeping. What was it she'd said? "There's a part of her that's no longer with us."

"She's barely a woman, not yet had her ceremony," my mother had replied. "You make too much of her dreaming."

I'd strained to listen, though Sela's words made no sense. "She may be one of those who goes beyond what we know, who seeks the place where earth meets sky. Some return to be our teachers. Others never come back. Either way, we can't help her."

Where earth meets sky? Was that where my dreaming took me? How would Sela know about that? Anyway, she was a worrier, seeing problems everywhere. But what if she were right? What if I didn't come back? I quieted my mind, watching the in and out of my weaving, until all I knew was the whisper of grass through my hands. I didn't want another world. I wanted the People. I'd apologize again for my carelessness and prove to Sela that I wasn't strange.

Silka strolled by, bringing food for the Old Ones, smirking as she passed. I turned my back to the group and looked instead at Tenja. She must not have watched the stars last night, since she was already awake, reclining against a log and making marks on a stone. Maybe Tenja saw another world inside of her, a star world cut by rivers of

111

light and rocks that floated. She might understand.

Suddenly Tenja jumped to her feet and shrieked. I turned my head. Just clearing the ledge was a powerful man, his black hair matted, his tunic stained as dark as his arms. "Ephus!" Tenja shouted, running toward him like a child. Sela would forget about me now, at least for a while. Ephus the Traveler had returned.

Tenja grabbed his arm before anyone else had even moved. She clung to him with one hand and rubbed the dirt from his face with the other. "Where have you been? We've waited and waited . . ."

"Some more than others," said Magla, stepping up to the grizzled man. She shook her head at her sister and handed Ephus a horn full of water. "Bring him something to eat," she ordered. Silka ran to get the food. All eyes were on Ephus.

For four summers we'd awaited his return. Ephus brought us news and treasures and told us the wonders of distant places. He was one of the People, born of a mother who'd left our group to join a reindeer hunter from the west. But the woman, the hunter, and most of his people had died in a rockslide, buried in their cave as they slept. Young Ephus and his father's father survived, coming to us for shelter long before I was born. Even as a child, so the story went, Ephus wouldn't sleep in a cave. He'd stay under the stars with the animals, making his bed in the forest, not returning for days. When he stayed with us now, he told tales around the fire until the moon was high and then slept outside with Tenja. He was one of us, but different.

"Let the man eat," insisted Magla as we crowded around him. Even Yarrow, leader for journeys and lover of order, could hardly stop speaking. Where had he been? What had he seen? Magla forbade questions to anyone with an empty stomach.

At last Ephus finished his rib bones and wiped the grease on his leg, leaving a lighter streak where the dirt had been. I held my breath. Then he did what he always did. Stretched and yawned and said in a voice scratchy from lack of use, "Good time for a nap." We gasped and moaned, while Tenja pounded his shoulder. Ephus just laughed. "All right, we talk first." We all began at once. "What did you see? What did you bring? What took you so long?"

"Quiet!" Yarrow shouted. "Sit down, all of you." We did as she said, Ephus sprawling like a bear come back to the den. Yarrow turned to him. "Well?"

"I have seen Strangers," he began, the laughter gone from his voice. "There are Others in the forest, north of here, heading south. I hailed them with our greeting, saying, '*Olan.*' They didn't answer, just stared." What strange people, not to know our words!

Yarrow frowned and looked hard at Ephus. In the past, he'd spoken only of wonders and dangers far away. I'd never heard of strangers in the valley. Why would strangers go where they didn't belong? "These Others," she said, "how do they look?"

"Their hair is yellow, their eyes the color of water, their men as tall as horses."

People glanced at each other, shaking their heads. Birch turned to me and covered her mouth. "Yellow hair!" she giggled, as if Ephus had told a good joke. Yarrow silenced her.

"I have never seen Others like these," he continued, "but I have heard of them. They are called Arn. They once had a home, northeast of here, beyond the mountains, in a place now covered by water. They travel without ceasing. They are quiet and keep to themselves. They'll soon move on."

"How many?" Yarrow asked.

"As many as the fingers on two hands. Their winter must have been hard. They have few children."

"We watched Yarrow's face to see what we should feel. She nodded, waiting for the voice inside that would give her a plan. Finally she spoke. "It will be good to see these Arn. Ephus, after they cross the meadow, you and Zalec go to them. Take them meat. Build them a fire so they can rest. When they have eaten, return and tell us. We will not bring them here."

Ephus nodded. "Wake me when the sun's straight up," he said, stretching out to rest.

All that morning the camp buzzed like a hive. Who were these people? To have no home, to speak different words, to have yellow hair, how could such things be! I dropped my work and motioned to Birch. Now that Silka had Rube, Birch was my closest friend. We ran to the ledge and huddled behind a boulder, watching the meadow for the first hint of movement. Birch was young and trusting. She believed everything I said, which made it easy for me to lie.

"What do you think they eat?" she asked, scanning the quiet valley.

"I have heard that some eat children." Her eyes grew wide. "But not these Arn. Different ones. These are friendly." Unlike Silka, Birch was truly good. It was no fun to torment her. She jumped up and ran to the cave, returning with a bulging pouch.

She opened the bag. "Here. Take some."

"What do you have?"

"Walnuts. For the Arn." I filled my bag.

Fire and Zale found us at the ledge. Both boys were naked, their feet hard as hooves, their brown skin grey with dirt. Fire's red curls hung about his face like the plume of some rare bird. "Magla says you're to watch us," he said. Why did he have to bother us now?

"I'm taking you to the river tomorrow, to wash you," I warned.

114

"And I am cutting off your hair." Fire pulled away from me. "We have to do it. Or birds will nest on your head."

Magla had put out the fire, not wanting the Arn to see the smoke, so I gave the boys dried apples and salted fish. They chewed contentedly, forgetting my threat. The day was getting warm.

Ephus and Zalec left at noon, slipping down the hill and moving west through the trees. They'd wait in the woods for the Others, meeting up with them after the strangers had crossed the open ground. Like birds on a long branch, the People lined up on the ledge, hidden by dark rocks. We waited, the sun hot on our faces. Finally we saw a movement.

Across the meadow, where a distant forest met the field, a small band of travelers emerged. They paused. I could just make out the shafts of their spears. Then they entered the grassland, lumbering under large packs, moving toward our hill. I tried to count them.

Suddenly Birch gasped. "Look!" she cried. "Wolf People!"

I stared harder, confused. Then I saw an amazing thing. Plodding along with the Arn were four-legged creatures, three of them, each carrying a small pack. Animals who walked with humans—how could that be? We stared in stunned silence as the strange group trudged across the meadow and disappeared from view below our mountain.

Zalec returned late that afternoon. Though he was a man who rarely spoke, we clustered around him like sparrows to seed. "Ephus says to join him," he said. "The Arn await." Birch jumped up and clapped her hands.

Yarrow nodded. "We'll go now." She followed Zalec along the ridge and down the slope, the rest of us hurrying behind.

"This way, just ahead," Zalec said when we approached a small clearing. It was a place I knew well, having gone there often to dig onions.

Yarrow held up a hand. "Listen." We hovered in the lengthening shadows, the sun hanging low in the sky. Surely we'd be safe. There were as many of us as the fingers on four hands, the Old Ones and babies having stayed behind. From up ahead came the sound of laughter. Ephus. "We will meet these Others," Yarrow continued. "Meet them in a place we know. If they should strike, run into the forest. Lose yourself in the trees. Ochre, Rube, and Bakar will stay behind to stop any who chase you." The three men nodded and faded into the woods. Zalec led us to the edge of the strangers' campsite. There sat Ephus, chewing on another rib bone, grinning at his new friends. He rose and waved. We stood speechless, staring across the fire circle at the hulking Arn. The strangers were huge. The Wolf People had been resting at their feet, but now they stirred, growling. Birch grabbed my hand. One command and the Wolf People lay down, stretched out their paws, and stared at us with yellow eyes. The power of the Arn was great.

We shuffled into the camp and stood in a crooked line. Never had I imagined such humans! They towered over us, with arms like sticks and hair like straw. Even the men's wavy beards were yellow. One of the boy Others stood in front of me, too young yet for a beard. I looked up at his smooth face. His eyes held the sky. I jumped back.

The Strangers had opened their packs and spread strange things on the ground; rolls of hides and a giant bone shovel, a pile of flint and a stack of pelts. They wore loose tunics cinched at the waist and open-toed shoes with thick soles and leather ties. Their biggest man, the one who'd commanded the creatures, stood over an unopened bag, his arms crossed. A curved horn hung at his neck. He towered above the rest of the strangers, his arms like the trunks of young trees. Perhaps he was a giant. I'd heard of such things.

I looked back at the straw-headed boy, my hands shaking as I undid my carrying pouch. "Here," I said, holding out the bag, "these are for you." He took it and stared back at me as if I were the strange one.

The Arn stayed in our forest for seven days. We never took them to our camp, but we went to look at them every day. They were hungry and weak, some sick with fevers. Yarrow tended them, Birch and I carrying her medicines. Besides the Giant and the boy, the Arn had two small children, two Old Ones, one Mother, and three men. The Giant spent his time carving small stones and staring at the fire. He had no woman. I wondered if there was a giant woman somewhere for whom he waited, until I saw the way he looked at Yarrow. None of the People had ever gazed at her that way.

Yarrow had been with Zalec since she was little more than a child. To us she was just Yarrow, a capable woman whose duty it was to lead us, heal us, and be our teacher. We never noticed how she looked. That Arn knew nothing of her skills. But he swept her with his eyes, staring at her round breasts where they pushed against her tunic and watching the curve of her buttocks when she bent over a sick child. By the second day, the Giant was no longer crossing his arms when we were in his camp. Instead, he reached out to brush against Yarrow whenever he could. She'd push his hand away and continue with her work. Once she smiled.

On the fourth day, the Giant opened the bag he'd been guarding. It was filled with red ochre, the powder for Earthmaker's ceremonies. The ochre rocks were quarried beyond the Ice Mountains, then crushed into dust for carrying. Never had I seen so much in one place. There was enough powder in that pouch to last for years. His face beaming, the Giant handed the bag to Yarrow. Her eyes met his and she froze.

Ephus was close by. She motioned him over. "What should I do?" she whispered.

"Thank him," Ephus replied.

"You do it."

Ephus grabbed the bag, grinning, and shook the big man's hand. "Nothing hard about that." He swung the pouch to his shoulder and lumbered away. The Old Ones would be surprised.

Around the Giant I felt a strange fear that was not unpleasant. When we left his camp that day, I stayed close to Yarrow, wanting to ask a question. She saw me watching her. "What?"

"Yarrow," I said, "will you join with the Giant?"

"No!" She glanced around and lowered her voice. "Why would you say such a thing?"

"Because of how he looks at you."

"I have Zalec. I have my baby, my medicine. We don't know these people. It displeases Earthmaker for us to join with another when we have a partner. Say no more," she muttered.

"But at The Making of Spring the People join with others. And at Sun's return."

"Thistle!" She looked around again. "We join our bodies at those times as a way to join with Earth. Our longing goes out to Earth, to all of life. But when you join with another for your own need, part of your soul stays with that person."

"Then what happens?"

Never had I seen Yarrow so flustered. "That part always calls you back. You can't be at peace. You're weakened and you invite in Chaos. Never join with another when you have a partner, Thistle, no matter how beautiful the other might be."

"And is the Giant very beautiful then?"

I could see the color climbing up her neck. "Yes, the Giant is very beautiful."

EPHUS WAS LEARNING SOME of the Arn words. After several days, he could speak with them of simple things. Most nights we sat at their fire while he pieced together their story. Ephus told us good stories and could make his own facts if any were lacking. "These people," he explained one night, "were made by Earthmaker." Ephus said that of everyone, even those who didn't know Earthmaker's ways.

The four-legged creatures sat with us, as well, making puffing sounds. By then I knew they weren't Wolf People, but some new kind of animal sent to help humans. They rested at the feet of the boy I called Strawhead. When I touched them, they were soft and amazingly warm.

In the orange light the Arn glowed like lions. The Giant sat cross-legged between his people and Ephus, the dancing flames illuminating his golden beard and somber eyes. That night the tall man held a pouch the size of four men's hands. I held my breath as he slowly drew the bag open and pulled out a large, flat stone.

"Ah!" Ephus exclaimed. "A marking stone." I'd seen smaller ones before.

The Giant turned over the piece of slate and a picture jumped out. It was the monster Ephus had told us about, the huge creature whose horns jutted from the front of its head while its snout hung to the ground. Had this monster taken their home?

Ephus haltingly told us their story. "I know the land from which they come. There are no caves there and few trees." Once the Arn had lived together, it seemed, many of them, beyond the Ice Mountains. Their home was a wide grassy plain surrounded by ice. They ate the monsters, which were taller than two humans. But now the monsters were gone. The ice had melted, leaving a shallow swamp in the summer and a frozen lake in winter. There was no grass for the monsters, barely enough for a few reindeer. So the Arn had left their homes, some wandering over the northern plains, some heading south. As Ephus told their tale, the Giant stared into the fire.

"Ask them where they're going," said Yarrow. At the sound of her voice, the Giant looked up. She glanced away.

Ephus asked the question in different ways, but the Arn just shook their heads. "Either they don't understand or they don't know."

"Ask them if they know Earthmaker's ways," she said.

"I have no words for that," Ephus replied. "The Arn once knew Earthmaker's ways, like all People do. But these Arn are restless and have no home. They believe in nothing, except perhaps the weather."

We looked at them in new amazement. To believe in nothing! How could one live?

"Ask them how they can live?"

Ephus was tired of our questions. "They live in huts," he snapped. What was this "huts"?

Ephus told us of the abandoned dwellings he'd seen, now only round spaces dug out in the tundra and encircled by monster bones. They dug their fire pits inside and covered the structure with hides, leaving a hole at the top for smoke. Like us, they laid hot rocks on the frozen ground to melt the earth for a floor. In the past, when they'd left their homes to hunt, they'd stayed in small tents, like the ones they were using now.

Arn Dwelling

"How did they kill the monsters?" That question was from Zalec, Yarrow's man. He'd taken to sitting next to her at the Arn fire, grasping her hand. He was our greatest hunter, but he'd never had to kill anything larger than a bison.

"They dug pits," Ephus said. "I have seen their traps. They cover the pits with long sticks and they cover the sticks with grass. The monsters come to eat and one falls in. Then the Arn kill it with clubs and spears. This is what I think they do."

Zalec nodded thoughtfully and Ephus continued. "They make their clothes from the bodies of the monsters and their tools from their tusks, then eat their flesh and soften hides with their fat. They make tent covers with the skins and tinder with the bones. They make all manner of things from these monsters and now they have nothing and no habits."

I looked at them in a new way. What was it like to live cut off from one's past, to not know the proper way one did things? Perhaps the Arn were like us in some ways, I thought, only we used antlers where they used tusks. I'd watched them around the fire. They laughed like us. Strawhead often sat with the Giant and talked. Could the huge man be his father? The boy seemed to have no mother there.

With rest and food and Yarrow's medicine, the Arn were getting stronger. We went to visit them on the seventh day and found them packing their camp. None of us knew what had called them. They'd just become restless. Zalec and Ephus fetched a reindeer shank from the frozen pit, so they'd have meat on their first night. Then we stood and watched while the Giant opened another bag and removed several items. These he placed in Ephus's hands; three amber beads, a handful of fox teeth with holes drilled at the bases, and a small clay whistle.

Then the Giant turned to Yarrow, his eyes covering her while his powerful arms hung motionless at his side. He reached into the bag again, dug around, pulled something out, and thrust it into Yarrow's hand, enfolding her fingers. Then he stepped away. She opened her fist. Laying in her palm was an ivory figure, perhaps carved from the tusk of one of their beasts. It was Earthmaker's symbol, the gleaming body of a woman, her swollen breasts and ample hips rendered in tiny detail. Yarrow closed her hand and looked away quickly, but not before I saw a crimson flush spread from her neck to her face.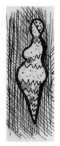

The Arn loaded up their camp, leaving no sign of their passing but the fire circle and the trampled grass. The Giant and Ephus stood with their heads together. Then the big Arn pointed south. We walked with them to the river, showing them a shallow place to cross. We grasped their hands as they pulled away, called out to them as they clambered up the other shore. The rough travelers turned back to wave, then headed south.

"Good-bye, Strawhead!" I called, waving broadly.

"His name is not Strawhead," Yarrow snapped. "It's Anish."

Anish. I wondered if I'd ever see him again.

Earthmaker's Daughters

SOON AFTER THE ARN'S DEPARTURE, THE RAIN BEGAN. The weather made the Old Ones cranky and kept the hunters home. Yarrow's boy was ill. Zale, a spirited child of three, usually followed my brother everywhere and feared nothing. But now he hardly moved. One night I was awakened by the sound of his coughing. I sat up. When my eyes had adjusted to the darkness, I saw Yarrow in the back of the cave, rocking the boy in her arms. Zalec stood over them. I crawled to Yarrow's side. "Is he all right?"

"Thistle, get my bag," she whispered. I sorted through the pouches by the cave wall, finding the medicine bag by its smell, an earthy mixture of pine and mint. Yarrow and Zalec spoke in low tones and Zalec went outside. I crept back to Yarrow.

"I can hold him," I said, trading the medicine pouch for the boy. He was hot and his chest made a rattling sound. Yarrow dug through the bag.

"Lay him down," she said. She'd wrapped Zale in a small hide, which she now pulled back, rubbing a pungent paste onto his chest, up his neck, and under his ears. She covered him again and sat back down, holding him close. This was the way her last baby died.

Zalec returned at dawn. Some of the people were stirring. He nodded to Yarrow and picked up the boy. The three of them went outside. I followed, out of the shelter into the drizzling day, across the mud to the ceremony cave. Zalec had made a steam tent just inside the entryway, stretching hides over a curved wooden frame. A small fire flickered near a pile of stones. Yarrow's voice quivered. "I did nothing wrong, Zalec, nothing," she said. Her eyes in the early light were as wild as a rabbit's. She lifted a hand to her face and I noticed that her nails were chewed to the quick. I'd seen her like this only one other time. Fear crept like a spider across the back of my neck.

"I can take the baby in!" I said.

Zalec nodded and handed the boy to me. Yarrow clasped her hands. Zalec pulled aside the opening flap. "Call when you get too warm," he said.

I crept inside, holding the boy, staying away from the hot rocks in the center, sitting cross-legged in the back of the tent. Running my hand along the ground, I found the bladder bag full of water. "I'm ready," I called. Zalec dropped the flap and darkness swallowed us.

I sprinkled a few drops on the stones and a hot cloud of steam swirled around us. The heat made me gasp. Zale whimpered, his little breaths coming fast and shallow. I unwrapped the hide and let the steam wash over his body.

"Give him a drink," called Yarrow.

I poured water into his mouth and over his head. And there we sat, gulping in steam like the lungs of some dark beast, sweat dripping from our bodies, our nostrils pierced by the smell of hot pine. I reached for his hand and felt a small, clenched fist. "Little boy, come back to us," I whispered. "Your mother is afraid. Your father is afraid." We sat in silence. I felt myself shriveling like a fish on a spit. I couldn't see Zale, but as the heat swelled around us, I could feel the beating of two hearts. Little by little, his breathing began to change.

"Thistle?" Yarrow peered through the tent flap.

"He's better. I think." I crawled out, lifting the boy to his mother. She wrapped him in a dry hide. I stepped outside, welcoming the bite of cold rain. I stood just long enough to cool my skin, then ran to the shelter.

The Old Ones and a few of the others sat just inside, talking softly. It would probably be too wet again to work outside today. Sela glanced up as I walked by, silver hair framing her face. Then she went on speaking. Thought Holder, Ephus, and Tenja clustered around her, as serious as owls, hanging onto every word she said. Perhaps she'd forgotten my carelessness at the fire for some new concern. I walked to the back of the cave, turned my back, pulled off my wet tunic, and wriggled into a dry one. Maybe I'd rest for a while, pretend to sleep, find out what thoughts gripped the old woman now. I learned the most when no one knew I was listening.

"The structure has changed," Sela was saying. I wrapped my sleeping cloak around me and lay down. "The structure has changed. I have seen rocks topple when I sleep. I have seen birds in flight turn to stone and fall. I have seen a she-bear crying for her cubs. I have seen a hawk returning, time and again, with empty talons. I have seen a falcon perched on the shoulder of an Arn. Why do they come here now?"

I peered at the four of them through narrowed eyes. Thought Holder was drawing lines in the dirt with a stick. Like Sela, he had a mountain goat's grey strength. "Ephus," he said, holding the stick, "you have walked these hills for the length of a man's life. Tell us what you've seen. Large things and small, that we may see the pattern."

Ephus scowled and wrinkled his brow. Before the Arn's arrival, he was the largest man I'd ever seen. Now he rested his elbows on his strong thighs, his hair as wild as a horse's mane. Ephus seemed restless even when he was sitting. I remembered Idra's story of the Horse People. Surely he was one of them. If it hadn't been for Tenja, he might have left with the Arn.

"These things I have seen," he answered. "I have seen saplings grow where there was once only grass. I have seen sparse meadows filling with young trees. I have seen the geese come earlier each year, their cries greeting us even in the month of Melting. I have seen shallow rivers rise, filling low places like a sea."

"And Tenja," Thought Holder continued, "what have you seen?"

Tenja hesitated. Always thin, she was leaner than ever, as if food had lost its interest. "The stars turn as ever, Grandfather. "I've had only that one dream, two summers ago, the dream you dreamt as well." She paused.

"What else?" the old man asked.

I strained to listen. "Ah, sometimes a thought comes to me—of a tree in a great storm." I glanced at her wide eyes. Of all the People, I most wanted to be like Tenja, gazing into the distance, studying the Mystery.

Thought Holder nodded and sighed. "We approach Change," he said. "Perhaps Earthmaker tires of us. More than this I don't know."

Magla began passing around dried fish and the talk shifted to simpler things. After a while, Yarrow appeared at the entryway, her child in her arms. She was smiling. "We need some broth," she said. Zale would recover.

As if in celebration, the rain ended the next day. Silka had awakened before me, for once, and hers was the first voice I heard that day. "Get up!" she ordered, grabbing my arm and pulling me back from the dream world.

"What? Where's everyone?" Sunlight streamed into the empty cave.

"The men left at dawn. Sela says we're to meet the Mothers outside. Hurry!"

I stumbled out and saw the women: Yarrow, exhausted and happy; Magla, busily shaking out the bedding; Tenja, who'd slept inside during the rain; Litva, Reen's mother, her gentle face now haggard; Frightened Eyes, with her secret memory; and the other two Old Ones, Lida and Ivy, grandmothers to Silka. Even Magla stopped moving when we stepped out. Anticipation hung in the air like smoke. Sela walked to the front of the group. How could one be so small and yet so frightening? "The time has come for the Woman Making ceremony," she said. "Silka and Thistle are ready."

Silka had spoken of this for two winters until I grew sick of hearing it. But now it was real. Birch stared up at me.

"Change is upon us," Sela continued. "We will go to Earthmaker and bring Her new servants. Birch will stay with the babes." We followed Sela and the others to a stand of pine trees west of camp. A cool breeze danced through the boughs. "Yarrow will prepare you for this night," Sela said. She folded her arms and settled against a rock, lifting her chin as she watched us.

Yarrow brushed a hand through the hair that blew across her face and smiled. "Earthmaker brings blessings as well as Change. Soon you will see the faces of the Mother. There are some things you should know before we go to the cave tonight." Her eyes seemed to be looking through us and beyond:

Long ago the People knew only the whirling embrace of Being. Many of us watched, many of us listened, many of us prayed, and now we see the parts as well as the whole. For the Mother comes to us in many ways, feeds us, clothes us, buries us.

She is there in the baby's tugging at the breast, in the mixing of medicine, in the hot pulling of our bodies for another.

Many are her animals: the snake that sheds its skin, the humming bees, the bear and its fierce protection, the bison and its slow strength, the vulture announcing death. We will dance in the night until you see the faces of the Mother, rising up within you and exploding in your minds. We will dance with the children of the night, the moon and the stars. We will dance and you will shudder to feel Her body become your body. And you will carry Her within you from this night on.

Silka and I returned to the camp to await the dark. No one asked us to work, so we sat down. Perhaps we'd have no tasks today. Magla had made rabbit stew earlier that morning. She brought some to both of us. I stabbed a turnip with a stick and blew on it.

"I'm going to be sick," Silka said. "How can you eat?"

"I've seen the dancing before. We've danced many times."

"But never in the Mother's cave. Never have we gone there. Nor seen Her markings on the animals."

"We know Her body," I said, remembering the naked fullness of a woman's figure carved on the wall of the larger cave, pointing our way underground. We'd sneaked in many times to look at Her. Nothing bad had happened.

But Silka's fear was real. Like a stream in the rain, it steadily grew. All day we sat, alone with our thoughts. I wasn't given to that much thinking. By the time the last streaks of gold faded from the sky, Silka's fright had crept into me. Magla gave us dried apples for supper and disappeared with the women to prepare for the night. But now I couldn't eat. I put the apples in my bedding for later. What were we waiting for? The men had returned from the hunt long ago. Now they rested by the fire with Birch and the children. I was too nervous to sit any longer.

"Come on," I said to Silka, "let's get ready." We wrapped our cloaks around our shoulders. The large cave would be cold. Then we walked over to it and stood outside.

Silka shifted from one foot to the other, hugging her cloak around her. "What's taking so long?" she said.

At last, the three Grandmothers, Sela, Ivy, and Lida, stepped from the shadows. Sela silenced us with her hawk eyes. "It's time," she said. She walked to the fire to light her torch. Silka and I followed the three of them into the ceremony cave. The rest of the Mothers stepped in behind us. I felt an urge to run, but their bodies blocked the entrance. The women lit their torches from Sela's. By now the sun had set and the walls danced in the flickering shadows. Sela turned and began walking. Her light led us on, the Mothers shuffling behind.

At the end of the outermost chamber, we came to a narrow room. Beyond that room was a branch in the path. The Grandmothers raised their torches. Looming before us on the rough wall was the body of the Mother, Her belly bulging with life, Her flesh trembling in the light. I heard a tapping sound. Silka's teeth. Was it that cold?

"Turn here," Sela growled up ahead. We ducked into a narrow passage and crouched to keep from hitting our heads. Sela bent down and disappeared through a black opening in front of us. Lida and Ivy dropped to their knees and followed, leaving us in total darkness. I began crawling after them. If the Old Ones could do it, so could I. The tunnel sloped downward and went on for perhaps a man-length, maybe longer. Above the huffing of the Grandmothers, I'd begun to hear the pounding of my heart. At last I emerged and stood. The ground was uneven. The sound of dripping water came from somewhere up ahead. I slid my hand against the cold wall as I walked, so I could catch myself if I stumbled. On we moved, into the silence.

"Wait here," said Sela. She went ahead with the other two, while we hovered in the dark. I strained for the sound of the Mothers behind us, but heard nothing. I held my hands in front of my eyes. I saw nothing. No night had ever been so black, no sleep so silent. What if no one came? Suddenly all but the darkness fell away and I was nothing, nothing but my thoughts. Silka whimpered. I was frozen to that spot and couldn't reach her hand. Our breathing merged and grew louder. The darkness was unchanging. I stood until my legs ached. Still no hint of light. And then even my thinking stopped. I became some raw animal, flesh without memory. But no. There was another darkness. I remembered an earlier time. I'd once thrust myself through another passageway in ignorance and dread. Then I understood. I would be reborn.

At last the Mothers came up behind us. I felt a gentle push and gasped. Keeping a hand on the wall, I moved forward, taking small steps. It felt like we were descending. Far ahead I could see a faint light. I hurried toward it, slipping on the rough ground. Silka tumbled behind me. I pulled myself up and moved on, with Silka clinging to my arm. We entered a brightly lit chamber. The Grandmothers stood together with their torches.

And then we saw them, the images of the Mother.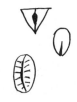
Up and down the walls they ran, tumbling over each
other, ancient and fresh, delicate and bold, terrible and
kind. She was here. Her symbols wound about the room.

 The meandering triangles and the two joined lines
pointing downward, signs for Her sex. Rippling
streams and the wings of birds. Round-
headed owls, with great disk eyes that
had never blinked. Stacks of white bones. Tiny painted
moons repeating their waxing and waning, telling us of
renewal. Cowrie shells, like tiny vulvas, strewn about the floor. A black
and gold bison with bulging belly ambling along one wall.

 I turned to gaze at the wall behind me, where round-
bodied women watched and waited, while around them
danced a circle of naked men, organs thrust upward,
servants of the Source. Layered over the chamber walls
were the marks of the Mothers who had gone before,
handprints in red and black, high and low, leaving a memory for those
who followed. A high wail pierced the silence. I jerked around to see
Yarrow blowing a whistle of eagle bone, telling the Mother that we
were there. Yarrow's voice filled the space:

> *Earthmaker, we bring you our daughters. Let them be like*
> *water, nourishing the land. Let them be like food, sustaining the*
> *People. Let them be like memories, upholding the past. Let them*
> *work and learn and heal, bringing Your vision to us. Let their*
> *minds and bodies be penetrated by your power, that they may*
> *bring forth life in their words and wombs.*

Magla and Tenja stepped from the shadows, each carrying large shells. Tenja's shell contained water. "Here," she said, holding it before me. My fingers trembled as I dipped them into the cold liquid. Magla offered me the other shells, one filled with powdered ochre, the other crushed coal. I placed my hand in the red one. Magla nodded.

"See this small hand here," she said, pointing to a handprint at the level of my head. "This is my mark. And here is your grandmother Sela's. And here is the mark of her mother and the marks of the ancestors. Join your hand with them."

I pressed the sticky paste onto the wall, leaving my mark with those who'd gone before. Then I repeated the words Magla told me. "I am Thistle, daughter of Magla, granddaughter of Sela. I pledge myself and all my daughters to the Mother, Goddess of All. I pledge myself and all my sons to the Mother, Goddess of All."

Silka made her mark next to those of Lida and Ivy and her own dead mother. I saw a new light in her eyes when she glanced toward me. Then we sat without moving, the air heavy with the weight of our past. Finally, we stepped out of the chamber, through the narrow passage, and into the night, new people.

The Old Ones were waiting when we emerged. I heard drums and the clack of bone striking bone. Yarrow led the women to the fire circle, chanting strange words. I joined them. Our voices were high and wild, but no words came from our singing, only sounds like the shriek of the wind in open places. We danced into the night and images burst in my mind like shooting stars, images of cliffs and valleys, streams and caves, babies and crones, bones and blood. All of these were within me and then I was within them, no longer separated by a frail sack of skin. We danced into the night until we became the night, our feet throwing off stars.

When the Reindeer Didn't Come

THE HUNTERS SET OUT THE NEXT DAY. The rain had left behind a bright green world and a cloudless sky. It was hot. Birch and I spent our afternoons on the ledge waiting for a breeze. We were making things for Fire and Zale, stuffing straw into hide-covered balls. They'd lost their old ones on the hill. Three days after they'd left, we saw the men trudging up the hill, led by Zalec. I always recognized his walk because of his bowed legs. They were empty-handed. Zalec and the hunters walked past us, stopping where Thought Holder sat. The Mothers dropped what they were doing and joined them. I stood with Birch at the back of the group. Zalec's face was gaunt. "The deer are gone," he said. "We walked for three days. They're gone."

Yarrow stepped closer. "Gone where?"

Zalec shrugged. "The valley where they run is empty, the grass not eaten, the ground not trampled."

Yarrow frowned. Something was wrong. Had Earthmaker tired of us then?

"Show me your path," said Thought Holder, handing Zalec his

drawing stick.

The younger man smoothed the ground with his foot and drew two jerky lines for mountain ranges and a path in between. That was the way the deer always traveled. In dry years, we could see the clouds of dust stirred up by their hooves. The old man nodded.

Yarrow once told me that Thought Holder could look into his heart and bring forth knowledge. He could see the ways of animals and humans, of land and stone and growing things. His mind held pictures of the People, in the past, as they were now, as they'd become. When the pictures weren't right, he saw how the trouble began. "Tell me what you saw," he continued.

Zalec shook his head. "Nothing different." We went to bed hungry.

I awoke before dawn. A lean shape stood in the entrance, framed by an indigo sky. Thought Holder. He slipped out of the cave. I didn't see him for the rest of the day. He returned at dusk, hobbling on ancient legs. We moved aside to make way for him.

"I have seen them," he said, smiling. "I have seen the deer. Two days away, in a different valley, just beyond the range." He pointed to the northeast. My eyes followed his hand. The same question rose from everyone. Why had they left us? We fell silent when he spoke.

"Change has come to the old path. There is a ridge above the valley where the deer once ran. And a gap between two mountains." I remembered the place. "The gap was filled with boulders held fast by ice. Heat and rain destroyed the ice. The stones shook loose and rolled. Filled the valley. Blocked the reindeer's way. Now the old path is gone."

It was only the stones that had changed! No horrible thing, only stones. Earthmaker hadn't forgotten us. The deer were nearby.

"We must leave soon to find them," he added. "They're two days from here, moving north." We'd all be going, it was decided, to butcher the animals where we took them and pack them home. Otherwise we'd go hungry waiting for the men's return. The hunters would travel quickly. The rest of us would meet up with them at night. We'd leave at dawn.

I was to watch my brother while Magla packed. Zale joined us for a skimpy meal of turnips. Birch and I gave the boys the leather balls we'd made. By the time the Mothers' work was done, our fire had burnt to embers. I walked sleepily to the cave, pleased about tomorrow's trip, but something in the shadows caught my attention. Glowing in the blackness at the camp's dark edge were four pairs of yellow eyes.

The hunters were gone when I awoke. We followed soon after. Down the hill, north across the meadow, and up other slopes we walked, clearing the foothills. We followed a goat path up a mountainside, sending loose shale down behind us. The air grew colder as we climbed. We stumbled over the roots of dead pines. Never had I been this far north. We'd always lived where the reindeer ran. Would the cave still be our home if the deer were gone?

Weary and shivering, we spent the first night in a small clearing. Before the last stars left the cold sky, we were gone again, plodding toward the summit. We cleared the mountain at midday and picked our way down the other side. Far ahead, like pointed clouds, the Ice Mountains thrust up their peaks. Below us opened a rough valley, not as wide as the one near home but lush with grass. Was this the valley Thought Holder sought? We hurried on. Then we saw them, below and to the west. Reindeer. A river of deer, pouring into that green valley, their antlers rocking in a great animal river, their breath rising like fog. We'd found them.

We clambered down the hillside. Just to the west, on a rocky slope ahead of us, stood Ephus. He'd heard us coming. Waving his arms over his head, he motioned for us to stay back. We stopped and dropped our packs, looking for the others. Then we saw them. Near the bottom of the hill, on an outcrop of boulders and broken shale, Ochre stood with Bakar, Rube, and Leu. Their backs were to us, their eyes on the valley. Below, between the men and the meadow, Zalec crouched behind a stone. Just beyond Zalec, where the land leveled off, the hill swelled to create a slender pass. The herd had slowed down to accommodate the narrowing.

The lead deer stepped timidly into that thin neck of land. Zalec sat motionless, waiting. But he didn't wait for long. Once the first deer ventured through, the others surged into the passage. Zalec stood and heaved against the stone. It rocked briefly and rolled down the hill, picking up speed as it careened toward the herd. Lurching over the rough earth, it bounced twice, then crashed into the animals below. Those in its path staggered and fell. Some tried to right themselves. But they had no chance. The terrified deer that followed trampled everything in their path. We'd have food to last all summer.

Zalec turned to make his way toward the men. Suddenly, before our shocked eyes, he lost his footing on the loose shale. He began to slide. Grabbing for a hold on the rocks, he fell to his knees. Again he clutched at the rocks. He couldn't stop himself. Now he was on his belly, slipping toward the deer. He covered his head with his arms. Yarrow screamed as Zalec's legs disappeared under the thundering hooves. We stood helplessly as the herd ran by.

"Zalec!" Yarrow called again, running toward him. We followed. Ephus was ahead of her. He reached Zalec first. The herd veered off to the side, away from the mangled carcasses, giving Ephus a chance to pull him to higher ground. Zalec's legs dragged behind like bloody pelts. The last of the crazed deer raced by. Yarrow dropped to her knees and grabbed Zalec's hand. His face was white, his eyes wild, his body shaking so hard we heard teeth. Yarrow herself began to shake, but she stopped suddenly, as if she could command her fear. "Zalec!" she yelled, "stay with us." She moved her hands over his writhing body. The deer seemed to have crushed only his legs, missing his stomach and chest. "Magla," she ordered. "Cover him! Build a fire."

She hacked off his leggings with her knife. Blood seeped from the gouges on his legs, but she had no interest in that. Instead, she stared at the purple blotch spreading like night over his right thigh. "Press here!" she said to Ephus, placing her hand on Zalec's groin, below and inside his hipbone. "Press hard! Don't stop." Zalec moaned and shivered. Ephus kept pushing. Yarrow looked around. "Berry, Leu, get some snow from the mountain. Run! Ochre, get some branches. We'll set the bones. We have to keep the swelling down. But he can't get cold." She spoke choppily, as if she could remember only one thing at a time. Her mouth continued to move even when she was done speaking. Magla boiled water for willow tea. Ephus stood. The bleeding had stopped. Zalec couldn't be moved, so we made camp there. The men dragged seven deer carcasses up the hill and stashed them behind a rock, building a second fire to guard them. We roasted a few chunks of meat on sticks, but no one was hungry. Tenja and Ephus went to sit with Yarrow, adding wood to the fire.

"Will he live?" Birch asked me as night came on.

"Maybe," I answered. Whenever I drifted off to sleep, I was awakened by Zalec's screams. Morning dawned grey and damp over the stark land. Magla was making tea when I awoke. The world was strangely quiet. I looked at Zalec. He wasn't moving. Yarrow hovered over him.

"Here, bring this to Yarrow," Magla said, handing me a steaming horn cup with a leather strap. I rubbed my eyes, took the tea, and walked to Yarrow. Her face was ashen.

Tenja was speaking as I neared. "Go to sleep. He's better. I'll watch him."

Yarrow shook her head. "After the others wake up. I want to tell them first."

"Tell us what?" I asked.

"Thank you," Yarrow replied, taking the tea.

"Tell us what?" I persisted. "Will Zalec die?"

"He's better. But we can't move him. I'm staying here. Ephus will stay with us."

"And Zale?"

Yarrow shut her eyes and shook her head. "Will you take care of him for me, Thistle? He's not safe here, out in the open."

"Of course."

So we were to separate and go on without them. That seemed like the only choice. Still, I couldn't remember a time when we hadn't all stayed together, except when the Old Ones couldn't travel. Earthmaker had given us the deer, but She'd taken Zalec and now Yarrow and Ephus. What was it She wanted?

Well, at least if Ephus stayed, I'd have Tenja to myself for a while. She'd spent so much time with Ephus, she'd had little time for me. Yarrow had been too busy with her son to talk much lately. Most of my questions, I couldn't ask Magla. Magla liked questions that had one answer. Tenja had many answers. We could talk on the way home. "I'll take care of Zale. I promise."

We wouldn't be leaving for several days. The time just after a hunt was always busy. My questions would have to wait. Everyone worked quietly, trying not to bother Zalec. That first day we skinned the deer and butchered them. We'd scrape the hides more closely back at home, then salt them down or smoke them so they wouldn't rot. I sat with Birch and Silka, slicing flesh from a hide with a piece of flint.

"Thistle, look! This would just fit me!" Birch said, holding up the hide of a young deer.

"Well, you'd have half of a tunic."

"Oh," she replied.

Our tunics we made by sewing two hides together at the shoulders and sides. With the seven animals we'd brought down, there were hides for three large tunics, with a small one left over. "But there's enough to make you a pair of leggings with that little animal," I said.

"There is?"

"Sure. Look. It takes four deer legs to make one pair." I laid the hide down to show her. For each legging, we sewed two leg skins together with two long seams. Birch's face lit up again.

I myself was hoping for new boots. We made our boots from the reindeer's heads, one boot from each head. We'd sew the eyeholes shut, and the mouth, and wear the fur on the inside. With six large deer, we'd have boots for three people. And one little boot for Birch. Maybe I'd mention to Magla that we needed another small deer before winter.

I sat close to the fire, holding my hands over the flame when they got cold from butchering, listening to the sizzle of fat. Hands on her hips, short legs apart, Magla stood on the bloody ground, planning her next move. A mound of fresh bones lay nearby. She was already roasting the flank of the young deer. "We'll leave two hides for Yarrow to work," she said. "Zalec will need new clothes. And we'll roast one flank to leave behind." She bent to toss another log on the fire, and before she straightened up, an idea came to her. "When you finish there, you can help Sela cut the meat for drying. Make sure your slices are thin. We'll start a rack for Yarrow." By the end of the third day, most of the work was done. There was enough grease to fill five pouches. We'd use it for soups and torches and softening hides. In the winter, the Mothers put it on our hands and feet and faces, as well as the babies' bottoms. We had more meat than we could carry. Some would have to be stored.

"Bakar," said Magla to the sullen hunter squatting at the fire, "you and Leu go up the mountain. Bury the meat in the snow. Cover it with rocks." Bakar pushed against his knees and rose slowly. Ever since Reen's death, Bakar had treated Leu like a son, teaching the ungainly boy the things he'd taught his own child. It was strange how good could come from bad.

Ochre had made carriers for the meat, tying two poles together with leather strips. Over the strips, he'd draped a hide. He'd stacked the meat on top of that, coating each layer with salt, then covering the load with another hide. The carriers were heavy, but two men could manage.

Finally, on the fourth day, we were ready to go. I hadn't minded the work, since the faster we got out of there, the sooner I could talk with Tenja. Zalec showed little change, but maybe that was good. No infection had set in yet. I was eager to leave that forlorn place, though I knew the trip wouldn't be easy. The load would slow us down. The smell of blood would draw the cats.

I'd had no teacher since before the Arn. I could learn without a teacher, but what I missed was talking. Not since Idra's death had I had a friend who knew the joy of words. I'd hardly spoken to Tenja since Ephus came. Now I tried to remember everything I wanted to ask. She, more than anyone but Thought Holder, knew Earthmaker's patterns and the People's trails. Tenja knew of high mountain caves, strewn with the bones of humans from the past. What did she think of, alone at night, staring toward the horizon and beyond to the stars?

The men hoisted up the meat carriers and the Mothers stuffed the final things into their packs. Zale and Fire wrestled on the rocky ground by my feet, laughing as they rolled down a slope. Once again Zale followed Fire everywhere, his illness like a bad dream. He hadn't minded at all that he'd be staying with us. I grabbed both boys by the hand and squeezed their fingers. "We're going home," I whispered. Tenja strode toward the group, as lithe as a young elk. Maybe she'd walk with us.

She stepped before the People. "*Aeii*," she said. "I will speak." The men lowered the carriers. The women put down their packs. All eyes were on her. "I will stay here."

There was a murmur of surprise, then a few questions. No one was telling her not to stay.

"But you're our Starwatcher!" I blurted out.

"Ssh!" said Magla. "They have the same stars here."

"But mother!" It was too late. They'd accepted her decision. So our hunter, our healer, our traveler, and now our star watcher would all stay behind. I looked around at their calm faces. This wasn't right. Everyone said farewell to the other four. For a moment, I thought about saying I'd decided to stay as well. What reason would I give? That I wanted to talk to people who didn't care if they spoke to me? I said nothing, just turned and marched up the hill with the boys. My eyes burned.

Halfway up the slope, I passed Silka and Rube. "Tenja would rather sleep under the cold stars in Ephus's hairy arms than come home with us," I muttered to her. Silka smiled her annoying smile, as if keeping some great secret. I was tired of her and walked on alone.

The journey home was uneventful. I didn't even feel excited the next afternoon as we climbed our own hillside and trudged into camp.

I looked around, bored. Right away I knew something was wrong.

The waste pile near the ledge had been knocked about. Gnawed rib bones were strewn all over. Storage bags, packed with dried meat and hung high, had been dragged from the cave and strewn about the entryway. Deer hides stored for the winter lay trampled on the ground. The drying racks were upended. Even Ochre's lion pelt lay in tatters at our feet. The muddy paw prints left us a clue. Wolves.

I remembered the yellow eyes the night before the hunt. The wolves must have waited for us to leave. Famished from the deer's disappearance, they'd torn into our camp, eating everything. Never before had they ravaged our home. We knew the creatures only by their paw prints, rarely coming close enough to see them. Except for the one on the path that day just after Sun's Promise. Were the wolves now braver and more clever? Or just hungrier? Everyone scurried around to put things right, talking angrily. I looked at the woods in a new way. There were many things we couldn't see. Now there was even more I didn't understand.

Tenja's Return

NOW THAT TENJA AND YARROW WERE BOTH GONE, there was more work. I helped Magla around the camp, once again feeling Sela's eyes on my back. Birch and I hurried through our tasks in the morning so we'd be free in the afternoon. There was so much I wanted to learn. I had to do it on my own since I had no teacher. But at least I had Birch. I was working on a bird trap. I'd told no one my idea but Birch. One bright day, when the trap was ready, I grabbed a piece of raw meat, dropped it into my pouch, and nodded to her. We headed into the forest, pine needles crunching underfoot.

"Birch," I said, glancing back toward camp, "no one must know of our plan."

Wide-eyed, she whispered, "No one will."

We walked to the foot of a giant pine on the far side of the woods. Its lower branches were bare, its high boughs merging with the other trees. I'd try my trap here. I pulled the net from my pouch, a simple thing made of six strands of sinew tied together, then climbed the low branches and straddled a limb. Birch stood below. Next I draped the

143

net loosely over a few branches, leaving an opening at one end. Then I took another piece of sinew from my bag, tying one end to the net and looping the other around a flat stone. Finally, I stuck the meat between the stone and the knot, ramming it in tightly. I climbed back down.

"Now what?" Birch asked.

"We wait. When a bird comes to peck at the meat, he'll knock off the stone. When the stone falls, it will pull the net over the bird." Or so it seemed to me. We hid in the shadows, listening to the rustle of small creatures. Nothing happened. "The birds know we're here," I said. "Once we leave, they'll come."

It was late afternoon when we got back. Magla looked cross. "Birch got lost," I explained.

"I got really lost," she said, her voice quivering.

Magla shook her head. "Bring the Old Ones some food, then get yourselves something to eat." Birch grinned at me when Magla wasn't looking. Then she ran off while I ladled out stew for the old men. Otok, Zlatar, and Thought Holder sat together as usual, heads bent low, carving and talking softly.

Sela sat nearby, sopping up stew with a slice of turnip. She glanced at me and raised her eyebrows. She'd think the bird trap was foolishness, a waste of meat. Anything that hadn't been done before was foolish to Sela. "Hello, Grandmother," I said with a smile. I turned toward the old men. They were better company. They wouldn't notice if I was gone all night, unless they got hungry. And they were interesting. Of course, it was easier to spear a trout than get a direct answer from them. But sometimes, when they forgot I was near, I overheard some great secret meant only for themselves.

"Here, Grandfathers, stew."

"I can see that, girl," said Otok, Sela's man. Maybe he got his crankiness from her.

"Thank you, Thistle," said Zlatar, looking toward me with clouded eyes.

On the ground by his feet lay an antler. He'd notched a line of tiny v's up and down its shaft. I gave him the first serving, pressing his rough fingers around the shell. Zlatar had been quiet for a long time after Idra's death. But now he'd found his voice. I felt close to him, knowing he was a Changer like myself. I smiled when I remembered his geese. After serving the other two, I filled a bowl for myself and sat down.

"Too much rain, eh?" Otok was saying. His curled fingers hurt in the damp.

"Ah, Change, it's harder when you're old," Zlatar added. Thought Holder and Otok nodded. Then Zalec mentioned the strange ways of the reindeer. This was my chance for a question.

"Grandfather," I said, "the wolves in the camp, is that Change?"

Zlatar shrugged. "Hunger is always with us," he said. "Maybe their hunger is growing."

"But the wolves have never been here before," I said. I wanted answers, not riddles.

"They're always here," he said. "You've just never seen them." He continued eating. I finished my food, wiped out the shell, and went to find Birch.

"Hurry up and get done," I said. "Let's go check the trap."

"But it's almost dark!"

"That's why we have to hurry." I waited for a moment, then we slipped into the woods. The forest was darker than the camp, but we could see well enough for a while. The tops of the trees were black against the golden sky. The wind was rising. Shadows swayed and pine

145

boughs creaked. The dead needles were sharp against our feet. A crow questioned our passing. Suddenly, I heard a hoarse scream.

"The trap!" we said together. We plunged on. Another scream followed. We hurried toward the sound, letting the branches snap behind us. Something was in the trap! A raven? A hawk? I could hear a wild, thudding sound. The thrump of trapped wings. And then we were at the tree. I looked up. Through the black branches, I saw a writhing, white shape. Curved talons grasped a branch. Round eyes stared down at me in yellow rage. It worked! The trap had worked! I'd captured the most beautiful of all birds, a great snowy owl.

Birch clapped her hands. "What should we do?" she asked.

I hadn't thought that far. "We'll get some feathers and let him go." We'd never eaten an owl. Maybe one day we would. Maybe one day the deer would be gone and Earthmaker would force us to do strange things. I started up the tree amidst a great squawking.

I couldn't see the net, but it must have caught the beating wings. I wedged myself between the tree trunk and a limb, looking to the upper branches. I could almost touch the bird. What now? Mindful of the talons I reached upward, my arm brushing the warm body. The owl lunged but the net held. I braced my-self and reached again, grabbing a fistful of feathers. The bird shrieked and flapped his wings. One pulled loose. Slapping the wing free, the creature lurched from the net and hung sideways, one wing still trapped. Birch screamed as a talon raked my arm. Grabbing my blade, I slashed the string that held him. With a rush of wings, he was gone.

"Thistle, come down," Birch cried. I climbed part way, then jumped. "Thistle, your arm!"

The blood was rising like a black line in the deepening night. The gash stung but it wasn't deep. I picked up the feathers that had floated to the ground and we headed home. For once I was glad we'd be returning after dark.

AN ENTIRE MONTH PASSED without Tenja and the others. Bakar and Leu had returned to the reindeer mountain ten days after our return. They'd brought back some of the frozen meat and told us that Zalec was mending. Meanwhile, we dried the meat and sewed, savoring the heat of midsummer. The days were so warm we didn't need leggings. Birch and I sunned ourselves on the flat stones east of the cave, talking and watching Fire and Zale throw rocks down the hill. Frightened Eyes joined us some days. She was older and never spoke, but she was no bother. We liked to talk about Silka and Rube. They'd had their joining soon after we returned. The last joining ceremony I'd seen had been Zalec and Yarrow's, when I was still a child. Birch remembered nothing about that time. I explained what I could.

First Magla had gone to Silka to tell her that the time was right and the Old Ones approved. The men had built them a small enclosure far from camp which Magla stocked with food and water. Then we'd gathered and cheered and sang as the two of them hurried away. We didn't see them again for three days.

"Do you think there's a baby growing in her yet?" Birch asked one day.

"Maybe." I picked up a small, flat rock. I knew something about marking days, since I'd watched Tenja make her calendar. "You can make a notch for every full moon and count the months from their joining. Then, after the baby comes, you'll know when it was made."

Birch frowned. "Would you do it for me?"

"All right." I was already keeping a record for each month we'd been on the mountain, three now. I could just knick an edge right before the third full moon to mark Silka's joining. If I wanted a more detailed record, I'd need Tenja's help. I'd already chipped off a full cycle of the moon without her. One month gone since Zalec's fall. Maybe I could figure out more myself, but it would be better if Tenja were here.

Then one day, when we were sitting in the sun, Zale shouted, "Ma!" I looked up to see Yarrow and Tenja clearing the ledge. Finally. Yarrow hugged her boy. Ephus and Zalec followed soon after, the big man almost dragging Zalec up the hill. Zalec had one leg in a splint and couldn't stand on his own. His face was sunken, like the memory of pain. Once they made it to the fire circle, Ephus eased him to the ground. Ephus grinned and waved at us, the same big bear as ever. Yarrow looked haggard. Tenja seemed different. She smiled thinly and said nothing. I was too excited to dwell on that for long.

We brought them water and let them rest. Magla started a stew for the next day, lining the cooking pit with a hide, filling it with venison and apples, then dropping in hot rocks and covering it with another hide. We slept outside, talking into the night and awakening to the smell of cooking. I went to the cave to look for something, waiting until everyone was fed to show them my treasure.

"Tenja?" I said, feeling awkward. I remembered my frustration, first when she'd said she'd stay behind, and many times since as I tried to make my calendar. But it was hard to be angry at someone you needed. "Tenja, I have something for you." I held out two hair ties made from the feathers of the white owl.

"Thistle, they're beautiful!" she exclaimed, her face softening for a moment. She wrapped one into her straight brown hair. When she smiled, she looked almost like the old Tenja.

I'd made ties for Sela, too, hoping a gift would make her less cranky. I tried to look happy as I handed them to her. "Here, Sela, for you."

She reached for them slowly, as if expecting a trap. "Where'd you get the feathers?"

"I picked them up in the forest."

She closed her hand around them and held them close. "Humpf." For Sela, there was a certain way things should be done. She was not accustomed to gifts. I myself liked surprises. "Nice for you that the bird left them behind."

"Put them on," I said. Her old fingers fumbled with the ties, so I wrapped them for her. Sela patted her hair, her face flushed. I handed a pair to Magla and Yarrow as well.

Then we listened as Ephus told us of their month. Yarrow said little, just rubbed oil into Zalec's legs and played with Zale. Everyone had questions for Ephus and Tenja. I lingered, curious about their trip, happy that Zalec was still with us, hoping for a turn to speak. After a while, I grew tired of waiting and left for the woods.

"Birch! Where are you?" I called. Maybe we could go to the river. A branch snapped behind me and I jerked around. "Sela!"

"Thistle," she said, stepping toward me, the owl ties tangled in her grey hair, "Thistle, I have been watching you."

"I know," I replied.

"Girl, you dream more than most."

"Yes."

"Your people need you. There's a time for dreams, but your duty comes first. Who is it that feeds you, brings you hides to keep you warm, shelters you, protects you from the Unknown?"

"The People," I mumbled. Why was she saying this now? I'd done my work. What could I say to make her go away? "Grandmother, I'm one with you and all the People." That would have been a good answer, but my mouth kept moving. "But there are things I want to learn, things of which we rarely speak."

"What things?"

"I want to learn about the wolves. The geese and the stars. The Fish People and the Others." I didn't tell her what I most wanted to know: Earthmaker's plan for us.

"Is there anything else you think about?"

"No."

She moved her hands as if chasing flies from her face. "Very well. Go on. Perhaps Tenja can teach you these things now that she's returned."

"That is my hope."

Tenja's Secret

LIFE WAS AS IT SHOULD BE ONCE AGAIN, everyone together. The golden
days filled us. Yarrow spent her time with Zalec and their son. Ephus
and Tenja were always together, so if I wanted to talk to her, I had to
talk to him as well. I didn't mind Ephus. Still, Tenja seemed irritated
by my questions, telling me "later" as if I were a child. So I came up
with a plan.

One night, after the stories were finished and everyone was heading off to sleep, I whispered to Zlatar, "Wait." The old man, never in a
hurry, just smiled and sat motionless while the others left. When we
were alone I asked him, "Will you teach me about Spirit?" He nodded.
If I learned all I could from Zlatar, maybe Tenja would begin to take
me seriously. "Good," I said. Zlatar was eager for a listener. I talked to
him in the day when Otok wasn't around. It didn't matter if Thought
Holder was with us, since he could barely hear. We sat together in the
night as well, after the fire burned down and the others went to sleep.
Sometimes Tenja and Ephus joined us before she went off to track the
stars. But usually we were alone.

"I know Yarrow and Ephus are Travelers, running with the spirit of Horse," I said one night. "Your woman, Idra, told me that. What is Silka?"

"Silka is a Golden One. She shines like the Sun. Everything turns around her. Her heat draws people to her. Their praise makes her glow. The power of the lion moves through her. Whatever she wants, she feels she deserves."

"And Sela, what makes her so cranky?"

Zlatar laughed. "Sela was born old. She's an Elder. Even as a child, she thought of structure and form. The Elders keep the right habits alive. But they're as stubborn as goats."

It was probably good we had someone like that. I was glad it wasn't me. "My mother, too?"

"Yes, Magla, even Yarrow, though Yarrow's way is softer. Spirit takes many forms. Any of us can teach, or lead, or hunt, or dream. Each brings something different to the task."

Some nights, after we'd talked and Zlatar had hobbled back to the cave, I sat outside alone, too excited to sleep. Then I thought of the People as animals, whinnying horses, placid bulls, sturdy goats. I felt my own arms becoming wings. Some nights, I slept outside with Tenja and Ephus, waiting to see the silver streak of a falling star. Sometimes I looked at the stars in different ways, as well. What if the sun were really a star that we saw in the day? Could the stars be suns for other creatures? Did they know Earthmaker? She'd have a different name.

Some nights I thought about a story Tenja once told me, taught to her by Thought Holder, taught to him by the Ancestors, the story of the Great Tree. I tried to imagine that tree, branches reaching for the stars, roots so deep no one knew their end, trunk uniting the world above with our flat world and the world below. When he was young,

Thought Holder had taken journeys in his mind, so Tenja said, journeys that let him climb that tree and bring back songs. He'd taught Tenja everything else he knew. I wondered if he'd taught her how to make that journey.

There were other things I wondered about Tenja. She and Ephus seemed happy with each other, yet she slept poorly and roamed alone at night while Ephus snored peacefully. Some mornings, when I awakened early and slipped outside, she'd be sitting by herself, staring at the grey horizon. I'd join her then, waiting for whatever words might come. Little by little, as the days went by, she began to talk. Maybe she thought I was ready. Or maybe she was eager to talk about the stars to anyone who'd listen. Either way, I was happy for the change.

One clear night, after everyone was asleep but the two of us, I huddled on the ledge with Tenja. I wore my new tunic. I'd outgrown the old one and given it to Birch. The night air was chilly. When I pulled the garment around me, the stiff seams poked my skin. The world was silent, except for the hoot of an owl.

"Tenja," I whispered, "tell me about the stars and the Great Tree."

"Again?" Her voice was weary.

"One more time. Please." I lay my head on a log and hugged my arms around my chest.

"All right. The Great Tree grows through the center of the earth. The world turns endlessly about its trunk. Even as we sit here on firm ground, we are spinning. All the stars are spinning, and the sun and moon, like the songs of different creatures in the same dark wood."

I stared at the stars as she spoke, trying to imagine them turning.

"The stars you see now are the stars of summer. Later the stars of winter. The sky is always changing. You already know that the place sun rises shifts just a little each morning, moving farther and farther north for half the year, turning, then moving gradually to the south. This you can see with your eyes."

I nestled further down. We were getting to my favorite part.

"But there are other spinnings that we will never see, giant spinnings we can only glimpse in our minds. Our short years measure the lives of the People. There are much longer years that measure the life of the sky."

Like night birds, her words flitted by me. I knew something was there, but I couldn't see it yet. My eyelids had become too heavy for me to think any more about stars. But I had Tenja with me now and years in which to learn all she could teach. I drifted to sleep, part of me lifting with the night birds, spinning and swirling in the black, glistening sky. When I awoke, she was gone.

I finished my work quickly that morning, then went to the woods to bait my bird traps. I'd promised Fire I'd take him with me later to see what I'd caught. We liked to pluck a few feathers and let the creatures go. Birch stayed behind. She was sewing another ball for the boys, their last two having disappeared over the hill.

I entered the woods quietly, pushing aside branches to make my way, moving slowly so I didn't disturb my quarry. My bare feet were soundless on the damp pine needles. I always went to the same far corner of the woods, leaving my traps in different trees each time. I liked going alone. No one ever went there but Birch and me, sometimes Fire if he was with me. I'd come to think of this part of the forest as mine.

From up ahead came the sound of voices. How strange! I stopped to listen, puzzled. Was someone curious about my traps? I took a few more steps and crouched down. Someone was sobbing. I peered around a tree trunk, my face hidden by the foliage. Tenja sat on a stone, Ephus at her knee.

"Something is not right," I heard her say. "Something is not right. They look to me to explain it. I have no answers." She rubbed her eyes.

Ephus shook his shaggy head. "Go on," he said.

She sniffed and continued. "I've known something was wrong. Ever since that last gathering. The sky looks no different, but my dreams tell me terrible things. I'm afraid I'll look up one night and see in the sky what I now see only in my sleep." She pushed her hair from her forehead and looked away from Ephus. I ducked. "I have no answers. My questions haunt me. The People know something is wrong. We've done the ceremonies, made the promises, but they know."

Ephus just sat there, his big hand on her thigh. Finally he said, "Perhaps we should just trust Earthmaker. Trust and go on."

"That is what I've tried to do for more than two years," she said, her voice rising. "It's not enough! If it's possible to know what's happening, then I must know. Keeping my fear secret is what tortures me."

"Will you tell them then?" he asked.

"No. Not yet. Fear will weaken them. Thought Holder knows. He felt it first."

"What does he say?"

"He agrees. It's better to say nothing. The People must continue to hunt and to hope. I'm to speak only when I'm sure. But what if I'm never sure? What if I never understand? I'm the one who's supposed to know the stars. If I can't explain my fear to myself, how can I ever tell them?"

A branch cracked under my foot. I held my breath. Had they heard? Neither looked my way. Tenja held her head between her hands as if it were a burden.

"What will you do?" Ephus asked gently.

Tenja straightened her back. "Try harder," she said, smiling bleakly.

"Study and watch and pray. But it could be a long time before the answers come. If I stay here, I'll be interrupted. Worse, the People will see my fear and worry more. So I have to go."

"No!" The word was out of my mouth before I could think. A limb snapped back and scraped my face as I pushed through the brush. "No, you just came back. You can't go!"

Tenja jumped to her feet, looking dismayed. "Thistle, what are you doing here? You shouldn't be here! You're to say nothing of this!"

"Then take me with you!"

"Don't be foolish. I can't take you with me. You belong here."

"I belong with you. I need you to teach me. I belong where I can learn the things you know." My words tumbled, unthought, from my mouth. "I can help you. I know I can."

"No!"

"If you leave here without me, I'll tell the People all you said today."

Tenja's face was growing red. "Stop it!" she hissed.

"I will. I mean it. I'll tell them everything."

She softened her voice then, as if coaxing a child. "Thistle, you're too kind to tell them. You would never do that."

"Part of me is kind. But part of me speaks whatever I think, kind or not. You know that. Can you trust that part of me?"

Tenja stepped toward me, finger to her lips, but I wouldn't be silenced.

"Your leaving will make a hole in the thoughts of the People," I said. "Only the truth will fill that hole. How long could I be silent? Can water run uphill? Tenja, think! You'd have to take me with you even if I didn't want to go."

Tenja was angry then, angrier than I'd ever seen her, angrier than that fine white owl, but not yet ready to admit she was trapped. I'd learned from the forest the danger of getting too close to irate creatures. And I'd learned from my own life the loneliness of having no teacher. That was far worse. Stepping back, I stared at her red face. "Tenja," I said, "I'm going now to tell my mother that you have an important question to ask." I turned and plunged back into the woods, crashing through the undergrowth as crows screamed above me.

Magla was dozing in the sun when I returned, her hands on her belly. She opened one eye. "What?"

"Tenja will be back soon. She and Ephus. She has a question to ask you.

"Very well," she said, closing her eye and sighing.

It wasn't long before Tenja strode into camp, jaw set and eyes blazing. She glared at me but I was prepared. I hurried over to Birch and sat with my back to the Star Watcher. "Birch," I said, reaching for the little leather ball in her lap and admiring her stitches, "what fine work you do!" She looked at me in surprise and smiled. Tenja's eyes were like hot coals on my back. "Let's make some more balls, Birch, different sizes," I said.

"Really?" We sat there for the rest of the afternoon. Birch worked contentedly. I'd never sewn so fast.

"Thistle," said Birch after we'd finished four balls, "shouldn't we get something to eat?"

"Not yet. Wait until Fire comes, then you go. I'm not hungry." I turned around, keeping my eyes down, afraid that Tenja's wrath would weaken my resolve. Where was my brother? Fire came along shortly, his face smeared with blueberries. I grabbed him and held him, smiling as if his words were the best I'd ever heard, making sure I wasn't alone for a moment. There could be no chance for Tenja to argue with me. She would be my teacher. Of that I was sure.

That night, Tenja stood before the People. "*Aeii,*" she said. All eyes gazed at her. She chose her words with care. "Earthmaker has called me away. She speaks to me of Change. I don't yet see this change, whether it is large or small, good or harsh. I must listen more closely. I will return to the winter cave to do the ceremonies, hear the spirits of the stars, and pray. I'll listen for Earthmaker's voice. When you return in Autumn, I may know Her message."

These were good words. The People looked surprised, but not frightened. They were used to her absence. Sela, stroking her jaw, was the first to ask a question. "Will you go alone? How will you eat? How will you live?"

"Ephus will come with me as far as the winter cave. Then he will travel on." She paused. I stretched and turned her way, peering over Fire's head and staring until she looked toward us. My eyes met her sullen gaze. She sighed and continued, "I must seek Magla's assistance on one matter." She turned to my mother and muttered. "I want to bring Thistle with me. She is strong. She can fish. And you will see her again in two months."

"Thistle!" Magla exclaimed. Her mouth fell open. "Thistle? She's a dreamer, a wanderer. I need her here." The request had confused my mother's thinking.

I set Fire down and stood, forcing myself to speak slowly. "It is true that I am used to walking far. I study many things, animals and fish and stars. I can bring Tenja food so she'll be free to work. I am happy to help her." I turned to Sela and added, "In this way I can also help the People." She stared at me curiously and I saw in her an old woman whom I didn't yet know.

Magla glared at me. "You want to do this? You want to go with Tenja?"

Sela turned to her daughter and patted her knee. "Let her go," the older woman said. "She'll be fine."

My mother looked at the ground. She was not one to let other people make her decisions. Perhaps it would have been kinder had Tenja come to her alone, but then Magla would have been more likely to say no. "Very well," she muttered. "But only this time. Thistle returns with us in the spring."

"We leave in two days," Tenja said. She strode away.

I was going! Joy surged through me, followed quickly by fear. What had I done? I had only two days to play with Fire, to talk to Silka and Birch, to visit Reen's grave, to get my things. What if something happened to me while I was gone? Or, worse, what if something happened to Tenja? For the next two nights, I slept fitfully. My thoughts rushed on, though I spoke very little. It was my words that had brought me this far. I was no longer sure I trusted them. I was to have what I wanted. I'd yet to consider what I might lose.

On the third morning, I rolled up my bedding, tied it snuggly, and ate two plums. Tenja and Magla were talking in the entryway, gazing at me. I knew Magla was giving her instructions. It was still early when we left. The People walked with us to the bottom of the hill. Then we stood in the meadow, Magla clutching my arm, Fire clinging to my tunic. "We'll get another goose when you come to the sea," I promised him. "Two more, one just for you."

And then we were gone, Ephus, Tenja, and I, loaded with packs, picking our way back, across the golden grasslands, through the sparse forests, along high ridges, over tumbling streams, and down at last to the blue-green sea. Now my learning would begin.

Of Numbers and the Stars

TENJA WALKED FOR TWO DAYS WITHOUT SPEAKING TO ME, but I was happy. No Grandmothers, no babies, no Silka, only the azure sky and my friends. Ephus didn't seem to mind my presence. Maybe he was happy there'd be someone to look after Tenja once he was gone. I promised myself I'd be a great help to her. I'd find new foods, new routes, new ways. She wouldn't be sorry. I brought down a rabbit with a stone on the second day and gathered kindling each night. By the third morning, Tenja had forgotten her anger. We reached the West Sea on our fifth day.

Surely the sea was higher. Our beach was smaller than I remembered. But something else caught our attention before we could talk about the shore—a powerful stench coming from the cave.

We'd chased out animals before: owls, foxes, wolverines, bears. That smell could only be one thing. Hyenas. Those powerful scavengers feasted on the flesh and bones the lions left behind, their sharp side teeth gnawing through hides no other animal would touch. This bunch must have dragged the carcasses home to finish them. The rocky beach in front of the cave was littered with bones. The high yelp of pups told us this was no temporary abode. An entire pack lived there. They'd be in no hurry to leave. Two adults rested near the entrance, their wide heads turned in our direction. We dropped our packs at the bottom of the hill. I looked at Tenja.

"Get some dry wood," she muttered, keeping her eyes on the creatures.

Few trees grew near by, but driftwood was plentiful. I dragged a few large logs closer, leaving them about four man-lengths from the entrance. Ephus stood by with a stout branch, his eyes darting from the creatures to me and back again. Tenja had removed the iron stones from her pouch. She began striking them together. I dropped a handful of dry grass on top of the wood. Soon the sparks caught fire. By now the animals were standing, sniffing the air, growling. Their rough yellow coats quivered. I tossed some brush onto the tinder and the flames shot up. The hyenas drew back their dark muzzles, baring long teeth. As the fire took hold of the wood, six fuzzy pup heads popped out of the cave as well.

Tenja grabbed a torch from the blaze. "Follow me," she said. "Don't get too close to the mothers."

I grabbed a burning branch as well and we rushed the cave. The two large females nudged the babies back inside. Barks and snarls told us there were others in there as well. Following Tenja's lead, I hurled my torch into the entrance and ran back to the fire for another. Once again we rushed the entryway. Smoke was drifting from the mouth of the cave, though there was still no sign of the animals. We made another trip. At last the creatures bolted, choking, nudging the pups before them, nipping when they were slow. Two of the big ones turned to yelp at us. Then they all slunk away, seven adults and six scuttling pups, tails between their short hind legs. We left the sticks burning to take away the smell and spent the night under the stars.

The next morning when I awoke, Tenja was coming from the sea, twisting the water from her hair. Ephus was still asleep. She dropped down next to me. We sat with the wind in our faces, listening to the rolling waves and the cry of gulls. "Tenja, I've been thinking," I said after a while. She rolled her eyes. "No, listen. We left in The Time of Ripening Fruit. So we have The Month of the Fat Deer and The Storing of Food before the People return. If I did all the work, you'd be free to watch the sky in the night, sleep in the morning, mark your calendar, and still teach me."

"First you have to learn to count."

"I can count already. I want to learn about the stars."

"There are more stars in the sky than fingers on your hand."

"But once I learn the numbers, then you'll teach me?"

"Yes, yes," she replied.

So we began that day. I gathered up stones as she instructed, then put them into ten piles of ten stones each. "We'll work with these first," she said, "then talk about stars."

When I was done counting, I gathered the bones the hyenas had left behind and piled them in the back of the cave. We could burn them when the wood ran low. Then I helped Ephus look for food. He carved a harpoon head from an antler for me, notching it twice. I speared trout at the river and set nets for dace, the little silver fish that swam in clusters. On the third day I caught a burbot in the net and roasted the fat fish on a stick. Grouse pecked and preened in the grass just up from the

vendace

burbot

beach and I went to work on a trap for them. Tenja would see she hadn't made a mistake.

Each day I went to a different place. There was no one to tell me, "be careful." Tenja slept late and Ephus didn't know those words. Never had I been so happy. One morning I awoke early and found myself heading for the salt marsh. I'd forgotten to say where I was going. Or maybe I just hadn't known until I was on my way. Tenja had mentioned she wanted clams and I hated clams without salt and then there I was. I'd been to the marsh before, years ago, once with my father and later with Ochre. Ephus said the sea had once flowed there, until part of it was cut off, leaving only a shallow pool. When the seawater disappeared, it left behind a crust of salt which we could easily scrape and carry.

The marsh was a strange place where dwarfed trees twisted in the wind. They must have grown there long ago, before salt water flooded the shore. A few saline pools dotted the area but most of the beach was dry and encrusted with salt. It wouldn't take me long to pack what I needed, leaving plenty of time to explore. I knelt to scrape the hard white surface, breaking off several clumps and dropping them into my bag. A dead tree floating in a nearby pool caught my attention. Its trunk was almost submerged, the loose bark floating in the muddy brine. Strange thing.

Earthmaker caused me to wade into the pool and lift the bark. The limp, fibrous sheet fell apart in my hands, separating into strips. I tugged at the strips and they in turn pulled apart into long, looping threads. Never had I seen such a thing. The strips were so strong I could hardly tear them. Some magic had been done to the bark in the water. It would be good for something, I was sure. If we had no sinew, perhaps we could use it to tie things. I gathered all the wet bark I could find and dragged the strips home, almost forgetting the salt. If I had one of those wolf people, like the Arn had, I could have brought more.

It was midday when I returned. Tenja was working on the beach. I slipped into the cave unseen, leaving the bark strips far in back until I figured out what to do with them. Then I dropped the salt pouch by the wall and ran to join her. She was deep in concentration, arranging round stones in a curved pattern on the ground. I watched curiously as she bent over her creation and rolled the stones into place. A shape was beginning to emerge. A crescent moon! She began working on another form, laying out a line of stones as long as a person and angling a second line to the first. I watched as a five-pointed star emerged. Finally she stood, stretched, and pushed back her damp hair. I waited for an explanation.

"Earthmaker came to me in a dream," she said, "telling me how to draw down the power of the stars."

I stepped closer. The moon figure was made up of twenty-eight stones. The star was not so simple. Four central stones marked out a shape on the ground. Each side was made of twelve stones. I didn't know the name for the total number of rocks, just many. "Did Earthmaker tell you the numbers, too?" I asked.

She nodded. "The twenty-eight you already know. The twelve in the star points are for the twelve different ways Spirit moves through us. The sixty-four stones in the star are for the sixty-four sparks that make up life."

"You'll teach me about these numbers?"

"Just watch. You'll learn."

And so I came to know of numbers and the stars. The shapes were like a shrine. We sat at them each night. I'd drag out an elk hide to put under us and we'd wait for the darkness, even on hazy nights. "Night's power still reaches us," Tenja explained, "even if we can't see the stars." She told me that the stars were fires and that even the sun was a star. Earth was round like the sun, she said, but had no lights of its own. So the part of the Earth that turned away from Sun was dark. I didn't see how that could be, but I let her believe it.

Sometimes she awakened me before dawn, while the stars still glistened in the black cloudless sky. I'd shuffle from the cave, rubbing my eyes, then sit sleepily against Ephus's warm shoulder, letting her words wash over me. Some of the things she told me made no sense. Maybe she thought I'd understand if she said them often enough. "The cycle of day and night, sun and moon, heat and cold," she'd explain, "is the root of all order in the world. We are the creatures of that cycle." Her voice would float by like a cloud. I'd yawn. She'd tell me how the sun brings renewal and the moon brings rest, explain how we sometimes longed for the sky because we feared our own death. "Earth, with all its loss," she'd say, "reminds us of our own dying." I'd usually decide to think about her words another time and move closer to Ephus, who snored like a tired bear between us. Then I'd wait for the dawn, watching as the snowy summits to the north turned pink in the rising sun.

Tenja was waiting in the entryway one day when I came back from fishing. I handed her two spotted trout. She passed them along to Ephus, picked up a bag from the ground, and motioned for me to follow her outside. "I have a new task for you," she said. I sat next to her on a log, wondering what it was she was carrying. "It's time for you to start keeping a moon calendar of your own," she said. "You can start with this." She opened the bag and pulled out a flat shoulder bone, probably a bison or auroch, and handed it to me. It was as long as my forearm and wider.

"What am I supposed to do?"

"Every evening, you're to make a mark as I show you. I'll still keep my moon calendar. Then, before the People return, we'll compare the two. Just mark the moon's passing for now. Later, I'll show you how to track its shape as well. One day your calendar will look like mine."

She lifted another bone from the bag. Tiny moon shapes crawled around it in a curling line. Gouged-out circles representing full moons clustered in the center of the calendar. The little circles moved to the right, gradually becoming crescents. Then the line of moons curved to the left, through half moons and reversed crescents, and up and to the right again, where the new moons were rendered as delicate outlines. The line again curved right, then left, and down to the right again.

"So many moons! You can count each month this way?" I'd seen this fine thing before, but never understood its purpose.

"We can do more than that. The calendar keeps the year for all the People. I have a second one that I keep hidden, should anything happen to this one. Look." She placed a finger on the first full moon and counted out loud. "There are too many moons here for only one month. Follow the twenty-ninth moon as the line continues right and curves upward. There are thirty-nine more marks."

"Why so many?"

"A month doesn't last exactly twenty-eight days. Sometimes it changes between twenty-nine and thirty. We learned long ago that we couldn't mark off an exact year from the moon alone. The numbers will always be off. In ancient times, long before Thought Holder or Thought Holder's grandfather's grandfather, the People watched and waited and studied the sky. And when they deserved to know, Earthmaker showed them Her secret."

I watched as her slender fingers tapped off the days.

She continued. "We tally the months at the top of the calendar and then, one time each thirty-three months, we count off a month thirty-one days long before we begin a new month. This we call The Long Month. Because of it, we can count the years."

Perhaps the teacher I loved was crazy. "I can never count so many marks," I said. "I'll make marks for the moon, but perhaps Earthmaker just wants me to fish."

Tenja smiled. "See where I notch each night? Start like that, then knick those lines a little deeper each month." So I began to mark my first bone calendar. On the narrow end of the shoulder blade, I started carving a little goose head. It was on this beach that I last saw Shine.

Tenja was busy with her calculations and I with my counting and fishing. But Ephus was restless. Some days he sniffed the air like a wild animal, clenching his

geese from bison shoulder bones

muscles or pulling back his unruly hair. Other days he sat close to Tenja, like a wolf pup with its mother. He puzzled me. One night, while he wandered along the beach, I sat on the shore with Tenja and listened to the slosh of the waves. "Ephus is like a man who holds the spirits of many animals inside himself," I said. "Some days those animals seem to fight."

Tenja nodded. "We all hold many spirits within us, each of them wanting a turn. With Ephus, the same animal always wins."

"Zlatar told me you're a Changer like me, a Bird person. I think that's a good thing to be."

Tenja settled back and shook her head. "The world of Spirit is not so simple, Thistle. The ways that Spirit moves are neither good nor bad. Sometimes we must heed the reasons for a person's actions even more than the actions themselves. That's how we become wiser."

"But you're already wise. Think of all you know!"

"Oh, Thistle, we always want to look at what is strong in us and say, 'This is my best.' Sometimes what is most vulnerable may be our best. Earthmaker gives us all the gift of a special weakness. When we overcome that weakness, we become who we truly are."

What a lot of trouble. "But surely it's good to be with others like ourselves," I said. "I like your strengths. I like what's already best in you, how you want to know more and do more and understand more. When I'm with you, I'm excited and happy. When I'm with someone like Sela, my strength is hidden. Isn't it best to be with those who make you happy?"

"Sometimes," she replied, looking out to sea. "But we may learn more from those who make us angry." She picked up a stick and began tracing lines in the sand. "We never know what a thing is by looking at the surface. What things truly are is embedded in a pattern, held together by invisible roots. Sometimes the pattern throws up a clue. But the clue is never the pattern. We can only watch the clues and approach the pattern."

A chilly breeze was roughening the sea. I pulled my tunic tighter. Sometimes Tenja hinted at things to see if I was paying attention. I had no idea what she was talking about, but I took a guess. "These clues, do they include the stars and Moon?"

"Yes. And all the animals. The stones that roll from high places, the creeks that branch to new ground, the lines in the forehead of an Old One, the faces that appear in dreams, the swirling of clouds, the pain that lurks in your body, the anger you feel when someone tells you No. All of these are clues." She waited for her words to settle, then continued. "You're very good at seeing what's before you, Thistle. I'll teach you to see what's above. You yourself must learn to see what's beneath you."

"And this is what you do? See what's beneath you?"

"That's what I try to do."

"Then I'll watch you and learn from you. I feel at home whenever I'm with you. Even if I still need to learn from others." The moon shone high above the sea, throwing a path on the waves that ended just beyond my feet.

"Remember, Thistle, everyone carries a little of the Bird spirit. It's just stronger in some than in others." She was quiet for a moment. "One thing you'll learn about Changers, Thistle, as you watch the pattern: they, more than any others, feel at home everywhere and nowhere."

I heard the scrunch of feet on gravel. Ephus was returning. The moonlight added a silver streak to his hair. He sat next to Tenja, his eyes on the horizon, his elbows on his knees. "I've been thinking about a story I once heard," he said. "A story about a place far to the south where humans live like giant ants, scurrying about in great numbers and throwing up earthen domes. It is said these people have special ways and great power. I would like to see such things."

I heard a small gasp from Tenja. Then she whispered, "You must return to tell us of these great wonders."

Nothing more was said, though the night seemed bursting with words. I went to the cave, where my thoughts were quieter, and fell asleep.

I slipped out in a drizzling dawn. Ephus and Tenja were neither in the cave nor on the beach. Maybe they'd gone to the woods to wait out the rain. I climbed the hill behind the cave, crossed the meadow where the grouse ran, and headed for the thicket beyond. Then I huddled in the brush, eating blueberries. I'd smeared a paste of pine resin and fat on my face and arms, so the mosquitoes left me alone. By midmorning the sky was clearing. After I'd eaten my fill, I stretched out on the damp, sun-warmed grass, the clouds floating like fat geese above me. After a while, I filled a bag with berries for Ephus and Tenja and set out for home, happy with myself and the bright day.

My path took me back across the meadow. The once-lush grass was turning gold. A sudden sound startled me. A moan. I stopped short. Just ahead of me lay Tenja and Ephus, sprawled naked in the tall grass. They were mindful only of each other, their gleaming bodies twisting in the bright sun. Never had I seen Ephus with no tunic. His muscular body amazed me, as white as driftwood in an amber sea. He was caressing Tenja's flesh, his arm sliding from her shoulder to her thigh, his rough hand rubbing her smooth places.

As I watched, Tenja slowly wrapped her legs around Ephus's back, digging her heels into his pale flanks. Ephus rose to his hands and knees, holding himself above her, his body starting to sway. Her legs clutched more tightly. He moved harder, shoving himself against her. She gasped and moaned, arched and fell, with each lunge of his body.

Perhaps I should go, I thought, but I seemed to have no legs, only eyes. Ephus thrust his head forward and down, grabbing one of her breasts in his mouth and sucking hard. Then he rubbed his hairy face over her chest. Tenja screamed, her piercing yell followed by sharp gasps. Ephus growled and panted, pushing himself forward with his legs. Their bodies shook and moved as one, a tree of flesh caught in a storm. I turned and ran back to the brush.

There I lay, panting, until I caught my breath, and even long afterward, waiting for the images of their bodies to fade. I'd seen Earthmaker's fierce power that day, seen how She moved through their bodies and claimed us again. Would She ever move like that through me? I took a long path home, leaving the crushed grass undisturbed.

Tenja and Ephus were quiet when I returned. She was studying her calendar and drawing chalk lines on a flat stone. Ephus sat oiling his tunic. Tenja looked up when I approached and said brightly, "Ephus goes tomorrow. We'll walk with him as far as the Fish People's camp."

My thoughts raced. Ephus going? The Fish People? They lived just two days south of us, though I'd never been to their home. We'd missed the solstice gathering this past summer because of Zalec's injuries. Now we'd have a chance to see their colorful ways and hear Ziva's chirping speech. Another idea jumped like a trout. Perhaps Tenja wanted Ephus to know he wasn't the only one who'd have exciting journeys.

"The Fish People!" I said. "What a great adventure."

It took me a long time to fall asleep that night. And when I finally did, I dreamt for the first time a dream that was to visit me for the rest of my life, the dream of a jagged mountain, the highest of seven peaks, its summit tipped to the side like a wave about to break.

Part 2

She Who Walks Alone

Son of man,
bathe yourself in the ocean of matter;
plunge into it where it is deepest and most violent;
struggle in its currents and drink of its waters.
For it cradled you long ago in your
preconscious existence;
and it is that ocean that will raise you up to God.

Teilhard de Chardin
Hymn of the Universe, 1924

Have the People Known Chaos?

ZIVA WAS THE FIRST TO SEE US TWO DAYS LATER, as we trekked along the beach just north of the Fish People's home. She'd been wading in the sea at low tide when she spotted us. She ran toward us, clapping her hands, jumping like a child, then leading us into camp as if in victory. "Look, look, from the north!" she sang. "Thought Holder's People!" The others crowded around us, naked except for their feathered hats and necklaces of clacking shells. "We missed you, we missed you," Ziva said as she embraced Tenja. "There was no one to do the ceremony, no one to greet the sun, no one like you." The others hugged us as well. The Fish People always made a person feel welcome, knowing beyond words what another needed.

Ephus had said little during our trip. When Ziva asked him to sit, he smiled and shook his head. While Ziva badgered Tenja for news about our year, he slipped away, continuing south as if late for another destination. I stood at the edge of the gathering, watching until he rounded a curve on the shore and disappeared. He never looked back.

Ziva chattered on. She stood with hands on her hips, her brown breasts hanging almost to her belly. Shorter than Tenja, she had the strong arms of one accustomed to work. Like the others, she wore a feather hat draped with strings of fox teeth and the round spine bones of fish. Tenja seemed to lose herself in the mirth of our hosts, though I felt shy in the unfamiliar noise. "Where were you, where were you, and why are you here now?" Ziva asked. "Where are the others? How long can you stay?" She turned to me. "And who is this, who is this? I remember this one, she was sick, you were sick. And are you well now?"

Her warm eyes melted my awkwardness. "I'm fine," I mumbled.

"Ah, you're well. I see." Ziva nodded and smiled. Then she threw her arms around our shoulders. "We will feast!" she announced. She called to two boys about my age, as brown and gleaming as eels. They ran toward the sea and returned with a huge turtle they must have kept for special occasions. The women spread grass mats on the sand and we settled onto the beach. That evening, I filled my belly with roast turtle and clams and listened to our hosts, who twittered like larks late into the night.

I awoke to the laughter of children and opened my eyes to see a boy and girl kneeling over me, pointing at my tunic. When they realized I was awake, they ran screaming toward the sea. The sunlight dazed me and I shielded my face with my hand, looking around. The Fish People were already up and about their work. I'd been too fascinated by the people themselves last night to notice my surroundings. Now I took some time to observe the beach. Unlike our home, the shoreline here was smooth and sandy. A long, high cliff followed the beach. These people had no large cave, though small caverns dotted the face of the cliff. They were too small to live in, but handholds dug into the rock told me the little caves were used for something. The Fish People had strung hides from posts to make shaded areas on the shore. Like us, they made lean-tos by hanging skins from poles and anchoring them to the ground with stones. Maybe they stayed in the lean-tos when it rained and used the caves for storage. Their group was much larger than ours, maybe twice the size.

Six more children had joined the two who ran away. Now they all stood at a safe distance, pointing at me and giggling. I looked away from their laughing faces. At first I'd thought perhaps the size of the group kept them safe from predators while living on the beach. But maybe these people were just too noisy to be eaten.

Tenja was already up and gone. I pulled on my boots and went to look for her, finding her near the water with Ziva. Just behind them, six men trudged from the sea pulling a large net between them.

"Ah, Star Watcher's Helper, you join us," said Ziva. I smiled and yawned and splashed seawater on my face. The men started emptying their shimmering catch onto the shore. Ziva turned back to them. "Good work! Good work!" she said. "Can you take our visitors on the boat? Take them on the boat to Fish Island. Let them ride on the sea!" She pushed me toward the men.

"Go, go now, you must see the island. I'll go with you!"

The men grinned. All six were brown and lean and looked like boys, except that three of them had grey hair. Two of the younger ones began wading out to a bobbing structure tied to a rock, while the other four stayed with the fish. I'd noticed that floating thing yesterday. It looked like an inverted turtle shell. It was as long as two humans, as wide as one, and made of hides stretched over wooden braces. So this was one of their boats we'd heard about at The Gathering. I felt no desire to get inside.

The Fish men pulled the vessel over and steadied it, while Ziva motioned for us to come closer. "Come, come, come. You can fly on the water!"

"I'll watch," I replied, backing up.

"Watch from inside! Oh, the things you'll see!" She pulled me into thigh-high water like a salmon on a hook, while I kept shaking my head. Then the men lifted me and pushed me over the side. It swayed and I grabbed the rim. "She's ready!" Ziva cried. "Come, Tenja."

Tenja crawled in and hunched down on the bottom next to me, her face as white as a haddock's belly. The two men hoisted Ziva into the vessel next to us, heaved themselves over the side, and grabbed two long paddles. "We go. We go!" cried Ziva. The boat rocked and swayed and headed out to sea.

The waves slapped against the side of the vessel as we rose and fell like a leaf. I lay on the bottom, my hands on the sides, watching the brilliant sky and the dark bodies of the men, their arms rising and reaching, their faces upturned to the wind. After a while, I pulled myself up to look over the side. The tiny beach shimmered behind us and the entire world was blue.

Up ahead was a dark speck of land. As we approached, I could see that the island was made of the same familiar sponge stone of home. A few low trees clung to its rough surface. We sloshed nearer. Terns strutted along the shore, then rose up and flew away as we approached. Gulls screamed and soared and dived at us. The place was strewn with nets, broken boats, and scattered shells.

"Fish Island, Fish Island!" Ziva exclaimed, as if coming upon a treasure. One of the men jumped from the boat and grabbed a rock, pulling us to shore. I climbed out, happy for solid ground. Near a blackened fire pit lay a pile of driftwood. I was about to sit on a log when I noticed that the rocks themselves were moving. "Get some crabs, get some crabs," yelled Ziva, running after the creatures that inhabited the stones. "Find some snails!" We dashed around, Ziva and the Fish men grabbing the scuttling creatures, Tenja and I lifting a snail or two. I stayed close to Ziva, wanting to be sure the boat didn't leave without me. "See," she said, gesturing at the rope and wood and debris strewn across the little land, "we keep our old boats here. And everything we need for repairs."

Ziva and the men put the crabs into the bottom of the boat. Where was I to sit? "Let's go," she said. "Time to eat!" Tenja had managed to squeeze into the back of the vessel. She smiled weakly and looked away. I crawled in between the round creatures, pushing several aside, drawing my legs up under me, and hugging my shoulders. "Make sure they don't get away!" Ziva cried. We returned to shore with our breakfast.

Ziva fussed over me all morning, bringing me the first roasted crab, again telling her friends that I would have died two years ago if the Fish People hadn't saved me. By midday, I was exhausted. She showed no signs of slowing down. We moved to a lean-to and sat in the shade. I hoped she was done with me.

"She's one of us now," Ziva said, patting my head. "Let's make her a hat." Two of the women began weaving something of sea bird feathers, white and brown and black, and set it on my head. "Get my cape," she said to one of the girls, who ran off and returned with a lustrous, grey cloak. Ziva tied the heavy piece around my neck. I saw that it was made of gull wings. "Come, let me paint you," she chirped. I stood in the sun while she drew black circles around my eyes and mouth. "Now you look like a fish!" She gave me a necklace of shells and turned me to face the others.

The women agreed merrily. "Now she's a fish. Now she's one of us."

"Come," Ziva commanded, "you must swim in the sea." I was used to dashing into the water to wash. But we stayed away from the sea at home, where the waves smashed hard against the rocks and sucked you underneath, spitting you out elsewhere. I looked at Tenja, who sat cross-legged on the beach as if anchored there. She just shook her head and shrugged. Ziva led me to the shore. The naked Fish People were already ambling into the water. "Take off your clothes," Ziva ordered. I dropped my beautiful headdress, my gull wings, and my tunic. The breeze was so chilly my nipples tingled. Then I stepped one foot into the cold green sea.

"Take this, you need this," Ziva said. She handed me a long, hollow quill from some huge wing. "Take this to visit the fish!" She showed me how to bend the quill slightly and place one end in my mouth, keeping the other above water. "Let the sea carry you!" she cried, plunging into the water and floating motionless in the gentle swell.

I did as she said, gasping at the cold water. My entire body tingled. I walked out further. In a little while, my limbs began to warm. I laid my face on the dark surface and began breathing through the quill. Then I kicked off, trailing my legs behind. The sea did carry me! Beneath me I beheld a new world, skimming and shining and swirling, a world where tall grass swayed and wide-eyed creatures darted, where slow clams opened and closed their shells, and things that had no name crawled and bobbed. The sea carried me and I was hers.

I returned to the beach much later, filled with the blue wonder of all I'd seen. Quickly pulling my tunic over my head, I sat in the sun with Tenja. Ziva soon plopped down beside us, glistening. She'd slowed down at last and lay silently as the sun dried the water from her flesh. I listened happily as she shifted her attention to Tenja.

"Tenja," she said, "I don't understand why you're away from your People. And Ephus, why the hurry? Where's he going?" More women had joined us, seeking the shade. The men seemed to stay to themselves, gathering in their own lean-tos when the fishing was done. The newcomers drifted closer, eager for the story.

Tenja glanced at the crowd, then yawned and stretched. "Ziva, I am so stiff. Maybe you and I should walk for a while. There's not really that much to say."

"All right, a walk," Ziva replied. She turned to the disappointed women. "Time for stories later. Stay here and take care of our guest. Tenja and I will stretch our legs." I'd been ready to join them, but Ziva's words stopped me. The two of them stood and strolled away.

I looked at the pleasant faces around me. I'd had enough company for one day. "I'll just sleep for a while," I said with a smile. I picked up my feathered hat and hurried back to the lean-to where I'd spent the night, lying down before anyone could ask a question. The others went back to visiting each other. Peace.

It didn't last. In a little while, I heard the crunch of feet on the sand. I opened my eyes to see two narrow ankles before me, encircled by bands of woven grass and tiny, dangling shells. I looked up, into the lovely face of a girl about my age. "I am Luba," she said in a lilting voice. "Remember? I know your friend Silka."

"Of course." I nodded. Luba was Ziva's daughter. We'd met at the Gathering two years ago.

Luba grabbed my hand. "Come," she said, pulling me up. Three other girls and two boys stood nearby. One of them was a boy who'd helped bring up the sea turtle last night. We stepped toward them. "Come and see the marks of the Fish People," Luba said, using our words in an odd way. Luba herself looked like a sea creature, her skin more gold than brown, her hair braided with cowry shells and blue feathers. I felt strange to be the only one wearing a tunic, but not as strange as if they'd been staring at my white body.

"Wait!" I ran back to get the feathered hat. I placed it on my head.

"I'm ready."

The seven of us headed south along the beach, Luba in the lead. Their graceful bodies seemed to glide across the sand, dancing eyes lighting their tan faces. Their eyes were the same color as ours, dark, almost black. Except for one of the boy's, whom I'd never seen before. His eyes were as yellow as a cat's. Unlike the others, his dark hair curled tightly about his head. My mouth fell open when I noticed his eyes. Everyone giggled. Luba stepped closer. "His name is Belov," she whispered. "He is one of my brothers. His father didn't come from here."

We walked on. The cliff that bordered the beach became higher, going on as far as I could see. "Where are we going?" I asked.

Luba put a finger across her lips and ran ahead. The others walked faster. My eyes followed her down the beach. The high rock wall we were approaching had a bluish cast. How strange. I hurried to catch up with the others.

"There!" Luba announced, pointing up at the cliff face. "There they are. The markings of the Fish People. We did not make them, but they belong to us now."

Above me was another world, a painted world with writhing swimmers, glorious birds, and colorful creatures. The drawings were well above my head, too high to touch, but large enough to be clearly seen. I'd never known such a thing! The shapes appeared to be outlined in coal, the surfaces stained in blue and gold. Best of all, the eyes of creatures and swimmers were inlaid with golden pieces, their bodies decorated with blue stones.

"Who made them?" I asked.

"Belov's father," she said, standing straighter. "He came from the south and loved my mother. Then he left us this wall and his son."

I looked back at the one called Belov, staring into his sun-flecked eyes. "Your father was a great artist," I said. He nodded and smiled.

We returned late in the afternoon. Ziva and Tenja were already there, sitting with their heads together. I went to join them. Something about Ziva had changed. She was quieter now, thoughtful. "So, you saw the wall?" she asked, turning away before I had time to answer. "Belov," she said, "call the people."

The strange young man ran off. A few moments later a loud wail swept across the camp. I turned to see Belov holding a large shell near his mouth. Had the sound come from a shell? Everyone stopped what they were doing and walked toward Ziva. I helped her to her feet.

"Listen, my people," she called. "Tomorrow our guests must go. They have important work to do. We must not delay them. Tenja, as you know, is the greatest Star Watcher of all the People. Tonight, after we've eaten, stay with us by the fire. I have stories for Star Watcher and her helper and all of you. Stories to bless their journey." The small woman walked to the edge of the circle, stopping to talk to some Old Ones resting in the shade. I was glad for some time alone with Tenja.

"Did you tell her? Does she know your fears about Chaos?" I whispered.

"Hush. I told her just a little. It's impossible to keep secrets from these people. Our thoughts flow into them like water. Ziva will watch. She'll tell us if her people sense change."

"But she talks so much. Won't she scare them with her words?"

Tenja shook her head. "Ziva is like the sea on a breezy day. You notice the choppy surface, not the water's depth. She says nothing she doesn't plan to say."

My eyes followed Ziva as she made her way around the group. If she stopped to talk with everyone, she'd be awhile. I decided to look for Belov and the speaking shell, watching when he sounded it again before we ate. Ziva took her place between the people and the water, so that, watching her, we also saw the sea. We filled ourselves with fish and walnuts as the sea turned silver in the evening sun. Ziva finished a piece of roast bass and licked the juice from her fingers. It was time. She gestured to someone behind me. Suddenly, the high, twilling sound of a flute arose and floated along the shore. I breathed in the sharp salt air. From somewhere in the dusk, a woman's voice rang out:

Earthmaker, my large self comes to meet you,
my small self stays behind.

Earthmaker, my large self awaits you,
hollow as sky I am, fill me, fill me, fill me.

Earthmaker, my large self awaits you,
heavy as stone I am, lift me, lift me, lift me.

Earthmaker, my large self awaits you,
near your flame I am, keep me, keep me, keep me.

The shore was silent except for the slap of the sea. Ziva began, her voice gentle and slow:

Earthmaker, The Great Mother God, made humans long ago
when She commanded Sun, The Great Father God, to shine on
Her.
All manner of life came forth. The Great Mother God watched
with love. About humans She said, 'Of all My children you are
the wildest. I never know what you will do. Of all My children
you are the most like me, for you would create. I'll hold you to me
to protect you, so that no harm comes your way.'

184

*Then one day, The Great Father God said, 'These children
are too wild. It is not enough that we protect them. They must
learn many things before they can create.'*

*And so The Great Mother God told Her children, 'I must
send you out into the dark world without Me or you will never
learn. My heart breaks for you. The rivers are My tears. But in
your minds I will leave a lantern. When you have learned all that
the world has to teach you, that lantern will be lit and, in its
bright glory, you will find your way back to Me.'*

*And so The Mother told them goodbye and the children trav-
eled alone into the world to learn the things humans must know.*

The sun was setting over the water as the story ended, Ziva only a
black shape against the golden sea. I sat in the stillness, puzzled. Perhaps this was a good story. I'd never heard of The Great Father God. I
hoped I'd never be sent alone into the world.

My reverie was interrupted by a piercing cry. The Fish People
jumped up to begin their dancing. Their movements became faster,
their shell bracelets clacking, their bodies spinning. Luba and her friends
pulled us up to dance with them, pounding their feet, kicking up sand,
and twirling until the moon was high. Then all found their places
and slept.

Tenja and I left early the next morning on our lonely journey home,
waving wearily at our new friends. Tenja walked in silence.

After a long while, she said, "It came again last night, the dream I
had two years ago, before the Gathering, the dream of a great tree
in a storm."

To See the World Dancing

THE LONESOME FEELING STAYED WITH ME even after Tenja and I returned to our shore. Ephus's departure had left a hole in our lives. Tenja seemed to have retreated within her own thoughts, perhaps looking for answers to her puzzling dreams. We'd come to the time called The Storing of Food. Next month was Return to the Sea. Another month before the People returned. I marked off the days on my moon calendar, longing to see my fat little brother and Magla, Birch and Grandpa Zlatar, even Sela and Silka. I marked and waited.

Tenja had given me a new task. I was to learn how the waxing moon changed the tide. She'd told me to stay awake in the dark and mark the highest water line with a pile of stones. I did it happily, falling asleep when the tide began to recede. But no matter how long I stayed awake, I was always up at sunrise. I'd pull on my boots, make my way up the hill and along the ridge, and look for travelers. All I ever saw was the browning meadow, the first of the grazers picking their way south, and sometimes a high hawk circling in a search of her own. I'd wait until I got hungry, then walk back home.

Finally, one bright day, I saw them, moving in a rough line in the distance, descending a hill on the horizon, heading toward the sea. The People! "Tenja!" I yelled, running all the way back to the cave. "Tenja! They're coming!"

I hurried back to the east again to meet them, leaping over stones, forgetting to watch for cats, running across the meadow, through the thicket, and up the smooth hill. "Fire," I called, as they came into sight, "Fire, it's me!"

And there they were—Fire scampering toward me, taller and lankier than when I'd left; Magla, looking ready to cry; Frightened Eyes, shuffling along as usual; the Old Ones; gentle Birch. Everyone was back, even Zalec, lurching along at the end of the line, Yarrow and Zale beside him. And Silka, her face glowing and her belly plump, Rube at her side. My eyes burned and my loneliness disappeared.

Magla grabbed my hand. "Thistle, did you have enough to eat? Have you slept? You look tired. Did Tenja keep you up?"

"I'm fine, I'm fine. We saw the Fish People. Ephus left. I learned the names of the stars."

Tenja met us at the shore, walking slowly toward us. She'd been in no hurry for the People's return. Sela looked at her with raised eyebrows, but Tenja ignored her, greeting everyone the same, welcoming them back and saying little. "My work is not finished," she explained. "But I know more now than when we parted. Without Thistle, I couldn't have done nearly as much." Magla beamed. We walked back to camp and settled into another autumn.

TENJA'S PRAISE HAD MADE ME more confident. In the days that followed, I taught Birch and Fire their numbers up to twelve. Fire was only six and didn't stay long in one place, but Birch learned quickly, when she wasn't dreaming. I'd cleared a place on the beach where we could work.

"Doesn't Silka look beautiful?" Birch said one afternoon as she counted out stones.

"Pay attention. I said twelve, not ten."

She sighed and added two more to the pile. "I hope I have a baby soon. Did you keep a calendar to figure out when Silka's baby was made?"

"No, I forgot. We could start one now." I preferred Birch as she used to be, more interested in adventures than babies. Maybe if we worked on a calendar, she'd learn her numbers and forget about babies for a while. I considered the matter for a moment. "It's been five moon months since Silka's joining, at the end of The Ripening Fruit. Her belly's not that big. I'd say the baby was made around the time of the joining, probably not before. It will come late in Journey to the High Meadows or early in The Gathering of Medicine."

"Really?" She handed me a flat stone. "Make the marks for me."

"You make the marks. I'll check them."

"You'll be the next one to have a baby," Birch said. "You, then me."

"I have Fire to take care of. That's enough."

"But you're too skinny. And there are dark patches under your eyes. If there were a baby in you, you'd glow like Silka."

Birch was right about Silka. She seemed to be lit from within. I marveled at how everyone in the group came to tend that fire. Never one to hurry, Silka now moved as slowly as a blossom lifted by a breeze. The Mothers fussed over her. Rube was so anxious to serve her that he could hardly leave to fish. Some mornings, Ochre had to practically drag him down to the sea. One day I had asked her, "Doesn't it bother you that Rube can't do his work?" She'd looked at me with wide eyes.

"I am his work," she'd replied. And everyone else's, I'd thought.

"If there were a baby in me and thirty-seven people waiting on me, perhaps I'd glow like Silka," I said.

"There's thirty-seven of us?" said Birch.

"You figure it out, then come tell me." I went to look for my brother.

He was outside the shelter with Magla, being fitted for winter shoes. They both looked up and smiled as I approached. My mother had changed over the summer, becoming softer. Some mornings she hovered over me, as if reluctant to have me leave. I missed being able to roam wherever I wanted, but I didn't miss the loneliness. She knew the stars and the sea just from watching. But she had little need for numbers, except to figure out that everyone was there. I sat on the ground, wondering what question she'd have for me today.

She finished Fire's second shoe and patted him on the rump. "Go play," she said. He ran to join Zale. She picked up the worn leather. "Fire tells me the Fish People took you on the sea."

"Once," I replied. "I like the river better. At least, if the raft goes under, you can swim to shore."

"Still, it must have been beautiful. The sea." I followed her gaze to the west, where the bright water disappeared into the haze on the horizon. She twisted the worn leather in her hands and closed her eyes.

"Well, it was nice."

"Your life reminds me of journeys I will never take," she said.

I couldn't think of anything to say.

THE WINTER PROMISED TO BE A GENTLE ONE, damp but not too cold. Though the days were growing shorter, the river never froze. The men fished contentedly, teasing Zalec that he'd become a great hunter of fish. Darkness came soon after our last meal. Most nights, I'd sit on the beach with Tenja, shivering as we studied the winter sky. She said it was time for me to learn about the Great Star Path.

We walked away from the fire circle one brisk night to begin my lesson. She'd wrapped a wolf pelt about her shoulders to keep out the wind. I'd borrowed Ochre's lion pelt. "Not all objects in the sky are the same," she began. "See." She pointed to a distant reddish light.

"That's a planet."

"I know."

"And how do you know?"

"It moves separately from the stars?"

She nodded. "Planets have no light of their own," she said.

"Then why do they shine?"

"Perhaps they are lit by the sun." We walked a little farther. "All the night sky turns in a great circle, so slowly you could never tell, unless you watched for many years and knew the stories of the ancestors." I stared at her, then the sky, and back at her again. "Like the Earth, the stars turn. But they turn together, each cluster in its own special place. There are twelve great star groups that spin above us. And smaller groups as well. The people have watched them since our beginning. Now your vigil begins."

The wind tugged at her wolf skin so that it seemed alive. Tenja gazed upward, looking as if she herself were ready to whirl into space. Sometimes I felt I should grab her to keep her on the ground. Only when Ephus was with us had she been satisfied to be a creature of Earth.

"What are we looking for?" I asked, my breath rising into the blackness.

"To understand the pattern." Her thoughts returned to the ground. We headed back toward the fire. "Once we know the pattern, we can see any change."

"What kind of change?"

"Any change."

"Because that would be Chaos?"

"Perhaps."

"Tell me about Chaos. Why do the People fear it so?"

"Thistle, I've told you all I know. Quit asking."

"Just one more time. I promise."

She sighed. "Chaos happens when the structure falls away, when what holds us collapses."

"Are there stories about Chaos? Do the People have memories?"

"I told you, Chaos leaves few memories." Just ahead was the moon shrine. Tenja walked over to it, stopped abruptly, and picked up a stone. "I made something for you," she said.

"What?" I asked, aware that she was changing the subject.

She'd scraped several marks on the stone, though it was too dark to see them well. We walked back to the fire. "It's time for you to learn the star groups. Look here." She held out the stone. I could make out several carved circles scattered on the surface. She touched the largest one. "This star, far to the north, is Vega. Look for it to keep your direction. And this star group, which is just above us, is the Hunter. See, these three stars are his belt. This little star to the side is the wolf pup that follows at his heel."

I looked into the night and back at her drawing, as she described Hunter's journey across the winter sky. I'd known those stars since I was a child, but I'd never seen pictures of them before.

This became our pattern. On clear nights, I learned the names of star groups; the Great Horse and, directly above us, her Colt; the Crane, low on the horizon; and the Fish, above the Crane and to the side. In the day, I used a sharp stone to cut their positions into rock, so I'd never forget.

"Ask the stars to show themselves to you," Tenja said. "Then watch and listen." So I waited. And while the world outside me never seemed to change, something deep and nameless had begun shifting within.

When I wasn't making pictures of the star routes, I wandered along the shore with Birch and Leu and Fire. Zale joined us sometimes, but he was only three. We pried oysters from the rocks at low tide, roasting the flesh at night, and tossing the heavy shells back on the beach. Some days we followed the river, looking for mussels upstream. Their black shells stuck to the rocks in the river grass, held by bundles of thread protruding from their bodies. From time to time, eels drifted upriver and became tangled in our nets. Winter was the only time to catch them, since they returned to the sea in the spring to spawn and die. Their oily flesh was a welcomed change from the lean fish we usually ate.

Some mornings we wandered to the tide pools to discover what the sea had left behind. One day, while I was picking up shells, I heard my brother's excited voice. "Thistle, come here!" He yelled. I scrambled over the rocks and found him peering into a little pool. "Look!"

I crouched next to him. A scallop was moving in the water, propelling its shell along in a series of small jerks. A starfish writhed above it, its liquid movement graceful but deadly. Suddenly, the starfish caught the fleeing creature, clamping its star body over the scallop shell. The starfish held tightly, slowly sucking out the scallop's meat. We watched until it relaxed its hold and let go. The empty shell began to sink. I plunged my hand into the cold water and grabbed the little shell, handing it to Fire.

"Here, it's yours. We'll make a pendant for your neck." He grabbed the shell, hopped up, and turned it over in his hand. Then he ran back to the cave, probably eager to show Zale. I followed him home.

I passed Thought Holder and Sela, sitting with Tenja by the fire, as they often did. Their heads were together and their voices low. Sela was smaller than ever now, as if all that was unnecessary had fallen away, leaving only skin and bones and shining eyes. What serious matter troubled them now, I wondered? The three of them looked up as I walked by. Had they been talking about me? I had no time to ask, since Magla called to me right away. I walked over to where she stood, turning fish on a drying rack.

"Thistle, Silka wants some chestnuts. I can't fix them just now. Can you help her?"

I went to the cave, scooped a few handfuls of nuts from a bulging bag, and got out my knife. It took forever to cut away the fuzzy outer layers and peel back the hard coverings, especially when I didn't want to do it at all. "I hope you're in no hurry, Silka," I called to the back of the cave where she rested, her plump form reclining on a pile of furs.

"No hurry," she replied.

I put the raw nuts into oyster shells, crumbled a bit of salt over them, and laid them in the coals, half for me, half for her. I'd have to watch the fire closely to be sure they didn't burn. I picked up the rabbit furs I'd been working on and continued sewing a little pouch for Silka's baby, waiting for the sweet smell from the fire that told me the nuts were done. After they cooled, I scraped them loose from the shells and brought them back to her.

"Silka," I said, setting the shells beside her, "did you ever wonder what it would be like if your baby turned out just like you?"

She looked away quickly, her black hair swirling like a cape as a delicate hand reached for a chestnut. She placed it in her mouth. "You never cook these quite right, do you?"

I went outside to eat mine. Tenja, Sela, and Thought Holder were still deep in conversation. I strained to listen, but heard nothing of what they said.

One strange night, not too long after, we gathered at the mouth of the cave. It was the night of the winter solstice. The drizzle on that short day had finally cleared, though the cooking fire still hissed when droplets fell from the cliff. My brother had been coughing, so I'd draped him in Ochre's lion coat to keep him warm. The pelt covered all but his red hair and dark eyes. I was telling him about the stars, passing the time before the real stories began.

"*Aeii*," called Sela, standing before us on the wet beach. Everyone stopped what they were doing and looked up. "We come to the longest night of the year." She held a sputtering torch. The wind whipped around her, so that she looked like a sea bird ready for flight.

"Once again, the time has come for Earthmaker's promise and our renewal. And that story will come. But first, a new part of the tale."

Pulling her cloak around her, Sela walked past us and back into the shelter. Though the shadows hid her body, I could see that she was reaching for something from a high shelf. She returned with a small bundle, stopping in front of me.

"Thistle," she said, her mouth as close as it came to smiling, "you've learned the stars quickly and kept to your duties. You are taking your place among the People. Someday you'll be a teacher and a leader." She untied the cord on the bundle and reached inside. A chill ran across the back of my neck, as if spiders were walking there. Silence swelled around me. I held my breath. "You will now keep this for the People." She pulled out a strange rock and placed it in my hand. Black as a beetle and smaller than my fist, it was heavier than rocks twice its size. Its smooth surfaces shone like water. "This is a stone tossed down by stars," she said. "The People have kept it since our first days. As the sky gives us the gift of mystery, I give this gift to you."

I held the little rock and looked around, unsure of what to do. The features of the People were soft in the shadows, but I could see they were turned toward me. I looked into their eyes and what I saw there was hope. Suddenly, the burden of their hope seemed heavier than any stone from the stars. I looked from them to the rock and back to Sela. What was this gift that I'd been given? Could I ever give it back? I clutched the stone and felt a new heaviness, the weight of my aloneness. I looked out at the sky's vaulting black beauty, the stars gleaming like ravens' eyes.

"Thank you," I said.

AS THE WET DAYS LENGTHENED and the last of the salted venison disappeared, my thoughts turned to the high country and the green journey before us. It was the end of the Month of the Reindeer Calves. I was getting sick of the crowded cave and the grey beach. I'd finished sewing the little rabbit pouch for Silka's baby. Birch had kept track of the days, as I'd instructed. We figured Silka was in her eighth month. The baby seemed as large as a bear cub. Silka was already moaning when she walked. I hoped, for her sake, that the child came early, so we could help her carry it over the mountains.

I awakened in anticipation one morning in Journey to the High Meadow, early sunlight streaming into the cave. Maybe this would be the day Magla would give the order and we'd prepare to leave. I crawled out of my coverings, groggy from a late night watching stars. Magla and Tenja were standing just outside the entryway. Magla's hands were on her hips. Both of them were as rigid as trees. I stopped, hoping they hadn't seen me. Maybe I'd get to hear them fight.

"I told you, just one time. That was our agreement," Magla was saying.

"But I need her another summer," Tenja replied. "I can't do the work without her. I need just a little more time."

Magla lashed out. "For what? What great thing are you learning, that you must keep her away from us?"

They were talking about me. Stay behind another summer? Tenja had said nothing about that. I stepped out of the shadows.

Magla turned on me like a cat about to pounce. "Thistle, what do you say to this?"

"I, ah, not go with them?" I looked at Tenja. To be away from the People another summer, to miss the high meadows for another year, not to hold Silka's baby? To be lonesome again? "You never told me," I said. My eyes burned and my throat was tight. "You never told me."

"I just decided, Thistle," Tenja said. "I've been thinking about this for days. I don't know what else to do. I can't force you to stay here with me. But I hope you will."

I looked again at Magla. Her eyes were shut, her hand covered her mouth. How could I stay here without the People? "Would you stay alone, Tenja, if I left?" I asked.

"Yes. Maybe an Old One would stay and help cook."

If Tenja remained here and I went on without her, I'd forget most of what I'd already learned, my time with the night sky becoming only a dark memory. I looked from one face to the other, at the two sisters who, more than anyone else, had shaped my life. Magla had molded my past, but I knew my future belonged with Tenja.

"Then I should stay . . . just this one summer," I said. Magla lowered her head. Tenja looked off into the distance. A shiver passed through my body. Spring would bring my people northeast, in pursuit of the reindeer. I'd stay behind with Tenja, pursuing the stars.

The Threshold

THE EMPTINESS STARTED TO CREEP BACK into me soon after the others left. It would take a while before I relished my freedom again. I tried to stay busy, clearing the campsite, fishing, butchering the reindeer calf Ochre had left for us. A few days after their departure, an idea came to me while I was gathering wood. I rushed back to camp to tell Tenja. She was tending the fire, watching a flank of venison roasting on the spit. Strange that she'd be cooking, I thought.

I blurted out my plan. "Tenja, maybe if you find what you're looking for, we can go after them. The People, I mean. To the mountain. We could make it, the two of us together. They'd be surprised."

"No," she replied. "Not this summer. There's another journey I need to make."

I laid down the firewood. "Where?" Where are we going?" I wouldn't mind an adventure.

"I'll make this journey alone." Tenja's head was bent over the fire. She didn't look up. "Into the world of spirit. All you'll have to do is watch my body."

"What? You never told me that!" Without thinking, I glanced toward the path that left our shore. It was too late to run after the People. "Tenja, look at me!" Her eyes met mine. "I know nothing of these journeys. Why didn't you keep Thought Holder with you? Or Sela? Why me? Why did you wait so long to tell me?"

"I'll teach you all you need to know."

"When? When are you planning to teach me? When it's too late for me to escape?"

"Thistle," she said, as if speaking to a child, "I can't always know ahead of time what I have to do. Remember, I didn't force you to join me. You begged to come. From the beginning, it was your choice."

"That was when I still trusted you." She stood quickly and glared at me. "I'm sorry," I said. "I just need you to tell me things."

She nodded. "No, you're right. I should have told you. I planned to tell you. Let's eat first. Then we'll talk."

Again she leaned over the fire, turning the meat on the spit. The juices hissed as they hit the flame. Now I understood why Tenja was cooking, a job that had always been mine. She thought the news of this strange journey would sit better on a full stomach. I wasn't even hungry.

"I'll just walk for a while," I said. "I'll eat later."

I scuttled up the hill and toward the thicket. A few tender blades of new grass pushed through the damp ground. The bare trees were happy with birds. Even the thought of springtime brought me no hope. All I had to do was watch over her body? She'd teach me what I needed to know?

I looked to the hill beyond the woods where the path met the horizon. Deserted now. It was there that I'd last seen the People. For the first time since Reen's death, the huge sky seemed unfriendly. There was a coldness in my belly. Not loneliness. Not anger. Fear.

It was almost dark when I returned. Tenja sat with her arms around her knees, waiting. Her moon pendant, carved from a shell's blue lining, hung from her neck. Who would be watching over my body, I wondered, if I were watching over hers? I wasn't ready to hear about her journey. Maybe knowledge wasn't such a good thing after all. "I'm tired tonight," I said. "Tell me another time."

"I'll just tell you a little tonight, a little every night."

Just a little then. The coldness in my belly crept into my chest. "These journeys, why do you make them, you and Thought Holder and the others?" I asked.

"We make a journey inward," she began, "because thoughts can hold the memories of the world. When what we see outside ourselves is not enough, we go within."

"Not enough for what?"

"Understanding, healing."

"This journey, then, anyone can do it?"

"Yes. Not everyone chooses to."

"Why not, if they learn so much?"

"Because they must first cross a threshold." I shifted my legs and rested my head in my hands, sick of talking. I liked the outside world much better than the inside one. Still she continued. "Words can't make this journey, Thistle. They can only point you in the right direction." I looked up, frowning. Maybe if she thought I was confused, she'd stop. Moonlight glinted off her pendant. "That's enough for tonight," she said. I jumped up and hurried to the cave, pretending to sleep.

I was up early the next morning, heading for the salt marsh before Tenja stirred. I felt trapped at the cave, having begged her to tell me something I no longer wanted to know. Two of us wouldn't eat that much salt, I knew. But I'd get plenty. I'd bring back enough to salt down the meat. Maybe it would take all day. I could preserve some fish, too, keep working all month, all summer. Someone else could watch her body. Or no one. Then there'd be no journey. Just stacks of dried fish for when the People returned. I began scraping the salt crust, filling the bags.

It was almost dark when I returned. She was at the star shrine.

"Find what you were looking for?" Tenja asked.

"Part of it."

"What's wrong, Thistle?"

I stared at her. My teacher, my guide. As thin and brown as a wren. As stubborn as a crow. "I don't want to hear about this journey. Something isn't right."

"It's only that you don't understand," she replied.

"No. Something isn't right. I don't want you to do it."

"Thistle, I've never known you to be afraid of anything, not like this."

"Doesn't that tell you something?" I asked.

She just shook her head. "Someday you'll have to know. Now eat something. We'll talk for a while. You tell me when to stop."

I took a couple of deer ribs and some new greens, eating quickly so we could get this finished. Tenja watched me eat, shook her head, and resumed her story. "Within each of us is another world," she said. "An immense world, bigger than the one you see outside yourself. The world you go to when you sleep. Or when you're sick, like you were at the solstice gathering. The world of spirit. It can be a frightening place when you're not prepared. It is there that you are introduced to your death."

"Thank you for the story, Tenja." I stood quickly, tossing the rib bones in the fire.

"Where are you going?"

"For a walk."

"You just got back."

"I'm going the other way."

"Thistle, wait."

"You said I should tell you when to stop."

"But I've told you nothing yet."

"Let's do it like this then," I said. "You tell me this story in the day. It's not a good story for the night. You tell me when the sun is shining and I'll listen, if it's not too long."

She stared at me. "We'll never finish."

"The days are getting longer," I replied. I walked south for a little way, then circled back and slipped into the cave.

THE NEXT AFTERNOON WE BEGAN AGAIN. "I can't remember what I told you," she said.

"Something about the threshold and the immense."

"All right. Once you enter the Immense, you forget your name and lose your specialness," she continued. "Who you know yourself to be falls away and for a while it seems you disappear, becoming no more than the wind. That's why your body, your small self, resists the journey."

I thought about her words, trying to make them into a picture. "When we feel ourselves disappearing, that's the threshold?" I asked. I felt less afraid in the daylight, but a voice within urged me to keep looking down, as if I could be swallowed by the sky.

"The beginning of the threshold. It can be frightening at first. Once you decide to leave your body behind, to go beyond your small self and into the Immense, your thoughts race and your stomach churns.

Your legs say 'don't go.' Your body calls out, 'don't forget me, I am not finished.' You tell them to stay behind. You promise to return."

"And then you're at the threshold?"

"Then you're at the entrance of remembering," she said. "You enter it. All of your past is there. First you see the angry, frightening memories your small self keeps hidden. Then the lonesome ones. Even the happy ones, filled with deep longing. The memories rush at you and cry, 'don't forget me, I am not finished.' You wait and listen. You can't pass until they've spoken and you've understood."

"I'd rather be chased by wolves than memories," I muttered.

She continued. "And then, beyond the memories, the world of spirit opens into a vast meadow, a meadow where your ancestors walk. Some of them are waiting, longing to hear of the world they left behind, depending on you to bring them the knowledge you've won with your own mind, beaming with a love you'd almost forgotten. They grab at your ankles and cry out, 'don't forget me, I am not finished.' But you must embrace them and go on."

"And then you're there, then you're in the world of spirit?"

"Then you come before your helper, that one who takes you the rest of the way, who knows the way of power, who becomes visible to serve a purpose."

"Who's the helper?"

"It's different for everyone. Horse is the one I see."

"So when you see a horse, you know you've reached this place?"

"First I see the spirit of the horse. Then I see the world dancing. That's when I know I've reached the place."

I sat very still, not daring to look around. Perhaps the world was dancing now. One could have too much of mystery. "But how do you start? How does the journey even begin?"

"Just by going beyond the small self. You'll learn in time."

"Then how do you come back? What if you don't come back? Could someone never come back?" I imagined being snared in the threshold forever, the voices around you like the roar of wind through a canyon.

"I only know of one. She was lost as a child. Her loneliness trapped her."

I stared at Tenja, taking in her meaning. "Frightened Eyes! That's what happened to her?"

She nodded. "Can no one get her back?" I asked.

"Her small self is gone. She has nowhere to come back to."

The day was warm, but I was shaking. "Tenja, what if you're trapped? What will I do without you?"

Tenja smiled. "I'm familiar with my fear, Thistle. I've made it my friend. That's enough talking for now." She placed her hands on her knees and pushed herself up.

I walked back to the meadow, glad for the daylight that remained. These new thoughts weighed heavily. I'd need to walk for a while, whittling them down until they fit. There was only one journey I cared about—the People's return. But I didn't dare tell Tenja she'd been wrong to keep me there. If my anger separated us, I'd be truly alone.

By nightfall, I'd made peace with Tenja's words. I returned home, finding her on the beach with her moon calendar. "For this journey, then," I asked, "what do I have to do?"

"Go to sleep now. I'll tell you when the time comes. Until then, we watch the stars."

I glanced at the first twinkling lights in the purple night. How strange. I'd always thought the sky was filled with stars. Now, for the first time, it seemed empty.

Starwatcher's Journey

DURING THE MONTH WE CALLED GATHERING OF MEDICINE, I brought in extra food and wood. Tenja wouldn't be eating during her journey, she'd explained. I couldn't leave her at that time, so I'd have only the food I'd stored. Happy for the work, I tried not to think of anything else.

When we'd visited the Fish People, I'd watched them preserve their catches by smoking. We always dried or roasted our fish, but smoking didn't look hard. I decided to try. The cliff above the cave, pocked with holes in the soft sponge stone, would be a good place to start. First I worked with the little silver fish we called vendance, slicing their bellies and arranging them six-across on sticks. I chipped slots into a crevice, rammed the fish-laden sticks into the stone pockets, built a little fire below, and covered the smoking hole with a hide. My first racks caught fire, burning the fish so badly even the gulls didn't want it. Then I figured out that a mound of damp leaves beneath the fire kept the flames down. Soon I was smoking salmon and burbot as well.

I picked what I could for medicine, but I didn't really know where to look, since we'd never spent a summer by the sea. Nor did I know

what we'd need, for just the two of us. Chamomile grew
in the meadow. I dried handfuls of the tiny flowers.
We'd chew the blossoms for stomach problems or make them into a tea when we couldn't
sleep. I found celery for coughs, mint for stomach trouble. Willow bark was plentiful. We
kept it for fevers and aches.

chamomile

My nights remained the same. Tenja
listened while I described the star groups
and their routes. The answers to her questions came easily now. The
work and the learning hid my loneliness. When my thoughts became
longings, I'd walk along the shore. It seemed I'd traded the warmth of
my People for the separateness of my learning.

One night I sat with Tenja, working on my calendar. She counted
the notches I'd made for the past several months, praising me
for getting them right. "Tenja," I said, "the more I learn, the more
separate I become."

She was quiet for a while. Then she answered. "Life is a circle,
Thistle, not a line. Your circle loops around the People. It will come
back to them in ways you don't yet know."

The moon had once again grown round, luminous as an open
shell. Tenja had been quiet all day, tense. "What's wrong?" I asked.

"The moon is full. The time has come."

"For the journey?"

"Yes."

"No!"

"Listen, Thistle. I need your help. This is not the time for fear. You
are to remember everything I tell you before the journey begins, everything that happens during it. That's what I need of you. Can you do

that?" I said nothing. "Can you?"

I nodded.

"Good. Tonight we'll sleep. Tomorrow we'll get ready."

I awakened to a sound from the shore. Tenja was rolling a stone along the beach. She stopped just above the tide line, about two man-lengths from the sea. I wandered out to watch as she rolled three more stones into place, making a square about twenty steps across.

"What are you doing?" I asked.

"These stones will anchor me." She pointed to the first one. "The one on the north is for Vega, which always gives you your direction. Imagine a line between the north stone and the south stone. That line is for the Great Tree, the tree that holds up the world. You're to watch during the journey to be sure this line never moves."

"I don't see a line!"

"You haven't yet begun looking."

Then she cleared away the pebbles between the four stones and spread an elk hide on the ground. I waited while she went to the cave for her sky bundle and watched as she untied the doe skin pouch. She spread the contents on the hide. A clump of dried plants. A shell and three rocks, one a deep green, the others shiny black like my sky rock, but smaller. She opened the bag further, pulling back the sides to reveal the painted interior. I gasped at the delicate stars and moons, spirals and triangles meandering across the hide. I knelt to touch them.

"It's beautiful!" I said. "What's the triangle for?"

"Creation. The womb of the world," Tenja said proudly.

"And the color?" I traced my finger over the thin, brown lines. She must have drawn them with a sharp stick. "Blood?"

"Reindeer blood, for Earthmaker."

"And these?" I asked, lifting the clump of grey-green salvia plants, their stems woven together.

"For smudging." She took the fronds from my hand. "Someday, Thistle, this bag will be yours," she said dreamily. I was in no hurry.

"What do we do now?" I asked.

She frowned and looked around, returning to the task at hand. "Bring down some wood. I need a fire every night to keep the yellow-eyes away. Pile it here. Make the fire over there."

She pointed to the other side of the elk hide.

I did what she asked, then waited while she arranged her things. "What if it rains?" I asked.

"Cover me with a cloak, cover the wood pile, rekindle the fire later."

"What if the wood gets wet?"

"Get dry wood from the cave."

"What if someone comes? What should I tell them?"

"Who would come?"

"Strangers. What if strangers come?"

"Thistle, you'll be fine." She stood quickly and looked around, making sure everything was right. "Just watch closely. Pay attention. Do you understand? You're to watch and tell me everything you see, everything I say." Her voice softened. She reached for my hand. "I trust you," she said. My fingers were shaking. "Thistle, your fear comes from feeling separate." She covered my hand with hers. "You are not separate."

"Then why am I scared?"

"You don't trust."

"I trust you!" I said.

"Now you must trust yourself."

Tenja sent me back to the cave to bring a torch. She touched the fire to the circle of kindling, which burst into flame. The bundle of salvia she placed in the shell, lighting it with a twig. Then she fanned the smoldering leaves toward her face, breathing deeply. Standing and turning slowly, speaking softly, she sent the smoke to the four stones, to the earth, to the sky.

> *Mother of the Universe and all that lives,*
> *Mother of the Memories, Mother of the Prophecies,*
> *Mother of the Dancing, I call upon you now.*
> *I call upon the life yet waiting to be lived,*
> *I call upon the night and secret places,*
> *I call upon the streams that shine in darkness,*
> *I call upon the whirling emptiness.*
> *Mother of the Universe, I call upon you now.*

She handed me the shell. "Thistle, remember all I've told you. Leave me here on the beach until I reclaim my body. Don't be afraid." She sat, her back toward me, and stared out to sea.

The first day I spent by the cave, mending, cleaning, throwing branches on her fire, napping. Tenja sat like driftwood while the sky turned from orange to black, grey to blue. On the second day, I heard her sobbing and watched her shoulders shake. I ran toward her and stood in silence as her face twisted in some private agony and tears trickled from her closed eyes. Still I held back, remembering that I was to protect her only from outside danger, not from inner threats.

The third day she began to moan, hugging her arms around her, cringing at some unseen blow. I watched as she drew her legs to her chest and rolled to the ground, her body fraught with sobs.

Still I watched and waited. Words formed on my tongue but never left my mouth. From time to time she spoke, saying, "no, no," to invisible dangers. Sweat soaked through her tunic by day. I threw a fur around her shoulders at night, which she cast aside before morning. For three days she remained fixed to that place, never sleeping or touching food, rarely moving to pee. By the third night, she was shivering. I decided to stay on the beach, doze by her fire, and make sure she was covered. By then I was exhausted, worried that I wouldn't awaken if she needed me.

I draped a wolf pelt over her and lay nearby, promising myself I'd hear any sound she made. I awakened with a start. The sky was black, the fire burnt to embers. Tenja was silent. The pelt was on the ground. I replaced it, added a few logs to the fire, stirred the coals, and waited until flames licked the wood. Again I lay down. Again I was awakened, this time by a scream. I jumped up, confused and terrified. Tenja. I glanced to where she sat. Her eyes were open wide, looking upward, her face contorted in horror. I followed her glance.

What I saw made no sense. Above us a glowing orb lit the sky, throwing the beach into a shimmering half-light. The beam of light was moving, rushing toward us, brightening the shore each moment, illuminating stone and driftwood, throwing tails of flame behind it as it flew. The light drew closer, aiming for the hide where Tenja crouched. Suddenly the entire beach blazed like midday, blinding me in the flash. I heard the roar of a dreadful wind, the thunder of boulders crashing from a mountain. The raging glare came closer, casting a golden circle around Tenja so that she seemed ablaze. As I watched in horror, a beam of lightning struck her, passing through her flesh, piercing the earth, throwing up sparks and sand. Her body heaved and shook and was thrown to the dirt, crumbling like an ember in a flame. The earth shuddered.

"Tenja!" I screamed, crawling toward the place her body had just lain. The shore was dark. I sensed something above me. I looked up. A wall of water, huge as a cliff, rolled toward me, yellow lather curling at its edge. The dark wave was gathering up the beach, swallowing sand and stones in its fury. Again I screamed, bracing myself for the blow. But as quickly as it came, it disappeared. No water, no wave. The surge was gone, the beach still, the black sky calm.

A crumpled form sprawled on the shore. Tenja. Farther away than I'd remembered. I made my way to her, sure that she was dead. But this time she slept peacefully, snoring softly, the wolf pelt snug about her shoulders. The beach was dry.

Now it was my turn to gaze out to sea. I waited, shaking, glancing from side to side, until grey light etched the horizon, still trembling when red dawn danced on the hills. How would I tell Tenja about my strange dream? The morning sun climbed higher. Still she slept. Never had a dream terrified me so. I jumped at a sharp sound. Tenja. Coughing.

"Thistle," she murmured, "I'm here."

I knelt beside her. She was haggard from her journey, her face drawn, but her eyes warm.

Relief poured over me like sunlight. "Oh, Tenja," I said. "You're back! I had such a dream."

Happening to glance behind Tenja, I noticed a strange thing. Somehow we'd moved far down the beach from our original site. Her fire, which still smoldered, was now perhaps six man-lengths away. In front of the fire was the smoothed-out area where she'd placed the elk hide. The four large stones still circled the hide, marking the directions. But between the stones where Tenja had once sat now rose the jagged trunk of a white drift tree. A deep crack had all but severed its top. Had the tree been cast up by waves? My breath caught as if I'd swallowed ice. I looked back at Tenja.

"Thistle, Thistle," she said, shaking her head and smiling bleakly, "I am so tired. Help me back to the cave." I took her arm. She shuffled along like an old woman, shaking her head and saying, "I saw so many things." I glanced once again at the tree, then headed up the shore.

"Are you hungry?" I asked at the entryway. I made her a broth and rubbed her shoulders, keeping my own strange tale to myself while she rested. All that day she dozed and sat, sat and dozed. In the night she slumped at the mouth of the cave, clutching her moon calendar and gazing at the stars. She'd started to cough.

"Tenja, don't you think you should sleep?"

She shook her head and silenced me, seeming to listen to some other voice. I'd seen enough of the night. Crawling to the back of the cave, I wedged myself between a boulder and the wall, pulling my tunic around me. Last night's dream was beginning to fade like a frightening memory. Perhaps it would soon be gone.

Tenja's cough awakened me in the night, but by dawn she seemed stronger. She still leaned against the wall, looking at the shore, hardly mindful of me. Her eyes were as empty as the sky, except for a sadness I hadn't seen before. I boiled water in a bladder bag and made us mint tea, then sat next to her and tucked my feet beneath me. Perhaps she'd talk today. Her voice was hoarse when she finally spoke. "Thistle, there is so much we don't know." I waited. "I saw just a little of it."

"What?" I asked.

"I saw that the air moves like water, wave upon wave, ebbing, flowing. And the stars burn as waywardly as a fire in a storm, throwing off sparks as large as the sun." I tried to imagine such things. "And the sun itself holds the power to draw objects to it and devour them."

"What kind of power?"

"A power not yet named." She pushed damp hair from her flushed face. "There are many things for which we have no record, Thistle. One of those things I've seen."

"The giant light flying toward the earth? Did you see that?"

"Yes. It seemed so real." She turned toward me with a jerk. "How did you know?" Tenja's face was ashen. I'd wait until she was stronger to tell her my strange dream.

"I'll tell you later," I said. "So Sun's power to draw things to it, is that Chaos? That power?"

"No. That happens all the time. Small things go to the large." Her voice was weary.

"So that's not bad?" I longed for a clear answer.

"Well, only if the small thing whips too close."

"That would be Chaos?"

"Yes," she said, "that would be Chaos."

Suddenly, she looked lost, in some silence beyond me. A tear was making its slow way down her face. I had to reach her, for my sake as well as hers. "Tenja, what is it?"

She spoke at last, more to herself than me. "So . . . it's come to this . . . all my longing . . . all my yearning . . . All my life was because of the People and the sky. Now the sky will destroy them." The tears came faster.

"Tenja, it's not your fault. You've done nothing . . ."

"No, I've done nothing. I've watched and waited and counted and prayed, but I've done nothing. All my work, all my life, has led only to this—that now I know the time they'll die."

No sound but the stirring of the sea and the curious cry of a gull interrupted the stillness. I stared at Tenja's face, then my feet, and back at her face again. My stomach growled. What terrible thing had happened to her on that beach? These journeys were horrible things. I would never take one. And then even as I watched, her countenance began to change. She seemed unfamiliar, no longer terrified, but certainly not the Tenja I remembered. Her agony was giving way to some new tenderness. What if she were crazy, like Frightened Eyes?

"Tenja," I finally whispered, swallowing hard, "what are you thinking about?"

She sniffed and wiped her hand across her nose. Then she smiled. "The light on stones . . . the tracks of birds in the mud . . . the hairs on Ephus's arms." She picked up a handful of gravel and let it fall through her fingers, her face soft. "The world is so beautiful, Thistle, trembling to be loved."

I swallowed again. "Well, ah, I'd better go check the drying racks." I stood up slowly and backed away. "I could make us something to eat," I said brightly.

Tenja was asleep when I returned. Perhaps she was strange, I thought, but at least she was alive. I had to keep her that way. "Earthmaker, help us," I prayed. "I can't stay here alone." I made some stew. Tenja awoke in the middle of the afternoon and ate a little.

"We still have some time, Thistle," she said once she'd eaten. "We have a little time. I just need to figure out what to tell the People." She lay down again, while I put things away.

I was aware of a prickly feeling under my skin. I hated it. Perhaps I'd walk for a while. I threw a log on our cooking fire and headed out, careful not to look at the phantom tree still embedded on the beach. I walked until I was exhausted. The tingling in my body finally disappeared. Maybe I should take a closer look at that tree, I thought. After all, Tenja had given me instructions, before she became strange. "Watch the line between the stone." I made myself walk toward it.

I stood over the white tree in the dusk. Then I reached out and touched it, rubbing my hand over the hard wood, following the smooth surface to the jagged break, running my fingers over fresh splinters. I pushed against the tree with my body. It stood firm, its roots buried in gravel. It was dead. But it was real. I went back to see about Tenja.

She slept poorly that night and woke early, leaning against the wall with her calendar in her lap. "Please rest," I begged her.

"Soon," she replied.

The journey had weakened her. Her cough was worsening. In a few days, she began rubbing her ears. I made her willow bark tea. She got worse, grabbed her ears and moaned. I tried to remember what Yarrow had taught me—prickly ash bark, red clover, wild celery, all good for infections. But I couldn't leave her while I searched the countryside for plants.

"Sit with me, Thistle," she demanded. "Tell me the names of the stars. Tell me the star clusters."

I cooked her different foods, broth, and rose hip tea. I gave her tiny pieces of fish and tangy roots. I picked new shoots and steamed them, so she'd have something fresh. The fear in me was growing.

"Tell me the names of the stars, Thistle. Count the months of the moon. You must know this."

There was a day when it seemed her ears were getting better. Then her head began to hurt. She screamed with pain. "Something is pushing in my head, Thistle, something is swelling. Make it stop!" One ear started to drain. Maybe that was good. The pressure might decrease.

I forgot all thoughts of Chaos for this new terror. I had to keep her with me. I had to hold on to her. But she grew confused, her thoughts slowing, her words dragging, her eyes distant.

Drowsy all the time, she rarely slept. Ten more days went by. One foggy morning I awoke to Tenja's moans. She hadn't eaten for days. Her cheekbones were sharp, her eyes sunken. Seeing that I was awake, she clutched my arm. Her fingers were like sticks.

"You must be the one to tell the People, Thistle. You must explain," she said. I pushed back the hair from her hot face. She tightened her grip. Her strength amazed me.

"No, Tenja. You'll do it. You'll see."

"Promise me, promise that you'll tell them. Please!"

"What, tell them what? What should I say?"

Her breathing was fast and shallow. "Tell the People, tell them a great light is trapped in the constellation of the Seven Women. Like a wild horse, it will break and run, kicking over planets, plummeting past Earth, crashing into Sun. No one can stop it. No one ever could. Tell them."

"All right, I will. I'll tell them. But you must rest, Tenja. Don't talk, just rest."

For four more days I watched her, helpless. On the fifth day, she awoke from a tortured sleep and looked around in amazement, her eyes wide with wonder and as radiant as new flowers.

"Thistle," she said, "Thistle, I see it. I see the torch inside my mind, the one Ziva told us about! It's so bright, it's brighter than stars, brighter than all the stars. Brighter than the great, glowing horse. They don't matter, Thistle, the other things I told you, they don't matter. Tell the People, tell Ephus, tell them none of that matters. Tell them of the torch they carry. Tell them the torch is the only light they need. Tell them that all that matters is their love."

The morning sky gleamed overhead, but its light never reached me. Tenja's eyes were the stars and her smile the setting sun. Even in her stillness, the joy never left her face. I held her all that day, her body as light as a hollow log. I sat alone until darkness covered me.

I buried Tenja in the back of the cave with Idra, who'd been her teacher long ago. Two days it took to dig the grave. I pulled her into it and covered her. First with dirt, then rocks. I hauled up the twelve stones from the moon shrine and counted each one before I dropped it.

"Tenja, take back the rocks for the moon."

I carried up the stones from the star shrine, the five star points with twelve stones each. I left the four center ones on the beach and counted up to sixty as I let the other ones fall.

"Tenja, take back the rocks from the stars. I bury them with you."

Then I stared, dismayed, at the seventy-two stones marking her grave.

"Goodbye, Tenja. I give you back your stones. And thank you for your great gift. For now, though I am nothing, I can count."

On the third day I began to scream.

She Who Walks Alone

THE HILLS FLUNG BACK MY VOICE and none of my kind could hear me. I crouched near the entrance, torn by grief. I couldn't stay in the cave, where thoughts of Tenja overtook me. Nor was I safe on the shore, with the memory of her last journey and the new paw prints of curious animals. Like the hollow shell of a crab whose life is sucked away, I trembled. Always before I'd been a part of something. Now the world was empty and the emptiness loomed like an evil stranger. Where could I go? The meadow? The woods?

My mind raced, unconnected. My body told me in its own way about its fear. The day after I buried Tenja, I felt a burning tightness in my hands. I looked down, startled to see the fingers of a stranger, red and stiff, fat as snakes, new scabs crusting on my palms. Had the stones done that? Even my body was no longer my own. Again my fear arose.

"Earthmaker, what were you thinking?" I cried. "The thing I feared the most, you gave me."

Silence.

My thoughts were wild. I had to tame them. I tried to remember everything I'd ever learned, hoping for a hint of wisdom. Willow bark for fever. Twenty-eight days in a month. Never eat mushrooms growing under an oak. Make yourself larger if you see a cat. Don't cross a frozen river in the spring. Nothing I knew could help me. I had to find something new, something beyond my habits.

"Earthmaker, help me!"

I waited, forcing myself to sit, though my body wanted to run.

Find a quiet part of you, a part that doesn't shake. Who said that? The voice seemed to come from within. I held my breath, listening. *Stare at the sea. Sit quietly. Stare again. Don't run. Stay close to the cave. Wait. Make a plan. Breathe. Wait. Don't run.* I shifted my attention to the rise and fall of my chest, sighing deeply at each breath. Yes. There was a still place, between breathing in and breathing out, a place where I could rest. Yes. I could do that.

I returned to that place again and again as the day wore on, getting up only to pee or take a drink. Each time I moved, I lost the calm. But by nightfall, I knew how to get it back. All night I sat, listening to my breath, dozing from time to time. By the fourth morning after Tenja's death, a still small part of me had been born, one that didn't shiver. Perhaps it could be my leader.

I stood and stretched. Thought about eating. Changed my mind. Crouched on the shore again, close to the cliff. Damn you, Tenja. How I hated her for leaving. My tears welled up. I sobbed, sad but less afraid. When I looked at the sea again, a different person stared through my eyes. I listened to my breathing. In a while, my quiet part began to speak.

You are older than Frightened Eyes when she was alone. You have reached your fifteenth year. You know your small self. You must tend it.

Yes, that's it. Tend my small self. Like a fire in the rain. Keep the flame alive. I breathed until I was calm again. Two things threatened my fire. Tenja's death and my aloneness. Those things would have to wait. I saw that I'd decided to live. I'd have to go slowly then, so I didn't make a mistake. I listened for the calm part.

Check the food.

I walked into the cave and counted. Four dried trout, part of a salmon, walnuts.

Make a plan.

A plan. What I would do in the future. For a moment, my fear lurched up like vomit. I swallowed it. A plan. I picked up a stick and began to mark on the sand.

What could I do? I could stay here. I drew a circle for the cave and a wavy line for the sea. I could stay close, fish, and wait. I went to the cave and pulled down Tenja's moon calendar, counting the marks. Eighty four. The People would return in eighty four days. Three months! Fear rose up, huge and menacing. That was too long to hear nothing but my echo and the howl of wolves.

I made a second picture, a mountain with a circle. I could go to the People. Follow the path they'd taken, head uphill, reach the summer cave in eight days. Home! I knew which peaks to follow if I got lost. But I wouldn't get lost. I remembered the way. Like I remembered the yellow eyes that stared from black forests, waiting for someone to stray. I'd never make it alone.

What else? One other place. I drew a little fish. I could go to the Fish People. I could be there in two days. I'd have to go inland, like I did with Tenja, so I'd get clear of the cliffs along the shore. If I got lost, I'd just follow the sea. I could tell Ziva about Tenja and the torch. Tell her about Tenja's awful journey. Make my marks on the calendar. I could fish there. Take care of their babies. Not eat too much. They'd keep me. I was sure of it. That was the best plan.

I looked at the calendar again. I'd forgotten to record the last five nights. Five nights with no counting. Tenja would be angry. I'd have to be more careful.

The calm voice continued. *Leave tomorrow for the Fish People. Build a big fire tonight.*

Only then did I realize the fire had burned out, probably gone dead when I was digging the grave. I walked to the fire circle and brushed my hands through the cinders. Nothing but charcoal now. Another mistake. I shouldn't have let that happen. Already the smell of death crept up from under the stones in the back of the cave. Some beast would be here soon. I went to look for the fire stones and struck them together over a few dry leaves. *Tend the fire of your small self.* I set the iron stones by the entrance so I wouldn't forget them. *Everything you can't carry, put up high.* The stone from the stars. Tenja's things. *Put the iron stones in a pouch. Lay the tools straight, the antler blades, the shovels, the clubs.*

I was still restless. I dragged three logs to the front of the cave, a man-length from the entrance. *Burn them,* my calm self said. *No animals will come.* At last I slept, awakening to the cry of gulls and the smell of smoldering wood. It was now the fifth day of my aloneness.

My calm self greeted me before my fear. *Splash water on your face, pack your things, roll the charred logs to the entrance.* Maybe the hyenas wouldn't come.

It was time to leave. I climbed the hill, looking back to the shore one more time. Then away from the sea, across the meadow, up a small ridge, and to the south. I kept my eyes forward, pretending that the People were following, naming the stones that had no names. The world was larger than I remembered. My wandering had begun.

Around nightfall, I came upon the deer path I'd followed through the forest with Tenja the previous spring. It wouldn't do to enter the woods at dusk. I retraced my steps to a stone outcropping I'd passed. I'd make my bed there. After a little water and some fish, I rolled a few rocks around me and lay down in my stone nest. And with the morning, the woods. The ravens were my closest friends. They seemed mindful of me, calling "Walks Alone, Walks Alone," as I entered the woods. One even followed me into the brush, flitting above the path few humans seemed to know. I was glad for the company, unfamiliar with the ways of the forest.

I was a creature of open spaces, accustomed to the horizon. My trip here with Tenja had been nothing like this. We'd come in the spring, walking briskly between leafless trees. But now, with the summer, the forest kept secrets, telling me little of what lay ahead. The day grew hot. Sweat stung my body and dripped into my eyes. Branches and roots clutched when I came near.

I slapped them inside, demanding to pass. But the brush scratched my face and stung my arms, as if to say, "you can't hurry here." After a while I began to listen.

The woods changed as I moved south. By midday, pine trees had given way to broadleaves. Hazel and hawthorn nestled under oaks. Ferns unfolded at my feet. Clouds of mosquitoes rose with every step. I ripped loose a frond to wave them away. How could other creatures live here? I wondered, as I swatted at the pests. The birds were beautiful, though. I saw a white-throated warbler flitting through the branches. A woodcock looked up from his insect feast, then resumed jabbing his long bill at the ground. "Tenja, look!" I called. Then I remembered.

Deeper I went, following a line of trampled foliage and deer droppings. Deeper. The path that had been so obvious last spring disappeared in summer's lushness. Now I stood in a wash of green, a sea of ferns rising around me.

"Walks Alone!" the raven called mockingly.

"I'm not lost!" I yelled back. The path behind me was still visible. I could return any time—if I wanted. But just ahead I heard the sound of water. "Do you hear that, stupid bird? The sea!"

I lunged into the tall grass, heading southwest. From this height, I'd be able to see a long stretch of coast. I was almost half way there. Probably see the Fish People tomorrow. I thrashed through the under-brush, tripping over fallen trees, eager for the familiar surge of blue.

No. There was no sea. I'd come upon a creek. A stream that plunged from a ledge and dropped at my feet, swirling over rotted logs and moss-soft stones, misting the green-black wood. Clusters of dead trees told the stream's meandering tale. Beyond it rose a dark wall of forest.

"Walks Alone!"

I looked up to see the raven perched above me, his head cocked to one side. I remembered my plan. Tend the fire of my small self. Don't give way to fear. I raised my chin, meeting his bright gaze.

"What a beautiful place, friend bird!" I called.

I crouched to take a drink. Slivers of light dappled the treetops but only shadows reached the ground. No grass grew here. The damp earth was covered with rotted leaves and scattered acorns. Night would come fast and early. I glanced at the trees behind me, remembering the di-rection I'd just come. If I were mistaken, it would be better to find out in the morning than at dusk. I'd stay here, I decided. The mosquitoes were already celebrating my arrival. I'd need to build a fire quickly. I looked around for a place to camp.

In the middle of the creek was a little island, maybe five arm-lengths long and three across. The fast-flowing stream ran on one side.

On the other, a dark pool moved quietly below a high bluff. I studied the water until Earthmaker gave me a plan. Then I measured the creek's width in my mind, rolled a dead log to the bank, and propped one end against a tree. Raising it slowly, I shoved hard, watching as it fell and straddled the stream. I glanced around for the raven. He still watched me, perhaps curious about the ways of humans. I was happy for his presence.

I tossed my pack to the island, then my spear, and crawled across the log. Standing on the other side, I brushed the rotten bark from my hands. The ground was even wetter here. It would take a while to start a fire. I scooped up a handful of mud and spread it over my arms and face, disappointing the mosquitoes. Dead branches littered the ground, plenty for a small lean-to. I made a loose frame and spread my sleeping robe over it. The fire took longer. But after a while a small flame trembled. Then I picked blackberries from the vines that looped round the island. Except for the rush of the stream and the little waterfall, the forest was quiet. I looked at my little house, my bridge, my fire. Maybe the woods was not so bad. I was safe from everything, I thought, except maybe bears and lynx. I was too tired to worry.

I took a fish from my bag, tied the bag to a tree, and stretched out. I was sick of fish. Perhaps I'd hunt tomorrow. I yawned. It was peaceful here. Maybe I'd live in the woods some day. The sky demanded so much and hid so little. You couldn't have secrets under the sky, especially from yourself. But the forest welcomed secrets, loved secrets. It took me as I was. Roots and branches sheltered me, cradled me, concealed me. The singing stream soon lulled me to sleep. As I slept, the forest lifted me and brought me softly to the land of dreaming.

The outside world fell away. Then the waterfall that had been whispering to me changed itself. I saw that it was really made of bird wings, of white birds who wafted down, flew away, and returned, over and over again. Who would have guessed? My sleeping self watched their flight. Other images rose and fell as well, visions of Tenja at night on the shore, Fire's laughing face, Ziva slowly beckoning as she receded into the distance. A dream path wound before me and I heard a raven laughing. I started to follow. Then a new creature appeared, one with glistening fur and eyes like tiny stars.

An otter. What did I know of otters? He was sitting on the banks of a dream creek. The whiskers on his narrow head twitched as he watched his six swimming babies. Odd to see webbed feet protruding from such sleek fur. He looked at me. I stared back.

"Do you swim?" he asked, eyeing me curiously. My dream had taken me to an old place where humans still knew the talk of animals and could answer.

"Some."

"Huum," he said, stretching his long body.

I wanted him to tell me all about the animals. "Little otter," I began. But before I could continue, there was a great rumble. The earthen wall above the dream creek gave way. The forest fell away behind it and a great mountain rose up far in the distance. It was the mountain of my dreaming, the same peak I'd seen my last night with the Fish People. It was as it had been the first time, a summit surrounded by six smaller peaks, its crest thrust upward like a breaking wave. Only this time it towered above a swollen sea. And there, at its base, preening his bright body, sat the otter. He was watching his young ones paddling around him, preparing to dive.

The shining otter jumped. I awakened to a "plunk" on the water, bolted up, and stared at the pool, expecting to see him. But there was nothing, no ripple on the smooth black surface. I looked around, puzzled. No otter. It had been a dream after all. I glanced down. Something shone on the dark ground, glowed silver beside my leg. I reached out. Three long white feathers lay in the mud. I took the feathers and put them in the pouch with the moon calendar. At least the birds were real. It would soon be light.

I had had enough of dreaming. I was hungry. The path to the Fish People could wait. Today I'd eat. Anyway, I could hardly be late if they didn't even know I was coming. I took up my spear and crawled back across the swaying log, imagining a roasted boar with juices dripping from its fat crisp skin. I'd build a fire so high no bugs would come near. Of course, a hunter only got one chance to strike at a charging boar. Even then, it would take three men to bring one down. Maybe I wouldn't get a boar. Something else then. I looked around, waiting for a plan.

Once again I noted the trees that marked my route, two big oaks with a little maple in between. To the west, beyond the ledge with the waterfall, the ground fell away into a deep, wooded ravine, a likely home for red deer. The chances of getting even a young deer were slim. My throwing ax was no good unless I came upon a herd. That would be unlikely in the woods. Still I felt hopeful. I'd head for the ravine. I started down the hillside, which was still damp with dew. I made my way down the slope, grabbing at the wet grass to slow me down.

The tree cover had blocked my view in the woods but on the hillside, I could once again see the sky. It was dark to the north where clouds were rolling in over the mountains. Maybe it was raining where the People were. What would it be like, I wondered, to move as fast as clouds. I started to slip in the wet grass and shifted my glance from the sky to the ground. Below me, at the bottom of the ravine, a creek ran between two bluffs. That's where I would find my animal, I reasoned.

I edged down sideways, finally sliding on my backside to the bottom, close to the stream. Looking back to remember my route, I realized that each tree merged into another. Each rock repeated the last. I'd come almost straight down. I could still see my path in the grass.

Still, it would be better to stay here and let the animals come to me than to wander in a strange valley and lose my way. I found a hawthorn bush close by, downwind from the stream, and crawled under it with my net and short spear. Then I waited for a plan.

The grass on the bank had been torn away. Probably the work of boars I thought, judging by the angular tracks nearby. I crawled further into the brush. Morning dragged on silently, the buzz of insects the only sound. I chewed a twig to pass the time. Should I fish? It would be easy to dam the stream. Or just hold the net. I glanced at the creek and shook my head. I was tired of fish. Was the water higher? The boar tracks were gone. Suddenly the strange silence of the forest hit me—not even a raven's taunt. Something wasn't right. I looked at the water again.

It was rising, flowing faster, the trickle becoming a gush.

I glanced to the north. There, where the little creek rounded a sharp bend, I was saw a wall of brown water churning through the pass. What was happening? Even as I watched, the wall grew higher, taller than my head. The rain! It was the rain from the mountains to the north. I tossed my tools aside and tore through the brush, hardly mindful of the thorns. All I could think of was getting to high ground. Already the swollen stream swirled at my feet. Just ahead of the rising water, I threw myself at the hill, pressing my body against the earth. I grabbed a clump of grass. It came uprooted in my hand. I grasped for the woody trunk of a bush, caught it, and held on. Pulling my legs close to my body, I hung sideways. I could hear the roar of the creek below me, though I didn't dare look down.

From a short way upstream came a dull thud. I glanced over to see a great hunk of earth plummeting to the water. The hollow space it left behind was quickly flooded. The water was coming faster, getting deeper. I couldn't stay here. I reached and pulled, crawling like a salamander up the hill, scanning the ground above me for a handhold. Up ahead a ragged juniper clung to a rock. I scrambled in that direction and grabbed a twisted branch. Surely I was high enough now.

Anchoring myself above the little shrub, I twisted my body and looked down. I'd climbed perhaps six man-lengths up the hill. Now the water was surging halfway between the creek bed and my feet. I clung there, watching the torrent. The floor of the ravine was gone, the trees and brush eaten by the rushing river. Tumbling in the current below me was a thrashing elk, his dark eyes huge with fear. I turned my head. Then I looked upward. A little way above me was a treeless shelf of earth. I'd try to make it there.

I waited until I could no longer hear the pounding of my heart. Then, without stopping, I clawed my way, one hand over the other, to the little ledge. I pulled myself over the edge and sat panting. It was good to be on a level ground. I'd never known of such a thing, a flood so fast. Who would believe me? No wonder I'd heard nothing all morning. Silence was a strong teacher, I thought. Thank Earthmaker I was safe.

Suddenly, I heard a low snort. I froze. I was not alone on this small ledge. Had I come upon a cat, a bear? I held my breath and slowly turned my head. Several large boulders lay behind me, fallen from a high rock face long ago. Something was behind those rocks, its raspy breathing near.

I had no weapon. My eyes swept the ground. A stone the size of my head lay close by. I'd have to stand up to throw it. Should I charge first or wait? Maybe the creature would go away. I didn't move, just listened. Surely the animal knew I was there. A sudden snort broke the silence, then several high squeals. Boars! Baby ones as well. Those creatures of low places, wooded glens, deep forests, the bottoms of ravines—how could boars be here? I glanced over the slope that plummeted below my feet, imagining my own path. How could boars, with their tiny legs and low bellies, climb up such a hill?

Yet they'd made it; somehow they were here. This narrow, forlorn ledge was surely not their home. I scanned the ground around me. A boar would never charge across this thin lip of land; he'd go right over the side. He couldn't gouge me unless I stood right in front of him. And I was protected by a wall of stone. I had him. I turned slowly, crawling to my knees, picking up the stone, scooting to the boulder that separated us. I peered over the top.

Six pairs of tiny black eyes stared back at me. The young ones squealed frantically, while the mother nudged them, pushing them back with her nose. The male, who stood between me and the others, pawed the earth and glared. His yellow tusks jerked with every snort.

"You've protected your family well," I said, "bringing them to such a place. But I'm protected, too." I edged my way onto a higher rock, well out of the reach of his tusks. He rammed the stones angrily. "You are safe here," I told him, "safe from everything but me." Standing above him like this, it would be easy to smash his head. Earthmaker had done well to put this creature before me. But what about the female? I could kill the male, but I couldn't take the meat until she left. What if she stayed there, hovering over her dead mate? Would I have to kill her, too? And let the babies die? I'd be happy to eat any one of the six, but I didn't need them all. What if another animal, drawn by the fresh scent of blood, found me while I was waiting for the female to leave? Thoughts passed quickly as I watched my prey, my stone raised above them.

I knew I could kill the boar and probably even get its carcass out. Something else held me back. The babies had stopped squealing and stood trembling behind their mother, their bodies against the hill. The male's eyes never left me. As I studied him, I noticed something odd. Blood, oozing from his legs. I glanced at the female and the young ones. They, too, were bloodied from their strange journey, the flesh torn from their legs, their chests rubbed raw. Did that father have a memory that told him to lead his babies up a ragged hillside before a flood swept through? All he knew was that he wanted them to live. Habit and memory were no help at such times. I saw in his terrified eyes the same fear that lived in me. Had Earthmaker saved him so that I could kill him now? Whatever the power that had brought him up that slope, it seemed more important than my hunger. I glanced one last time at the boar, then reached for a handhold in the crag above me. I pulled myself onto another stone and away from that lost family. Then I scrabbled back up the hillside, returning to camp empty-handed. Though I carried less than when I'd left that morning, my head was full of thoughts. I sat with them for a while, then made another net of vines. One more night of fish.

That night, as I roasted two trout by the lean-to, I saw that I'd been wrong about the forest. Like the sky, the woods asked much of me. Things might be hidden, but they couldn't be ignored.

I'd been lucky, lucky and blessed. I thought about that, too. My fear and loneliness were still with me, held in my thoughts like shadows. I wouldn't forget them. But that day I'd felt the preciousness of life. Something else was growing in me now, something like joy.

The evening sky was grey. I added wood to the fire and hoped there'd be no rain. At least the wind couldn't reach me. My body ached. The cuts burned. I was exhausted. "Earthmaker, let me rest," I murmured as I settled in. "I have to travel tomorrow." Would I see the otter in my dreams, I wondered? But I slept hard and remembered nothing. Sometime during the night, the fire burnt out. I awakened stiff and cold. Turning to stretch, I noticed marks along the muddy shore, new marks, indentations left by the feet of a creature crouching near my face. Pulling myself up on my elbows, I looked closer. The tracks were much larger than mine but they were clearly those of a human.

The *Elhaz* Hunter

SOMEONE HAD BEEN WATCHING ME, another human in the forest! I wasn't alone. Was this a good thing? I crawled to my knees and studied the ground. The tracks were from one person. One person with very large feet. Was this human a creature of the forest or a traveler like me?

The moon calendar! I looked up and saw my pouch, still tied to the tree. The visitor brought no danger, so it seemed. I'd try to find him. It had to be a male. Only a female giant would have such huge feet. Giants. The Arn! What if the Arn were close by? Surely they'd come back.

I wasn't alone. The Arn were Others, but they knew me. I'd belong somewhere. I grabbed my bag, eager to go. No, wait. My face was covered with mud. There were leaves in my hair. I stunk. I slipped off my tunic, jumped in the cold water, and washed quickly, rubbing my skin until it tingled. Combing my fingers through my hair, I wound it into one long braid. Then I pulled my tunic back over my wet body, took up my pack, and crawled across the swaying log.

"Goodbye, small home!" I called. The Arn! There'd be company, shelter, a fire, meat. I dashed into the forest, looking for the path.

My visitor's trail was easy to spot in the tall grass. I followed it to the deer path I'd walked two days before. Whoever had found me must have seen my fire from that path. But from which direction had he come? And which way had he gone? The trail to the north I knew well. The path to the south went deeper into the forest, finally ending near the sea.

I crouched in the grass. Deer had worn the path bare. The ground showed me nothing.

Maybe I should just run south, maybe catch up. I hated being slowed down, wasting time thinking. *Wait!* my quiet self said. *Remember the creek.* Yes, the creek that almost swept me away because I wasn't paying attention. Had I learned nothing? What was it Tenja always told me? "Look for clues. Try to find a pattern." I sat on the ground, forcing myself to patience.

Each time of day gave up its clues. Smoke, footprints, trampled grass. I had two clues, hardly enough for a pattern. I'd concluded that the Arn were nearby. Was I fooling myself? Why would the Arn be here at all? They'd headed south months ago. I tried to think. Hadn't Ephus said there were other Arn, many of them, restless humans with no homes? Maybe these were their relatives. Why would they be here? Were they going south to meet the others? Or heading north, following the grazers? Too late for that. Staying here then? The Arn weren't forest people, but creatures of the tundra. They'd never live here. And I'd seen the land north of the woods, rocky and sparse, with nothing to eat. No one could live there. So these people were travelers, on the move to somewhere. Or maybe it was just one person. One lost person.

Like me. Was he going north or south? Thinking did no good.

Suddenly I was afraid, too frightened to sit still. My legs were shaking. What if I'd lost him?

I'd tricked myself into believing I was all right alone. I didn't want to stay separate. Was there no clue to help me? Maybe one. The visitor had come in the night. No human traveled by night.

He must have been camping close by. The Arn weren't likely to sleep in the woods. They were people of the horizon like us. I was only here by accident. The only open country was to the north, too far away to see my fire. But they could have seen the smoke. I'd go north.

I jumped up and started running. It was a long way back. I'd taken half a day to get here. But then I'd stopped to rest and watch the birds. And I hadn't been sure of the path. I'd get back more quickly. I'd find them if they'd come this way. My hope carried me as I crashed through the wood, snapping back branches and jumping fallen logs. This time oaks gave way to pines. My heart pounded and my sides ached. I had to slow down. Still, I pushed myself on toward the open country and finally out into the sun. Once again the sky greeted me, throwing the world open all the way to its blue rim. I squinted in the bright light, shielding my eyes with my hand as I studied the rugged hills. Nothing.

I could see no sign of a camp, no sign of humans. I sat on a rock, the same outcropping I'd slept under three nights ago. Had I made the wrong choice? Had I failed?

Wait. Slow down. Listen to your breathing. Feel the sun on your face. Think.

I looked around. This was a place where cats might live. Maybe not. I hadn't seen any grazers nearby. I was back where I'd started, only this time I had no water. I opened my pouch. Two fish.

A sound. What was that? A cry from up ahead. I stood on the rock and looked to the north.

There was a movement on the ridge just beyond me. A human, just coming over the rise! And then another behind the first. Two of them, moving this way. I waved my arms and yelled. Had they seen me? Yes! I strained my eyes to make them out. Yes. I recognized the first one.

Taller and fuller than I remembered him, but unmistakable. Strawhead. And behind him, a burly man with a lurching gait. Ephus! Ephus the Traveler! I waved. And then I heard Ephus calling out my name. Great sobs welled up in me at the sound of his voice. I ran toward them.

Strawhead was closer, pointing at me and smiling and talking non-sense words. I ran past him and grabbed Ephus. "What are you doing here?" I cried. "Why . . . ? I've been so lonely." My sobs drowned out my words. I stopped trying to talk and nestled my head against his chest, losing myself in the comfort of another human, feeling his rough hand on my shoulder. Then my questions rose up again. Why was he here? Where had he been? How had he found me? I pulled away and sniffed, ready to talk again. Then I remembered that Ephus knew noth-ing of Tenja's death. I looked into his sad eyes. Or perhaps he did. "You saw the grave?" I whispered. He nodded and I cried again.

"Tenja would not have left the cave had someone died," he said. "So I knew it was you who buried her."

A shadow caught my attention. Strawhead stood beside us, his eyes shy but curious, his yellow hair matted as if small creatures slept there. Whiskers now roughened his face. I covered my mouth with my hand. "Why is he here?" I asked.

"We looked for you. I took the path north. Anish went south. He saw your smoke. It was he who found you."

I turned to the strange man-boy. "Thank you for finding me," I said, loud and slow.

He scuffed one foot in the dirt, perhaps the Arn way to say "you're welcome."

I looked back at Ephus. "You're staying with them?"

He nodded.

"In the forest?"

"No. East of here. We are here only to find you. Come back with us now and tell your story."

I went gladly, willing to do anything he said. Leaving the woods behind, the three of us headed over open country uncut by any path, walking in the direction of the morning sun. I held Ephus's hand tightly. Strawhead strode beside us like a tree with legs. He hadn't stopped grinning since they'd found me. "Why is he smiling?" I asked Ephus after a while.

"He's happy," Ephus replied.

I took Strawhead's hand as well, clinging to both of my humans. "Thank you, Earthmaker," I prayed.

We moved along quickly, the two of them speaking a language of our words and Arn words mixed together. I understood little of what they said. When I brought up my own questions, Ephus just raised his hand and shook his head, as if to say all would be answered later. I did break into their conversation with one question, something that had been troubling me since we'd first met up. "Ephus, why didn't Strawhead—Anish—why didn't he awaken me?"

"He didn't want to scare you."

"But to go all the way back . . . that seems foolish. What if I'd lost you again?"

Ephus just smiled and shook his head. "That was no distance for an Arn. Besides, once he'd tracked you, he'd never lose your trail."

"Oh."

A little after midday, we reached their camp. The laughter of male voices and the cry of a baby told us the Arn were near. But it was their creatures who saw us first, those dark, four-legged wolf people. All three of them ran yelping to Anish, jumping to look him in the eye and lick his hands. He pushed them away and spoke a soft command.

Coming upon the Arn again was almost like going home. They dropped their work and hurried toward us, the Giant leading the group. He grabbed my shoulders in his meaty hands and nodded to Ephus. "*Wunjo, wunjo,*" he exclaimed, shaking me.

"Yes," Ephus said, "I'm happy to find her."

I glanced around at the ragged little group. The Arn had built one of their large huts, the kind Ephus had described, elongated rather than round. The frame was made of wooden poles bent into half circles, crossed at the top, and draped with hides. Its base was ringed with stones. Smoke wafted through an opening at the top. Since that was their only structure, I figured the entire group slept inside.

"*Gebo,*" the Giant said, gesturing. "*Gebo.*" He turned toward the hut, reaching it in two long strides and stooping to dig through a pouch that lay by the wall. When he returned, a wide grin lit his face. He placed a red stone object in my hand.

"You made this?" I asked. I held a carving, almost the size of my palm, polished until it shone. It was a replica of their mother beast, the creature whose nose was longer than its legs. Could any animal really look so sad?

"*Gebo,*" he repeated, folding my fingers over it.

"It's a gift," Ephus whispered.

"*Laguz*," the Giant said, spreading his hand over the air before him. "*Laguz*." His voice caught as he spoke.

Ephus explained that the home of their mother animal was now a great lake. All such creatures had disappeared. The Arn kept them alive only in stone. I ran my finger along its smooth red flank. "The beast is *thurisaz*," said Ephus, "a thing of great strength."

I looked into the large man's glistening eyes. "Thank you very much," I said. "It's beautiful."

A white-haired woman, who would have been much shorter than the leader even if she wasn't so stooped, jabbed her finger from me to the ground. I sat, along with the men. The Old One and a younger female, both of whom I recognized from last summer, brought us horn cups filled with a steaming liquid. The women glanced at me curiously and spoke in whispers, as if concerned that I might understand their words. I took a sip of tea. It was the same beverage they'd served last summer, a mildly sweet brew made of crushed grass seed. I stretched my legs and yawned, glad I no longer had to think about my safety every moment.

Ephus swirled his tea to cool it, tossed it down, and held out the horn for another. I waited patiently, knowing he never went for long without talking. I'd soon hear his tale and learn how it was he'd come to find me. After his third horn of tea, he was ready to begin. He spoke to the Arn leader first. Both of them glanced at me from time to time. Ephus was gesturing broadly, his arms spread as wide as a peacock's tail. What nonsense was he telling these people?

"Ephus!" I said at last.

"What?" He turned to me in surprise, his arms dropping to his side.

"Have you come to the part where you save me from raging beasts?"

"I was getting to that," he said, smiling weakly.

237

"Tell me what you're saying. I want to hear the story, too."

So he continued, explaining to the Arn how they'd come to find me, then telling me the story in my words. Apparently, Ephus had been traveling with them for some time. They'd reached this place several days ago and made their camp. There was a river close by and animals were plentiful. Ephus had taken the young Arn with him when he returned to the cave to find Tenja and me.

"But how is it you came to be with these people at all?" I asked. That was the part of the story I didn't understand.

"When I left you and Tenja at the Fish People's home," he said, "I headed south." I nodded. "I'd never followed the coast before, only taken the inland route south of here. The shore was rough, too rough to travel. After two days, I left the sea and headed east."

"Where were you going?"

"To find those of whom I'd spoken. Those who live beyond a narrow sea. Makers of stone places."

"How could you find them if they lived across a sea?" I asked.

"They go about on boats."

"You've seen this?"

"I have seen the water. A long finger of blue. As a young man I traveled to that coast. I saw the shadowed trace of land on the other side." He stared dreamily at the sky, then remembered my presence. "It was then I learned of boats. I spoke with those who once lived across that sea. People who had come on boats and made their home on a new shore. They waited for those vessels to return. It was they who told me. To cross that water has been my longing ever since."

"Why didn't you?"

"I am getting to that part. Let me tell the story." Ephus stretched his legs and crossed them. "I left the Fish People, like I said. Even after

I turned inland, the country was rough, hilly and thick with trees. For eight days I walked, looking for the flat land that would lead me to that sea. Instead I found these people and a lake."

"A lake?"

"A lake where none should be." Ephus shook his head. "Always before, one could walk to the southeast, cross a wide plain that seemed itself the size of an ocean, and finally reach that sea. Now the low country is gone."

"What happened?"

He shrugged. "The snow from the mountains melted. For once, the slopes stand bare. The runoff filled that land and made of it a marsh. We tried to walk around it. It lapped at the foothills. We found no end."

"So you came back."

He nodded. "For a while. We'll rest, then try again. Maybe go east from here, farther east this time, then south. I've never seen what lies in that direction."

I suspected Ephus didn't care if he reached this other sea as long as he kept moving through new country. I myself cared less for journeys now and more for home. "How long will you stay here?" I asked. My heart was racing.

He shrugged. "Another month or two. The lowlands should drain by autumn, freeze by winter. We'll cross them then, after the reindeer and before the snow.

Yes. Good. The People would be back by then! I could stay with the Arn until their return. I had a home. I had two homes. The previous days fell away like a bad dream. I'd do whatever Earthmaker wanted of me, as long as I didn't have to be alone.

"So, tell me how you came to find me," I said, limp with relief.

"Did you look for long?"

"Anish and I went to the sea cave two days ago. We saw the grave. We felt the ashes, still warm from your fire. We called your name. Only ravens answered. We slept there, waiting. The boy dreamed. An otter showed him a pond in a forest. The next night we slept near the woods, not far from the path. The boy awoke and saw a white line of smoke above the trees. He followed it. That's how he found you. Then he ran back for me."

I looked at the young man. He was sprawled on the ground by the giant, Andor, his hand resting on the neck of one of their animals. I wouldn't call him Strawhead anymore. I'd call him by his real name. Anish. He smiled at me. I tried to smile back.

Ephus had learned more about the Arn the past month. While the women served us roasted rabbit, he told me about our hosts. Andor was father to Anish, it seemed. Andor's woman and baby girl had died four winters back. He was like a father for the group, as well. He had no woman and wanted little but to carve his stones and gaze at the horizon. Vor and Sambir were his brothers, a wild pair who snarled like hyenas and smelled no better. I watched them sharpen their spears while Ephus talked. They'd jab each other playfully until one got angry and pulled back to slug the other. Then Andor would shut them up with a quiet glare.

There were only two Old Ones left, the other two having left their bodies last winter. Osh and Ora, they were called. Toothless and bent, they were the parents of the three large men. I stared at Ora in amazement when Ephus told me she was their mother. She'd brought forth these monster sons? Though taller than the People, she was but a child compared to Andor. Yet the two younger men cringed when she lifted an eyebrow. Vor brought her a piece of honeycomb after she served the meat. Osh was a quiet, blue-eyed man. His knotted hands folded in his lap, he seemed to listen to some story within himself.

The Arn had one other hunter, Salo, a lean man who never looked me in the eye. His female they called Lohja. A bold woman with ample breasts, Lohja was the mother of two young children. Salo eyed the two younger men uneasily and stayed close to Lohja all through the afternoon.

"Andor seeks two women for his rough brothers," Ephus confided.

I nodded. "I'm sure that's quite a task."

Ephus snorted and stood, done with talking. It was a little before dusk. The other men picked up their spears, Anish with them. The wolf creatures leaped about and began to yap, cowering only at Andor's command. One of them was bulging with young. Anish tied her to a bush by the hut. Dogs, Ephus called them.

"Where are you going?" I asked.

"To the river. To await the grazers."

"I'm going with you!" I jumped to my feet.

Ephus shook his head. "Stay. The women are curious about you."

I dropped back to the ground. He was right about that, I thought. Lohja and Ora had been glancing my way all afternoon. With the men gone, they felt free to stare openly. I grew restless under their gaze and crept over to the mother dog, who lay panting in the shade of the lodge. Her yellow eyes were cautious, but less prying. I scratched behind her ears and smoothed her hair, once again surprised at the warmth of the creature's fur. She sighed and stretched.

From time to time, I took my eyes off the dog and looked around the camp. Roots simmered in a cooking pouch, their unfamiliar smell pungent but not unpleasant. Dried tubers with braided stems hung from the side of the dwelling. The old man slept in the sun. From the hut came the voices of children playing. Ora and Lohja tended the fire, glancing at me from time to time and muttering to each other. So, here we were, the women of the camp. A thought as annoying as a fly buzzed past. What if Ora wanted me for one of her two wild sons, men more like hyenas than humans. Better to run back to the woods. The next time the old woman stared at me, I stared back. She would see I was not one to be pushed. Her grandson, though, seemed very fine.

It was twilight when the men returned. The two hyena brothers carried an elk between them, while the other four hunters strode behind. I joined the two women to take a look at the animal.

"Ah," said Ora, looking at me and pointing to the animal, "*elhaz, elhaz.*"

Anish was at the end of the line. I caught his eye and smiled as he passed. "Good *elhaz*," I said. He smiled back.

Sowilo

AND SO I CAME TO STAY WITH MY NEW PEOPLE. Everyone slept together in the hut, just as I'd figured. They could cook inside when it rained, but since it was summer that fire was rarely lit. The floor was dug down about a hand's length underground to keep out the wind. I'm sure it was comfortable in the winter. But the summer nights were too warm. And we rarely had a breeze, since Ora wanted the door flaps shut against bugs and predators. That entire summer had been unusually hot. Maybe the hut was cooler in normal years. Our beds were comfortable, though.

Ora and Lohja had spread grass over the earthen floor. Each night I squeezed in between Lohja's children, yellow-haired creatures with skin as brown as berries. They were both younger than Fire and reminded me of home. Even the dogs joined us, dropping down just inside the doorway. They'd pant softly and whimper at strange sounds. I liked having them there.

The countryside was like the inside of a shell, smooth on the bottom with gently sloping sides. Several small lakes dotted the bowl of

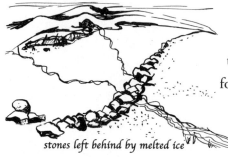

stones left behind by melted ice

the valley. Two long stone walls curved along the ground to the south of us, so perfectly formed that they seemed the work of giants. I asked Ephus about them. He said the stones had been carried there by ice and left behind at the melting. Perhaps.

Other boulders were strewn about the land as well. Great stones with blunted edges and smooth faces, some as large as the hut. Ice did that too, Ephus said, moved those rocks from their homes and dumped them there. For all I knew, he was making that up. However the boulders came to be, I was glad they were there, standing like friendly grandfathers all around the valley.

My first few days with the Arn, I walked all over that valley, exploring the rock walls, letting myself sink into a new place. I moved easily through the open land, the wind in my hair, the sight of the lodge never far away. I was happy to be moving. There were things to be said to Ephus that I wasn't yet ready to say. I felt his eyes on me each time I got up to leave, but he said nothing. Finally, on the third day, he asked about Tenja. I was ready to talk.

I'd tried to forget those last days with Tenja. For Ephus' sake, I now tried to remember. I recounted as much as I could about the star journey, about the giant wave and the shattered tree.

Then I told him about her last days. "Ziva told us there is a torch in our minds," I explained. "The Mother lights it when it's time to return." Ephus sat silently, his forehead furrowed. "Tenja saw that light," I continued. "She saw that light just before she left me. Her face glowed."

Ephus nodded. The lines on his forehead deepened. "Was there anything else?" he asked.

This was the part that was hardest to put together. I spoke haltingly. "She saw it, you know. Chaos. Tenja saw Chaos. Saw it race like a horse, wild and gleaming, across the sky."

Ephus frowned. "What do you see, Thistle?"

His question surprised me. No one had ever asked what I thought about anything. I'd never even asked myself. "You mean me? What I think?"

"Yes, yes."

I hesitated. I had noticed a few things, though I'd never tried to line them up before. "Ah, some clues, maybe a pattern. Warm days, new lakes, high beaches, the stones' remembrance of ice. I see Change. I'm sure of that. But the People have always known Change. Tenja spoke of Chaos. I know nothing of that. Just what she said. If Chaos comes, it will come from the sky. Of that she was sure."

Ephus looked away.

"Can I go now?" I ran back to the rock wall and walked along it, running my hand over the smooth stones. They felt hot in the sun. Despite what Ephus said, I liked to think that giants left them there.

I'd begun helping the women with their work in the morning. Before too long my life blended into the world of the Arn. Their days began like ours. Hang the sleeping robes in the sun. Plump up the grass bedding. Feed the children, a task I enjoyed. Their blue eyes followed me fondly. Feed the men. Their eyes followed me as well, but not so pleasantly. Tend the fire. Get the water. Not so different from us. Lohja and Ora spent their afternoons gathering plants and resting. The men usually left before sunset to hunt, though sometimes they'd depart in the morning. When they weren't away or resting, the men worked on their tools and made things, belts and pouches and shoes.

Ora made things too. Lohja's time seemed taken with the children. Ora was friendlier when her hands were busy. I watched her some afternoons. She was working on a hand drum made of hide stretched over an oval frame. Braided leather thongs hung from the sides. When the drum was finished, she drew a picture of their mother animal on the face, dipping a stick into a blue liquid made from berries. Around the edges she added waving lines and little moons. Though the Arn were skilled craftspeople, only Ora and Andor seemed to find much joy in their creations. Except for the two of them, the Arn were poor in memories. Perhaps they'd had a star watcher at one time, but I could see no signs of a calendar now.

I liked Anish. He was more like his father than his uncles, quiet but alert, with a ready smile. He seemed eager for a companion and began coming with me on my explorations. We'd hunt for eggs and tubers near the ponds. Then we'd stop to rest at the large boulders, finding hand-holds in the stones and climbing to the top. Anish usually got there first since his legs were longer. He'd reach out a hand and pull me up, though I could have made it easily enough. And there we'd sit, with the breeze in our faces. I liked to watch him on top of those rocks, the sunlight framing his yellow hair.

Most days he taught me his words; *sowilo* for sun, *ehwaz* for horse, *dagaz* for day. I'd watch his mouth move as he made each one, enjoying his generous smile when I pronounced them. My new friend was a gentle person, beloved by Lohja's children and the dogs. He was a good one for adventures too. Like me, only kinder. Since he didn't understand my words, I could rarely tell him what to do. But we took turns following each other.

He took me north to the river one bright day, a wide, slow river at the bottom of the ridge behind the camp. I'd never gone there before, since I always kept the hut in sight when I was alone. I didn't mind leaving the camp behind when I was with another person. It was near this river that the men came to hunt. Like a bowl too full, water spilled from the channel and sloshed onto the land. Autumn was near. I could feel a new hint of coolness in the air. The grass along the river was green, though the prairie beyond it was browning. Long-legged storks rose and fled in a rush of grey wings when we walked near. I knew those birds. They rested every year near the cave on the sea. This was not their home, just a temporary shelter.

I was seeking more than a view of the river that day. Ephus had shown me how to carve a harpoon point from bone. It was like the points the People made, except that this one had three notches. Anish carried a wooden fish lance, his prized tool, the same kind used by the rest of the Arn. I was pretty sure whose harpoon was better. My anticipation grew as we neared the water.

The ground was becoming soft and spongy. A snow goose called. Fat carp lazed in the marsh grass along the shore. When we finally reached the bank, Anish gestured toward the water and smiled, offering me the first try.

"Fish," he said, "fish." That was one of the words Ephus taught him.

It would do no good for me to go first, winning with my harpoon just because I'd had a head start. We had to throw our spears at the same time. How would I explain that?

"No, together, together," I said, gesturing back and forth between us.

He shrugged and yanked at his hair, as he did when my words weren't clear. I gestured again. He picked up his spear and got ready to throw. Finally. It seemed he understood. I reached for my harpoon. But before I could aim, he leaned over and dropped his spear on the ground. Now what? I looked at him, puzzled. The afternoon was golden warm, without a breeze. A line of sweat was trickling down his face. Anish stood and pulled off his heavy tunic, tugging it over his damp chest. That was it. He was too warm. He tossed the shirt aside and again picked up his spear. I aimed, ready to throw when he did.

The first catch should have been mine. But in that moment my gaze shifted from the languid brown-green water to his golden back. It was as smooth and muscled as the flank of an elk. Forgetting about the river, I stared at his flesh. Anish plunged his spear into the water and pulled out a huge turbot. He tossed it behind him. The flopping creature woke me from my reverie. I grabbed my harpoon and got the next two, another turbot and a carp. Stupid to let him win like that. I shook my head.

"You cheat," I said.

Anish looked at me, eager to please. He gestured to the river. "Fish?" he asked again.

"Never mind."

Who cared which harpoon was better. I went back to jabbing the fish spear at the dark water, watching Anish's rippling back between throws. His hair bobbed up and down with each thrust of the spear. An idea came to me.

"Anish," I said, stepping into a shallow inlet and motioning him toward me, "come here."

"Not fish?" he asked.

"No fish. Later." Gesturing and pulling, I nudged Anish deeper to the water. "Like this." I dunked my head, soaking my hair and combing it smooth with my fingers. He came closer, bending his knees until the river lapped at his shoulders. He went under and jumped back up, shaking droplets of water from his head. "Come on, you can get out now," I said, leading him to shore. He sat on the grass patiently, trusting me.

My plan would take a little while. I lined up our catch on the fish spear, stood it in shallow water, and looked around. Too bad my shell combs weren't with me. I'd left them at the cave. I'd have to use a stick instead. "Wait," I said, placing my hands on his shoulders. There was no wood here, so I ran back to a little thicket we'd passed. I found the stick I wanted and returned.

"Comb," I explained, making little notches in the wood. He nodded politely. I pulled it through my hair a few times. Not too bad. "Now you."

I began smoothing his wild mane, tugging gently to get rid of the snarls. He closed his eyes, grimacing when I pulled too hard. Sometimes the knots were too tight and I had to cut off a few clumps. My arms ached when I was done. The little stick was broken in several places. But at last his golden hair lay smoothly on his back. "There," I said, sweeping my hand from his face toward the sky, "you are as beautiful as the sun."

"*Sowilo?*" he asked.

"Yes, *sowilo*, the sun." He ran a long brown hand over his head and down one shoulder, smiling. But I wasn't quite done. Pulling the hair back from his golden face, I braided it into a long, yellow plait, cutting a strip from my tunic to tie the ends. As beautiful as the sun. That he was. "Braid," I said, patting his head. "Come on, let's go show the others." I picked up our fish, eager to show off Anish's transformation.

"Fish now," he said. This time it wasn't a question.

"All right. Fish." I put the spear back in the water and sat down to wait. It was mid-afternoon when he was ready to go. I ran on ahead, then circled back for him. What would the others say, I wondered, when they saw the new Anish. He just plodded along, content with the day as it was.

Vor and Sambir, the hyena brothers, were the first people we encountered when we returned. They sat near the hut, their tunics stained with sweat, snarling over a game they played with pegs and stones. I avoided them whenever I could, since they usually stared at me like hungry wolverines. This time there was no escape. They looked up from their game when they heard us coming. I glared back at them.

But that day they had no time for me. Their gaze shifted to Anish, who was walking just behind. Their jaws dropped. Then the two of them burst into laughter. I watched in confusion as they leaped to their feet, slapped their legs, and pointed. "What's wrong with you idiots?" I yelled.

But they were mindless of my presence, focused only on Anish. They howled and pranced, cupping hands over their breasts as they called out an Arn word I took to mean "woman." Anish, his face bright red, strode past them and into the hut.

What had I done? I hurried across the camp and sat next to Ephus, angry at myself for my stupid idea and at the two louts still laughing nearby. Ephus just shook his head and sighed. All that night I waited for Anish to leave the hut. Andor glanced in that direction a few times, but said nothing.

It wasn't until the next morning that I saw Anish again. I'd been awake since dawn with the others. We'd eaten and the men were lounging around the camp, in no hurry to start the day. All except for Andor. He'd left long ago, heading north toward the river. I sat next to Ephus with Tenja's moon calendar on my lap, not really working on it, but needing something to do with my eyes. I heard the silence when the tent flaps opened. I glanced up. Anish emerged, still wearing his braid.

Looking straight ahead, he crossed the dusty fire circle in two long strides and dropped down next to Ephus. Lohja brought him a breakfast of berries and fish, keeping her eyes down. No one spoke, though Ora glared at her smirking sons. Tension settled over us like smoke. My face grew warm and I glanced sideways at Anish to see if he was angry. But he was as calm and quiet as usual. I looked back at the calendar and notched a tiny moon with a piece of flint. I sensed Anish and Ephus watching me work.

"Tell Anish I'm sorry about the laughter," I whispered. "Tell him he looks very handsome."

Ephus and Anish exchanged a few words. Then Ephus grumbled, "Ah, those two. Don't mind them. They're fools. They've seen little of other humans and can boast of nothing but their ignorance. Andor says we'll meet up with more of the Arn on the eastern route. He hopes the two men will learn from them."

I glanced at the two sullen brothers. "I doubt that."

Andor sauntered into camp just before midday, his long arms swinging at his sides. Everyone looked up. Though no questions had been asked, I'd sensed their curiosity about his absence. My mouth fell open when I saw his chiseled face. Andor's yellow hair fell in a rough braid down his back. He nodded to the group. Then he picked up the rock he'd been carving, leaned against a log, and resumed his work. This time no one laughed.

The women got up to cook and the children tossed sticks to the dogs, while the men pretended to sharpen their tools. The camp was strangely quiet the rest of the day.

The next morning I stood with Ephus outside the hut, listening while he talked of something, probably fish. He'd been curious about my luck with the three-pronged harpoon. I'd told him little about my day with Anish, just that the new fish spear worked well enough. I smelled them before I heard them, Sambir and Vor, standing a short distance away, shuffling from side to side as though the ground was too warm for their feet. Sambir made a growling sound and jerked his head at Ephus, his way of saying "come here." While it was hard for me to tell the brothers apart, I knew Sambir was the one with no front teeth.

Ephus sighed and walked toward him. I heard Sambir mutter a few words and strained for Ephus's reply. I couldn't make out what he was saying. His beard moved up and down quickly as he spoke, all the while jabbing a finger at the big Arn's chest. Sambir shrugged and looked at his feet, having nothing else to say. Ephus came back, the brothers plodding after him.

"What? What is it?" I asked.

Ephus's eyes twinkled when he spoke. "They want braids."

Braids. I looked at their thatched heads, dark with dust and sweat, more like underbrush than hair. It wouldn't be easy.

"Tell them to go to the river. They should wash their heads. Then they can come back here and wait until I'm ready."

A few words from Ephus and the pair trudged off in the direction of the river.

I notched more sticks, slapped some deer fat on a stone, and waited. When the two returned, their hair was the same color as the other Arn. I went to work on the two of them, breaking four sticks before I was done, perhaps going a little roughly. Both men sat still, grimacing, but saying nothing. By suppertime they had their braids.

All of the camp lined up to see. Vor and Sambir stood grinning and nodding, admiring themselves in each other's eyes. Then Sambir edged up to me, hunching up his shoulders as he patted the back of his head. "Thank, thank," he said.

"You're welcome." And it was an improvement. "But tell them," I whispered to Ephus, "tell them, if they want to find a woman, they'll have to wash the rest of their bodies as well."

He looked at me out of the corners of his eyes. "I'll tell Andor," he said. "He can tell them himself."

Thurisaz

I CONTINUED TO TEND THE CALENDAR. Some nights, I sat outside with Ephus after the others had gone to sleep. Ephus didn't mind being in the hut, not like he did the cave. But he still preferred sleeping outside. He'd tell me about other places, some he'd seen, some he'd dreamed. I'd listen happily and watch the night sky, wondering at each perfectly blazing star. Some nights a spark would shoot across the blackness and fall like a swallow weary from flight. That was the best part.

Some nights Anish joined us. He was curious about the world and must have sensed that Ephus was a good teacher. And Ephus was always glad for a chance to retell his stories. The Traveler explained other things as well, the kinds of things Tenja had once taught me. Anish learned quickly, even though Ephus didn't have words for everything. As much as I loved the older man's tales, I enjoyed them even more when Anish was with us. His presence also gave me a chance to discover more about the Arn and learn some of their words. It seemed that Anish knew only the kinds of things a person learns in one lifetime. His people had no stories from the past. They did have names for the star groups, different names than we had, and not as many. Just as I'd thought, the Arn had no calendar. When they lost their homes, Ephus told me, they lost the order in their lives. That was why their hearts were so hungry.

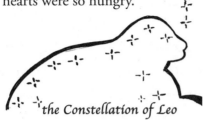

the Constellation of Leo

It was early Fall, in The Time of the Lion, when the constellation of the Great Cat ruled the sky. That was the star group that rose in the eastern sky each spring, in the exact place the sun came up. Ephus had tried to explain that to Anish, with little success. It was too bad we wouldn't be together half a year from now, so I could show him exactly when that happened. But I was trying to find other ways to teach him. I'd drawn the twelve stars of the constellation on a rock like Tenja had done for me and had him do the same. Sometimes, on clear nights, I'd wake him up and point the star group out to him. Eventually, he'd see exactly what we meant.

The Great Cat rose just before dawn. I had to do the same, if I were to find the best time to show the constellation to Anish. So, for several nights, I roused myself early, crawling out of the hut and into a dew-black world to sit and watch the sky. Then, if the night was clear and all twelve stars were visible, I'd awaken Ephus and Anish.

Anish came willingly. All I had to do was crawl back and shake his arm. Waking Ephus was a different matter. I went to get him one perfect fall night, our third viewing of the Great Cat. As usual, he was outside the hut, rolled tightly in his sleeping robe. Even his head was covered.

I crouched next to him and put a hand on his shoulder. "Ephus," I whispered, "it's time."

"Time for what?" he growled.

"The Great Cat."

"Go away. I've seen it before. Let me sleep."

"No, you can't. You have to explain it to Anish."

He muttered something under his breath and threw the robe aside.

I motioned to Anish. We went a little way from camp, like we always did, so that we didn't bother the others. I'd never leave the hut alone at night and sit without a fire, but there were three of us, and Ephus always took his spear. It was a cloudless night. The moon was a tiny crescent, the air just cool enough to keep us awake. Ephus stretched his arms over his head and yawned. Anish was wide-eyed and quiet. I sat silently for a moment, thinking of what I wanted to say. Then I pointed to the horizon.

"Look," I said to Anish, "the Lion. Keeper of our Age."

There it was, The Great Cat, composed of twelve bright stars hovering above the horizon, each star a point on the creature's body. Join them and you had the outline of a lion, the mighty paws, the reclining belly, the mane. I looked at Anish. The moonlight was reflected in his eyes.

By now he knew these stars well, but he was listening. I continued.

"The Great Cat watches over us for a very long time, the length of one hundred generations. Then the constellation moves on and another takes its place, again watching over us for another one hundred generations. This is what the People know." I turned to Ephus. "Now you tell him."

The two of them talked for a while. Then Ephus spoke to me. "He wants to know why the Great Cat is the keeper of this age. Why not something else?"

"Tell him the keeper of the age is the constellation that rises in the east every fall, in the same place the sun appears. Tell him to watch. In a little while, the sun will come up just under the Lion's belly. That's how we know."

Anish's eyes were intense but puzzled. Once the light began to tinge the horizon, I could see his doubtful look. He kept staring at the constellation as it slowly faded in dawn's orange glow.

"Tell him not to take his eyes off the Great Cat," I said to Ephus.

I held my breath, watching. Then, in the bright hush of dawn, the curve of the sun burst forth exactly where the Lion had been. The stars disappeared.

Anish whispered, "*Sowilo.*" Joy, like the sunrise, spread across his face.

"Yes," I answered, "*Sowilo*, the sun."

All through that sleepy day, I smiled when I thought of Anish, remembering the wonder on his face. I'd begun noticing other things about Anish as well. Going with him to the river for water, I forgot the countryside and saw only his hands, the blood pulsing through the raised veins, the callused palm reaching for the bladder bag. Walking back, I saw how he strode through the brown grass, as smooth and sinewy as a cat himself.

And then one day a sickness came upon me. We'd gone to the river as we often did, to search the tall grass for crane eggs. I'd seen a nest and rushed to it, bending to pick up a large egg. Anish must have seen the same one. I didn't know he was beside me and, when I stood, my shoulder brushed against his leg. At that very moment, a fever flashed through my body. I dropped back. I felt dizzy and embarrassed, as if I suddenly stood naked before him in the meadow. And then I heard a pounding sound, like running hooves, except the sound came from me. I needed to rest. It could be I was dying.

I motioned for Anish to go on. He stood for a moment, then shrugged and left. I sat with my head in my hands, watching his receding back. In a little while, he turned, smiling and beckoning me to follow. I waved him on, looking down, afraid to meet his eyes. But before too long, I got up again. I didn't want to be left alone in the valley, whether I was dying or not. I followed him from a distance, listening to the pounding in my chest.

When we reached the camp, I slipped past Ephus. He looked up in surprise, but I kept going, avoiding his eyes, rushing to the hut. I tore the flaps open and ducked inside, dropping down into the shadows. My shoulders were shaking. What if I died here, far away from the People? Would the Arn know to bury me under rocks? Or would they leave my body for the wolves? I pulled a sleeping robe over my head and waited in the darkness for the pounding in my chest to stop. After a while I heard the sound of someone lifting the tent flap. I lowered the sleeping robe just far enough to see Ephus's burly shape outlined in a shaft of light.

"Go away," I said. "I'm sick." He left.

I heard the sounds of cooking coming from the camp, logs thrown on the fire, women talking.

The thought of food made me sick. Evening was coming. Maybe I was a little better. The pounding wasn't so loud. If I stayed in there too long, there would be questions. I decided to go outside. Maybe it was dark by now. I crawled out, keeping my head down.

Ora was chopping turnips. She raised her head, her eyes lit by the fire's orange glow. She looked at me strangely. I glanced away. Anish was sitting between his father and Ephus. He looked up and smiled the same way he always did. Ephus patted the ground beside him. I dropped down next to him. They'd already eaten. Empty clam shells lay on the ground. Maybe I should clear them. I moved to stand up. Ephus reached out an arm and pushed me back down.

"Sit," he said. He picked up a shell, walked over to the fire and ladled out a grey mound of stew. Then he returned and handed it to me. "Eat."

The men were talking of hooks and fish. I pretended to listen, all the while moving the food around with my finger. When no one was looking, I set the shell down behind me. I soon heard the slurp of a licking dog.

My sickness continued all night. I lay awake, tired but restless, listening to the soft snores around me. Lohja's boy sucked his thumb and curled closed to me, clucking like a steppe hen. I heard the sounds of night, naming each one. Andor and Ephus snorting from time to time. Lohja's sigh and the thumping of the dogs as they scratched. Frogs from the ponds. The tap of field mice. What could be wrong? Was I sick from my bleeding? It had never caused more than a twinge of pain. Rotten meat? Mushrooms? My thoughts circled like vultures but they always returrned, lighting on a long, sleeping body, sprawled at the back of the lodge. Had Anish made me ill?

Ephus was awake when I went out the next morning, sitting on the worn ground with Andor, drawing lines in the dust. "So," he said, as I passed him, "the dogs like turnip stew."

I walked to the fire and fixed myself some tea. Ephus turned his back and continued talking with Andor, studying the lines he'd drawn. When Ephus wasn't traveling, he liked making routes to places he wanted to see. I sat close by and sipped my tea. This could go on all morning. I had to speak with him.

"Ephus, uh, can I talk to you?" I asked.

"What?"

"Not here." I looked around. I was glad Anish was gone.

"Get us some tea."

I brought them both a horn full of tea, cleared up the eating shells from breakfast, then went to help Lohja drag out the bedding. From time to time, I glanced at Ephus. He was still making lines with his stick, smoothing them out again with his foot. I stepped closer.

"Four days east should be enough," he was saying. "Then we turn south. East of here is an ocean of grass." He marked the place with his stick. "Could take longer if the grass is high."

Andor nodded. Both men stared at the lines, their thoughts having taken flight. I couldn't wait any longer. I walked over to him and stood on top of the imaginary ocean of grass.

"I need to talk to you before you leave for this trip."

Ephus threw the stick aside and stood. "What?" he asked.

"Away from here."

He nodded to Andor, shook his head, and followed me. I took him a little way from camp and sat on the ground, motioning him to join me.

He dropped down, rubbing the back of his hand over his mouth. "I know nothing about sickness or women's things," he said.

I stared at his lined face. "Ephus, you're the only one I have."

He pulled back as if he'd swallowed an insect.

I continued. "New thoughts have come to me. Strange things."

"Are you leaving?" he asked, his voice rising. That was something he could understand.

"No, I'm not leaving." I shook my head. Was that his answer to everything?

"Well, then, what thoughts?"

"Thoughts about Anish."

"Huh. Anish. Well, what thoughts are those?" He raised his chin and narrowed his eyes.

"I look at his body in a new way."

"A new way?" he said. Color crept up his face.

"How Tenja looked at you."

"Huh. How Tenja looked at me? Well, how was that?"

"Ephus, you know. Stop it. You know what I mean. What should I do?"

"Tenja looked at me a long time before she did anything."

"And you, what did you do?"

"Well, I waited for her."

"Ephus," I cried, "I can find out more talking to a goat!"

I jumped up and left him there, heading toward the giant rocks. If only Tenja were here. She'd know what to say. I covered the open ground quickly and stopped at the first boulder. How could I go back and face Anish and the others, feeling like I did? Ora would look at me. Ephus would be thinking about what I'd told him. Sambir and Vor, would they know? Would they laugh at me? And what about Anish? He'd think I was strange. I'd have to figure this out for myself.

I climbed up the face of the rock. A chunk of stone was missing on one side, leaving a notch in the surface, like a resting place for giants. That was where I stopped. I decided to wait there, hidden in the rock, until my thoughts calmed themselves. Maybe I'd be there a long time. I was in no hurry to go back. The Arn camp wasn't my real home, anyway.

The day was windy but the rock kept me from the breeze. I leaned back into the curve of the stone, resting in its hot hardness, studying the land before me. In the distance, a small band of reindeer picked their way over the northern ridge, early travelers to their winter home. I watched as they came toward me. They were so calm, knowing without thinking. The warm stone eased my mind. After a while I dozed.

Held by the stone, washed by the sun, I rested, dropping into the land of dreaming. Humans. I didn't understand them. But dreams I knew. Before me a dream field unfolded, stretching golden at my feet. I sighed. Seven bronze elk grazed in a meadow, nibbling placidly, their muscled flanks burnished by the sun. A dream sky blazed above the creatures, bathing the land in sunset orange.

I slept. One of the creatures, a radiant animal, slowly turned his head. His liquid eyes and gentle muzzle were melting, becoming a familiar face, becoming the face of Anish, gleaming like the sun.

A warm pleasure surged through my belly. I awoke as the last band of yellow faded from the sky.

I sat up, jolted by a new understanding. What if this was the way Earthmaker called us, lighting the body from within, tingling the skin with a strange heat? Did Anish feel it too? Did everyone? Could my sickness be Earthmaker calling? A dark mantle of blue had wrapped itself around the horizon. I could no longer see the lodge, only the faint glow where the fire burned.

Climbing down the rock, I made my way home in the darkness, warmed by the light of this new knowledge. Perhaps I had nothing to fear. Perhaps some good would come of it.

THE LIFE HAD GONE OUT OF THE SUMMER GRASS. It was hard and brown. I sat at the edge of the camp late one afternoon, studying Tenja's calendar. Everyone was there, the men staring at Lohja as if that would hurry their supper. I kept my eyes on the calendar. When was it the first frost came and the herds began to move? I counted twenty days until Return to the Sea. The Arn would probably leave sometime that month. The People would return. My brother would be almost six.

Silka would have her baby. "Come with us to the south," Ephus urged each night by the fire. But he knew I'd return to the winter cave. I had to go back. I had to tell the People about Tenja and continue her work. Life would be different without Ephus. I glanced at him across the circle.

He was already restless to be on the move, full of stories about the places he'd seen or wished to see. I'd miss him. And Anish. I tried not to think about Anish's leaving. Seven days had passed since my dream of the elk. My skin still grew hot whenever he was near, but at least I knew I wasn't ill. Perhaps with time the heat would go away. Or at least the Arn would.

After we had eaten, Ephus began a familiar tale, describing for the Arn the land they'd cover when they left their lodge. First he told it in Arn words, then he told it in mine. Anish and his father knew a few of our words, but none of the others did. Still, everyone listened to both stories, understanding some things just from the sound of his voice and the movements of his hands. "Beyond here, to the east," he explained, "is a broad treeless plain, an ocean of grass, surrounded by hills as smooth as the bodies of women." When he finished the tale in my words, he stared at the horizon. "I followed those paths when I was no more than a boy," he said.

"How far is it to this sea of grass?" I asked.

"Oh, a morning away," he answered, shrugging. "Just over that rim." He pointed southeast.

"I'd like to see that," I said.

"Come with us."

"No, I just want to see where you're heading." Maybe I wouldn't feel so lonely if I saw their route. Maybe I just wanted to see an ocean of grass. Have my own adventure. "Ask Anish if he'll go there with me."

He motioned for Anish to come over and they exchanged a few

words. Anish nodded.

"He says he'll go tomorrow," Ephus said.

There. I wouldn't really be left behind if I saw the road first.

I awoke at dawn and crawled over to Anish, shaking his arm until he opened his eyes. Then, moving between sleeping bodies and angry grunts and sighs, we made our way outside. I'd packed some dried turnips and a few deer ribs, as well as two bladder bags of water. That would be enough.

We walked fast. By midmorning we were halfway up the eastern slope. Anish's long legs took him easily up the hill, but I was out of breath. I was thirsty, too. One water bag was already empty. "I have to stop for a while," I said, panting. I sat down, put my elbows on my knees, and looked back at the ground we'd covered. Below us was the shallow valley that I'd called home for a little while, the lodge just a speck in the distance. Above us was an immense and cloudless sky. Anish dropped down next to me. I held up the empty bladder bag. "You'll need to carry plenty of water," I said, "when your people come this way." He smiled and nodded. I never knew if he understood me, since he smiled at everything I said.

Anish could surely figure out for himself that they needed water. But I was worried about them just the same. Ephus knew nothing about caring for people. Ora was old. Lohja was overworked already. It would all fall to Andor, who was something of a dreamer. These people needed a strong woman. Maybe they'd come upon more Arn when they reached the great grass ocean.

After a short rest, I was ready to go. We started the last leg of the journey, heading for the stone-capped ridge. It felt good to walk beside Anish, with the day and the world before us. We might not know each other's words, but he was the best friend I'd had since Reen. My eyes stung for a moment. I glanced up at Anish. It would soon be time to say goodbye. At least I was able to be with him now without wanting to run, as long as I didn't get too close.

A high spine of white rock jutted from the top of the slope, all that kept us from the valley on the other side. Anish cleared the stones easily. It took me a little longer. "Wait!" I yelled, the sweat dripping from my face. "Don't get there before me!" He made it to the top of the stone, then turned around, lay on his belly, and reached down to me. I grabbed his hand, happy for the help, feeling a familiar spark leap through my body. He pulled me up and over the edge.

A few more steps and we were ready to see it, Ephus's sea of grass. We hurried across the narrow plateau and looked down. There was no ocean of grass! Instead, a vast forest of saplings stretched below us, thousands of them, tiny birch trees heading north like an endless, wooden herd. I looked from the valley to Anish's surprised face and back to the valley again. Where was the waving grass? In a slow, awkward cadence, I heard Anish say, "Ocean of trees." I looked at him in surprise. He smiled, repeating the phrase. "Ocean of trees." We hurried back to tell Ephus.

At first Ephus refused to believe us. Then he grew cranky, as if he were angry that change could come to things he knew so well. But in a day or so, he was excited, eager to leave the hut and see the trees for himself. It wouldn't be long before the Arn disappeared. That was good, of course. It meant the People would soon reach the sea. I'd be happy to join them.

But as the days slipped by, I found I was thinking less about the People and more about Anish. His hands, his face, his hair. I didn't know which was worse. Anish must have sensed my tension, for some dark brooding had replaced his easy smile. Why couldn't things be simple like they'd once been, just the wind, the sky, and the walking? Well, Anish would be gone soon enough, I told myself, through the ocean of trees, south over the marshlands, away from here. I didn't want to think of that.

I was walking through the valley one day, in the lowest part, near the ponds, trying to remember my brother's face. The male dogs were with me. The female had given birth to four black pups a month ago and still spent her days at the camp. A few early geese flew overhead. Their cries were making me sad. I began looking for happier thoughts. What if the Arn headed southeast and found that the marsh wasn't frozen? They'd have to come back. Maybe they'd stay at the West Sea. Fish. Put their hut up there. People needed a home. It wasn't right, how these humans lived, letting the days slip by, just waiting to see what happened. Squirrels planned their lives better. Still, if I didn't already have a home, maybe I'd want to join them.

A large bone protruded from the grass in front of me. I bent down. A shoulder bone. A bison, most likely. Already picked clean. I held it up, turning the smooth, white form in my hand. Just like my calendar, maybe a little smaller. Earthmaker suddenly gave me a plan. I'd make a calendar for Anish! I'd notch it for him, just like mine. I could teach him a few more things before he left. He learned quickly. Then he could keep track of the days, figure out how long it would take them to return. The Arn would again have order. Well, maybe not right away, but eventually. I put the blade under my arm and ran back to camp.

The men were gone when I got there. Sometimes they hunted in the afternoon now, rousting the geese from the river grass. Ora was asleep. Lohja was sewing a small tunic, while her children played with the pups. The mother dog watched them with large eyes, her mouth drawn back at the corners. She was thin. I brought her a deer rib from the butcher site and rubbed her ears.

Next to Anish and Ephus, the mother dog was my favorite one to talk with there. I sat down by her, holding the bison bone and my flint. "Black Dog," I said, "If you came to the sea to live, I'd give you fish every day. Tell the others." I cut thirty lines on the rim of the shoulder blade. Under the first one I gouged out a circle, so Anish would know to start the counting at the full moon.

The dog watched me earnestly. It didn't take long to finish. I held the shoulder blade in front of me, proud of my work. Nothing complicated. Just a beginning calendar. But it would do. I'd give Anish a piece of flint too, so he could make sharp marks.

Andor and Ephus returned to camp, each with a goose in hand. Vor and Sambir came soon after. I could have waited for Anish. But I was eager to show him the calendar and not sure I wanted the others around when I gave it to him. I was pretty sure where I'd find him.

I headed for the boulders. The two male dogs followed me for a little while, then went chasing after something in the grass. At the largest stone, I stopped. This was the rock we usually climbed. Sometimes Anish came here alone to sleep. Maybe I'd surprise him. I held the shoulder blade under my arm and pulled myself up with one hand, crawling awkwardly up the side of the rock.

I peered over the top. There he was, stretched out in the sun, his chest bare. I nudged the shoulder blade up first, caught my breath, then swung my legs over the ledge. I laid the calendar at Anish's feet. Should I wake him? Or just leave it there and let him find it when he awoke? Maybe I'd just watch him sleep.

I crouched down beside him, watching his chest rise and fall with every breath. How peaceful he was. My eyes were drawn to the path of yellow hair that ran between his nipples and his belly and disappeared under the belt that hung around his hips. I remembered my dream of the elk. Anish's skin was that same golden color. And how Anish had come to me in my dreaming, turning, waiting, melting. Did Earthmaker move through him in dreams? My gaze moved to his sprawling legs. Then to the bulge underneath his tunic, rising and falling with a life of its own, like a sleeping pup.

The dogs' wild barking brought me back. They were on to something, probably a rabbit or some other burrower. I glanced at Anish. The sound had awakened him. I was startled by his eyes. He showed no surprise at my presence. His gaze was level and serious, his eyes as grey as a river in the rain, as urgent as thunder.

"I brought you . . . ah . . . something," I stammered.

He reached out a long, brown arm. I caught my breath. And suddenly I was with him, startled by his rough hands and the heat of his skin. He pulled me closer, crushing me with his arms. My fingers flew to his face, tracing the bones of his cheeks to the curve of his neck, following the hollows of his chest to the warm flesh of his stomach. He shuddered beneath my hand. My mouth brushed his face, tasting the saltiness of his skin. I slid my hand down his belly, my eyes frozen by his gaze, my fingers slipping under the band that encircled his hips, gliding past the bristles low on his stomach, sliding down to the moist warmth of him, soft as a ripe mushroom, my breath catching in my throat. And there we stayed, long after the dogs had wandered home and the purple twilight slipped into night.

And then we were together each day, by the river, at the rocks, in the meadow, his wildness calling, my hunger growing, until I no longer knew whose belly was lurching, whose legs were pushing, whose voice was wailing in the still, bright air. "*Thurisaz*," I called him, "thing of great strength." Each day I held him tighter, in a place beyond thought, forbidding the future.

268

But once again the geese gathered by the thousands in the marsh grass and cried farewell in a great rushing of wings. Once again Ephus paced the ground as if tethered there. And once again came the day Andor held a finger to the wind and said, "It's time."

It didn't take the Arn long to pack. Even the puppies went into a bag, which Anish hung over his shoulder. "Come with us," Ephus said one last time. And one more time I stood and watched as the Arn moved on. But this time, the one I once called Strawhead did look back. Reaching into his pack, he pulled out a squirming pup, walked toward me, and put it in my hands. He looked away quickly, but not before I saw a new wildness in his eyes. I held the squealing dog and watched as Anish joined the others. And then the rough travelers were gone, moving in a crooked line across the meadow and into my memory.

I'd sleep at the hut that night and the next day go to the sea.

The Return

MORNING WAS A LONG TIME COMING. The Arn had taken most of the lodge with them, leaving only the frame. Ephus had given me a hide, which was large enough to cover one end of the open structure. I'd hung my sleeping robe next to it and kept the fire burning all night. The dog was no help. She whimpered unless I held her. I was up at dawn, more tired than when I'd lain down. But the crisp early air awakened me, reminding me of other journeys. I kept my thoughts on the people coming toward me, not those walking away. I was anxious to leave.

Still, I'd never covered so much open space alone. I'd have to plan the trip well. It would take one day to reach the sea, maybe a little less. Of course, the days were shorter now than when I'd crossed the countryside in early summer. I scanned the tan hills to the west. The land would be dry. Grazers passed through in the autumn and spring, but never stayed. There were no rivers. But that was good. If there were no water, there'd be no grazers. And without the grazers, there'd be no cats—coyotes and hares, and not much else. I'd still need to be careful, move quickly. I'd make do with dried meat and whatever roots I found along the way. And take three water bags. That should be enough for the pup as well.

What would I do with her? No doubt she was hungry. I tried feeding her jerky which she licked eagerly. But even torn into little pieces, it was too hard for her to chew. So I chewed some for her, munching until my jaws were sore. She ate it as fast as I softened it, then looked back at me, crying for more. I had to get out of there or be in open country at dusk.

I put the dog in a bag like Anish had done and hung it around my neck. Then I loaded my pack, the calendar, the rolled-up hides, and the bladder bags. Finally, I picked up my spear. I'd keep it in my hand, since it made a good walking stick. I started out, heading west, the pup yelping all the time, telling the countryside a baby was near. What a fine gift Anish had given me! The People's babies never cried on the trail. "Hush, something will eat you!" I said, patting her hard. At last she fell asleep. This would be a difficult trip.

I walked as fast as I could, wanting to cover plenty of ground during the dog's silence. She awakened midmorning. I stopped at a stand of yellow-needled larches and set her down. Her belly almost dragged on the ground from the jerky, but still she looked at me hopefully, smelling my hands, wagging her stub of a tail. "You wait!" I said. I took a sip of water and poured some in my hand for her. After she'd had her drink, I put a hand under her belly and lifted her, studying her for the first time. Black as coal she was, with little wolverine eyes and needle-like teeth. "What will I call you?" I asked. "Perhaps I'll call you meat." She yelped again and I returned her to the bag. At least she kept my thoughts from wandering.

By midday the rolling plains had given way to gravel-covered hills.

A new thought began to nag. What if the People got to the cave before me and found the grave? They'd be confused. Magla might think it was me buried there! I had to reach the shore before them. I tried walking faster, but my feet slipped on the shale. Before too long, I came to the place where I'd found Ephus. I could see the oak forest far to the south, red now on this late autumn day. Anish's memory rose up and I wished it away. I did stop for a moment to look north, at the trail that disappeared into the jagged horizon a good day's walk from where I stood. It was a route I knew well. We took it sometimes in wet years. I squinted into the distance, hoping for some movement, a dark cluster of travelers. Nothing. What if the People were already there?

I quickened my pace but the dog bounced on my chest with every step and the load on my back lurched sideways. Hurrying did no good. Besides, I had to watch the countryside. I slowed down, reminding myself it could be days before the People came. Anyway, the path was familiar now. I'd walked this part of it several times. It was easier, too. The land had begun its downward slope, the faint trail winding between tufts of yellow grass and white sponge stone. I hoisted the pack and walked along happily, telling the dog about her new home. In the middle of the afternoon, I caught a glimpse of the sea. Before dusk, I reached the hill above our camp. I started down slowly, but was soon sliding over the loose stone, my heart pounding.

"Mother, Ochre?" I yelled, running onto the beach. "I'm here. It's Thistle. I'm back!"

Silence. The camp was deserted, the burnt timbers still laying across the mouth of the cave where I'd left them. So, I was early. I glanced around. The shadows of the rocks were lengthening. Maybe that's what gave the place such a lonely feel. I lifted the pup from her bag, happy for her soft warmth.

272

"See, dog creature," I said, holding her up to look, "this is where my people live. It's just as well they're not here yet. You're not ready to meet them."

What would Magla say about a dog? There were some who'd want to eat it.

What was that sound? A growl had come from the cave, a low, canine noise. I shoved the pup back into the bag and backed up slowly. Something was in my cave. I edged toward the hill and tied the pouch to a high branch. What creature had claimed my home? There were no gnawed bones, no squealing litter, no stench this time. If not hyenas, what? Wolves? I decided to see for myself.

The rock wall above the cave was about four man-lengths high. I climbed it quickly, grabbing at shrubs and stones to pull me up. Then I lay on my belly and looked over the ledge. Protruding stone hid the mouth of the cave, but I could make out a dark stain in the entryway. The animal was hurt. Maybe it was just one creature, come here to die. It was too early for a bear surely. I'd just have to watch the entrance. If it was a wolf pack, they'd leave at night to hunt.

I dropped back down and made camp, the rock wall behind me and the fire circle in front. No wolf would come near a fire. The pup and I went to the river to drink, then shared a small fish. She was quieter when her belly was full, so I let her eat all she wanted. Then I tied her to my pack with a short strip of hide. If there were danger, I could push the dog into the bag and pull it shut. It had been a long day. I settled in to watch the flames, the pup whimpering at my feet.

Wolves. I tried to remember what Yarrow had told me. They'd rarely kill a human unless the pack was starving or the human seemed weak. They did take children when the reindeer had few babies. But I was full-grown and game was plentiful. I had nothing to fear, as long as I didn't turn my back. Unless there was a pack.

I patted the dog from time to time. When she bit me once too often, I gave her a piece of jerky and shoved her back in the bag. The night was clear. Nothing stirred. No sound came from the cave. I wondered if the animal was already dead. But as the darkness deepened, I saw two yellow eyes, watching me from the entryway. It had to be a wolf. "The People will drive you out," I yelled. I drifted off to sleep, awakening several times. The creature never moved, as far as I could tell, never ate nor drank nor ventured out. Morning came quietly.

This was no wolf pack, but one dying animal. Its silence was making me bold. No animal that sick could be much of a threat. I picked up my stick and edged toward the cave, keeping close to the hill. Then I saw them just inside the entryway, two large paws protruding from a dark shape. The blood that had pooled around one of the legs was now dry, hard and black. Was it already dead? But then I saw the eyes, yellow eyes, too weak for fear, but still alive. I kept my stick in front of me and near the ground.

"Have you come here to die then?" I asked.

The wolf didn't move. It was full-grown, I judged, but not old, with the wide muzzle and broad forehead of a male. A jagged gash ran along one puffy foreleg. A flap of skin hung from its mouth. Its right ear was almost torn away. Perhaps it was a loner, driven out by his group. The wounds didn't look deadly but, without the pack, the animal would die of hunger and thirst. I moved the stick closer. Still no movement. I wanted to get into the cave. What should I do?

It would be easy enough to kill him here, take the pelt. Winter was coming. I needed a coat.

I'd have to drag the body to the sea before I skinned it, to keep down the smell of blood. Or I could just let him die here. That wouldn't take long. And I'd still have my coat.

"It's no good to be alone, eh? No good to live alone. No good to die alone."

The wolf's eyes shifted, meeting mine. There was some life left in him. If he ate and drank, he might even mend himself and slink away. A strange plan was forming in my mind. Magla would think it was the stupidest thing I'd ever done. That was the only good part about being alone. No one else knew your stupidest actions.

"All right then. I'll feed you. But you must leave before the People come," I said. "I'm getting this place ready for them." He'd have to be gone by then. Magla would have him killed and skinned before I could argue.

Keeping my body near the wall and my stick in front of me, I slipped to the back of the cave, grabbed a bag of dried apples, and picked up a large shell. The wolf never moved, didn't even turn his head when I set the shell in the entryway. I stopped at the tree to check on the pup, then picked up the bladder bags and hurried to the river. I returned quickly, filled the shell with water, and pushed it toward the wolf with my stick. "Here. Drink."His mouth curled back, but the wolf took nothing. I moved the shell closer, but the creature didn't move.

"I want you out of here," I said. "Don't make me kill you."

This time I dripped a little water onto his jowls. He licked at it, wincing when he moved his mouth.

"Were you left behind or did you go first?" I asked.

Wolves were like us, happier in groups. He was a fine, strong animal, with a healthy pelt.

Maybe he would survive. Even if he did become vicious, it would still be days before he was strong enough to turn on me. I'd know before that happened. Just to be sure, I dragged a few more logs into the cave and stacked them at an angle across the entrance. The wood separated me from the wolf, but allowed us both to get out. I'd light a fire behind him if he growled at me or refused to leave. And, I thought, adding to the reasons his survival was a good idea, no other animal would enter the cave with a large wolf lying across the entrance. He was a guard, of sorts. No harm could come from this.

I brought my pack into the cave and reclaimed my home, at least the back of it. The pup yelped and jumped at the wolf, so I tied her to one of Tenja's grave stones. I'd keep her leashed when I was in the cave, I decided, and take her with me otherwise. Then I sat in the dark with my stick on my knees, waiting for the wolf to leave or die. It was odd, being there with those four-legged creatures, my own kind far away. It was odd, but better than being alone. Maybe Magla would understand that.

The cave was too quiet. I was beginning to feel sad when Earthmaker whispered a plan. I decided to go fishing. That way, when the People arrived, they'd have fresh food. I'd have to listen carefully for them, since I couldn't see the path from the river. When I heard them, I'd run back and explain about the wolf. Holding the pup in my arms, I slipped out past the injured creature and headed for the river, happy there was work to do. I returned late in the afternoon with an eel, two turbot, and a salmon. I tied the pup in the back again, letting her strain at her leash and yap while I chopped the eel for her and the wolf. The salmon I cooked for myself. Earthmaker had given me a good day.

The wolf ate nothing that night, but by morning the meat was gone. He'd taken some of the water, as well, and had started licking his wound. That was a good sign.

For three more days I followed that pattern, bringing in fish, listening for the travelers, feeding the two creatures, and waiting. I'd set up two of Magla's drying racks, filling them with salmon so none of my catch would be wasted. The animals were doing well. The dog I called Thur, for the time she'd become strong, and for the memory of the one who'd given her to me. She'd sniff the ground and pull toward the wolf whenever she was near him. The larger creature sometimes showed his teeth. Otherwise, he had no interest in her. On the fourth day, he moved for the first time, limping out to pee and dragging himself back in.

A story was forming in my mind, a story about how I might save him. But I'd have to be at the cave when the People arrived. "This wolf is a guard wolf," I'd say. "He's saved me from things."

Badgers, lynx, bears? I'd think of something. "He got hurt, saving me from a . . . badger." It was as good as one of Ephus's stories, though I needed more practice. I began telling the tale to Thur at night, adding details. Someone might doubt my story, but its telling would give the wolf more time.

And so we settled into our days. Wolf's leg was still draining, though the swelling had gone down. Some days he ate a bit, but mostly he just lay there, sleeping. He showed no interest in leaving. If they liked my story, maybe the People would decide to keep him. I worked hard, loading in firewood and fish, netting rabbits, keeping myself busy so that the time would pass. I picked rose hips. Apples spilled from two large bags. While I never went too far or left for too long, the cave had begun to fill with my harvest. At night, with my creatures, I'd look around at my work. I'd done a good job. Magla would be proud.

Magla. What was keeping her? What was keeping all of them? The month we called Return to the Sea was almost over. I'd slept in the cave for twelve nights. There was frost on the meadow every morning when I went to the river. The northern sky had been dark for days, heavy with snow. You couldn't be in the mountains when the snow came. Everyone knew that. First you get to the sea, then the snow comes. Where were they? This was no time to linger.

Then one morning something changed, something that turned my anticipation to dread and offered an answer to my question. I'd slept well the night before, our coldest night so far, holding the pup next to me for warmth. When I awakened I sensed the change, even from the cave. A strange new brightness. Snow. I jumped up and hurried outside to stare at the shore's grim beauty. The world glistened. The edges and angles of the rocks were gone, each stone as plump and round as fruit. Winter never came to the sea before it came to the mountains. And it never came to the mountains when the people were there. The snow was already melting, but my uneasiness grew.

I grabbed Thur and ran to the meadow to check the path. Reindeer tracks mingled in the slush. Herds were gathering in the valley, picking their way south. But there were still no people. And then the geese overhead, the frenzied work of the squirrels, the early morning ice on the river, the broken skin on my hands, and the white smoke of my breathing all whispered the same eerie message that I'd tried not to hear.

Winter had returned, but not the People.

Earthmaker's Gift

I STOOD IN THE MEADOW, THE DOG AT MY FEET, thoughts washing over me like choppy waves. So, the People had been delayed. A storm perhaps. They'd wait it out. No one stayed in the mountains in Winter. Snow starved all but the sleeping bears and the burrowers. Wind raged for months. Maybe I should find the Arn. No. They were fourteen days ahead. I didn't know their route. No. The People would get here. The weather had changed. That's all. Change. Not Chaos. That's what it was. They'd get here if they could. My fear rose again. I forced it down, as Earthmaker had taught me after Tenja's death. Think. Plan. Work. Think again.

What if there'd been an avalanche? No! Stop. I waited. Well then, if the People weren't coming, I would need a coat. I would need a heavy coat. I tapped my stiff fingers against my thigh as I gazed out over the valley. New snow fell from the stone-grey sky. How would I get a coat? Think. It was too late. My hand was no longer tapping, but trembling. My aloneness rose up like a sudden blizzard, blinding me to everything else. All I knew was the pounding of my chest and a world gone white. I looked north, to the hills, and took a step. I should go after them.

Thur's cry called me back. I looked behind me. The pup hopped about on the frozen grass, lifting her paws. I bent down and lifted her, putting her under my arm. Shutting my eyes against hot tears, I rubbed the little dog's back. "Winter is coming," I said, swallowing hard. "You don't know Winter, Thur. It's the lonely time." I swallowed again. "I'll tell you about it. I'll tell you what happens. We are like you in Winter. We always wear coats. In the winter we rest and wait. In the winter the babies die. In the winter the Old Ones fall asleep and don't awaken. You can't bark at me now, Thur. Winter is coming and I need a coat."

There. I'd spoken my fear. The dog squirmed and I loosened my grip.

Carrying her back across the crunching grass, my breath hovering before me, I began telling her a story. "The best coat to have is a bear-skin," I said, my voice trembling. "The People have had a few of those. We get them in the spring. Those Who Serve go to a high cave and choose who will wake the bear." Thur snuggled closer. The sound of my voice was making me stronger. "You should see how brave the People are. The chosen one sneaks into the cave. He holds his spear. He follows the sound of breathing in the darkness. Goes to where the Old One sleeps. Calls out, 'Grandfather, Grandfather.' Then he jabs the bear and the bear awakens. The hunter runs out and the bear roars after him. The others spear it then."

The little animal squirmed in my arms, watching the frosted world from her perch. My words kept tumbling out. "In those years, we have a feast. You would like it. So much meat. Those Who Serve put Grand-father Bear on a sleigh and pull him to our shore. And we honor him for his flesh. We eat and sing. We take his skull and put it with the others. In a special place. The Bear Cave. Their spirits fill that valley."

I'd been a child at the last bear hunt. All I could remember were the mountains, rising like the palms of two hands, and a narrow valley enfolded in fog. And Ochre lifting me over the steep places.

A blast of wind whipped my thoughts back to the present. This was no time for dreaming. I had to hunt or freeze. I would never kill a bear. Then I remembered: A wolf pelt waited for me. I had my coat. And at that same moment, I realized I would never kill the wolf. I knew now why I'd kept the wounded animal with me. I held the dog closer. "Thur," I said, "you and Wolf are my family now." Perhaps some day they'd help me hunt. This time I'd have to get my deer alone. I came to the path that led down the hill and made my way down sideways in the slush.

Wolf raised his head weakly at our return. This was a creature I would always recognize, I thought. His leg was healing, but the scar went almost to the bone. And he was missing half an ear. Nothing remained of the meat I'd left him but a tuft of grey fur. "So, you like rabbit," I said as I filled his water shell and added a log to the fire. "We are alone for now," I told him. "I have to make a plan." I sat by the fire with the dog.

My best chance would be to try for a deer. Most of the herds were gone by now. The busiest route lay a day to the east and then south across the plains. Their path would probably take them to that new lake the Arn had found. Reindeer could easily cross a frozen river. A frozen lake might not be a problem. I didn't care about the herds. My target would be the stragglers, those deer still ambling out of the mountains, nosing at snow-covered rocks to gnaw lichens and moss. Only a few more days and they'd be gone as well. The cave held all the tools I'd need to flesh out my animal and sew my coat. But how to kill him first? I fell asleep trying to answer that question.

I was out the next morning before dawn, walking over fog-covered ground, carrying the pup in her bag. She was as big as a raccoon now, and heavy, but far too young to leave behind. I had a plan of sorts, depending on the deer. I'd made a torch, wrapping leather around straw at the end of a stick. I was heading for the woods, first crossing the meadow where Tenja had loved Ephus, then stopping where the grass met the trees. I leaned my torch against a pine, dropped my pack, and tied the dog.

I turned to study the meadow. The fog was too thick to see much, but this was a place I knew well. Morning was brisk with a northerly wind. The copper grass was frosted. In the distance was a mound of white logs, all that remained of a beaver dam. A shallow slough drained in the middle of the area, guarded by the stumps of long-dead trees, and now covered by a thin sheet of ice. It was here that the browsers, and those that followed them, stopped to drink. The animals came at sunrise. I didn't have much time.

Going to the edge of the bog, I took out my flint and began hacking at the frosted grass. I spread the straw along the edge of the frozen pond, tossing a little beyond my reach, covering the ice. Then I hurried back to the wooded patch, maybe thirty steps away. After I'd taken the fire stones and dry branches from my pack, I settled near a juniper. Soon a small fire crackled, the smoke blowing south along the meadow. I held my unlit torch and waited. An owl called through the low clouds.

"Earthmaker, send me a deer," I prayed. The world was silent. Even Thur sat quietly, looking at the mist. A raven cried, "Walks Alone, Walks Alone." I was happy the bird had found me. Still I waited, breath rising like smoke and mingling with the fog. "Earthmaker, send me a deer."

The grass parted in front of me and a mouse scampered by, eager for the day. Across the meadow, a band of grey trees stretched into the dawn, their bare branches tinged with gold. I listened for the crunch of hooves on the frozen grass. The world held its breath with me. And then, beyond the silence, I heard it. Not the sound of a herd, but the sound of a single animal, large and slow, picking its way over the tundra step by step, cracking tiny sticks as it came, snapping back branches, lumbering toward the water. What was there?

A dark shadow rose from the mist and loomed between me and the water, a shadow taller than a man, taller than a reindeer, broader too. Antlers took shape in the grey light, thrust out like giant hands, wider than the creature's flanks. The beast brushed through the hard grass, moving slowly, its head bobbing under the burden of the strange autumn horns. Earthmaker had given me a deer, but not any deer. It was one of the great deer, a creature that roamed the meadows alone, now all but vanished, destroyed by the power of its own protection.

Once, in the springtime, walking with the People through the forest, I'd come upon the remains of such a creature. It must have entered the woods to feed, and somehow locked its antlers between two pines. There it had died, its bones picked clean and lying neatly, beneath the horns that still spanned the trees. Now such a deer had come to me.

I waited, not moving, hardly breathing, letting him edge forward, letting him reach the water. I watched in the dim light as his massive head dipped down to drink, his neck straining to support the rack. The animal's labored breathing was the only sound. I stood and lit my torch. Then I leaped behind him, screaming and waving the fire. The startled deer reared and jerked his head, snorting wildly, hot breath rising and round eyes huge. He towered above me, enraged, but hindered by the weight of the horns. Avoiding the powerful hooves, I jabbed his flank with my torch and urged the deer into the water. He took a step and halted, planting his feet in the shallow pool, entrenched.

Suddenly a black demon sprung from the shadows, lunging at the deer's other side. Thur had broken her leash! The deer lurched around to ram the dog. But in that moment, he lost his balance, jerked back, and fell into the bog. Another deer could have righted itself, but one side of the rack was lodged under a log. The great deer managed to stand again, but his head stayed down. He turned pitifully, trying to free the antler, all the time hooking himself more tightly. Thur jumped at his feet, barking wildly. The deer thrashed and twisted, strongly at first, steam rising from his haunches, then feebly, as the weight of the antlers slowly pulled him down.

I stood quietly in that awful dawn, the torch flickering, the dog yelping. The great deer slumped to his knees, his head now underwater. Bubbles rose. Then the animal fell, his back legs buckling underneath him. I laid my hand on his warm flank as the cold water pooled around my thighs. His coat was reddish gold, thick and fine, with a heavy mantle about the neck. I was one whom life had blessed.

By sunrise I'd hacked off the antlers. My satisfaction was seeping away with the blood. How would I get the deer out of there before the cats came? If I could drag the carcass whole, the blood smell might not give me away. But not even an Arn could drag that deer. Sometimes the People made sleighs, using antlers for runners. But that worked only when there was snow. I'd made a second fire near the carcass. It sputtered in the damp air as I studied the meadow and listened to the silence. I'd been there far too long already. At last, Earthmaker whispered. Yes, that might work. It would be almost impossible, but it might work.

I decided to follow Her plan. I stayed at the marsh for two days. When my work was done, there was little sign that someone had been there, little sign that someone had loaded a carcass on logs and pulled it through waist-deep water to the beaver dam, little sign that someone had tugged out the tightly-wedged branches to make an entrance. And after I'd made just enough room to crawl into the mound, I'd dammed up the underwater passage, using sticks from the inside and enlarging the lodge. After that I no longer had to think. Earthmaker told me all.

Hack off the hide, roll it, store it in the beaver lodge; set aside the head to save the brains; gut the deer and throw his entrails in the water; butcher it, stacking the meat inside; pack a little to take to the cave; wash the blood off Thur and me; build the lodge back up again, weaving the sticks together with freezing hands. I'd keep my food and pelt in the dam until I was ready and do my work there in safety. I laid the massive antlers on the top of the lodge, marking the time that Earthmaker had shown me a great thing.

I was proud of my work, proud of the meat I carried, proud of my dog. It was time to go home, time to get my tools and feed the wolf, maybe sleep one night at the cave, then return to take care of the hide. I'd have to work fast before it got too cold. At least the meat would keep. I looked around the meadow one more time. Then Thur and I entered the woods.

A marten sniffed at us from behind a pine tree. "Even you can't get my deer," I called. Jays cried. A brown nutcracker hopped along the ground between the fallen pine cones. I let Thur run ahead for a while, then called her back. She knew the way, but I didn't want her reaching the cave before me. When we were near, I carried her. Thur knew she'd done well, but there were things she wasn't ready for.

"Wolf will be happy to see us, to see what we've brought!" I said, scratching her ears. "We'll have a good winter. You'll see." I hurried down the slope to the beach. "Wolf! Wolf, we're home. Food!" Thur jumped from my arms and raced to the cave before I could stop her. I yelled and ran after her, stopping short at the entryway. The wolf was gone.

The Face of the Mother

"Damn you, Wolf! Why did you leave?" I dropped the bag of meat on the floor, tears burning my eyes. Thur ran about the cave, sniffing and whimpering. "He's gone, Thur. He left us." I sat and patted the ground beside me, trying not to cry. At least the dog came running, unlike that ungrateful wolf. But with Wolf at the entryway, I'd felt safe. Even more, I'd had a reason to come home. The space inside the cave had never seemed so empty. I held the dog, wondering if I should tie her so she didn't run.

After a while, Earthmaker whispered, *Get up.*

I looked around. Without Wolf to guard the cave, I'd have no peace, not with winter coming and fresh meat in my bag. But Earthmaker gave me a plan. I was to make a gate. I wiped my nose on the back of my hand, thinking things through. My arms ached. I was exhausted. But this needed to be done that day. I waited until I could see the entire gate in my mind. Then I plodded to a stand of young trees just up from the beach and began hacking off branches.

By afternoon, I had a pile of stout sticks, longer and narrower than the beaver logs. My hands were bleeding from where the branches scraped them and from the cracks around my fingernails. I carried the sticks back to the cave and threw them in a heap. Thur tried to drag them away as quickly as I put them down, so I tied her and let her bark. "Damn Wolf," I muttered. It was his fault I had to do this at all. But I didn't need him. I'd take care of myself. I sharpened the top of each branch, then laid them flat and lined them up, twenty in all.

It was time to go to the back of the cave, to the place I stored things that didn't yet have a purpose. The long strips of bark were still there, the bark I'd found two summers ago in the rancid backwater of the salt marsh. The memory of that day was vivid. The bark stunk so bad Tenja had made me leave it outside to dry. Then I'd rolled the strips and stored them until their time came. Now I brought a bundle outside and unwound it, jerking the strips to test their strength. Almost as tough as sinew, but easier to get, I thought. I'd bind the sticks together in three places, top, middle, and bottom. That should make it sturdy. I began weaving the strips around the wood, leaving two finger-widths between each branch, and wrapping every one several times. "There. That will hold," I said, admiring my work.

The sun was sinking by the time I'd finished, but I couldn't rest yet. I dug a hole on both sides of the entrance and hammered a post as thick as my arm into each one. Then I lifted the gate, dragged it to the entrance, and jostled it into place, tying it in four places at one end. The gate needed work, but it would do for now. I'd fasten the other side once we got in.

The dog had been following my movements with sad eyes all afternoon. I kneeled to untie her and scratched her head. "Look, Thur," I said. "No animals will bother us now." She ran off to pee and I placed another log on the fire just outside the entryway. "Come on girl, let's go," I called. She padded inside and I dragged the gate shut, tying it behind me. We were safe.

That night, as the moon streamed silver on the beach, I dreamed about a grey creature with long, thin legs that came sniffing at my door. I woke late, stiff and tired. My fingers were swollen, but I was eager to get to work on my hide. A heavy snow could come at any time, trapping me at the cave. I packed some tools, called the dog, and tied the gate behind us. Then I dropped a rib bone outside the entrance, close to where Wolf had slept. "Just this once," I told Thur. "In case he changes his mind." As we headed for the meadow, I sensed a shadow skimming along the ground to the left, just beyond my vision. It paused if I stopped, disappeared if I turned. I leashed Thur, not knowing if the shadow was hungry.

I'd decided to work the hide at the marsh. It was too heavy to carry back unscraped, the fat still clinging to it. And I'd have to stake it before I could remove the flesh. The smoking I would do at the cave, since it would be hard to keep a fire going for long in the damp grass. But the scraping and softening I'd do at the marsh. When we reached the slough, I unpacked some kindling and started a small fire, adding a few damp logs one at a time. They smoldered, then burned, as I sat and thought about my task. After the scraping, I'd haul the hide home. That would take most of the day. And it would be all I could carry. I'd come back another time for food. I'd thought of everything. The fire was burning well. Magla would be proud of me. I went to work.

Into the marsh. The water was freezing. I made my way to the middle of the pond, holding Thur at my shoulder. Something had been there before me, leaving new claw marks in the wood. A marten or mink, I guessed. Maybe a wolverine. I climbed out of the marsh and leaned against the beaver dam. My legs were numb. Bracing myself against the side of the structure, I worked the branches back and forth, tugging until I had an opening. I looked in. Everything was as I'd left it. I dropped Thur inside with the nearly frozen meat. "You stay here and eat. I'll be back." Now I wouldn't have to worry about her. I pulled out the rolled hide, replaced the sticks, and floated the hide back across the pond on two logs tied together.

All that day, I followed Earthmaker's orders: *Haul the hide to the shore, feed the fire, stake out the pelt, you've done well, scrape off the flesh, feed the fire, go back to the beaver lodge, return with the deer head, watch your back, watch the shadow that stirs at the edge of the forest, strike the deer skull with four sharp blows, pull out the pink brains, ladle them onto the hide, smear the soft paste, work it into the edge of the hide, rub hard to keep the skin soft.* I worked quietly and quickly. The dusky creature still lurked in the bushes, exposing his head from time to time as he peered between the branches. "Wolf, I know you're there," I called.

By late morning I was crouching on the shore, the fire at my back, the sky heavy, working the staked hide. A raven swept down, brushing my arm as he dived for a shred of flesh. "Get!" I cried. As the day crept on, my arms grew sore from scraping and rubbing. By midafternoon every part of me ached, but I was finally done.

I'd have to rest before I started back. I looked at the heavy skin still staked to the ground. Could I really get that huge thing home? Would it be safe there in the grass while I slept? I rolled two logs on top of it to be sure. Then I gathered up the fleshy pieces I'd scraped away and carried them part way to the trees, dropping them in a pile. "You were bad to leave us, Wolf," I called. "But I'm leaving these scraps for you. Just this once."

I slogged back through the water to the beaver lodge, removed some sticks, and crawled inside. If I pushed the meat to the edge, there was just enough room to lie down. I hugged the warm dog close and closed my eyes. When I awakened, I made my way back again, closing the lodge and carrying the dog to the other shore. Just as I anticipated, the scraps were gone. I pulled out the stakes and rolled up the hide, ready to go home.

The trip was slow. I tried carrying the pelt on my shoulder, but soon gave that up and dragged it. To keep from thinking about my weariness, I imagined the coat I'd make. I'd carve buttons from the horn tips and from the mantle make a hood. By the time we reached the cave, moonlight was dancing on the sea and I could hardly move one foot ahead of the other. I untied the gate, dragged in the hide, tied it again, and dropped to my sleeping robe, too tired for loneliness.

In the days that followed, Wolf was never far, lingering beyond my sight, but near enough to grab the bones I left. I dropped his food a little closer to the cave each day, waiting for him to slink over and dart off, his silver body floating above his slender legs. Sometimes when he loped away I tried to follow. He'd crouch and wait, then run if I got near. Still, I liked the game we played. Wolf was a friend of sorts. And then one day a new companion came.

I saw him first when I was on the beach hanging venison in the drying racks. Wolf was skulking in the brush just beyond, watching me, when I heard the familiar call. I swung around to see a raven lighting on a pine branch just above the wolf. "Walks Alone, Walks Alone," the bird jeered. Then he turned his head and preened his shaggy feathers.

"Is that you?" I cried. The raven cocked his head. I took a step closer. In that moment, the bird dived for a piece of venison and disappeared into the brush, Wolf bounding after him. So, Wolf had taken on a partner.

291

As the cold settled in, so did those two creatures. They were always together. Had they come to stay? It seemed I had something they wanted. Wolf was bolder when Raven was around. Some days the animal sat in full view while the bird pecked away on bones I'd left for Wolf. One morning, I looked up to see Raven circling overhead, looking for something. Wolf was lying low in the brush as usual, just up from the beach. The bird spotted him, swooped low, turned sharply, and flew east. Wolf jumped up and ran off in the same direction. Could it be that ravens showed wolves where to hunt, I wondered, signaling when they saw a weakened animal, waiting for the wolf to make the kill? The two of them were certainly nice and plump.

That was partly because of me, I knew. I'd removed the drying racks from the ground and wedged them into the rocks, beyond Wolf's reach. But the jerky had never vanished so quickly. It seemed that Raven came when I wasn't looking, taking much more than one fat bird could eat.

One day I came home from the river with three full water bags to find Raven perched on his usual limb. I was sure Wolf was somewhere near. I'd checked the meat racks before I left. Setting the bags on the ground, I climbed up the sponge stone to take another look. Just as I suspected. There were so many gaps where the meat had been that the first rack resembled an Old One's smile. I jumped down and looked hard at the bird.

"So, you both want my food, is that it?" I asked. He cocked his head. "The deer is mine," I yelled. "Tell Wolf no more. You neither!"

The raven pulled back. Then he hopped from the tree and strutted down the beach, his black plumage gleaming in the rainbow hues. "*Wraack*, we'll see," he said.

Magla would have never put up with this. I'd show them. There'd be no more drying racks. I'd smoke the venison just like I smoked the hide. If Raven was foolish enough to get caught in the smoke tent, he'd be cooked along with everything else. As soon as I finished taking care of the hide, I'd salvage whatever meat was left in the drying racks.

This would be the first hide I'd smoked by myself, though I'd helped Magla several times before. I wished she were here. I dug the fire pit first, then lit a fire and let it burn to embers, adding damp wood to make it smolder. Once the flame died down, I stood three tall sticks above the pit, binding them together at the top. Finally, I draped the hide over the logs like a tent so that the smoke billowed up and darkened it. The hardest part was keeping the fire right, not so hot it burned the hide, but not so weak it died altogether. It was confusing, trying to remember how the People had done things in the past, but trying not to think about what they were doing now.

It would take several days to finish the hide. I'd have to stay close by and tend the fire. No more trips to the meadow. I didn't mind. For one thing, it gave me a chance to empty the drying racks. I'd started feeding the animals in one place, giving them a few good pieces along with the scraps. Maybe if they got used to that, they wouldn't steal. Sometimes Raven forgot and I'd send a rock flashing past his head, though I never really tried to hit him. I liked having him there. Wolf too. It was like having bad children. I couldn't recall that the People ever had bad children, but maybe it was better than no children at all.

But there was another reason I didn't want to go anywhere. I was tired. Maybe I'd been working too hard. Maybe the cold air wearied me. My nose wasn't running, so I knew I wasn't sick. But I was exhausted. Some mornings all I could do was sit. Fortunately, the cave was full of the supplies I'd put aside for the People, surely enough to last until the tiredness lifted. And I had plenty of meat. I'd made two more trips to the beaver dam since I brought down the hide. Anyway, I was tired of meat. Some days all I wanted was currant tea and dried apples. That would probably pass, too. I had enough venison for at least a month.

The hide had dried to a beautiful reddish-brown. I spread it out to cut. There was easily enough for leggings as well as the coat. I didn't have to worry about boots. Last year's still hung from the ceiling of the cave. I was eager to start stitching, eager to keep my hands busy while my body was resting.

THE DAYS FELL AWAY LIKE LEAVES. A few bright aspens were all that remained of fall. Geese no longer flew overhead and the rushing streams were still. Winter soon overtook autumn, floating in on tiny flakes. The snow drifted down slowly at first, unsure of its welcome, growing more confident each day. We'd rarely had snow in winters past, not here by the sea. But the summer rains must have had nowhere else to go. The days were just cold enough to keep the snow clinging to the rocks along the shore, wrapping a white mantle around my home. Birds still gathered on the bare trees near the beach, but no other creature stirred.

No other creature but Wolf, that is. Every night, I'd leave scraps outside the cave. In the morning, they'd be gone. I'd look out at the fresh snow cover and see a trail leading south, then disappearing into the trees. And always the same round paw prints pressed into the snow.

Raven was not so elusive. Some mornings I awakened to Thur's wild barking and found the bird perched on top of my gate, shifting from foot to foot, poking his bill at whatever struck his interest. He'd cock his head and pull up his chin when I spoke to him, but was never in any hurry to leave.

Thur spent her days running in the snow just outside the cave and chewing strips of rawhide I tossed her way. I was glad she had no interest in running off without me.

IN THOSE EARLY WINTER DAYS, I rested and sewed and kept the calendar. And when the sewing was done and I had my new coat, I brought up stones from the sea, not sponge stone, but hard grey rock. Then I carved little animals with my flint, like Andor had done, but not so fine. I lined them up around the wall; a wolf, a fish, a goose, a hare. Each creature was a friend. I kept my hands busy, but my thoughts still roamed.

Some days I myself felt like a skittish animal, afraid of wind and darkness and my own thoughts. I knew it was loneliness and nothing more. But it would do no good for my mind to suffer. I tried to remember what Tenja had told me, about the small self and the large. After I'd done my tasks, if the wind wasn't too cold, I'd sit on the shore and watch the grey, rolling sea. I'd breathe deeply, as Earthmaker had taught, calming myself, trying to match my breathing to the breaking of the waves. And then, very slowly, something strange started to happen. As I stared out at the waves, forgetting my small self in the endless, churning sea, I began to go beyond my loneliness and leave my thoughts behind, becoming as much shore as human. Was it my large self emerging? I didn't know. But it seemed at those times that the one I'd known as Thistle disappeared, leaving in her place only the breeze and a remembrance of joy.

THAT WORKED WELL ENOUGH FOR THE DAYS, but nights were still a problem. Like Winter itself, night loomed endlessly. And the days were getting even shorter. Raven was nowhere to be seen once the sun went down, while Wolf was only an occasional shadow. Thur would lie at my feet after we'd eaten, her head on her paws, looking at me as if I were to blame for the darkness. Some nights I brought out the calendar, drawing lines in the snow to help me count and to mark the path of the stars, hoping that would pass the time. But I'd forgotten so much. Like the winter sun, Tenja's teaching was growing dim. Sometimes it seemed my learning had been for nothing so I set a challenge for myself. I'd figure out precisely when the shortest day would come. I didn't know if my calendar was exactly right, but I didn't think I'd missed marking any days. I could at least come close. And once that was done, I could mark the days until spring.

I started my task the moment I thought about it, in the middle of a clear, bright night when the moon was almost full. First I counted backwards from the present to the day the Arn had left their camp. That was a time that I'd notched deeply. Thirty days. Then I counted ahead, figuring the number of nights left in the year. Sun would make the winter promise in twenty-one days, or so it seemed to me. I wouldn't think any farther than that. So. Twenty-one days until the solstice. They'd go quickly. I'd have a celebration. I started planning.

Did the People have celebrations for one person? I didn't know of any. Perhaps I'd invite the animals. Raven would come, and Wolf, if I put out food. Maybe others, too. Just to see. I could have a feast. But what would I do for the celebration? What did we do other years? Well before a special day, the Old Ones told stories. Maybe I'd begin with that, tell a story every night. Thur would listen. Maybe none of the other animals would be interested, but I hoped they were. They might like to hear the words of a human, so different than their own. Animals knew many things, but humans were more able to sum things up. Anyway, it would be good for me to talk. It would help me remember better. And the sound of my own voice always made me stronger. Maybe the animals wouldn't mind.

I didn't begin the story that night. I wanted to think about it first. But the next night I was ready. I waited until it was totally dark, which was not so long to wait. Then I opened the gate and sat on the shore with my small fire and my dog. And each night, for twenty nights, I told a story. At first, each story began the same.

"This is what the People know," I'd say, speaking to any creature who might be listening along the dark shore, my timid voice becoming stronger every time. I went through all I'd learned, about Earthmaker and Sun's Promise, about the Tree at the Center of the World, about Chaos and Change, about the Watcher within us, and the stars' great whirlings. About the seasons and the numbers and the stones. I hesitated and stumbled, trying to remember, and then, on the fifth day, all my thoughts came back.

Soon after that, words started to come to me that I'd never heard before. I let them fall from my mouth for the thrill of them. And then I realized that the words were the thoughts of animals and that the animals were using me. They had stories of their own, from which our stories came, but they had never heard them told before. So I changed the way the tales began and started out by saying, "This is what the People know, some of it told to them by animals and some of which they figured out themselves." And on those nights, it seemed as if more creatures came. All along the shore, pairs of eyes lit up the darkness, like stars fallen to the ground.

◻ ◻ ◻

SOMETIMES IT SEEMED MY DREAMS spilled into waking, and waking flowed over into dreams. Then one night, the night before the shortest day, Earthmaker, The Mother of All Things, appeared to me. She was as a fir tree standing in the night's blue snow. *Walks Alone,* She whispered, forgetting my true name, *you will see My faces.* Then I saw that the branches of her tree were made of snakes. The serpents, in their writhing, beckoned me. As I approached, the tree burst into flame.

I am the longing in your loins that calls you to another; the embers in your mind that kindle you, no matter how far you've fallen; and the blaze in your soul that summons you to the Source. I am what conceives you and my element is blood.

The boughs of that tree fell away, and then the trunk, leaving only ashes. And from those ashes, something rose and began to speak. I saw that it was a mother deer, swollen with her young, and that behind her rose the moon.

I am what is left of your desire and so much more. Your hunger lives in my own belly. I nourish what is planted in you and give of my own flesh that you might live. I am what nurtures you and my element is tears.

The deer gave birth and the young one walked away. Then the mother animal went forth across the earth and fed upon those plants that heal. As I watched, she ambled into the future and grazed in a field of tall grass tended by humans.

I am what tends your life, making it fruitful and giving order. Healing all of Earth, I bring balance to your body and the power of gentleness to your mind. I am what cleanses you and my element is rain.

The deer lay down and where she lay the fir tree grew again. Earthmaker took back Her form, turning slowly, showing me Origin, Nurture, and Purification, her eyes first fierce, then soft, then bright. Before She left me, Silka's face appeared, asking the same eager question she asked of Tenja long ago, "Does she not love babies?" I awoke to sunshine dappling the walls of the cave and lay there watching the dance of shadows. Raven called in the distance, making almost a human sound.

Night of the Blue Snow

IT WAS THE MORNING OF THE SHORTEST DAY. I awoke early and pulled Ochre's scratchy lion pelt tightly around my shoulders, settling back to rest in its warmth. There was nothing I had to do. I yawned and dozed again. Most winters, I had to be up early, making several trips to the river for ice. Not that the entire river froze, just the shallow part close to the shore. We were glad for the freezing, since carrying ice was better than hauling water. But this year, with the drifts on the beach, the water had come to me. All I had to do was scoop it up and let it melt in the basin. On really cold days I'd drop in a hot rock.

Watching my breath rising, I thought about other winters; short Magla, dragging a block of ice half her size; Silka, daintily lifting her water bag; Birch, trying to haul as much as the Mothers. But my memories weren't very good company. Thinking about the others made me sad. I ran my fingers through my hair and rubbed my eyes. The day stretched before me, unclaimed. It was supposed to be a celebration. What would I do?

I could think of only one thing that would be different, something I hadn't done in years. Thur and I could walk to the north, out of our little cove, along the rocky, windswept shore, beyond the place I'd once found Shine. Few people ever traveled that way. Adults didn't want to and children were not allowed. The coastline was too treacherous for fishing. But I'd gone there alone sometimes, whenever I longed for the bite of wind in my face, a glimpse of foam churning through rock, the sound of waves crashing against stone, and the feel of what was forbidden. I decided I'd go there that day.

It didn't take long to get ready. Thur jumped at my legs when I took down my carrying bag. As large as a fox now, she loved nothing more than a day of roaming with me. I packed a handful of dried apples and a fish and we set out under the bright blue sky. The sea, cut by white strips of waves, reflected back a darker blue. It was a breezy morning, but I didn't think there'd be any storms that day.

We followed the coastline north, walking toward distant snow-covered peaks separated from us by unseen valleys and black ridges of pine. Humans never ventured into those mountains, especially in the winter. But Earthmaker had shown us a way around them long ago, a pass to the east, the same trail the People still used. My eyes followed the jagged northern horizon until a pang of loneliness caught me and I glanced away. Better to watch the ground before me than to follow memories leading nowhere.

The way was getting rougher. Large boulders dotted the shore. I stepped over driftwood draped with seaweed and listened to the crash of the waves. By late morning Thur and I were rounding the shoreline at its northernmost curve and heading west. Now I felt the full brunt of the wind as it swept across the unprotected sea. I walked into it, taking its strength, forgetting all other thoughts.

We stopped at a quiet place, a sheltered area between two tall stones.

I sat with my back against a rock and stretched my legs. There I rested, the wind whipping above me and the waves pounding beside me. I was protected from both, though a bit of spray reached me from time to time. "Listen, Thur," I said, breaking off a piece of dried cod, "nothing can harm us here." She wasn't interested in the terrain. Her small black eyes followed the fish in my hand. I offered her a few bites and settled in, in no hurry to face the wind again or to return to the cave. It was a day of celebration anyway. I had no need to hurry. And I was sleepy. Walking made me tired now.

I rested. When I awoke, the sun was well beyond its high point and far to the southwest. Time to leave if I was going to get back by dark. "All right, Thur, let's go." I stood and stretched. I'd told myself not to look at the mountains, but I glanced north anyway before I could stop myself. What I saw made me gasp. I stared harder. From those distant peaks, as ragged as waves in a storm, rose a thin white line. Smoke. Humans were staying there, where none had stayed before! My humans, surely. Distant, but nearer than I'd dared to hope, trapped by snow.

Even if they weren't my people, the smoke proved that humans could survive in those mountains.

Magla, Ochre, Fire, they could all be at that fire. It might be months before they made it out, but I'd know they were alive as long as I could see the smoke. I began to tremble.

I don't remember how I got back to the cave that day. Perhaps the wind took me and set me down on my shore. All I recall was adding a log to the fire late that afternoon and roasting a little meat. And the dog and I staring at the blaze. "Thur," I whispered, when I could finally speak, "Earthmaker has shown us a great thing. The People live. They are caught in the mountains and will return." Maybe they could even see my fire. Thur crossed her paws and stretched out, thoughtful, while tears rolled down my face. This had been a day of wonder. My People, or at least some people, were only three days walk from here, once the snow melted. They'd return in the spring and life would again be tender. "Thank you, Earthmaker," I said, hugging my knees and staring north. Was there a way to make my praise stronger?

The sky was still bright, but not for long. I went inside, took down a pouch of shelled walnuts, and hurried back out. Then I flung a handful onto the snow-covered shore. As if waiting all winter for this moment, the beach came alive with the twittering surprise of sparrows. Jays and starlings swooped down. A red crossbill skitted in and darted off, the nut still in its beak. I ran back for a bag of dried currants and tossed those as well, just for the thrill of watching the wings. Earthmaker had brought the People close. I felt bountiful.

The birds disappeared and quiet descended again. Purple shadows lengthened. The air grew cold. I'd almost forgotten what day it was. I held the dog on my lap, this being her first solstice. We lingered on the shore, waiting for the shortest day, which was also the beginning of Sun's return.

I looked out over the sea, my eyes following a golden trail to the southwest, across the water and upward. Sun hovered in orange splendor over the still world. Finally, when it had gathered all the light back into itself, Sun paused, satisfied, then dropped into the sea. Words were too small for the night. I sat quietly. Stars winked in the twilight and a great owl swooped down. I felt no need for any other ritual. The world was already a celebration and I its guest. When I finally stood and called to Thur, the stars were already high in the clear black night. I shuffled into the cave and tied the gate.

That night, in my dreaming, the animals called. Wolf howled on the shore and Raven cawed, "The woods, the woods." So my dream self followed them, floating down the beach and up an incline, clambering through snow as high as my knees, coming to rest at the edge of the woods. And there I waited, the forest floor lit blue by a pearl-round moon and the trees themselves aglow. In the silence, a murmuring began to rise, like the sound of a breeze in high branches. At first I thought it was the moaning of the wind. But as I listened, the trees began to speak a common language. It seemed as if they spoke to me. The still forest trembled at their sound.

"You will be our child," they said. "Raven told us you were here. Wolf has been waiting."

Then into the woods I went, following their voices, past the naked larches, past the sleeping pines and cedars, the snow around my ankles now. But Earthmaker had blessed the night and I didn't feel the cold.

"Come into the forest and dance," the trees sighed. "Dance before the rooted ones."

On I continued, deeper into the night. I could see each glowing branch, the boughs illumined by the eyes of owls. Farther into the forest I crept. The spruce and pine reached out their limbs, encircling me. I slipped by and came upon a little glen.

Again the trees called, "You will be our child. We have been lonesome for the dancing."

All around the forest edge, the animals were waiting. A roe deer gazed at me with liquid eyes, slender antlers rising straight from the top of his head. Partridges, round as little moons, chortled and bobbed. A moose lumbered through the trees, his rack bumping from side to side. He stopped short, curled back his upper lip, and gnawed off a strip of bark. Then he turned to gaze at me, chewing slowly. And there was Wolf, hovering on long, slender legs, his silver hair blue in the moonlight. In the middle of the glen was a frozen pond. On its bank an otter slept, curled into a little ball. As I watched, the creature awoke, stretched and scratched, and raised his muzzle to gaze at me with familiar eyes.

Suddenly a wind arose. The branches began thrashing and clacking and the trees cried out, "Dance for us that you may hear our message. Close your eyes that you may see our secret." In the blustering night a strange wolf howled. The woods wailed more urgently. I felt my body begin to move, swaying with the elder trees as the wind clapped their branches. "Be the child of our spirit. Bring forth a child who will continue," they moaned, "a child who will continue the spinning of the forest dreams. We will hold up the sky that you might dance."

Around I twirled on that blue ground, in a motion my body knew without learning, taught to my blood by stars. The forest spun above me, my feet flying through the snow. Even when I stood still, my heart pounding, the branches continued to swirl. From their great whirling a message came, growing stronger as it roared into the sky:

We have chosen a strong vessel through which to speak. We have chosen a strong vessel through which to speak. Do not try to hold us back. We mean no harm. We must be heard. We must come through. In us live the memories of stones, the raindrops on ancient seas, the lifting gills of long-dead fish, the tongue of the fox mother licking her pups, the scent of blossoms in the mist. We are life and we will not be held back. We will burn forth and cry out somewhere in the universe long after that which would crush us is gone. We are powerful but raw, urgent to live more deeply. We gather strength from speaking and when our power is spoken, it becomes love. Speak now, human, for it is your duty to turn life's longing into love. And so we have chosen a strong vessel through which to speak.

Then the wind died down and my dream self huddled in the hushed darkness, listening. The words continued, in a slow, steady cadence, as if I should remember each one.

"Come back, human. You leave us at your own peril, you and your kind, the Separate Ones. You have forgotten why you learned to speak. Worse for you now, you have forgotten your past."

The forest was strangely quiet, the tree branches still, the world tense with waiting. My dream self peered around and saw, beyond the trees, the horizon tinged by the first hint of grey. Was it time to awaken? The voice began again, this time as tender as sunlight after rain:

> *Our child, we call you. For we have watched over humans from your first gentle stirrings when you slipped from our arms and crept over the earth. You are not the first to come before us, nor will you be the last. Your childhood is repeated over and over again, for so few among you have memories. You come upon Mystery not your own and claim it. Mystery flees. Earth falls victim to Chaos and Chaos remains unnamed. The past is washed away like your footprints at high tide. There is no one to tell our story, only more humans claiming, 'We are the first to travel this road.' Go now. We seek a strong vessel to hold our story and bring it forth. Speak now, human, for it is your duty to turn life's longing into love. Leave a message of your passing, that those who follow will grow beyond their childhood.*

My dream self slipped away then, back to the warm darkness of home and the quiet breathing of the dog, leaving behind the memory of trees. I awoke late, roused by Raven's scolding cry. The scruffy bird annoyed me. I wasn't ready for morning. Yesterday had exhausted me, or maybe last night's endless dream. At least Winter would be easier now, I thought sleepily, knowing that the People were close by. I stretched and looked at the nagging bird, perched on my wobbly gate. He was rocking back and forth, making the whole frame sway. Something wasn't right. I stared harder. Then I saw it. The gate was untied.

"Raven, bad bird!"

I tossed Thur's bone at him. The bird jumped and squawked, flapping his wings. But he came right back. Regaining his rickety perch, he cried, "The woods, the woods."

The woods? A chill of familiarity shot through my body. I had latched that gate, tied it tightly, surely too tightly for some rough bird to undo. I groped around for my boots and pulled them on. All the while, Raven was rocking madly, pitching himself back and forth.

"Stop that! I'm coming."

I pushed the gate aside, followed the excited creature out onto the beach. My dream had been about a forest, that much I remembered. In the bright daylight, the images faded quickly. Still I followed as Raven flitted down the shore, leading me up a wooded hill and through deep snow. The dense brush was full of low shrubs. Branches snapped against my face and dead logs tripped me. I never walked this way. But I tramped on, curious about the bird's odd behavior and the strangely familiar cast of the land.

We came upon a low clearing. Perhaps at one time the area had been a little lake. All that remained to tell that story was a circle of dead cattails standing around a frozen pond. Glancing down, I noticed a large, round paw print in the snow.

"Wolf!" I cried, looking up at the bird. "Does he live here?" I glanced around nervously. What if something had happened to the great grey creature?

The snow was disturbed by other tracks as well, intermingled with the paw prints. I stooped for a closer look. Most were too jumbled to make out, but I noticed one clear one. I scooted closer in the snowy field, crouching to examine the marks. Five little round toe prints on a long foot. I sat in the snow and pulled off my right boot, placing my foot next to the track. The marks were the same.

So. The forest was quiet. I heard my heart pounding and no other sound. Even the bird had shut up, watching me from a branch. So. I walked in my sleep. I had heard of such things. Good that Raven was there to follow me, if I ever forgot the way home. I could certainly recall the route now, I thought. I pulled on my boot, stood up, and glanced around. Then I turned and bolted back through the trees, the branches grabbing at me as if they wanted me to stay. Down the hill and across the beach I ran, stumbling over snow-covered rocks. At last I dashed into the cave, shut the gate behind me, and tied it, my heart still pounding. There were worse things than being alone.

All that day I kept myself busy, never going far from home. I brushed out the cave with cedar branches, fished the river with a net, cleaned a fat burbot and two silver dace, and sliced them to smoke. Not before nightfall was I calm, calm enough to consider the dream. But first I tied the gate shut in three places and dragged my bedding to the back of the cave, next to Tenja's grave. Then I sat to think. The images of the past night were vague, like stories told by Old Ones. A few words stood out. I was to bring forth a child? Could trees know such things? At last, I drifted into sleep.

I woke early, overcome by a sudden sickness. Choking down the gorge in my throat, I rushed for the entryway, striking my head on a stone. My fingers tore at the gate, but I couldn't even get the first knot undone. Nor could I wait. Grabbing my belly, I heaved the night's food on the floor, shuddering at the taste. This was not a sickness I'd ever had before. But Magla had had it when she carried Fire, and Silka after she joined with Rube. The trees knew. And now so did I.

"I Am What is Before"

I SAT WITH THE MOON CALENDAR, counting, adding, thinking. Between the making of a baby and the birth were nine or ten new moons. The baby would come in the early summer, during the month we called Journey to the High Meadows, or maybe during The Gathering of Medicine. Surely the People would be back by then. And the Arn? Where would they be? Would Anish ever know?

I was familiar with babies after they were born, but not before. Magla had always been hungry. That much I remembered. My brother had come to us in a lean winter. Ochre had trouble finding enough for my mother to eat. It was hard to imagine myself wanting food. But that could change. Everything could change. I had to get through six more months. Once again Earthmaker's admonitions returned. Think and plan. Think and plan.

I looked around the cave. Venison, fish, roots, apples, currants, nuts, even a few dried mushrooms. Enough for four more months of hard winter? There was still meat at the beaver dam. What if the snow got deeper and I couldn't get there? Or the People couldn't make it

310

back until late spring? Or I became ill? Or the baby came early and I couldn't leave? I had to have enough food to make it through the winter, to the birth of the child, and even a little longer, until my strength returned. And I'd have to be strong enough to take the baby out with me when I hunted. I couldn't leave it here alone.

I decided to bring the meat back from the beaver dam and store it at the cave before the snow got deeper or I got weaker. I was strong now, just sleepy. I'd save the venison as long as I could, try to bring in a little fresh food so my stores didn't run low. Making a few more trips to the beaver dam would be no problem. However, hunting could be difficult.

We were in the month called When the Babies Cry from Hunger, the leanest time of the year, just after the Winter Solstice. And this winter was worse than most. We'd had colder seasons, but never so much snow on the shore. The trees moaned under their burden of ice. Branches cracked and fell. Only a few creatures ventured out, their tracks quickly covered by new snow.

Animals who didn't sleep shivered in their burrows, gnawing the bark and moss beneath the drifts and growing thin. Even Wolf was leaner now. When the sunlight hit him a certain way, I could see the shadows of his rib bones beneath his fur. Once I'd watched him stalk a mouse. He'd waited patiently for that tiny bite, tracking it earnestly, sending snow flying when he finally pounced. Hunting would not be easy.

But it would not be impossible. The animals were harder to find but they were also weaker. In their hunger, they took chances. Thur would help. The well-fed dog learned quickly. I'd feed her less, I decided, to get her ready. This might be the leanest month, but I'd find a way. The dog and I made two more trips to the beaver dam, bringing back all the meat, and hanging it high in the cave. Then I began watching tracks, waiting for a plan.

But as my belly grew, so did my worrying. By day, I worked hard. At night, I worried. Why had Earthmaker left me here like this? And with a baby inside? I didn't know how to do the things I had to do. There was no one to teach me. I knew how to be part of the People, but not how to be alone. I couldn't hunt in snow. I'd freeze. I'd be lost. The baby would die. The People wouldn't even find our bones. Fear nibbled at me like a rat.

Then one night I saw two yellow eyes gleaming from the beach, steady, calm. It was Wolf, come to remind me of something. I watched those eyes and felt pulled into the darkness, as if the night itself was calling, "come down, come down. You have forgotten all you learned."

Once again my small self slipped away. I remembered the voice I'd heard after Tenja's death, the presence that came from something larger than my fear. As the black world throbbed around me with its own hidden life, my larger self returned. *Your fear is a door. Open it. Step through. Prepare for your future.* It would do no good to turn back now.

I slept little that night. Instead, I lay with the lion pelt around me, listening for the first birds of the morning. By the time the stars grew dim, Earthmaker had left a message in my thoughts, an image of a fallen tree trunk, ancient and hollow, rotten through. Why that, I wondered, as I rested in the cold, clear dawn? But a plan had already begun to take shape. I'd need a forest, big and old. Not the woods around me. Not these stands of straggling trees lined up like cranes along the shore. An aged forest, full of life and death, where hollow trunks lay scattered between time-worn trees. That was the kind of place where I was to hunt. I knew of only one such place close to here. "Thur," I said, once the image was clear, "follow me." I threw the robe aside and took down my carrying bag.

And that was how we came to hunt in the woods where the trees

312

had spoken. I remembered little about that night or my dream, except that it was these trees that told me about the child. It felt strange to return, many days after my last visit, even in the bright sunlight. My uneasiness persisted through several trips, though I had no idea why. Wolf's were the only canine tracks I ever saw there, his and Thur's. Wolf was my friend, I was sure of that. There was no reason to fear him. Still, I was anxious each time I approached those twisted trunks. A strange part of me came alive in that forest, a part forgotten or not yet known.

In time, I learned that this was Wolf's forest, his true home when he wasn't on the shore watching me. And I became aware of words rising up in me each time I neared those trees. If I refused to say the words, my fear returned. But if I uttered them, even though I didn't understand their meaning, I was no longer afraid. So I made the words into songs and sang them as I walked. Perhaps that was all the words wanted, all the woods wanted. The songs made no sense, but they brought me peace.

> I am what is before.
> The separation will come.
>
> I am what is before.
> The trouble will come.
>
> I am what is before.
> The wisdom will come.
>
> I am what is before.
> The planting will come.
>
> I am what is before.

I sang verse after verse. Before long, I could go into the woods easily, even stay there after dark, finding my way home between the shadows. I was becoming familiar with the night.

It took several trips before I realized what I was going to do. Then I fashioned a net, thicker than a fish-ing net, crossing long strips of hide over one another and tying them at each intersection. The spaces between the strips were two fingers wide. At each of the four corners, I sewed a pocket large enough for a stone the size of a goose egg. Once the sewing was finished, I practiced on the beach, throwing the net over a log. Finally, it was time to try my plan.

So, one cloudy afternoon, I rolled the net, put a club in my carrying pouch, leashed Thur and set out. Thur pulled at the leash, preferring to run free, but I couldn't have her frightening the animals. I'd teach her the dog part of the plan once we got to the woods. We followed the faint trail we'd made on other trips, along the beach, up a hillock, and into the trees. Our previous footprints were now iced-over and the ground was rough. I didn't mind going slowly. It gave me time to think. We passed a nutcracker on a branch, a handsome grey bird with a black-tufted head. He glanced up, watched us briefly, and went back to pecking a pine cone.

The snow slowed us down as we got farther into the woods. My feet sunk with each step. Thur flailed around, belly deep. I tried carrying her, but she kicked until I put her down. Though the day was cold, I'd begun to sweat. What good would it do to have my net if I couldn't get through the woods to use it? Ochre and the men always wore snowshoes when they hunted in the winter. Now I understood why. I tried to remember their construction. Red willow branches, tied at the ends, a loose net for the bottom. Maybe an old pair still hung in the cave. If my plan worked, I could always make my own.

By the time we reached a fallen stump, my boots were heavy with moisture. I was too excited to worry about that. I'd found the kind of place I'd been hoping for, a hollow trunk, open on both ends, laying in the snow. Most of the bark had been eaten away by beetles, I thought, noting the raised trails on the naked wood. But that wasn't what interested me. I stooped to take a look at the jumble of little prints beside the stump. Just the ones I wanted to see. Thur had been panting and pulling. I jerked her back, knotted the leash, and hung it over my arm. It wouldn't do to make the prey bolt too soon. Then I leaned the club against the stump and gathered the net. Thur stood tense at my feet, straining against the leash, her tail straight up.

Standing an arm's length away from the right end of the log, I opened the net. The next part I'd practiced over and over on the shore, until I rarely missed. But it had been only practice. This time was real. I held my breath and flung the net. It slipped neatly over the hole in the trunk and hung there, secured on top by two of the stones. In that moment, I let go of Thur's leash. She lunged to the other end of the stump, barking madly. I grabbed the club and leaped for the net.

A terrified rabbit burst from the stump and lurched against the snare. Long ears laid flat, he struggled and squealed. But when he tried to run, the stones fell down behind him, trapping him. He flailed about, kicking with his big back feet, twisting himself more tightly into the strands of the net. One blow with the club and he was dead. The plan had worked. Thank you, Earthmaker, I thought. I loaded up my things. All the way home I sang, swinging the rabbit at my side, letting the dog run free, repeating the words, "I am what is before." I knew it was Earthmaker's song.

In two months, I killed nine rabbits. None were as easy as the first. Eight tries failed. Once we almost got a badger. Sometimes the rabbits were gone when we got there. Most of them preferred to burrow under standing trunks. The burrowers we never got. Twice a rabbit slipped out of the net. Three times it bolted from Thur. One rabbit was too smart for us. She refused to come out at all and Thur was too fat to go in. Each time, however, we learned something new.

Thur was a good protector, but hunting was what she loved. At home, her eyes followed me, glancing at the carry pouch, hoping. When she got tired of waiting, the dog went out alone. Then she'd bring me things, panting proudly as she dropped them at my feet. I let her keep the rats.

I hung the rabbit carcasses in the back of the cave, to bleed them and make them tender, covering the bloody ground with dirt. Then I dressed the furs. Nine was just the right number for a baby blanket, but with ten I could make a little cap. We could have kept hunting all winter, improving each time we went out. But something happened on our last trip that told me we had had enough of rabbits.

It was late in the month called Waiting, just after When the Babies Cry from Hunger. I was no longer so tired, though my belly was larger and my back hurt. Thur and I knew the woods well by then. We'd set out that day, eager and sure. As always, I studied the snow for strange wolf prints. Wolves would roam long distances if they were hungry. They might not bother me but I didn't want to take a chance with Thur. All I ever saw was one familiar set of tracks. That day was no different. Wolf himself didn't seem to mind that we were in his forest. He still came to the cave some nights for rabbit bones or whatever I

could spare. I felt him watching from the shadows when we hunted, blending with the grey trunks. Perhaps he wished us well.

We'd been out all morning. I was weary. My feet were freezing. The conifers stood like open wounds, their flesh stripped away by elk. Life in the forest was growing leaner each day, as if the creatures had given up and only waited. Even the dog seemed reluctant, whimpering from time to time as I pulled her deeper into the woods. But I hated going home empty-handed. I wanted something, if only a cache of acorns. Besides, hunting made the days go faster. I'd decided to keep going, looking for a place we might have missed.

Up ahead was a fallen trunk, longer than an Arn. Surely something lived there. "Come on, Thur, let's go," I said, making my voice sound hopeful as I dragged her through the snow. I'd made myself some snowshoes like Ochre's. Almost like his. My feet just sunk a little way. I made it to the stump and bent awkwardly to check the tracks. As much as possible, I avoided coming upon a badger or a skunk. We were in luck. Little round rabbit prints. I held my hands on my lower back and stood. Thur held up one wet paw.

"Just one more, girl. Come on. We'll get this one and go home." My tiredness had lifted.

Still she cowered, her black body resisting. I looked around. There was nothing. Our prints were the only other marks on the snow. The forest was still. "Thur, let's go." I gave the leash a tug and readied the net. The People would be surprised to see how well this plan worked, when it worked. Casting the net now came as easily as throwing a fishing spear. I hurled it out, letting the dog go as the net drifted smoothly into place. But instead of lunging for the log, Thur turned and began barking wildly. I jerked around in time to see a white underbelly leaping down on us.

The lynx landed, flipped the dog onto her back. Thur yelped once. Pinned to the ground by the cat, the dog swung her head from side to side, trying to shield her neck. A red gash rose up across her chest. I grabbed my club and swung it hard across the back of the feline's head. It thudded dully against the thick fur. "Let go," I screamed, pounding him again. Thur's cry was like my own pain. I wasn't hurting the cat, but maybe I could give Thur time to run. I lifted the club for another strike.

Annoyed more than injured, the lynx turned to me. The cat was only half my size, but I was no match for his powerful mouth and claws. It was a young male, his white teeth gleaming under bearded cheeks. Laying back his tufted ears, he glared at me and growled. Frozen to the spot, I stared into his yellow eyes. The cat pulled back, ready to pounce, muscles rippling under tawny hide.

Another growl distracted him. I jerked around. Wolf crouched behind the lynx, opposite Thur, hair standing high on his shoulders, jowls drawn back to show his teeth. The cat scowled and pivoted toward the wolf, snarling at the intruder. Thur crawled to her feet. A lone wolf was no threat to a lynx. Perhaps it was the three of us together that made a difference. The feline turned his head slowly, looking from one to the other: the yelping dog, me with my club, the bristling wolf. Perhaps more irritated than scared, the cat snorted once and pawed the ground and turned. His body swaying from side to side, head low, he planted his paws before him and slowly walked away. The cat looked back a few times, jerking his head and growling as if to say, "The dog should have been mine." Only after he'd disappeared into the brush did I notice the long cedar branch that ended just above my head.

I hurried to Thur and knelt beside her. Blood oozed from the wound on her chest. At least the cut wasn't deep. I could feel Wolf's eyes on

my back. Standing again, I took a step toward him and reached out my hand. "Good wolf," I whispered. He didn't move. I stretched a little farther, laying my fingers on the side of his head and looking away. I knew he didn't want too much closeness. Thur whimpered. Wolf walked to her and touched her head with his nose, then bounded off, back to his own life. I glanced at the net. There was a rabbit in it, already dead, its neck broken in the leather strands. Picking up the net and the dog, I made my way home.

I cleaned Thur's wound and made a poultice of dried yarrow. She slunk into a corner to sleep. Then I slit the rabbit down the belly and skinned it. Long after the sun dropped below the horizon, I sat just inside the entryway, the gate hanging open, sipping cedar needle tea. The brew was nasty, but hot, good for my sore gums. I swallowed cup after cup, glad for something to do while I waited for a shadow to appear on the moonlit beach.

Something moved. A pale specter was stealing toward the cave, snow moving against snow. Though I could hardly make out the form, I knew he was there. I pushed the entire rabbit carcass out of the cave and held my breath. Clouds moved in and covered the moon. Then I heard it—the fall of padded paws, the crunch of flesh against old snow, a creature coming in like fog, trotting up, lifting the little mound of meat, and vanishing. "Thank you, Wolf," I whispered again, as his tail retreated like a banner along the dusky shore.

Gokihar

THE DAYS PASSED, TRAPPED IN WINTER, each one like the last. Only my belly changed. I sewed the rabbit blanket and the cap, softening leather strips with fat to make the little ties. I'd cut my old tunic into sections, as I'd seen Magla do, making squares to cover the baby's bottom. While I worked, I told stories, hoping the child could hear, stories of Anish and the Arn.

"Little One," I'd say, "you will not just be of the People. You have a father who comes from far away. His eyes are like the sea. He'll be back when you're older. For now you have me. And Thur and Raven and Wolf. The People will be here soon to welcome you. Wolf watches us until then."

Thur wanted me to hunt, but the memory of the lynx was still too fresh. And I was too big and slow for a day of walking. The tunic I'd made from the giant deer had once hung loosely. Now it hugged my belly. I was hungry all the time, though I tried not to eat too much. When I glanced at the food bags, I felt a shiver of fear. Would they last? What if I'd shared too much with the animals? Still, no predator had come to the cave all winter. I had Wolf to thank for that. Raven, Wolf, and Thur—they'd all been generous with me. One morning, I even found a dead badger by the gate, the blood still oozing from the tooth marks on its neck. Wolf's work, I was sure. The meat lasted for days. I planned to make a little coat with the fur. Anyway, I told myself, I could always drag the net to the river to fish. I'd be fine.

Raven came by most days, rocking on the gate, studying me with his shining black eyes, his dark feathers gleaming. I knew the bird grew plumper with each death in the forest. But he wanted more than just enough to eat. He seemed to enjoy my company.

I'd taken to sleeping in the afternoons ever since the day with the lynx. Dragging the lion pelt to the back of the cave, I'd stretch out in the darkness, Thur beside me. Then I'd listen to the sighs and soft breaths of dog dreams and doze for a while. The naps made the days go faster. More importantly, this had become the only time I ever really slept.

My life had taken on a new pattern. After the chores and naps of the day, night went on forever. Each night was the same. I'd lie down and doze, only to be jolted awake by a kick in my belly. Then I'd crawl out in the darkness to pee. I could never get back to sleep. I'd try for a while and give up, sitting at the gate until dawn instead, watching the great star road in the sky. On clear nights, I'd look to the south, over the sea, waiting for the Hunter to rise. I'd follow his three-starred belt through the clouds of my breath, to the Great Cat constellation, its paws outstretched along the horizon for a hundred generations, waiting. And I'd think of Anish.

But it was more than loneliness and the baby's kicks that kept me awake. The night sky called to a darkness within me that awakened other thoughts as well. Wasn't there something else I was to remember, something besides the sky's dark beauty and the warm mystery of my child? What was it Tenja had said about a great star horse breaking free and lurching across the sky? Had I already lost her message? Even the trees had spoken of humans forgetting. What did we no longer know? And how could we remember? My memories were like shooting stars, blazing and vanishing. Were my lessons to be for nothing? I was determined to understand, or at least remember, what had been given to me.

All through those long nights, I thought of the People and our learning. All we had to keep our knowledge alive was our stories. But stories vanished when they weren't told. I remembered how often sickness came and took an Old One before he'd spoken. Or a teacher, before her lessons had been learned. What if the People never returned? Would no one ever know their story? Or mine? Or my child's? Generations to come would forget us, as we had forgotten our past. It would be as if we'd never lived.

A few times, I fell back to sleep where I sat. On those nights, I'd awaken in the grey dawn, shivering, wondering if I'd always been alone and only dreamed the People. My memories of them were growing dim, but I was sure they were real. I longed for them more than I ever longed for dreams. I knew I'd never again hear Idra's voice, rough with years, telling us of Horse and Wolf and the Changers. Never see Tenja and the light in her eyes. But what if I never again saw Fire? Or Magla? Or Birch? Our words were fragile, our lives so fleeting. My thoughts always came back full circle, to the same conclusion. All that bound us, all that remained, were our stories.

Oh, how I longed for the sound of a human voice! I'd gone away because I'd wanted to learn. Now I had only myself for a teacher. I knew so little. And even that was slipping away. My mind seemed full of smoke, my learning replaced by longing. What we needed was a way to put our knowledge outside of ourselves, to have a voice that lived on. What a foolish thought! When we died, our past died with us. I tried to push the idea away and think only of possible things. But it nagged at me, refusing to let me sleep. And then one day something happened that changed my longing into hope.

I was resting on the shore, waiting for another morning, listening to the tide rising in surges and the sea feasting on shifting stones, in the time when dreams slip away to be replaced by the call of birds, when a new thought came to me. A thought that suddenly cleansed the smoke from my memory. For several mornings the idea returned, shining more brightly each time. Soon it began to haunt my days as well, so that I no longer cared if I slept or ate, the notion itself nourished me.

Later I'd look back and it would seem like such a simple thing, a wide path taken with my destination in sight. But in those early moments, the thought consumed me. What if we could save wisdom, know what others knew even after they were gone? What if we found a way to put our memories outside of us? What if it were possible to have a shared language, not spoken, that we could leave behind so anyone could understand? I was tinder in the heat of these questions.

Each thought led to another. How could we do it? Maybe I didn't know all the knowledge there was for us to save. But even if I didn't know what to remember, maybe I could figure out how. How could we put our thoughts outside of ourselves? The Arn had their carvings. When you saw the little statue of the mother animal, you felt its power. You knew their soul. That worked for animals. But how would you carve a dream or a fear? Even if it were possible to leave knowledge for those who followed, how would we decide that a certain shape meant dream, another danger, another water? Now we left a mound of stones to show others how to find us. But the Arn put their stones one way, the People another.

Maybe there was another way. Maybe we could make marks. Simple marks we already had: wavy lines for water, circle for sun, crescent for moon, little peaks for mountains, the forms of animals. The Arn made those shapes, too. We could learn others. But if we had more marks, where would we make them? We left shapes on stones to praise the animals and to track the stars. Some stones were good for that, some not. Slate was smooth, but it broke. Rocks were too heavy to carry from place to place. Cutting shapes on wood took too long. And it burned.

Hides? Would hides work? I looked at the little pile of diapers I'd stored for the baby. Could I use them?

That night I dreamed a familiar dream, seeing again the row of seven peaks, the high central mountain surrounded by three smaller summits on each side. This time, though, the vision was different.

Now the mountains appeared not as I'd actually seen them, but drawn flat on a piece of hide, their shapes outlined with charcoal. My dream self watched the unmoving image. The little animal skin was an extra step between me and the dream. The hide contained my dream! That was it. I awakened with a start.

There was a way to keep our learning alive! I lay in the dark, breathing fast. I already had a surface on which to make the marks, at least as long as the hide lasted. The People had always made marks on hides for counting, but never for keeping knowledge. Maybe someday I could remember my own story with marks. Maybe Tenja's words would come back if I could put them down. Then I could explain them to the People or even the Arn. And to my baby. Maybe dreams could be remembered in daylight. Or thoughts could come through my hands that couldn't come out of my mouth. The Old Ones' tales could be told even after they'd died. They'd never be forgotten. All I needed were the marks, the marks that told a story.

And so, in the month called The Waiting, I began to search for the marks. For days I drew shapes in the dirt and scratched with charcoal on the white stone walls, trying to make the marks appear. I drew on pieces of hide. I scraped and rubbed and cut. When the sun melted the snow on the beach, I waddled outside. Then I traced each shape with a stick in the wet sand, Thur's eyes following my hands. But the marks wouldn't let me shape them. There were all kinds of lines and wedges and circles, crossing and covering each other, standing alone. But nothing was right, nothing meant anything else.

From one day to the next, I forgot every line and shape. My frustration grew. Perhaps there was a magic to marks that I didn't know. Part of me said the task I'd set myself was impossible. Wolf left no marks but his tracks. Maybe that was enough, to know one by the footprints. Or the bones. Or a carving. Maybe I should listen to that part of me. Maybe I should just quit. Why, then, was I given a hint, a possibility, a hope, if it was to mean nothing and go nowhere? Back and forth I went.

The day finally came when I decided give up the search. I'd been awake for ten nights, sleeping a little during the day, sick with weariness, and no closer. I was frustrated and as fat as a seal. Throwing aside my drawing stick, I huddled on a log and cradled my belly, hot tears stinging my eyes. The beach before me was cut by lines and shapes, as if giant birds had walked there. How had I come to this?

It was loneliness, surely, loneliness that had pushed me so far, loneliness that made me so desperate that I tried to make words with sticks. I wiped my hand across my nose. What if the People returned and found that I'd become strange? No, better to forget about the marks and return to my old ways. Once the baby came, I'd get off this beach. I'd do real work. No more dragging branches through the dirt.

And this baby, this creature inside of me who gave me no peace, what if I didn't like it? It was bad enough that my thoughts no longer obeyed me. I was powerless over my body as well. Now another presence told me, *sleep, don't sleep, lie down, get up, turn, eat, pee*. How long would it be before I got my old life back? It seemed Earthmaker was punishing me. But that made no sense. I'd always tried to do Her bidding. I'd done everything She asked. At least I'd tried.

Reaching down, I picked up a stone and hurled it against a boulder. I'd wanted so much to make shapes that meant something. But that was only so I wouldn't be alone, so the shapes would talk to me. It was a stupid idea. I could put magic marks on all the hides I ever tanned, all the stones on the shore. None would be as good as the sound of one human voice. I closed my eyes, longing for peace, willing the shapes away. I'd stop looking, at least for now. Anyway, it was work for an Old One, not someone who knew so little. I'd done my best. I'd rest for a while, maybe go fishing.

Except the jumbled lines I'd drawn for days kept running through my mind. Even with my eyes closed, they rose up in a tangled mess. I wanted them gone. I opened my eyes again and gazed wearily across the beach, a deep ache in my back. There was no good way to sit. "Be gone, lines!" I said. But they danced before me like snakes, like sticks, writhing on the shore in the very place Earthmaker had once appeared. Then something happened that made me forget all about the pain in my shoulder. I watched in fear as a slow wind arose and began to stir the maze of lines before me. The twisted, broken, useless shapes reassembled themselves on the rocks, merging into a hazy form. Even the sea responded, the green waves surging in the new wind, swelling smooth as the shoulders of women, rolling and rising as a voice came from all around me and roared above the sea.

Who is it that would make the signs? Who is it that knows the ways of things and the heart of humans? Who is it that brings speech to forests and awakens your desire for memory? Your small marks mean simple things. I bring you symbols that come alive.

As She spoke, the lines took shape. Slowly, as if moved by water, the jumbled forms cleared to be replaced by new marks, ordered and precise. On the beach a tree emerged, made of three straight lines shaped into a Y.

If you are ready, human, I will bring these marks to you and you will tell the others.

And then as suddenly as it had come, the voice was gone, the sea lay down, silence returned to the shore. Earthmaker would bring the marks to me! My misery lifted. A new fire burned in my mind.

In the days that followed, different shapes appeared each time I took the charcoal to the hide. I studied every one that I scratched down, practicing them again and again, twelve marks in all and then they stopped. Each mark meant more than one thing. Y was the mark for Earthmaker, the three-part tree that contained, fed and anchored us. V was the mark for the part of us that drew in and held life. Reversed, , it became the part of us that thrust out and challenged life. Together those two forms, the valley and the peak, ◇, became the shape for wisdom. The diamond with a dot inside, ◈, was the sign of a powerful dream. But it was also Earthmaker's Eye, the Eye that saw all things. Now that I knew marks could have two meanings, I saw my dream of the seven mountains in a new way; not just a picture of valleys and peaks, but of the People in all their differences.

Once I understood the marks, I felt a new peace, as if I'd finished a good journey. Now I could keep our story alive. When the People returned, I could teach them the shapes. I'd teach the baby! Over and over I practiced until I knew each mark perfectly. Then I drew them on two hides, one to store, one to use. Someday I'd get a full hide, just for marking. Then I could begin my story and make marks for Tenja's words, and Idra's, and all of my teachers. I'd leave that hide for those who followed us, so we'd never be forgotten. For now, I'd done all I could. I was exhausted. I put the hides away and fell asleep, sleeping all of one day and the next night.

Glad to have that task behind me, too awkward to start anything else, I was now content to sit on the beach and toss sticks to Thur. Sometimes we'd take short walks, but we never went far.

"Thur," I'd explain, when I grew tired of trudging along the shore, "I can't hunt with you until after the baby comes." I'd pat her head and she'd sigh, dropping down with a thud.

The next month was the time called Melting. Though winter hadn't been that cold, it was wetter than any I remembered. Drifts still smoothed the jagged tops of the distant mountains, which had lost none of their whiteness. The days by the sea were milder, but winter was in no hurry to leave. Snow still fell on top of the slush. I longed for spring, not just for the warmth, but the food. Bird eggs and tender leaves. Maybe I'd be too big to climb a tree for a nest, but I could get goose eggs on the shore near the salt marsh. Or plover and gull eggs from the nests nearby.

One morning I awakened with a strange new energy. I'd slept fitfully, lying awake until almost dawn, waking restless and impatient. Thur looked at me eagerly, sensing the change. I knew she wanted to hunt. The air was moist with melting and bright with birds. Spring. That's what was calling. I took a branch and swept the cave, then dragged out the sleeping hide. Wispy clouds blew along like choppy waves. Maybe I'd go fishing.

Just then Raven flew over, louder than usual, flapping his wings and cawing.

"What now?" I asked.

The bird swooped near my head. I shook out the hide and draped it over the gate. Raven called again.

"All right, I'm coming." Maybe I'd follow him for a while. I'd had no strange dreams this time, but something was exciting him. Anyway, I was eager for a change and it would be good for Thur. "Just don't go too fast."

Ducking into the cave for my knife, I returned and strolled along the beach in the direction of the bird. I knew he'd circle back when I got too far behind. Thur ran ahead. We were heading north, back toward Wolf's forest, so I wasn't surprised when Raven turned at the trees, close to the path I'd made when I was hunting rabbits. Not since that day with the lynx had I been back there. I stopped short. The hill was too high, the trail too wet. "Not today, Raven."

The bird came back and flew off, returning again and screaming, "*Wraack!*"

What if something was wrong with Wolf? I shook my head and sighed. I'd better follow the bird. I looked up at the branches, afraid I'd see a cat in every tree, drawn up and waiting. Nothing. Yet.

I let the silence seep into me, straining for the snap of twigs, gazing at the ground for tracks. The only sound was the creak of branch against branch as the wind combed the upper limbs. I'd go slowly then, and only a short way. It wouldn't do to be far from home if my tiredness returned. And I'd begun to sense a pain in my pelvis, like a stretching in my bones. I had to be careful. I climbed the incline slowly and entered the forest.

The snow in the woods was deep, but melting fast. Sunlight streamed down from a brilliant blue sky. I made my way through underbrush woven together by thorny vines, slipping and stumbling all the way. I stopped to take a breath. This was far enough. "Raven, I'm going back," I called. The bird was somewhere up ahead.

Just then another raucous caw. I glanced around. To the left a little clearing opened in a stand of pines. A roe deer stood in front of the trees, one side turned toward me, the other toward the trees. I could tell from the two broken lines in the snow behind him, that he'd pushed through a drift. Now he stood still, rib bones protruding beneath his tawny hide. He'd cleared the snow, but seemed too weak to continue. He must have heard my voice. His head was turned toward me, the glaze of hunger in his eyes, his upright horns giving a look of permanent surprise. The deer took a few feeble steps, picking his way through the slush, teetering on skinny legs.

I saw a form floating through the timber behind the deer. Wolf emerged from the trees, moving deliberately, ears back, legs sidling, circling the creature's flank. The deer jerked at this new threat, his dark muzzle trembling, his brown eyes huge. Then, like a cloud that passes quickly across the sun, something changed in the creature's eyes. Terror fled. The deer again stood motionless, too weak to fight, too weak to fear, ready. Wolf jumped for the tan haunch. Grabbing my knife, I lunged a short distance across the snow and cut the deer's neck in one fast movement. The thin body shuddered and folded, dropping silently, blood seeping into the snow.

At my feet lay a gift. Raven perched above us, waiting for his share. Wolf stood aside, watching. I laid my hand on the warm muzzle. The deer was small, but too large to carry. The meat wouldn't last long, but the hide could last a lifetime. Now I could begin to make our story. Only Earthmaker knew how much I wanted a hide. These creatures had brought me one.

I looked around. It would be dark before long. I gutted the deer and skinned it, working quickly. I wiped the blood off my hands in the snow and rolled the wet hide. I'd leave the legs for Wolf and Raven. Carry a hunk of meat and the hide in one trip. Come back for the rest tomorrow. I stood slowly. The stretching pain between my legs wasn't that bad. Maybe a little worse. I cut the rest of the carcass into six pieces and shoved them into a hollow tree.

Twilight now bathed the woods in a soft purple, but it was easy to find my way against the white background. I'd been moving around for most of a day, not fast, but farther than I'd gone for a while. I'd have to be careful, not get too tired before I got home. Hoisting the hide over my shoulder, I began my slow journey through the wet snow. As I lurched along, I noticed a new feeling in my gut, a sick feeling, like pain and fear together.

Snowflakes had begun fluttering around me, dancing gently to the ground in the windless sky. I watched them as I walked, telling myself to ignore the clenching sensation now coming from my pelvis. It was getting harder to move my legs. They seemed to be too close together. I spread my feet farther apart, keeping my legs at a wider angle, so that I swayed from side to side at each step. Like a bear. That felt better. I was glad no one could see me. Fortunately, I could make out the edge of the forest a little ways ahead. I'd be home soon.

The wind came up and the snow began falling faster, swirling around me. I walked on, heading toward that dark opening between the trees. The world was white, striped with the dim grey of tree trunks and the blur of the black dog at my feet. I could no longer see the break in the trees. Suddenly, I felt a gush of warmth over my cold legs. No, surely this was a dream. I'd awaken soon. "Magla!" I screamed. "Come and get me!" But the mad vision continued. And then a searing pain, my body being ripped apart. I screamed again. This time no words came. Suddenly, in the white whirling forest before me, I saw the glow of two golden eyes. A large shape, tall as my thighs, nudged against me and I fell.

"Wolf, is that you? Wolf, the baby! Stay with me. The baby is coming!"

I crawled to my knees and spread out the deer hide, bloody side to the ground. Then I turned and leaned back on my elbows, pulling at the hide so the baby wouldn't end up in the snow. Another wrenching in my back. An agony in my pelvis. Dying could never be this bad. Surely this was beyond dying. In between the rips of pain, my breathing told me I was still alive. Thur whimpered beside me, even staying when I screamed. The wind picked up, driving the snow faster. It swirled around us. The stretching in my pelvis became a great burning as the baby pushed its way through. I stared into the two yellow eyes before me, steadying myself in their unwavering gleam.

Above the moaning of the wind came the sound of Grandmother Idra's voice: "Wolf will sometimes cross over to our world when what is about to happen to humans is also about to happen to Wolf, and he has grown lonely thinking of it by himself."

And in the next moment I heard another sound, an infant's cry. I fumbled for my knife and cut the cord, pulling the slippery creature to

332

my chest and covering us with the hide. Through all that long night the snow fell, gently and unceasing, piling softly around us. I hugged the baby close and waited for morning, not daring to sleep. And when dawn again lit the forest, in that early half-light that follows snow, I saw that Wolf slept near me, his body pressing against the hide, his fur shielding the baby. At my movement, the grey creature stood, stretched out his front legs, and padded away. I pulled the deerskin tightly around the wakening baby, a little boy. Gazing into his dark eyes, marveling at the tufts of yellow hair about his face, I whispered, "I will name you Gokihar, 'born among wolves.'" He looked at me with serious eyes and began sucking eagerly.

Coming Home

Dawn came as in a dream, light breaking softly over a pale world. At the first hint of daybreak, I struggled to my feet in the snow, holding the baby against me to keep him warm. He was as light as a rabbit. I took a step. My legs shook, but my body felt free. What was I to do about the hide? I'd have to drag it home. I pulled a corner of it through my belt with one hand and let it hang behind me. It wasn't that heavy. I looked around. It was late for snow, surely. The budding branches hung heavily with their wet load. Wolf's paw prints led into the woods behind me. Directly ahead I could see the shore. "Come, little one," I said, "let's go home." I took another step and the snow quickly covered the tops of my boots. We made our way slowly.

The beach was blurred by fog, the shoreline quiet except for the high cry of gulls. But already the sun was burning through the clouds. The snow wouldn't be here long. Oh, I was weary. The woods now behind us, I picked my way over the rocks, clutching the baby. A fierce love rose up in me with each step. Before long, I saw a dark spot in the haze ahead of us. The entrance. I stepped to the gate and peered in, startled by the cave's familiarity. I was a new person. Hadn't the rest of the world changed as well?

In the bright days that followed, I did Gokihar's bidding, feeding him often, sleeping when he slept, favoring my sore body. He was perfect. Unusual, but perfect. His eyes were like ours, as dark as beetles, but he'd be the first yellow-haired infant the People had ever seen. And, though he wasn't heavy, he was surely longer than Fire or Zale when they were born. "You are so beautiful," I told him. "When the People see you, they'll be proud. I'll be your teacher and you'll do great things. Earthmaker will watch over you, and Wolf, and the trees." Gokihar was a quiet baby, sleeping often. When he was awake, his dark eyes slowly followed everything, approving of the world.

I usually left the cave in the afternoons, to walk a little or get some water. Gokihar came along in a pouch on my chest. He wasn't safe alone. Badgers would get through the gate, or weasels and ferrets. On sunny days, we'd sit on the shore. I'd throw sticks to Thur. The dog was glad for the time I spent with her. Most days now she was on her own.

Plovers returned to the shore soon after Gokihar's birth, their presence a sure sign of spring. Hungry from their flight, the golden-brown birds spent days filling their bellies. Thur loved to run between them, barking and chasing them back to the sea. Once they'd had enough to eat, the birds moved far down shore to build their nests, laying their tiny, speckled eggs in the gravel. Both birds and eggs were invisible from a distance, but I was sure the dog could flush them out.

I gave the plovers time to settle in. Then, when Gokihar was twenty days old, I wrapped him up, tied him to my chest, and followed Thur south along the beach. I was ready for some new food. Plover eggs were too small to satisfy my hunger, but their taste would be a welcomed change. Thur began to bark as soon as we came upon the nests.

A brown cloud rose up in a twittering of alarm. While the dog dashed after the birds, I swooped in and filled my basket.

Back home, I rested on a rock and gazed at the northern mountains. Maybe I'd grab some geese hatchlings this year, I thought. Clip their wings and raise them. Then Gokihar would always have eggs. And the People, too, when they got here.

The tops of the northerly mountains were still white, but patches of dark ground were visible on the slopes. There'd been no new snow since Gokihar's birth. Chunks of ice floated in the swollen river. I couldn't see my breath. The birds were back, the trees were budding. It wouldn't be long before the People returned, once the snow melted from their path. I smiled, thinking how surprised they'd be to see my wonderful child.

Strange that I hadn't seen a fire for several days. Maybe they were out of wood. Maybe they were already on their way! They'd be hungry when they got here. They could be starving, after a winter in the mountains. Maybe I should be getting some food, go fishing until they showed up, find some large eggs, be ready for them. We could have a celebration! Yes. That was it. A celebration! I picked up the egg basket with one hand, held Gokihar against me with the other, and headed back to the cave for my net.

And so I went to work, Gokihar on my chest, Thur at my heels. The days rushed by as I hauled in fish and fetched goose eggs. We made five trips to the salt marsh for eggs, which I stored in a hold in the back of the cave. The shore was too wet for the drying racks, so I smoked some of my fish and salted the rest. Once again the cave was filled up with supplies. I hadn't seen Raven or Wolf for days, though I was too busy to miss them. Perhaps their work here was done.

One rainy afternoon, late in the month of Melting and just before

The Time of the Reindeer Calves, I sat in the cave, nursing Gokihar and looking over my provisions. I was exhausted, but proud. We had enough to feed the People for several days, surely long enough for them to rest and recover from their winter ordeal. "We should live at the sea forever, Little One," I said, patting him on the back, "you and me and the People. The Arn, too. Just take short trips. Never be separated again."

I tried to imagine what it would be like when they returned. They'd be exhausted. They'd have to sleep. And then they'd have stories to tell. But first I'd let them know about Gokihar. Later I'd explain what I'd learned about the marks that meant things, show them how marks could tell a story. Wolf and the talking trees? No, I wouldn't mention them just yet. And Tenja. What would I say about Tenja? That she'd had a bad journey? Or maybe just that she'd gotten sick? I'd think of something when the time came. I yawned and glanced outside. The sky was still dark. It looked like it could rain all day. I lay down with Gokihar and pulled the lion pelt around us, the dog panting close by. It was a good time for a nap.

I was awakened by a strange sound. I lay silent, startled. Nothing. The rain had stopped. All I heard was my heart and the dog's raspy breathing. I waited. I heard it again. A human call! A female voice, high and young, close-by. I felt a tingle in my spine. Thur began to bark. I spoke to her sharply and stood, leaning down to cover the baby. Then I stepped to the entrance and looked over the gate.

A ragged line of humans, draped in skins and loaded with packs, limped along the beach, coming from the north. They walked like creatures unfamiliar with the world, as if they'd just come out of the ground and into the light of day. Only one of them seemed to be awake, skipping and waving at the front of the group, as quick as a bee. Birch.

"Thistle!" she yelled when she saw my head. She ran toward me.

I fumbled with the gate. At last I got it open and stepped out. "Birch?"

She threw her arms around my neck. "Thistle! I knew you'd be here. I knew it. I told them everything was fine!"

I held her shoulders as the others trudged closer, slow as pain. They dropped their packs and themselves on the shore near the entryway. I looked from one weary traveler to the next, Magla, Ochre, my brother. No one smiled. Fire's face lit up when he saw me, but he grimaced quickly. It was then that I noticed his lips, scabbed and broken. Silka shuffled by carrying a black-eyed baby, Rube beside them. The little one peered at me from beneath a fur hood, looking like a startled fawn. And there was Yarrow, a hand under Zalec's arm, circles under her eyes. I looked around at the rest of the group. Some were missing. Where was Thought Holder? Otok and Zlatar? Grandmother Sela? Had the Old Ones lagged behind?

My eyes came to rest on a small group of strangers at the back of the group. Who were these people? A few looked familiar, probably other reindeer hunters I remembered from the solstice gathering. But there were three new faces as well, two grown men and an old woman, dark like us, a little taller. They had slender, horsey faces and long teeth.

I turned at the sound of my name. "Thistle," Magla whispered, clutching my hand. She seemed to hiss when she spoke. Her mouth was also cracked and bleeding.

I grabbed her arms, which felt like sticks. "Mother, what happened?"

"You all right?" she mumbled. "Talk later. Water."

All of them now watched me intently. I filled a drinking shell and handed it to her. Rube joined me and began bringing water to the others. Next to Birch and the two horse-faced men, he seemed the strongest in the group. The two of us kept refilling the water shells until everyone had had enough to drink. The two strangers helped a little, but they didn't know how to talk very well. Carrying the water around gave me time to study the rest of the group. Almost everyone's mouth was ringed with red sores and black cracks. Only Yarrow and her family and the horse-faced people had been spared.

Yarrow was sitting on the ground between Zalec and Zale. She grabbed my hand when I approached, her eyes staring out at me from some dark place. "To find you is a miracle," she said, grasping tightly. Warmth rushed through my body at the feel of another human hand. Now my leader was back, I thought. How good it would be to follow another's direction, instead of relying on my own thoughts. I patted her hand and smiled.

Once they'd had some water, all anyone wanted to do was rest. Fortunately, they were too tired to get up and haul their packs into the cave. My things were spread all over in there. I'd have to clear it out to make room for them. And I wanted to wait until the time was right before I brought out my surprise. The People and the strangers settled in, content to rest on the shore. I decided to get things ready for them while they slept and headed for the cave.

Magla was resting near the entryway, her back against the hill, Fire on her lap, and Ochre sprawled at her feet. She looked up when I came by. "Tenja?" she asked.

"In the back of the cave," I mumbled, watching the ground. Feeling her stare, I glanced into her watery eyes. "Tenja died last summer. I buried her." Magla winced and turned her head.

Rube had spread out a hide for Silka and the baby. Silka patted the ground with a thin hand. "Sit with us," she said, smiling weakly.

I knelt beside them, marveling at the little one's luminous eyes and dark curls. "Your child is beautiful."

"We named her Narta," Silka said, "after your sister who was taken by the boars."

The child looked almost old enough to walk. She leaned against her mother, one little hand by her mouth, staring at me with ancient eyes. You'd keep no secrets from this one, I thought.

"What a beautiful name you have, little one," I said, touching the baby's forehead. "Silka, after you rest, I have a surprise for you and Narta, a great surprise. You'll see."

Silka nodded and lay down. Narta continued to stare at me, no hint of sleepiness in her bright face. Everyone else seemed exhausted. Even Birch was lying at the edge of Silka's hide, her eyes closed. Narta's eyes followed mine as I gazed at the bodies sprawled about me, the mystery of their winter months still hidden. Snores rose up from some of them, while others stretched and moaned. I counted thirty-two bodies in all, including the children. Narta and I stared at them and then again at each other. Maybe there wouldn't be a celebration right away.

I left the little girl with her mother and went to add wood to the fire. These people must have had no fruit all winter, to have sores like that on their mouths. I'd straighten out the cave and start some rose hip tea before Gokihar awakened. Thank Earthmaker he was a good sleeper. I pulled the gate open. What could I feed them? They wouldn't want the salted fish. Anyway, they'd probably lost some teeth, so they couldn't chew much. I rummaged in the back of the cave, finding dried currants and a bag of wrinkled apples. I'd add the currants to the tea. Something hot to take the edge off their hunger. We could eat eggs later.

I crept past Gokihar on my way out. He still slept peacefully, the best of babies. "You'll have a new friend, my boy," I whispered, "a little one almost as beautiful as you."

I found Thur prowling around the sleeping people, sniffing at them and their skimpy packs. When one of them moved, she took off, running for the brush. I noticed her watching us for a while. Then she disappeared. It was probably best she was gone just then, but I hoped she wouldn't stray far. By late afternoon, the sleepers were beginning to stir. I touched Birch's shoulder and she bolted awake. "Help me bring them some tea," I whispered.

We added more water and currants to the pungent brew each time the cooking bag emptied. They'd need to drink as much as they could hold for the next several days. Fortunately, I had plenty of rosehips. I was passing around deer fat for the People's swollen lips when I heard Gokihar's cry. His long nap was over. I handed the fat to Birch and stood up straight.

"Silka, Magla, Yarrow. Watch," I said, gesturing toward the woman. "Someone has come to join us!"

Several heads turned toward me. I ducked into the cave and picked up the baby, pushing the hood from his head to give him a kiss, feeling myself smiling as I carried him outside. I stood before the weary bunch. Even the horse-faced people were looking our way.

"My baby!" I announced, holding him up.

Gokihar showed no interest in the rough group, but their mouths fell open when they looked at him. I hugged him to my chest.

Silka was the first to speak. "Thistle," she said, "your baby is an Arn!"

"Of course, he's an Arn. Well, part Arn. That's what his father is."

The People stared, their mouths too sore to move. Magla glanced at Gokihar, then shook her head and shrugged, as if she was so used to change that one more hardly mattered. The others looked to her to see what they should be feeling, then followed her example, nodding politely. All except for the unfamiliar old woman with the two dark strangers. She started at Gokihar with eyes like ice, her hands curling into fists. Then she looked up at me and glared.

There'd be no stories for a while, I was sure. The travelers were too weak and sore for talking. Rube, Birch and I took care of the weary group, the two newcomer men helping a little. They were a sullen pair, I thought, though they seemed devoted to the grey-haired woman I took to be their mother. She'd stare after them when they left for the river to fish, looking worried until they returned. I made fish stew every day, tossing in fresh greens, leaving out the salt, never minding the extra work. It wouldn't be long before everyone was healed.

The fifth day after their return, I sat near the fire nursing Gokihar. Rube and the two horse-faced strangers had gone to the river with nets, while the rest of the men quietly sharpened their tools, getting ready to hunt. I'd heard none of their familiar banter this year. The women seemed grim as well. They sat close by, mending the winter tunics, their thin fingers jabbing at the hides. Perhaps this would be a good time to tell them about my year, I thought. I was eager to talk. Maybe a story would take their thoughts away from whatever was bothering them.

"I was alone for a long time," I began, glancing at Magla and Yarrow. All of a sudden, my words tumbled out. I told them of the Fish People and of Ephus's departure, of Tenja and her sickness, of the burial stones and how Ephus and Anish had found me again, how we traveled to the camp of the Arn. And the dog. The Mothers listened politely, their eyes on their stitching. Only the old stranger woman dropped her work, fixing her gaze on me as if she couldn't miss one word. I went on about the winter and the loneliness. How I'd felt Gokihar kicking inside of me, how happy I was when he came to me, what a good child . . .

"Enough," Yarrow said. "Thank you."

Gokihar had fallen asleep in my arms. I laid him beside me and turned to Yarrow. Her son sat next to her, clutching the fringe of her belt. He must be three now, I thought, remembering his sickness and the steam tent. "Now you tell me," I said to her. "Tell me about your winter."

Yarrow shook her head and frowned. She was in no hurry to relive those days.

However, Birch was eager to tell the tale. "Thistle, it was terrible," the girl began. "You should have been there. The Old Ones died . . ."

Yarrow lifted her hand to silence the girl. "Very well . . . just a little then," she said wearily. "We left the summer cave late, trying for one more hunt. But the deer had already disappeared. We were hungry before our journey started." This was more than Yarrow had said since she arrived. I studied her sunken face. Like the others, she and her family were thin. But their lips weren't cracked. Maybe she'd had enough herbs to keep them through the winter but the months had eaten away at her in other ways. "The first snow fell soon after," she added, pausing to take a breath.

Birch jumped in. "It snowed for three days," she said. "So much snow. First we hurried to get off the mountain. But the snow piled around us like cold feathers, over our knees. We had no food or fire. All the babies cried. My fingers turned white. Yarrow cut off one." Birch thrust up her right hand like a prize, showing me the clean notch where the little finger had been, now replaced by a shiny red scar. "It was dead. That's why she did it," the girl explained. "Sela lost three toes."

Yarrow shook her head and continued. "We made a snow cave the first three nights, near a dead tree. We got the tree to smolder, but it never burned. Our food was going, so we couldn't stay there. We had to continue. The fourth day was clear. The snow was too wet for walking. Ochre made a sled to carry the packs, but the hills were too steep. It just tipped. The drifts in the ravines were so deep we couldn't cross them."

Birch took up the tale. "I got buried over my head. No one could see me. It was dark. Leu dug me out. Litva was screaming." I could imagine Litva's terror. A big-boned, slow woman with soulful eyes, Litva had been lost after Reen's death, lost and desperate for another child. Birch's own mother had died at childbirth, when something inside of her tore. So Birch had grown up as everyone's child. The last few years Litva had come to think of her as her own. "The snow was too deep. We couldn't go that way," Birch added.

Yarrow laid a hand on Birch's arm. "We couldn't go straight down the mountain," the older woman explained, "so we went sideways, toward the west, descending at an angle. For five days we traveled that way, moving like crabs toward the sea. We got a little lower, but not much. The mountains curve around to the north of the sea there. We couldn't get through the valleys. Never have I seen so much snow. Praise Earthmaker the winter was no colder or we'd have surely died. We found no deer paths to lead us. It was as if the snow had covered all of life and we were walking over a burial place." She gazed to the north.

"All we ate were squirrels. Squirrels and moss. That's all we ate." Pride swelled in Birch's voice. "We found trees with holes in them and yanked out the squirrels. We ate them raw."

"Anyway," Yarrow signed and continued, "since we couldn't climb down, we looked for a cave above us. That's when we saw some tracks. The reindeer hunters from the north. They were trapped, too. But they'd found a cave. We joined them. In time, the other three found us. They live beyond the West Sea. Only to them it's the East Sea."

I looked over at the elderly woman with the long grey hair. "Can they talk like us?" I asked.

I'd heard enough about winter for now.

"You can understand them when they don't hurry. They say the same words, but in a different way. Not like the Arn." Yarrow glanced at my baby.

"The Arn learn new words very quickly," I replied. "Then they know twice as much as us."

The story ended for the day. Yarrow had said nothing about the Old Ones. And I was in no hurry to be reminded of the snow. I hadn't spoken of Tenja's inward journey or the star-horse rushing toward the sun or the trees that spoke. These people had been through enough. My words could wait.

I was tired of suffering, mine and theirs. Grimness had settled like ashes over the camp. But there was still one thing I wanted to share. Something exciting and new. A vision. Something better than this waiting. I looked at the worn faces around me. The women had taken up their work again, stitching and cutting, their rough hands struggling to make their lives normal. When could I tell them about the marks that had meanings of their own? Making words on hides would seem foolish to these people. No one here would want to speak of such things.

Except maybe one. I glanced at the old woman from the west. She reminded me of an eagle ready to pounce. She'd taken her eyes off of me and now stared toward the river, waiting forlornly for her sons. What about this woman? Could I learn anything from her? Would she care about what I had to say? I'd rarely spoken to the West People. They were a smug bunch, the three of them, keeping to themselves, whispering together as if they had some great secret.

The old woman might ignore the rest of the People, but I knew she'd been staring at Gokihar and me since the day she arrived. What was she thinking? What did she want? Would she know what I was talking about? I watched her from the corner of my eyes. Perhaps I had a clue.

Around the edge of her worn tunic someone had once stitched long rows of deer teeth. They were handsome, but now unusual. Remarkable were the painted shapes decorating the front of her garment. I'd noticed them days ago and thought they were an interesting coincidence. It was those marks that now held my gaze. Long columns of Ys, exactly the shape Earthmaker had shown me. The People didn't use that symbol. I'd never seen it until this spring. Now I knew it and so did she. Were they just three lines drawn together to her? Or did she know a different story? I wanted to find out. Everyone else was working quietly, alone in their thoughts. Gokihar was still asleep. I scooted to the Old One's side. She turned, looking at me with fierce eyes.

"How do you like our home?" I asked.

She pulled back and made a snorting sound.

Very slowly, I asked my question: "Can . . . you . . . make . . . words . . . on . . . hides?"

She jerked her head back and squinted, her lips pressed together. Unhurriedly, she lifted a weathered hand to stroke her face, black rims showing under each cracked fingernail. Her eyes told me she understood the question, but she said nothing.

"Welcome to our camp," I said. "You'll find that we're a friendly people."

I stood up. I'd been kind to the old goat. She had no reason to shun me. I'd say nothing more about the marks, I decided. Let her come to me. Anyway, it was time to give Gokihar a dry wrap. And to think about supper. The men would be home soon with the fish.

We ate our fill of sea bass and curled up early to sleep. Ochre and Zalec, the two snorers, had made their way to the entryway and laid their bedding near the fire. Magla had asked them to sleep outside, for their own good. Before long, the sound of People's breathing rose up soft as quails. Too restless to sleep, I rubbed Gokihar's back and thought about the people around me. That West Woman, what had made her so horrid? Maybe I'd never speak with her again.

Fortunately, the People seemed to be getting stronger. A few more days of the rose hip tea and their lips would mend. Maybe they wouldn't lose any more teeth. Still, they had other wounds I couldn't see, a sadness that hadn't been there before. They were regaining their health, but their hope was gone. I bent my knees and curled my body around Gokihar's sleeping form. At least I had my son.

The River of Bones

AND SO WE WAITED AS SUN SKIMMED THE SNOW from the peaks and the green rivers surged clear and cold to the sea, the azure sky filling with the urgent cries of birds. Chunks of ice still tumbled down the river and out to the open water, bobbing for a day or two before they disappeared, little white boats becoming the sea. Winter's deep snow seemed far away in the warmth of spring, a warmer season than any of us remembered. Soon we'd feast and grow plump. We'd harvest cranberries from the bog by the salt marsh, grab great dripping honey-combs from the hives, search for gooseberries in the brush.

Surely the People's bleak memories would be forgotten and their joy return once summer came. I tried to imagine life as it had been, before the winter, before the separation, when I'd wandered the countryside happily, everything at home in its place. It would be like that again before too long, only better. Now I had Gokihar.

One morning I woke up early and went outside to pee. The others were just awakening and I was the only one on the shore. There was Thur, sniffing around the fire circle! She'd been gone for a month, disappearing the first day the others returned. I called to the dog and she crept over, head down. "Where have you been, girl?" I rubbed her ears, now thick with tics. She licked my hand and looked around nervously. I ran to the cave to get her a bone.

Magla stood over her mat, combing back her hair with her fingers. "Where are you going with that?" she demanded.

I stopped and turned. "Everyone, listen. Wake up and listen. There is a dog here, a dog named Thur. No one is to hurt her. She was a gift. And she kept me alive all winter. Her flesh is not for eating. No one is to hurt that dog." I looked down at their surprised faces, startled by the new strength in my voice. Yarrow was watching me strangely. "You can give her bones if you want," I added, then hurried outside.

I'd told the People nothing yet of Wolf or Raven. The two creatures had vanished. Or perhaps the forest had lost its magic with so many of us here. I rubbed the dog's belly and scratched her ears again. I'd put some pine resin on her ears later to kill the tics. And thank Magla for the meat. Sometimes I missed the aching loneliness of the winter days, just the silence and the animals. And not having to explain things. But I never missed it for long.

Thur ran back into the brush. I decided to bring Gokihar outside to nurse him. I sat with the rock wall against my back, glad birds and glowing sun warming the shore, the baby's lips making little smacking sounds against my breast. This was my favorite time to think.

By this time, in other years, we'd have already left for the mountains. No one had even mentioned the journey this spring. And it was too late to travel now, even if the People were strong enough to go. The warmth and wetness of this strange season had melted the marshes and hatched the insects even before the young reindeer were born. We'd yet to see the first of the herds, though the lowlands were already nothing but marsh and mosquitoes.

Ochre and Rube had talked of following the beach southward, trapping the deer in the cliffs before the herds headed inland. That would give us meat for a while. Hunks of fresh reindeer flesh, red juices sizzling in the flames. That's what the People needed to bring their spirit back. Rube and Leu, the young men, were ready to head out now. The older hunters were in no hurry. Perhaps too much change had crushed their confidence. Or maybe they were waiting for something, an order or a sign. In years past, Thought Holder would have told them when it was time to go. Who'd give the order now? Surely not Rube. What kind of people would have a young man for a leader?

Gokihar stopped sucking and looked up at me with curious eyes. I held him on my shoulder and patted his back. Rube and Leu slipped out of the cave, carrying spears, walking quietly. "Where are you going?" I asked.

"South," Rube whispered with a jerk of his head. "See where the deer are."

"Does Ochre know?"

They pretended not to hear, but moved on down the shore, Rube first, Leu plodding behind. Maybe they'd decided to get the deer themselves, surprise the others into action. A plan was beginning to turn in my mind as well.

We'd be here all summer. And we'd be here all winter. The weather was changing. Maybe we'd be here forever. Maybe not. But what if we were? Why couldn't we capture a few of the young deer, keep them with us? If only until next summer. Then, if the snow came, or the men got sick, or lost, or hurt, we'd have meat. If we could keep geese, why couldn't we keep deer?

How would it work? If we got the mother deer to run, we could easily catch the babies. If the mothers didn't run, we could catch them, too. Of course, they'd have to be tied close by and watched, so the wolves didn't take them. They'd be a lot of work. Well, I'd figure that out when the time came. First we'd have to catch them.

Ochre stepped out of the shelter and picked up a spear. He'd been sharpening it for days, but hadn't used it once since he returned. Magla joined him, adding a log to the fire.

"Thanks for letting me have the meat for the dog," I said.

"Humpf," she answered.

I'd need help with my plan. Who would I ask? Birch would gladly assist. But she wasn't much larger than a fawn herself and almost as skittish. Someone else. And someone not too old. Old people always thought the reason they'd never done something was because it was impossible. Leu? Leu was kind and dependable, but he only did what others told him. I had no idea what to tell him, since I'd never put a rope on a deer before. I needed someone who could decide what to do as he was doing it. Someone like me.

A sudden shout stirred me from my daydream. It came from the south, in the direction of the river. Ochre dropped what he was doing and stood up, Magla stepping beside him. I closed the button on my tunic and got up as well, hurrying into the cave with the baby. "Here, will you watch him?" I whispered to Silka, who was still dozing with Narta. She nodded sleepily. I laid Gokihar beside her and stepped back out. As if walking in their sleep, the others had also wandered onto the beach with Ochre and Magla. "What is it?" I asked. Magla shook her head. We headed toward the river, moving faster.

Soon I could make out Leu's cries. "The deer, the deer!" he was shouting. They'd seen the deer already? Well, it was late in the season. But odd that none had passed through our camp yet. Leu stood on the riverbank with Rube, pointing toward the water. Just ahead of us was the mouth of the river, where the current coursed over a few stones and finally met the sea, ending its long journey from the mountains. Except that today the water was sloshing beyond the bank and surging into a shallow pool. Maybe more ice chunks had come to jam it? The water lapped at my feet as I stood there with the others, staring stupidly.

No, not ice. Trees, it was floating trees, their naked branches rising like the tan flesh of ancient fingers. As far upstream as I could see, the twisted branches floated, plugging the river. I moved closer. How odd that the trunks of those floating trees were bloated. They reminded me of the rockweed air bladders that bobbed in the sea after a storm. But what trees were so tan and white? What hard bark so swollen?

Then the wind changed and the first stench hit me, the smell of death wafting across the river and into my face. And then I saw them. No ice jam, no washed-out trees, no rotted vegetation, but the swollen carcasses of reindeer, countless reindeer. I stared, dumbfounded, trying to make sense of the spectacle. I heard the gasps of the people around me, saw their hands rise to cover their noses. Still I stared.

How had their bodies come to be in the water? What history was held in that swollen flesh? Surely these were not swept up trying to cross the river from the south? This stream came from the mountains, fed by melting snow. These creatures must have frozen in the high valleys last winter. Their slender legs never even took them south. They'd lain buried in the snow until now, when Spring's rushing streams dislodged them and washed them down. What was it Yarrow had said about walking over a grave? Hundreds of deer stretched upstream, far beyond any number I'd ever tried to count, like stones on the beach. The thawing bodies at the front were heaping up, held fast by the rocks on the shore, trapping the others behind them. Now they rotted in the sun, rising like a yeasty foam. Legs and antlers jutted above the mass. And as the sea rushed in, the heap of flesh surged and fell. But it didn't move.

The first carcasses were wedged in tightly against the stones at the mouth of the river. Those that came later were piling up behind, several bodies thick, locked in place by the rocks and their own bulk. Stinging black flies had found the deer before us. The beach hummed with their frenzied drone. My eyes burned. My throat caught at the stench. Like the others, I stood speechless, staring at the strange destruction. When I could look no more, I glanced around at the people.

There I saw something which shook me even more. On each gaunt face was a look of utter despair, as if the agony of the winter had finally destroyed them. Their hearts were in the dead animals, their future frozen. I had to act quickly, while any glimmer of hope remained.

"Rube, Leu, get some poles," I shouted. They looked at me, baffled, until the words settled in. Then they wandered off toward a stand of pines. "Cut the longest ones you find, " I called after them. "Ochre, help me!" Startled, the big red-headed man followed me, moving as if in a dream. Never had I given my step-father an order. Now the fierce man shuffled beside me like a child. "We have to get the deer out of here, Ochre. Now." I grabbed the spears from the two nearest hunters, the men from the west, and thrust one into Ochre's hands, pushing him along toward the river.

"Magla," I yelled over my shoulder, "cut some hides. So we can cover our faces!" I prayed for the wind to change. We moved toward the putrid water.

First we jabbed at the bodies on top of the heap, but the flesh simply fell apart and moved nowhere. So we began working on the carcasses underneath, those bobbing closest to shore. Pushing together, Ochre and I dislodged one. It splashed into the water, sinking briefly, then bobbing up and floating out to sea. We'd need help on the other side. Still, the People stood motionless, except for Birch, who'd found a small stick and was uselessly pushing at a carcass. "Birch! Find Rube and Leu!" I yelled. "Tell them to go upstream, find a place to cross. Now!" She dropped her stick and ran.

"Ochre, help me. Push them from below," I cried, ramming a spear into a mound of flesh and leaning my body against it. Nothing moved. I felt a rough hand on my elbow and looked around to see one of the newcomers. It was the one called Lugo, a lanky, raw-boned man from the west, come to take back his spear. He jerked his head as if ordering me aside and joined Ochre, jabbing at the deer. I gladly stepped away.

Shouts from the other side told me that Rube and Leu had made it across. Maybe they'd found a downed log and used it for a bridge. Maybe they'd walked over the packed carcasses. But there they were, yelling and waving on the opposite shore. They'd both found long poles. Now the four men, two on each side of the river, began to work together, shoulders down, backs low, groaning and pressing, loosening the fleshy dam, pushing it toward the sea.

Magla had returned with her little strips of hide. Seeing her, Yarrow came to life as well. Soon everyone was covering their faces, except the two on the other side. Four more hunters joined the men at the river and then everyone was working, some pushing, some shouting. Even the children joined, clapping and running each time another body was shoved out to sea. The sun grew higher and the flies louder. But still we worked, bending, shoving, yelling, sweating. Magla was the first to realize we had no drinking water. She sent Birch and Litva upstream, telling them to keep going until they found clean water for the bladder bags.

For once I was glad for Silka's laziness. I knew she'd never bother to come down and see what was taking us so long. Gokihar would be safe with her, never near this mess. The mound was slowly subsiding. The carcasses kept coming, but the dam of flesh had been broken. By nightfall the river ran unhindered. The corpses bobbed freely and floated out to sea, feeding the happy fish.

Once again, purple shadows gathered on the shore and the sea turned black, the last glimmer of light throwing sparks on the waves. The river was back in its channel, the slippery bank gouged by our footprints. Either the stench was gone or it had become part of us. We trudged home, covered with mud. I saw the West Man just in front of me and walked quickly to catch up. "Ah, Lugo . . . thank . . . you," I said.

He turned to me. Even in the moonlight, I could see the smirk on his face. "You . . . are . . . welcome," he replied.

Silka must have been too busy to tend the fire. Nothing remained but coals. Everyone dropped down by the fire circle, anyway, ready to sleep. That was not to be. Yarrow stepped to the front of the group. Something of her old strength was visible in her stance. I was glad to hear her old voice.

"Eat nothing tonight and drink no water," she said, "except that from Litva's water bags." She looked slowly from one tired face to the next. "Take those scarves, those tunics, all the boots. Pile them away from camp. None are to come inside. Death is inside of them. In the morning, Magla and I will hang the clothing on stones. There it will stay, in the sun and rain, until the stench is washed from it. The boots will all be buried and never used again."

A sharp protest went up from the crowd. It was the other West man, the one I took to be Lugo's brother. "Waste of good boots," he muttered.

"Shut up, son," growled an elderly female voice.

We did as Yarrow ordered, pulling off our clothing, tossing them in a heap downwind from the cave, then scrambling back naked. I grabbed Ochre's lion pelt before he could get to it and quickly sat down at the fire circle, Gokihar in my lap. The others wrapped themselves in pelts or bedding or our few extra tunics. Then we huddled by the fire, shy as children, glancing at each other and laughing nervously.

"Tomorrow," Yarrow continued, "we'll weave tunics from grass. We'll wear them until our old ones are ready or we hunt again."

Grass clothes! Never had we worn grass clothing. Grass was for mats. Things that had never happened before were continuing to happen now. What did it mean? Was it good or bad? No one had said a word. I glanced around, wondering what the others were thinking. Everyone sat looking up at Yarrow, hungrily feeding on her words. All except the man called Lugo. He was staring at me with a hunger of his own. I looked away quickly. The night was warm, but I was shivering under the lion pelt.

"For now," Yarrow continued, "we will thank Earthmaker, who teaches us to live with Change. And we will thank Thistle, who woke us from our dreaming." Me? She reached down and picked up a hand drum.

Ochre began the drumming, since he was now the oldest man. At first the sound was weak, but he gathered power, remembering, and the beat became strong and true. I glanced around again. The People were peering out from their small selves, cautiously, and looking into the huge night. Our voices began timidly, reaching for the old songs, scratchy from lack of praise. But soon we found our level and were made whole again.

The Capture

YARROW'S CAUTION HAD WORKED. No one became sick from the dead deer. The shock of that terrible day had awakened everyone. I sensed a new impatience now, a need to make up for lost time. Little annoyances had begun to occur.

For one thing, the cave was crowded. It had been cramped when it was just our familiar group. Now there were more than thirty of us, ten of them strangers. And we needed to have somewhere to store the food and everyone's belongings. Every cough and runny nose was shared by all. When one of us crawled out at night to pee, someone else awakened. Tempers were growing short. This place was never meant to be a summer camp, only a winter shelter.

The Mothers and the men had talked for several nights, finally deciding that the newcomers would build houses on the shore. I'd seen the dwelling places of the other reindeer hunters when we'd gone to the solstice gatherings. Moving to the beach would be no hardship for them. They were used to living outside. At least, it seemed like living outside to me.

There were seven of the northern reindeer hunters with us. Five adults, three men and two women all in their prime, probably none of them over thirty. And a boy and a girl the same age as Fire, eight or so. The group seemed happy to get away and set to work immediately. They dug a circle of postholes on a level spot just north of the cave. Then the women scooped out a fire hole and surrounded it with stones while the men went to work cutting poles. They dragged a dozen long, supple pine logs to the beach. The children helped them strip the branches.

The men anchored the longest pole in two post holes on opposite sides of the circle, bending it into a high curve in the middle. They arched and anchored the other poles in the same fashion. The final result was a large round tent, able to accomodate several families, like the Arn's. But, unlike the structures the Arn made, this tent looked more like a circle than a long tube. The women bound the poles where they crossed and made a mantle of sticks to drape over the structure. They'd cook outside in the summer. In the winter, Magla explained, they replaced the stick covering with hides and cooked inside.

It was hard to tell how the three West People felt about moving. Since they'd continued to keep to themselves, I figured they didn't mind. Their house was the strange one, unlike anything I'd ever seen. It was shaped like a little two-sided hill, sloping at one end. The two men did the work, while the woman stood with her arms crossed, watching. No one ever spoke her name, but I'd come to think of her as Wild Eyes and said it to myself when we passed.

Despite their crankiness, or maybe because of it, I was curious about the strangers. Since I saw nothing special about them, I felt no need to honor the line they'd drawn between us. One afternoon, shortly after they'd begun their work, I left Gokihar with Silka and went to the shore to watch them. I would have helped if they'd asked, but they rarely spoke to me, so I didn't talk to them.

Lugo was a good worker. His brother, the younger and quieter of the two, followed the older man's orders. They'd already chopped down some white pines and dragged them to the shore. I saw two stout trunks, both forked at the top, each taller than a man and almost as thick. A large pile of thinner logs lay near by. I looked on as the men dug two post holes three man-lengths apart. Then they dragged one of the large logs over and stood it in a hole.

The younger man stepped away and Lugo steadied the log by himself. I was surprised at his strength. Maybe they'd just balanced it well. His brother rolled four stones into the hole, securing the log at the base. They did the same with the other trunk. Two sturdy posts with forked tops now stood on the beach. I was too curious to sit silently any longer. I walked toward Lugo, who'd picked up one end of a long, thin pole.

"What next?" I asked the tight-lipped man.

"Hold this," he replied, placing the tip of the pole in my hand.

His brother picked up the other end and walked toward one of the standing trunks, forcing me to follow or drop the pole. I followed. He hoisted up the pole and dropped it neatly into the fork of the log.

"Your turn," Lugo said.

I approached the other log, keeping my eyes on the cleft in the trunk. Once I was under it, I lifted the pole above my head, reaching as high as possible. But the fork in the log was another arm-length above my reach. How would I get it in? I glanced over my shoulder at Lugo's brother, who shrugged and made no move to help me. Lugo stood to the side with his arms crossed, waiting, seeming to find humor in my predicament. I felt my face getting hot.

It should have been easy enough to ask for help, but I couldn't do it. Instead, I took three steps backwards, continuing to balance the pole above my head. With each step, the end of the wobbling stick jutted up just a little higher. On the fourth step, I took aim and gave it a slight heave. It shot up and dropped down, slipping into the cleft with a solid clunk. I wiped my hands on my tunic. "There," I said. "It's ready."

Lugo raised his eyebrows, but said nothing. I watched from the side as the two of them leaned the shorter sticks at an angle against the suspended pole and secured them on the ground with stones. Then Wild Eyes did her part, covering the sticks with woven reeds. The result was a long, thatched triangle, open at both ends.

By then it was time to feed Gokihar, so I returned to the cave. That night the West people moved to their new shelter, the men with their skimpy packs, Wild Eyes with a bulging bag I'd never seen her open. Silka was curious about the place, so we took the babies and walked by at dusk. Lugo was adding a cobbled entryway to one end. He looked up and waved. The place was nice and airy. They'd have plenty of room. Unless they planned on someone joining them.

The cave was certainly roomier. I moved my bedding closer to the front that night, wanting more fresh air. The People had liked my gate. We continued to use it in the night, letting it hang open in the day. When I lay down with Gokihar, I couldn't help but notice the West people's fire through the gaps in the gate. What would it be like, I wondered, sleeping in a house like that? I was getting restless, wanting some kind of change. Once again I thought about the reindeer.

I'd have to act quickly if we were to have a herd of our own. Rube was convinced that some of the reindeer had made it back last fall, despite all the carcasses we'd seen floating out to sea. He thought they were still in the south, ready to migrate, but slowed down by the new marshes and the bugs. Ochre had his doubts, but everyone wanted to believe it was possible. We were eager for meat, having had only rabbits and squirrels all spring. And seeing the deer would somehow put things right again. Rube and Leu had left yesterday, crossing the river and heading south. If they found any trace of the deer, they'd let us know and we'd leave right away to hunt. And once we started bringing in meat, we'd be too busy for anything else. I didn't have much time. But it would be foolish to divulge my plan.

"Yarrow," I said early the next morning, "the People are still a little crowded. Perhaps we need more room as well."

"What are you thinking?" she asked cautiously. Yarrow no longer treated me like a child. Still, she was not a woman who welcomed change for its own sake.

"We could dig out more of the sponge stone. I'd do the work. Birch and I. Maybe make a little shelter next to this one, a place to sit when it's hot. A place to keep things." Like deer.

"I suppose. See what Magla says."

My mother was carrying wood from the back of the cave. I waited until Yarrow went out, then joined her.

"Magla, Yarrow says we can dig out a little shelter next to this one. We could keep wood there. Easier to carry. Fire and Zale can help me scrape the stone. Birch, too."

"There's no time. We're going south soon. For the deer."

"I know. That's why we have to start now."

"All right. Go ahead," she said with a shrug.

So while the others waited for word of the deer, I put the three younger ones to work. We started the digging four man-lengths south of the cave, scraping at the soft stone with antlers, hauling the chips and powder away. Whenever I wasn't with the baby, I worked beside them, telling them only a little about my plan. "It will be a great surprise. You'll see. And the three of you will be almost the first to know," I said. "Be sure to dig a water trough."

We scraped that day and then all the next. I stopped to observe our progress. One fawn could stand inside, I thought, if it never turned around. It was obvious the deer would be here before their pen was ready. I'd have to stay awake with them the first few nights. But, if I still wasn't sure how we'd take care of them, I had figured out who would help me catch them. I'd tell him, once I came up with the right words.

Late on the third afternoon of scraping, Rube ran into camp. "We found them!" he yelled. He stood, panting, as Silka brought him water. I dropped my antler and hurried over. He'd done it! He'd seen the deer. I wasn't surprised. I'd been aware of a new steadiness in Rube, ever since he'd become a father. He cared about the future. And he wasn't afraid of change. Ochre and the other men gathered around him. The women dropped their work. Once he'd caught his breath, Rube continued. "Not that many," he said, standing taller with so many eyes on him. The shadowy growth of beard made him look older. "But those that made it back ate well. They're fat. Moving slow."

"And the young? Are there many young ones?" I asked.

"As many as the fingers on four hands," Rube replied.

"Twenty," said Birch, who'd begged me to teach her numbers. "That's twenty deer."

Rube ignored her. "They should pass near here tomorrow, maybe the next day," he added confidently.

A murmur rose up from the group. Fresh meat. People nodded and smiled. In a little while, Leu trudged into camp. Having nothing to add to the story, he asked for something to eat. Once Rube has captured the deer, I thought, Leu will be the man to watch them.

All that evening the men sat together, honing their spears and talking, everyone with a story to tell. I was glad to see them happy. It would be their first real hunt together, the newcomers and the People. They'd need to trust each other. Even the West People were talking. Lugo, laughing about something, slapped his knee with a hand the size of a beaver tail. It was good to have another strong hunter.

As I rested by the fire, stroking Gokihar's back and watching the men's happy faces, I thought of Anish. Would he ever see his son? Gokihar might never come to know him. The baby had been with me less than two months, but it seemed like he'd always been part of my life. I was sorry Anish couldn't share that feeling, sorry Gokihar wouldn't know the man he so resembled. Sadness began creeping over me, but I pushed it back. This was no time to cry. We'd be leaving at first light. And I had something to take care of first.

I awakened while it was still dark and bundled Gokihar into his carrying pack. Silka was staying behind to take care of Narta and Zale. She'd wanted me and Gokihar to remain as well. But I couldn't miss this trip and I wouldn't go without him. Anyway, he was easy to carry. I stepped outside, waiting in the shadows for the camp to come alive, hoping to catch Rube alone.

One by one, the People awakened and walked into the trees to relieve themselves. Before long, Rube came out, rubbing his eyes. I nodded. When he returned, I grabbed his arm and whispered, "We need to talk."

"What?" he growled, not yet awake.

I motioned him away from the entrance and into the shadows. "I need your help," I said. He looked back toward the cave. "I have a plan," I continued. "But I can't do it alone. You're the only one I can tell. The others wouldn't understand. They're afraid of change. But not you."

I had his attention. I knew two things about Rube that not everyone realized. First, he was hungry for praise. The second thing was just as powerful. Though Rube and I had never been close, we had both loved Reen. Some dark bond had linked us ever since his death. Perhaps Rube blamed himself for the fall. I didn't know. Since that day, he'd rarely looked me in the eye. But he always listened when I spoke. Now he waited for me to continue.

"You know Change is upon us and the ways of the animals are shifting," I said.

He nodded.

"Change has taken the Old Ones and left the Arn homeless in a new land. Change has kept us from our summer mountain and caused us to eat squirrels. We must try new things while we still have choices."

He nodded again. My words were reasonable.

"I have watched you with Narta, seen your devotion. You are a fine father, a strong man."

He beamed.

Seeing that I had his interest, I added the line I'd saved for last. "Those who would protect their children must be ready for change." Then I explained my idea.

He frowned. "You think we can do this? Keep deer?"

"We can try."

Rube scratched his head. Maybe he needed some time to think. We walked back to the shelter where everyone was now gathering their things. Ochre and Yarrow spoke for a moment, then Ochre took the lead. Yarrow would be walking at the back with Zalec, who needed her beside him. Ochre gestured for Rube to join him and the young man ran to the front of the group. I hoped he wouldn't forget our talk.

We set out, trudging south until midmorning. The beach was

strewn with the empty shells, tossed up by some winter storm. Dark-winged terns soared above us. Had it only been a year since I'd hiked this shore with Tenja? Beneath the excitement of the journey, I was worried. What if Rube refused? What if he went along with my plan and got hurt?

"I'm bringing this for Zale!" I heard my brother's voice and glanced down. He'd been walking beside me. He'd picked up a long, curved whelk shell, bigger than the ones at home.

"Leave it. We're coming back this way."

It would do no good to worry. I might not have a chance to speak with Rube again before we came upon the herd. I could do nothing to change things now. In the middle of the day, we came to a place where a cliff jutted out to sea, leaving a narrow strand of land between the precipice and the waves. There the deep water surged around sharp stones before it broke into white spray. Rube turned to speak to Ochre. They were too far ahead and the waves too noisy for me to hear what they said. Ochre gestured for us to stop.

He motioned us closer, speaking loudly so we could hear him over the surf. "Listen. The deer have to cross this place. Three men will go ahead. Drive them from behind. Block their retreat. The rest of us will climb and wait." It sounded like a good plan. "Rube," the red-haired man continued, "take two men and go ahead."

Rube motioned to Lugo and his brother. The three of them left, slipping around the base of the cliff and moving south. Why Lugo? He seemed to get along well enough with the hunters. But I thought of him as distant and strong-willed. I hoped he wouldn't ruin my plan.

So the rest of us were to wait at the top of the cliff. It wouldn't be an easy climb. The bluff was made of sandstone and crumbled easily. We waited while Ochre found a route, then followed him up. Zalec had to stay below since his bad leg was too stiff for climbing. Yarrow remained with him, finding a fold in the rock face that offered some protection.

It didn't take us long to reach the top. There we came upon a grassy expanse that sloped to the edge of the bluff. Over time the sea had eaten away the underbelly of the ledge, dislodging trees and leaving the roots upended. We dropped our packs and rested, watching the water as a brisk breeze chopped it into little waves. After a while, Ochre gave a command and everyone went to look for stones, rolling them carefully to the edge of the cliff.

By now the sun was high and our bellies growled. My brother crawled close to the ledge each time Magla turned her back, wanting to be the first to see the deer. Time dragged. At last, the rattle of pebbles below told us that something was moving, moving fast. Deer would run in a place like this only if they were being chased. Rube had found them! I peered over the ledge.

The lead deer was hurtling along the rocky beach, a fine creature with sweeping antlers and flaring nostrils. The others ran behind him three-abreast. At the escarpment, he lurched to a stop. Trapped. The others fanned out. Then, one by one, following his lead, they began to pick their way through the narrow strip, trying for a foothold between the cliff and the sea. Stretched out in single-file, they were each a simple target.

We waited for Ochre's order. He raised his hand and, as he dropped it, we let go with a barrage of stones. From the beach came thuds and snorts and cries. I looked over the edge again. The lead deer had crossed the little neck of land. But the next three creatures had fallen. Those from behind kept coming. But they were soon blocked, trapped by the carnage before them and the crashing of the sea. Unable to advance, those toward the front pawed the ground and threw back their heads. Still more came.

Ochre heaved another stone. It rolled off the ledge and hit a fourth deer. Its legs folded and the animal tumbled to the ground. Then, in the midst of the chaos, the big male returned for his herd. Only this time, he rounded the shore by sea, his powerful neck bobbing above the waves, his front legs kicking wildly below. Seeing a way out, the remaining deer plunged into the water as well. Reindeer were good swimmers, but never had I known them to jump into the surf. We watched in amazement as the entire herd took to the sea.

Knocked back to shore by the waves and caught upon the rocks, the deer struggled free and kept on, gradually making their way around the promontory. I counted thirty adults and about half as many babies, the terrified little ones kicking madly during their short plunge. We slid down the cliffside. Four large deer lay dying at our feet. Yes. They would keep us for a while.

The two West men shuffled up the beach from behind, looking pleased with themselves. We shouted and waved. Maybe they weren't so bad, after all. Not as bad as their mother. There were enough of us present to carry the deer home and butcher them there, which was good, since we had no room here. Magla began calling out orders and we strung up the carcasses, tying the legs together, using spears for poles. I kept glancing south. Rube should have been back by now.

"What are you waiting for?" asked Yarrow, speaking to my back.

I jumped. "Maybe some more deer coming?" I answered.

She shook her head.

I glanced at Magla. She had plenty of help with the animals. Her hands were free. I hurried over to her. "Can you take Gokihar?" I asked, handing her the baby. "Go on without me. I'll catch up." I turned before she could reply, heading south.

I followed along the rocky path the deer had just traveled. Fresh hoof marks gouged the damp sand. At last I saw Rube in the distance, moving slowly, jerkily, along the beach. Was he dragging something? Then I spotted them, three deer, a mother and two young. I ran up to him. The deer bolted. But Rube had managed to tie them to three short leashes. He held tight, cursing and tugging. The frightened animals pulled against him, their legs splayed and their heads low. I'd never seen him look so angry.

"Rube! You did it, you did!" I grabbed the female's rope. Rube had fashioned a sort of anchor for her, a stone tied to one leg. She could drag it easily enough, but if she got away, she wouldn't go far. "You got them! You did it. You'll feel better soon."

I dropped into place behind Rube, who led the two young deer. The wide-eyed mother followed along easily enough, moving backward almost as often as she advanced, but trying to stay close to the babies. One of them must be hers, I thought, or I couldn't have pulled her at all. "Go, deer," I ordered. This would take some practice. We finally rounded the bend where the hunt had taken place. I was sorry to see that the People hadn't left yet.

They looked on as we approached, their mouths hanging open. They'd want an explanation before I had a chance to make one up. Unfortunately, Lugo was at the rear of the group with his brother. He stared at Rube and then me and back at Rube, again crossing his arms over his chest. "You people make the deer walk home before you eat them?" he asked.

Rube looked at me from the corner of his eyes, then down at the bleating babies.

"I asked him to get them," I said. "You'll see." They could just wait for more words from me.

"Now that Thistle and Rube have decided to join us, we can leave," said Yarrow.

Ochre shook his head and walked to the front. The deer carcasses were lifted and we fell into place, Rube and I remaining at the back. The journey to the camp was a long one, especially for Rube and me. Rube's two animals stopped often to raise their little muzzles and whimper. I plodded behind with the female, who was slowly settling down. The animals drank at the river near home and one baby nursed. The other stood alone and crying. We'd have to find a way to feed him. I was too tired to think of that yet.

We arrived home just before dusk. Everyone was lined up to watch as we trudged into camp. A few snickered. Most looked confused. I'd have to talk fast or these animals would soon be dead.

"Stop here," I whispered to Rube. I pulled myself up as tall as possible, nodded at the curious group, and gestured to the skittish beasts. "Thank Earthmaker for these animals," I said. "Earthmaker and Rube. As Yarrow told us, Earthmaker teaches us how to live with Change. If the People learn to keep deer with them, they will never starve."

The air was heavy with silence. People glanced at each other and back to the deer. I looked at Yarrow, who was smiling slightly. "Well spoken," she said. "Now everyone get back to work." They dispersed. The deer were safe, at least for a while. Birch ran up to the fawns and began stroking their noses. They tried to suck her fingers, eager to nurse. I hadn't fed Gokihar since midday. My own breasts were so swollen it hurt to walk. He'd be ravenous.

Rube and I pulled the deer over to the little dugout and tied them. "Birch, watch them," I said. "See if Leu will help." Holding my arms across my chest, I ran to find Gokihar, falling asleep as I fed him.

369

Several times that night I awakened to the whimper of the motherless deer. The People would never stand for that. I got up at dawn, put Gokihar in his carrying bag, and hurried outside. Birch had made a fire by the deer pen. She and Leu were sleeping there peacefully. The deer looked up at me miserably. "Birch," I said, shaking her shoulder. "Get up! Help me. We have to take the deer to grass. Bring a spear."

We left Leu sleeping and started out, leading our small herd. This time the mother went first. Still dragging her stone, she made her slow way to the river, then up the hill, and to the meadow. Birch pranced along with the young ones, who willingly followed the doe's broad hooves.

We staked the female in a grassy patch and let her baby nurse. The motherless deer was growing weak. Time and again he stepped toward the female, seeking a swollen udder, only to be kicked away by her free hind leg. Too young to graze, he stood on trembling legs, staring at the doe and her plump fawn. Birch tried feeding him broth from a bladder bag. He wiggled his muzzle in a sucking motion, but the liquid just ran down his neck. I watched helplessly. His suffering was my fault. We had perhaps one day to learn to feed him.

"Will he starve?" Birch asked, fighting back tears.

Gokihar's angry wail surprised me before I could reply. For a moment I'd forgotten he was with us. As long as we were moving, he slept soundly, awakening soon after we stopped. At the sound of his cry, my milk surged. My breasts began to ache. "Yes, yes, I'm coming," I said. I sat in the tall grass and opened the button on my tunic. His fists trembled in anticipation.

Birch was waiting for an answer. "Will the fawn starve?" she asked again.

"No. He won't starve. We'll find a way to make the mother feed him." I looked away from Birch's tight, little face and tried to ignore

370

the fawn's bleak cries. I had to think of something. Gokihar's wail soon gave way to a smacking sound. The pain in my breasts began to ease. An idea was forming. "Listen, Birch, here's what we'll do: keep the other baby away from her mother. When she tries to nurse, take her home."

She nodded. "Why?"

"Just do it. I want to try something."

We waited as the sun climbed higher, our flesh as warm as drying apples, the mother deer grazing while her baby rested. It would do no good to separate them yet. Meanwhile, the orphan cried weakly. In midmorning, the plump baby stood and again stepped toward her mother. That was the moment I'd been waiting for.

"Get the fawn, Birch. Don't let her nurse. Take her back now."

The girl jumped up and grabbed the leash, pulling the young one away from the mother. The fawn took a few steps and began to wail. The frantic doe pawed the ground, edging forward, dragging the stone behind her, urgent for her baby. "Wait!" I yelled. "Get another stone. We'll have to tie her front leg." I didn't have any more rope, so I cut a long strip from the bottom of my tunic. Eager to please, Birch found a boulder larger than her head and rolled it over. "Well, that should do it," I said. The fate of that deer was either with us or the wolves. Birch began to drag the young one away.

I looked around at the lush meadow. It was late morning, too late for predators. Still, there was no protection here. "Take the spear with you, Birch," I said. "You might need it going back."

"Are you sure?"

"I'm sure. Just send someone to stay with us. Don't leave Gokihar and me alone for long."

I waved as Birch left with the bawling fawn, watched until they disappeared over the hillside. Earthmaker, keep her safe, I prayed. And help her remember to send someone. I didn't like being here on my own. And I'd never get all of us home by myself—me, Gokihar, and the two deer. I scanned the dark trees that surrounded the meadow. Then the meadow itself, quiet except for the buzzing of grasshoppers. The mother deer hadn't started browsing. Instead she stood tensely, looking to the west where she'd last seen her baby. The other fawn lay hidden in the grass, his legs folded under him, gazing at her back. I glanced from side to side, listening, Gokihar asleep in my lap. This was no good. Even now some creature could be padding softly through the grass, sniffing, waiting, ready to pounce. I couldn't sit here with a baby, no weapon, and two captive deer.

Laying Gokihar on my shoulder, I crept to the edge of the forest and crouched down behind a bush. The deer weren't going anywhere. Anyway, my plan for them would work better the longer we waited. And it would go easier with another person's help. Protecting Gokihar was more urgent than saving the deer. No, we'd be fine. Birch would send someone before too long. Then everything would work out. I scooted back, letting the branches cover us, waiting.

In a little while I heard a whistle. A jarring sound, like the call of a giant crow. I looked around, unable to figure out its location. The annoying noise grew nearer. It was coming from the meadow. Peering around a branch, I saw the tall shape of a man in the distance, too far away to recognize, but carrying a spear. He was moving toward the deer. Then he walked past them and came closer, stopping just beyond the trees. Again the shrill whistle. This was whom Birch had found to replace her? The smirking newcomer who'd already laughed at my deer?

The Taming

"Over here!" I shouted, standing and waving.

Lugo turned and walked toward me. "Why are you hiding?" he yelled.

"I thought I heard a giant buzzard," I replied as I walked into the clearing. I regretted my answer right away. After all, he'd come a long way. "Birch asked you to come for us?" I asked, trying to sound more polite than surprised.

"The others were butchering. Anyway, I wanted to see what had become of the captive deer." He nodded toward the doe. "I see you've now tied two stones to that one. Will your men try to spear it soon?"

"Our men can spear any deer. We're doing something much harder; keeping them alive."

"Why?" he asked, sounding genuinely curious.

I waited before I answered, studying his face, not wanting to risk more ridicule. He had the dark skin of someone long in the sun. Like his brother, he wore his hair short, letting it fall in a smooth, brown line just below his ears. Little lines edged away from his eyes.

"Change is coming," I mumbled. "Perhaps the old ways won't

work forever."

He stared at me as I spoke, the crease between his eyes deepening. I could feel myself growing warm under his gaze. Just then the fawn let out a forlorn cry. The  little creature had pulled itself up on wobbly legs. It took a step toward the female.

"Here," I said to the startled man, "hold my boy. I'll show you what I mean."

Handing over Gokihar, I stepped toward the doe. Half a day had passed since she'd last fed her baby. Her udders were bulging. Surely she ached like I did when my baby went too long between feedings. I hoped my hunch was right. My face burned at the thought of that haughty man laughing at me again. I grabbed the leash. The doe balked, but couldn't move. It was time to try my plan.

Bracing my legs and digging my toes into the ground, I held the rope taut, waiting. I turned my head to the side to look at the fawn. The young one was moving closer to the female, looking hopeful but unsure. The doe raised her head and edged back, her brown eyes wide. Closer the baby came, nudging against her flank. She rocked back and forth, stomping her free feet, but anchored to that spot. The fawn lifted its head. At the touch of that strange muzzle, the doe lurched back. But there was no escape. Milk gushed from her swollen teat and the baby grabbed on, sucking hard. I relaxed my hold on the rope and stood quietly, while the fawn continued to feed.

Then came the mocking voice from behind. "So, you've taught a doe to feed a young one. Where I come from, they already know."

"And do they know how to feed an orphan?" I asked, glancing

back at his smiling face.

He raised his eyebrows again, but made no other reply. I returned to the deer, holding the leash while the little one fed, giving the fawn all the time he needed. I could feel the West man's eyes on my back. After a while the doe slackened her tense body. When the fawn had finally had enough, it moved away, lying down in the tall grass. I dropped the rope and turned.

"I'll take my baby now," I said, looking up into Lugo's tan face.

He ignored my words, lifting Gokihar higher on his shoulder. "My mother says this child has had no Welcoming," he said, his gaze too familiar. "She says that's because you've been too long alone."

My eyes darted between Lugo and the sleeping boy. I shivered, feeling as if ice made its way down my back. Then I pulled myself taller, meeting his dark eyes. This man had no power over me. "A Welcoming? I don't know what you're talking about. My People don't have such things." I stepped closer and reached up, ready to take my baby. The afternoon sun shone over Lugo's back, blinding me for a moment. I gathered up Gokihar and stepped back, startled by the hand that brushed against my breast.

Lugo seemed not to notice. "If she says there is to be a Welcoming, there will be one."

"How would she know?" I snapped, confused by the pleasure spreading across my body.

"She knows many things, especially about what is to come."

"Your mother has strong opinions. For one who knows little about us." It was time to go. Past time. Gokihar had awakened and was starting to fuss. I'd have to walk fast. Fast and alone. Maybe my boy would go back to sleep. But first I had to take care of the deer. I gestured toward the doe, avoiding Lugo's face. "Untie the large stone. Please. If you lead the doe, the fawn will follow."

I started for home, not looking back. Lugo would surely see that I didn't want him with us. But before long, he caught up, his long legs striding easily through the grass, both deer moving behind him. "And you, the one they call Thistle, whom do you follow?"

No man from the People would speak in such a challenging manner. "I prefer to make my own way," I replied. "Why are you running those deer?"

"We can slow down if you like," he said.

I slackened my pace, trudging on in an uncomfortable silence, farther from home than I'd realized. When the quiet grew too heavy, I offered a few words of conversation. "Maybe I'll remove the other stone in a day or so, see if she runs." Lugo said nothing. I kept walking, holding Gokihar tightly, my eyes fixed straight ahead.

The smell of roasting venison greeted us as we approached the beach. Birch must have been waiting. She called my name and came dashing across the rocks. I hurried toward her, Gokihar bouncing on my chest. "Birch," I cried, my voice sounding louder than usual, "the fawn drank milk! I told you. Everything's fine!"

"We're having a feast!" she exclaimed. "Tomorrow! And after that, a special time. The old woman talked to your mother. She said your baby was brought by wolves! But the ceremony will make us safe!"

Lugo and the deer came up behind us. Birch rubbed the surprised fawn's muzzle and took the leash from the man, leading both animals toward the pen. Lugo watched her go, then looked down at me, speaking slowly. "It is as I told you. My mother knows the future and the things that happen there."

"We'll see about that." I took Gokihar to the cave, wanting nothing more than to sit in the dark alone. I leaned against the cool wall. It had been a long day, but I was more angry than tired. It seemed that my baby and I had been talked about behind my back. Plans had been made for us by strangers. "We have secrets, now," I whispered to Gokihar, to whom I told most things. His dark eyes followed me. "I have secrets from the People. They have secrets from me. And some old goat has come to us with secrets of her own." As I fed him, I tried to think back to when the furtiveness had begun.

Had it always been with us? Did I just sense it now that I was older? No, it wasn't just a difference in me. It was more than that. Magla and Yarrow may have never been lighthearted, but at one time they'd been content. Had it started with the terrible winter? No. Before that. Even before Zalec's injury. Before my last gathering three summers ago.

An image came to me of Tenja. Tenja crying in the woods. Ephus trying to comfort her. And me, making her take me with her to the sea. With that picture, something fell into place. I'd been a child then. There were things I hadn't known. But the unspoken words, the hushed conversations, the veiled glances, those had come just before that time. Just before the last gathering. Before the wolf stopped Tenja in her path and stared her down. Around the time that Tenja and Thought Holder shared their dream and heard messages of Change. That was when the fear began.

And the fear itself had made us different. Tenja hadn't trusted us to live with it. She'd kept it to herself, protecting us, trying to understand it fully before she spoke. But she'd died trying to learn more about it. She'd died before she told the People anything. Her death had forced it down farther, hidden it deeper. But it hadn't disappeared.

I'd done no better. Like Tenja, I'd tried to protect the People, waiting until they were stronger to tell them her messages. And I'd tried to protect myself, saying nothing of Earthmaker's gifts, keeping to myself the shapes that meant things, the language of trees, the fellowship of creatures, afraid of my people's derision. And afraid of what it might mean for my son. What if my silence had made them more suspicious? Left them open to lies about Gokihar? The People's minds were hungry. Only answers could nourish them. Wrong answers were more tempting than no answers at all.

A stranger had come among us who might give us wrong answers, fill in the gaps with her fantasies, with her lies about my son. Fright could hurt us as much as change if it made us distrust each other and if it opened our minds to the ravings of a mad woman. It was time for the secrets to be spoken. I'd give them the truth, as much as I knew it. They'd have to grow to accept it. I'd have to trust them enough for that. And I'd demand the truth from them. Whatever happened, I wouldn't allow them to blame Gokihar for their trouble.

I changed the baby's wrap and took him outside. Yarrow and Magla were cleaning the butchering area, draping the last of the venison on drying racks. I stepped up beside them. "I have yet to find out what happened to the Old Ones," I said. "Thought Holder, Zlatar, Otok, Sela."

"Not now, Thistle." Yarrow wiped her arm across her forehead, her hands red with blood.

"Now. I don't care which one of you tells me, but one of you will."

The two sisters looked at each other. Yarrow nodded. "Very well. I suppose it's time. But not here. Nobody wants to relive that story. Come to the river so I can wash my hands."

We walked in silence. I waited while she cleaned off the blood. We sat on a log and she began. "The old men had no meat on them. They refused to eat. Said there wasn't enough. Otok was the first to go." Otok with the Curled Hands, her father, my grandfather, a cranky old man grown impatient with the world. An image of him in his younger days passed like a cloud. I remembered a stern man whose hands were not yet bent. "He died soon after we found the cave on the mountain, the cave with the hunters from the north. One morning, he just never woke up. We buried him in the snow."

"And Zlatar?" Kindly Zlatar, a Changer like me, a herder of geese.

Yarrow stared at her feet. "The next morning, when we awoke, Zlatar was gone. Ochre was the one who found him, lying in the snow where we'd buried Otok."

I swallowed hard. "And Thought Holder?" I asked.

"Thought Holder ate nothing. He took no food from the time we left the summer shelter. We begged him to eat, but he only smiled. 'I have seen my future,' he said. 'I don't need my body there.' He lasted even longer than the others. He just sat in that little cave, staring out into the whiteness, smiling. One morning Ochre touched his arm to ask a question. The old man was dead. But still he smiled." Yarrow folded her hands in her lap.

Tenja and Thought Holder, our travelers between the worlds. Now both were gone. Who was there to take their place? Too late, my vision of words on hides. Too late for Thought Holder to tell his story.

"He left a message for you, Thought Holder did," Yarrow said.

"A message?" I sat up straight. Gokihar stirred in his little sack.

"It made no sense to me, but I planned to tell you when the time was right."

"What message? What did he say?"

She paused, gathering her words. "He said, 'Tell Thistle, when she makes the marks, that I have seen the shape with the dot inside.' Does that mean anything to you?"

He saw the marks? Thought Holder knew the shapes? Earthmaker had come to him as well! "Yes," I said softly. Yes, the shapes were real. Gokihar twisted and yawned, clenching his little fists. I sat without moving, thinking about what Yarrow had said. The shape with the mark inside, Earthmaker's Eye and the sign for wisdom. Yarrow stood.

"What happened to Grandma Sela?" I asked, jumping up after her.

She turned, as if looking to the horizon for the answer. Sela was her mother, as well as my grandmother. She'd been a difficult old woman, but maybe Yarrow remembered her from more tender days. "We lost Sela four days before we got here. The river took her. We crossed where it roared down a canyon, after we rolled a log in place for a bridge. I told her I'd climb back up with her, cross where it was narrower. She refused. Said if the young ones could do it, so could she. Magla told her to sit and scoot across. You know how she was. She tried to walk like everyone else. Her body never came up again."

Now my questions were answered. "Thank you, Yarrow," I said.

She took a step and stopped. "Thistle, there's something else. What I said about the Arn, about their talk being different, I didn't mean anything by that. Your baby is beautiful. I was just surprised."

"Oh, it doesn't matter."

"I was just wondering . . . well, his father, is it the Giant?"

I looked up, puzzled. Why did she sound so worried? Then I remembered the tension between her and that powerful man. Apparently she hadn't forgotten it either. "The Giant? His name is Andor, Yarrow. Don't call him the Giant. Anyway, Andor is my baby's grandfather. Anish is his father."

Relief flooded her face. A younger woman looked back at me. "Oh, well, then, I just wondered . . ." She walked swiftly toward the camp.

By now it was dusk. The cooking fire glowed in the distance. The evening star, which we called the Mother Star for its brightness and beauty, was twinkling on the horizon. A wolf cried and wasn't answered. I sighed. Wonder coursed through me like blood. So many farewells. One strange message. Some secrets revealed. One misunderstanding put to rest. I'd been wise to try to end the secrets, uncover what was hidden, look at it directly. Nothing bad had come of it. Perhaps that was what Earthmaker wanted. What other illusions were yet to be corrected, I wondered? I waited for the darkness and the pure aloneness of the stars.

The night grew chilly. Gokihar began to fuss. By the time I headed toward home, the clear sky was black and the wind brisk. As I approached the line of brush just beyond the river, I heard a shuffling noise. I stopped short. Then came a raspy cough. This was no wild beast. The shadow of a human veered in front of me.

"I see you are acquainted with the darkness," the shadow said, "you and your child." I knew that gruff and mocking voice, though I'd rarely heard it. Wild Eyes. The new moon gave too little light to make out her features. How had she ever found me?

"What are you doing here?" I asked.

"The darkness calls me as well," she said. "So Earthmaker told you about Her marks, did She? I have not forgotten your question. Did She tell you anything else?"

"About what?" The woman made me uneasy, but I was curious about her just the same.

"Many things. That baby of yours, for instance, the Wolf Child." She gestured toward my son, her hand moving like a white bird against the night. "We should have a Welcoming for him. It's getting late."

"Don't call him that. His name is Gokihar. What do you mean, a Welcoming?"

"Your people do not do that, I hear. Greet a young one when he crosses from the soul world to this one."

"No, we have no ceremony for that." I looked around, wanting to get away. The old woman stood in front of me, branches on either side. I hoped she was almost done.

The gravelly voice continued. "Ah, but you should. When we come into our bodies, we leave behind everything familiar, no longer recalling the place from which we came." She stepped closer, her tunic smelling of smoke from her seasons by the fire. I held my baby tighter. Her voice was soft when she continued, a fleeting sadness in her words. "This new world can be a frightening place," she said. But the hardness quickly returned. "There will be a Welcoming for this child!"

Was she mad or wise? Or both? It would be best to ignore her, I decided, ignore her and give myself more time. "Thank you, not just now. Maybe later."

"No, the time has come. All has been arranged. We mustn't wait." She turned, stepping into the shadows.

"What do you do at this Welcoming?" I called after her.

"You'll see!" she answered, disappearing into the night.

"Wait!" I heard the crunch of branches and nothing more. The night no longer seemed friendly. I picked my way home across the beach, wondering what this woman wanted with us. Was she using fear for her own power? Or was fear using her?

Part 3

Children of the Twilight

I was the blazing, the brilliant fire,
I was the fire whose flame and sparks
rained down on the rebel land.
I was the conflagration which shone forth
in the heavens when the heavens shook
and the earth quaked.

inscription attributed to
Sumerian Goddess *Inana*

The Welcoming

I WAS MORE TIRED THAN I'D REALIZED. The day with the deer and the evening with Wild Eyes had exhausted me. Even Gokihar slept late. When we awakened the cave was empty. I fed the baby, stepped outside, and glanced around. The men had left to fish, but all the women were there. Birch had been right. There was going to be a feast. Magla was at the fire with several others. She could tell me what was planned. I started toward her, but at my first step, something else caught my eye. Last night we'd staked the deer in front of the little pen. Now that place was empty.

"Magla, where are they?" I shouted, swallowing hard. "Where are the deer?"

"Birch and Leu took them to the meadow," she called back. "Birch said that's what you wanted."

"Oh." I sighed. Magla shook her head. Those deer were making me jumpy. Maybe no one was going to roast them while I wasn't looking, but something else had occurred to me last night. What if Thur returned? I hadn't seen her since before the hunt, but I was sure she'd be back. I should have warned Birch. I'd do it tonight. I turned my attention to the women, rolling turnips into large flat leaves. "So, this feast . . . are we celebrating anything special?" I asked.

"Litva, get the salt," Magla said. "Thistle stored some for us. In that bag." The slow-moving woman stood and walked toward a small pouch. Magla continued her work, keeping her eyes on the wilted leaves as she spoke. "You did well, daughter, making the camp ready for us. I've spoken to Yarrow. You are grown now, we agree. Time for you to join the elders at the fire."

"Me? Really? Is that why we're having a feast?" Every night the Mothers and the men sat together to talk about the day. I'd never really thought about joining them. A woman didn't sit with the elders when her babies were young. "What about Gokihar?"

"Leave him with Silka when we meet." Litva was back, standing over the greens with a handful of salt. Magla reached for her arm. "Not yet," she said. Then she turned back to her cooking. I doubted I'd learn much more from her.

But there was someone who always had time to talk. And who paid close attention to such things. Silka. Feeling sure of where I'd find her, I headed for the shore. In the distance the men were tending to their nets. Silka and Narta were closer, Narta standing on wobbly legs by a driftwood tree, dark hair framing her pink face. The little girl was even lovelier than when I'd first seen her. Silka had dressed her in a soft tunic and pulled her hair into two small tails, wrapping each in a band of rabbit fur. Since her first glimpse of him two months ago, Narta had been fascinated by Gokihar. I sat down beside her, holding the boy on my lap. The little girl smiled and walked toward us, taking a few steps on her own before tumbling into my free arm. I held her on my knee as she stared at the baby, her eyes as round as little flowers.

"Greetings, Silka. How are you?" I said.

She looked over at me. "Well enough."

"Rube did a fine thing when he caught the deer. Please thank him again for his help."

"I suspected that was your idea," she said. "It seems silly, bothering with them like that." Her mouth settled into a familiar pout.

"He did it for you and Narta, for the future. You'll see . . ." She shrugged. "Silka, there's one other thing. This feast. Do you know anything about it?"

She twisted a long strand of black hair around one finger and smiled at her little girl as she spoke. "It was the old woman's idea. That's all I know. Yarrow said you'd be sitting with the elders from now on and I was to watch your baby. The old woman wants you in the fire circle."

"She wants me there?"

"I guess." She tossed back her hair and held her arms out to Narta.

Why would some stranger care if I joined the circle? I could think of no reason. Narta and Silka had begun playing a game, patting their hands together and making little sounds. I leaned back, listening to their laughter and the slosh of the waves, the sun warming my face. Maybe I'd stay on the beach while I fed Gokihar. It had been a long time since Silka and I had talked about babies. I was ready to forget the deer and the fire circle and the secrets, at least for a while.

Silka's next words brought me back. "You should get a man," she said. "For you and that baby."

I sat up quickly. My face was burning, but not from the sun. "What man should I get, Silka? Have you figured that out as well?"

"One of the West Men," she replied with a shrug. "They don't have anyone. I think that's the plan. Choose one now before they have to argue over you."

The plan? Whose plan? Why did I know nothing about it? More

387

secrets, more deception. "When do you find time to talk about these things, Silka? You and the Mothers and that woman. Why do any of you care?"

"When you're out hiking around, or whatever it is you and your boy do. The old woman says you've been alone too long."

I stood up, ready to get away from there again, away from all the talk and trouble. But I stopped myself. What if more decisions were made in my absence? I needed to stay close by. I'd remain in camp all day, I decided, let Birch and Leu take care of the deer, pretend to be interested in how well the meat was cooking or when to salt the leaves or what was said around the fire. If these people were worried that I liked my own company too much, I'd give them all a chance to enjoy my presence for themselves.

I smiled through clenched teeth. "Silka, will you watch my boy? I think I'll help Magla with the meat." She nodded. I hurried back across the beach.

The day passed quickly enough. For a while, I helped Litva turn the roasting vegetables. Once the cooking was well underway, I went to get Gokihar. We went to the house of the northern hunters and I listened as their women spoke of other feasts. I heard nothing new at either place, just the familiar sounds of a feast day.

Throughout the afternoon, I noticed Yarrow wandering among the people, as she always did at such times, asking questions, nodding, remembering what was said. A ceremony was a time to ease our minds as well as fill our bellies. She'd speak to everyone before we gathered, even the quiet ones, hear their hopes and fears and ideas. I smiled and nodded each time we passed, eager for my turn. The two of us had spoken briefly the previous night about the Old Ones and the Arn. But I'd promised myself there'd be no more secrets and had yet to say anything about Tenja's premonitions. They'd have to be spoken as well. Not just Tenja's fear of approaching danger, but the light that called her before she died. I'd bring them all to Yarrow. She could decide how to best tell the People. I waited, but Yarrow didn't seek me out.

Birch and Leu returned early from the meadow, the deer following. I greeted them, noticing that the orphan was stronger. People began to gather while the sun was still bright, urged on by the smell of cooking food. I saw Wild Eyes leaving her little house and hurrying toward the fire. She had a slight limp, which gave her a rocking appearance when she rushed. I tied the deer and headed for the circle, not wanting to miss anything the old woman said.

I heard children's laughter near the cave and came upon Zale and Fire wrestling in the dirt, Fire squealing and pretending to struggle as the younger boy pinned him. I glanced around. Almost everyone was there. The circle of elders shifted from time to time, people usually joining when their children were old enough to run with the others. The Old Ones were always part of the group. Only two remained from our people: Silka's grandmothers, Lida and Ivy. Wild Eyes lowered herself next to them. Magla and Ochre were there. It was the first time all day I'd seen her sitting. Reen's parents, Litva and Bakar sat next to them. Yarrow had joined Zalec. The two West men strolled over, looking as if they'd been interrupted in the middle of an important nap. Lugo was toting a large pack which I recognized as his mother's. I'd heard the name "Vasto" earlier in the day. That was what they called the younger man.

Frightened Eyes had no interest in the matters the elders discussed and preferred to sit with the children on the opposite side of the circle. Birch and Leu were in front of her, so close together that their knees touched. I'd been right. Herding reindeer seemed to agree with them.

Rube was with Silka, Narta on his knee. How fortunate for that little girl, to have a father.

Yarrow motioned for me to join them, so I kissed Gokihar and handed him to Silka. "Thanks for watching him," I whispered. "Be sure smoke doesn't get in his face." I walked around the back of the group and slipped in by Magla. The northern reindeer hunters, two women and three men, slid in beside me. They never had much to say, but I was happy for their presence. Everyone was present.

In the old days, Sela had been the one who called the elders together. Now that task had fallen to Yarrow. She stood before us, her tunic painted with the same marks Sela had once worn, charcoal moons and ochre stars, the signs of a leader. She was a fine handsome woman, I thought. It was easy to see why the Giant had been attracted to her. I remembered Andor and Anish and their lost little bunch, trekking alone somewhere through strange country, without the vision of a strong woman. I glanced around, pushing my sad thoughts away. Everyone was watching Yarrow, waiting.

"The time has come for our first ceremony," Yarrow began, "for we have become a new people." Several heads were nodding. "There are those among us who have different ways. Change has brought us together." She paused and gazed from face to face, passing quickly over me. "We gather tonight to celebrate, to greet those who have joined us, and to welcome a new life to our midst. And to ponder Change. For there are some among us who say Earth itself is changing." Yes! She'd speak of it. How had she known my premonitions? Had Rube said something? Or Thought Holder, before he died? Yarrow was smart. Maybe she just knew. I looked up at her in appreciation. Yarrow was staring at Wild Eyes, the old woman nodding her head. Had the newcomer gotten to her first?

"It may be that Earth is changing," Yarrow continued. I didn't take my eyes from her face. "Thought Holder, our oldest one, a man who saw both worlds, believed this. Tenja, the Star Watcher, warned of it as well. Thistle, who learned some of Tenja's ways, may agree." She glanced my way. "Tonight a Grandmother from the West will speak, the Story Keeper for her tribe. She will tell a tale of Change and offer a Welcoming for the new child with us now." Wild Eyes bowed her head briefly, then smiled at the group, as proud as a fox with a duck. "I have yet to hear all of her story," Yarrow continued, "but her words stir memories and awaken my ancestors' voices. So it is that she will speak to you."

Magla took over then, rising to her feet and brushing the dirt from her tunic. "First we eat. Then we hear the tale."

The camp came alive, the hunters lining up for a hunk of venison, the children scrambling after them. Magla and the Mothers held out skewers of turnips and roasted mushrooms. We ate and talked until moonlight spilled upon the sea. Once I felt a chill on the back of my neck and glanced around to see Wild Eyes watching me. A heron soared across the purple sky. When at last the embers burned low and words gave way to silence, the old woman rose and stood by the fire.

"*Aiee*, I speak," she said sternly. "I am Eda, Story Keeper for my people. I know not just the small stories from the West, but the large stories of all people; not just the tales of the past, but the patterns of the future. Some of us know a way to keep thoughts alive." For a moment she fixed her eyes on me. I felt like a rabbit in a hawk's shadow. "Lugo," she said, "bring my things." He hauled the bag over, laying it at her feet, then dropping back quickly. Perhaps he'd grown tired of her story. "Thank you, my boy," she murmured. She dug through the pouch and pulled out a rolled hide.

"Large stories must begin with protection," she said, unrolling the bundle. By then all that lit the night were a few glowing embers, a sliver of moon, and the stars. She held up a sleeveless tunic, decorated on the front with dark shapes. This she slipped over her head and smoothed across her chest. A sudden wind stirred, flaming the cinders. In that brief instant, I saw the symbol on her vest. It was the two wedged shapes, fit together at the open ends, the dot within. Earthmaker had spoken to her as well. The old woman began her story:

Long ago, when Earth was but a child, before the lizard people lived, the first stars were already old. They'd been born in the middle of the universe, at a time when nothing else had yet been made. How they gleamed! How they shone in the darkness, those first lights! First they gleamed, then they groaned, then they died. Before anything else ever lived, the first stars died. They died, but the dead star bones were never buried. No place was large enough to cover them. Sky itself became their grave.

What a strange story, I thought, looking upward. The sky a grave for stars! The old woman held up a hand, as if forbidding any thought but her own. "The story is a long one," she said. "Listen well." She continued:

Nor did they stay in one place. Round and round they swerved, knocked into bits and pieces and some into dust. Wind blew upon them. Like ripples from a stone thrown into a pond, the star bones began to move outward. Farther they moved from the center, never resting. In time new life came, changing all it touched. But the star remnants never changed. Farther they blew, for they had no home. And then one day they saw the Sun.

'Is he not one of us? Perhaps Sun will take us in,' the star bones said. And so they swirled closer to that light, for Sun himself had a power to pull them near. As they floated through the quietness of space, they saw something else. 'Look!' they cried. 'Sun is not alone. He has his own small followers. Surely some of us can stay with them.'

In those days there were other people on Earth. It was in the time before the ice, when humans had already gone forth. They did not know Earthmaker, for they were simple ones and followed the ways of animals. When the people looked up, they saw hurling toward them the stones and dust of long-dead stars. And then a great heat arose, so that the remnants glowed and smoked and coiled, trailing fire in their flight.

To those first trembling people, the smoke and flame appeared as tails and legs, teeth and jaws, glowing eyes. The firmament seemed full of animals and gods. 'Have we displeased the Sky?' they moaned, leaving offerings and tearing at their clothes. But they could find no protection. 'Behold,' they cried, 'Sky makes war on us!'

The star bits smashed the planet as if it were a dried pod. Some of the remnants, like swallows weary from flight, dropped hissing into the sea. A great shudder went up from the darkening earth, throwing up the moon, scattering the people. The bodies of creatures glutted the sea. The Great Tree was heaved to the side, its branches split like twigs.

Nor was this the only time that such things happened. Sometimes the dead stars thrust up ice, sometimes fire. Earth shuddered and tumbled in the darkness, knocked about by stars, shaking off the life that was before. The humans who survived, for there were some, looked out like frightened children, seeing a new heaven and a new earth. The memories of their ancestors were but mist in the morning and the old ones' voices were heard no more. 'Behold,' the survivors said, 'we are the first people.' In time, the new people themselves became old, believing that the sun always rose the same way, that Earth always turned with the same tender beauty, and that morning always came.

The People stirred uneasily, shifting on their haunches from side to side, frowning at one another. Was it not time to sleep? Gokihar made a little cooing sound at the other side of the fire circle. He would be hungry by now. I crawled over and took him from Silka, prepared to leave. But at that moment the old woman picked up the story, no hint of weariness in her swelling voice. This time she was looking directly at me and my son.

Ah, the little one, the Gokihar, 'born among wolves.' We must welcome the babies, for then we welcome the future. This small one has crossed over from the world of spirit to the world of flesh. It is a silent, lonely journey. Look into his eyes and remember the trip.

Before I knew what she was doing, Eda swooped down like an owl and plucked up the boy. Holding him with both hands, so that he faced the surprised crowd, she turned in a circle and held him for all to see. I crawled to my knees, ready to grab him. The baby made no sound.

Look at the little one, 'born among wolves.' There were some
who said the dead stars themselves were wolves, flaming wolves
with tales of fire, chasing burning swans. Such a wolf was caught
by Earthmaker when he fell, the story goes, caught and bound in
some dark place by cords that none can sever. To this day, he writhes
and moans and throws up fire, growling for his freedom. Some
humans hear his cry.

Slowly she turned, holding him before the perplexed group so that
all eyes were on my child. A sudden wind sparked the embers, rekin-
dling the flame. I jumped up. "Here, I'll take him," I said, grabbing
Gokihar under his arms.

Eda let him go and I stumbled back, regaining my balance just
before I fell. I squeezed in next to Birch. "Watch this boy well," the old
woman cried, pointing toward us, her voice rising on the wind. "Watch
him, this son of Thistle. Is he the one you want to carry on your
memories?"

Sheltering Gokihar, I looked around at the People. Yarrow's face
was stern. Birch's lips trembled. Everyone was silent, puzzled. What
kind of Welcoming was this, the old goat using my child to frighten
them? An unfamiliar rage rose up in me. I wanted out of there. But I
couldn't leave now, not like this. I had to find a way to break through
their fear. Holding Birch's thin arm for support, I pulled myself up
and laid Gokihar on my shoulder.

"A good story on this dark night," I said heartily, stepping to the
center of the circle. "But perhaps the Story Teller tires with its length,
since we have yet to hear the entire Welcoming as she explained it to
me. I'll finish the tale so that she can rest." The old woman took a step
toward me. I held out my hand. "Grandmother, you have done your

best. You are done for tonight." Her eyes flashed, but she sat down.

"Here, look into my little one's eyes," I said softly. "Greet him. Look into each other's eyes. Remember your own dark journey, the harsh shock of your birth. This one has come but recently from the Source. There his soul was bathed in love. He has yet to learn our rough ways. See? He trembles among us like a little tree, his roots twined in another place. Remember that world he still carries within, the large world, the root world. That is our true home."

I turned again before the silent group, waiting for Earthmaker to tell me each thought. "Night's shadows haunt us with wild imaginings. Release them. Remember the Source. There the fears of this flickering world are consumed. It is not so far away, nor must we wait." Had my words broken through? Ochre was rubbing his beard sleepily. Birch had begun to smile. Even Yarrow looked relieved. From the corner of my eye, I saw Eda struggling to get up. Lugo was holding her back, his large hand gripping her arm. Yawning and patting Gokihar's back, I said warmly, "Well, I for one am tired. And there's work to do tomorrow." I headed to the cave.

Before long the others stumbled in to find their places, the cave soon resounding with snores and sighs. Gokihar's little body was warm beside me, his breathing slow and even. Only I was restless. Dead stars, wolves, ancestors' memories, what did they have to do with each other? Or with my son?

The Sighting

THE OTHERS SLEPT LATE, WHICH WAS GOOD. It meant their bellies were full and their hearts untroubled. Perhaps my parting words had helped them. But the previous night had left me uneasy. How long would it be before the old woman bothered us again? I decided to take Gokihar to the river for a bath, since I was in no hurry for anyone's questions or stares. Soon after dawn, I crept from the cave with my boy.

Soft voices met me as I stepped out. Birch and Leu were by the deer pen. I waved and hurried toward them. "What are you doing?" I asked.

"Leu wants to go back to the meadow with me!" she whispered. "To watch the deer." Leu smiled and looked at the ground, his dark hair almost covering his eyes.

"Be careful," I said. I'd warned them about Thur.

"We will."

I walked with Birch and Leu to the river, waiting while they watered the deer, watching as they headed northeast to the meadow. I continued east, following the river upstream to a shallow inlet I knew well, where the water was warm enough for Gokihar. It was a lovely, quiet morning. Perhaps too quiet. Even the birds were silent. Soon after we parted company with the deer and their keepers, I began to sense that my boy and I were not alone. I had my knife and walking stick. Still I felt uneasy. I scanned the land, seeing nothing unusual.

I turned my attention to the river grass ahead of me, just in time to see the tops of the tall fronds parting. Some creature was running there. I lifted my stick. Thur burst from the rushes with a yelp. Just behind her, the grass separated again as another animal took off in the opposite direction. "Thur, my girl!" I cried as she ran toward me. Was something tracking her or had she found a friend? I reached into my pack, pulling out a dried fish which she took eagerly. "Come with us, girl!" I cried. She stayed by my side until we reached the inlet, leaving to chase some quail into a stand of evergreens. I felt happy knowing she was near.

I laid Gokihar in the grass, letting him feel the sun on his body. Then I pulled off my own tunic as well, eager for a swim. We usually bathed in the sea, but the water there was colder. Anyway, I wanted some privacy. And it would feel good to wash without salt.

"Oh, Gokihar, my good boy," I said as I picked him up. "My fine and handsome boy." He was already longer than the People's babies, stronger, too. Couldn't they see how fine he was? I stepped into the water, warming his body with my skin, twirling around slowly, swishing the surface with my free hand, lowering him until the water just covered his chest. Little pockets of cold nudged my feet. And then silence, sweet silence. I found myself wishing that the others had never returned. I missed Wolf and Raven. Humans were too unpredictable.

When we'd had enough of the water, I took him back to shore. How hot the summer was becoming! The morning breeze didn't even chill us. I laid the baby on my tunic and smoothed deer fat into his skin. Then I stretched out on the grassy bank, my own flesh longing for the heat. The mosquitoes had yet to find us. All I heard were Gokihar's little sounds and the twittering of the crossbills in the pines. My eyes closed. Perhaps I dozed awhile. A sound startled me. The brush of footsteps in the grass. I sat up quickly and looked behind us. It was Eda, slinking like a weasel to a nest. She jumped when she saw me.

I moved closer to Gokihar. "Hello, Grandmother," I said. "Come to frighten the fish?"

Her grey hair framed her head like a storm cloud. She took a few more steps, until she was almost standing over us. "You can't save them, you know," she said. "Not the fish nor the people. The time is coming. Not just yet, but it's coming."

"And you would terrify them until then?" I asked.

"Not terrify. Prepare."

"You came all this way to tell me that?"

She paused, pushing the hair from her flushed face. "We don't have to be enemies, you and I," she said softly.

"No," I replied, "we could be strangers."

Her face hardened. "You know so little about these matters. Would you still say that, I wonder, if you feared you were to lose your own son? And the memory of all your ancestors with him? Who are you that your boy should be spared?" Seeing that I had nothing to say, she turned and headed back. I watched as she became smaller, wondering what it was she wanted from me. I had no power over the future.

Longing again for Sun's hot breath, I stretched out, ready to reclaim the silence. A quick movement at the edge of the pines caught my eye. Too tall for a dog, surely. Pulling myself up on my elbows, I squinted at the line of trees, recognizing a tall, lanky shape. Lugo, retreating into the forest. Had he followed the old woman or me? Or had he just been hunting nearby? Whatever the answer, the peaceful morning was gone. I was ready to leave.

I wrapped Gokihar's bottom, pulled my tunic over my head, and started home. When I reached the beach I saw Lugo up ahead, talking to his brother. He turned to say something as I passed, but I kept my head low and hurried by the two of them. I'd heard enough from the West people already. There was one person I did want to speak with, though.

Yarrow was sitting on the ground when I found her, rubbing the stiffness from Zalec's leg. She looked up without speaking as I approached. "I'll wait here until you're finished," I said, hoisting my sleeping boy higher on my shoulder. "Then we need to talk."

"What is it? I have no secrets from Zalec."

I knew of one secret, I thought, remembering Andor, but I let that go. She must have sensed my anger and wanted her man nearby. It made no difference to me. "Very well," I said. Zalec looked off in the distance, as if he wished he were elsewhere. Never had I wanted to challenge her before, but my rage was greater than my fear. "You are our leader, Yarrow, the wisest one here. Is it not your duty to guide us?" She nodded once. "Then why do you allow a mad woman to speak?"

She hesitated. "Your harshness is unnecessary. Eda asked to speak. She is an elder, a Story Teller for her people. I didn't know all she planned to say."

"So you allowed her to say anything?"

"What she first told me sounded possible."

"Perhaps some of what she says is true. But only part of the truth," I replied.

"Would you have me forbid her to speak? We've never silenced anyone before."

"Then I trust that you won't silence me?" Yarrow looked up, her eyes wide. "If it's truth you want, Yarrow, I'll try to help you find it. The People can look for it together. We've had enough of silence. But half-truths and lies are also dangerous."

"What are you going to do?" she asked.

"From now on, every time the old woman speaks at the circle, I will speak after her."

"Very well," she said, looking tired. She folded her hands in her lap and I noticed how the veins stood out. Her leadership weighed heavily on her, I thought. Before this summer, she'd had the Old Ones to advise her. Now, except for Zalec, she was alone. Perhaps that was why she'd trusted Eda.

I hesitated. "Yarrow, you are our true leader. Thought Holder knew that. Tenja, too. They had no doubts. You need no stranger to direct you."

She smiled, but there was no joy in her face. What if Eda's words had shaken Yarrow's confidence? My fear crept back. I rubbed my hand across Gokihar's back. Yarrow was too smart to have suspicions of him. But if she were frightened by Eda's ravings about Sky attacking Earth, her work would be difficult.

I walked slowly back to the cave, ready to feed Gokihar and rest. As I lay in the cool darkness, thinking, I came to a conclusion. My days of wandering the countryside were over, at least for a while. I needed to stay close to camp, listening for undercurrents. As long as Eda was at our shore, some danger lurked for Gokihar. Maybe for all of us.

And so, while Birch and Leu tended the deer, Gokihar and I settled into the life of the camp. I cooked with the Mothers, dried fish, played on the beach with Silka and the children, listened to the men talk of their hunts. All the time I kept an eye out for Eda. Surprisingly, the old woman became friendlier following the day by the river. Someone must have scolded her, I thought. Or maybe she was trying a new way to win my trust. I sensed that she was watching me as much as I watched her.

Yarrow continued to motion me over to the elder circle, but we'd had no more stories for several days. We had happier things to think about. The animals were growing fat in the forest and the talk had turned to hunting. Every night the men sharpened their tools, teased each other, and made their plans. It was different now, not following the reindeer. Different, but not bad. Elk were plentiful. And red deer. I missed the mountains, but it was good to be near the sea in the summertime. I relaxed into the pace of the people, keeping an eye on Eda, but thankful for her silence.

Late one afternoon, I walked into the fire circle with Gokihar and dropped down to join the others. I nodded to Eda, who was sitting between her sons. As usual, Ochre was taunting Lugo about whose people had superior weapons, his red beard moving up and down as he spoke.

"A man can have nothing better than this," Ochre said, holding up a flint spear point.

"Not so!" argued Lugo. Those West People were cantankerous. "Vasto and I saw it!"

Zalec jumped into the discussion. There was not a tool he didn't know. "A flying spear, thrown from a stick? Who would make such a thing?" Maybe the newcomers were liars as well.

"Those to the west of us," said Lugo. "Bird hunters. They passed through last summer, after the rains." Vasto nodded.

"How thrown from a stick?" Zalec asked, frowning.

"They take a branch and stretch sinew from end to end. Then they bend it and the little spear flies." Lugo thrust out a lean, brown arm to demonstrate.

Ochre was listening intently, never taking his eyes off the long-faced man. He was wavering, I could tell, torn between scoffing at a lie or discovering a marvel. He could finally stand it no longer. He wanted to believe. "They hunt birds?" he asked, rubbing his hand across his red beard. "The spears go that fast?"

Lugo nodded.

Ochre nodded slowly. "Could you make one?" he asked.

"Of course he could, couldn't you?" said Eda, popping up like a gopher from a hole. "Lugo makes many things. He was the leader of our men." She beamed at her son. The surprised man frowned and covered his eyes. "Life will be hard for our people now," she added.

"What happened to them?" I asked. I'd forgotten that she had other people. Or perhaps I'd never imagined there were others like her elsewhere.

Eda hesitated. "Separated. We were separated, crossing a mountain in a storm. My boys could have made it back, but they stayed with me," she said. "Winter trapped us in the east."

"When will you return?" I asked, trying not to sound too eager.

"Earthmaker came to me in the winter," she said, talking to the ground. "I saw that our future was here."

"Why here?"

"So, Lugo," Ochre interrupted, rubbing his hands together, "you can make this thing? When will it be ready?"

"He'll be done in no time," Eda said.

I felt a moment of sympathy for the raw-boned man and grinned up at him. He glanced back, his lips tight. Magla called us to eat just then and all talk of weapons ended. I joined Birch and Leu, letting them hold Gokihar while I helped myself to rabbit stew. The two of them told me about chasing a fox from the meadow that afternoon. So far the deer-keeping had gone well. No one minded the absence of their young hands at camp. I was proud of them and the deer.

Eda's silence was not to last. We'd barely swallowed our food when the old woman rose to speak. I sat up straighter. Birch glanced my way. "I'll keep the baby," she whispered. I looked for Yarrow across the fire circle. Our eyes met and she shrugged. I turned toward Eda.

"Many nights ago, I began a story," she said. "Some say it is a frightening tale." She looked my way, her voice like nectar. "So I will tell you only a little each night. It is a story you must come to know. The past of all humans is contained there. And the future." As she spoke, I watched her hands. They floated around her like fish.

You have heard how Earth shuddered when the dead stars fell.
But what happened next?

Earth writhed and turned. Dust and smoke spewed from the star graves. Sky became dark. Earth shivered and grew cold. A great white land rose up in the west, beyond a distant sea, stretching in a wide curve and devouring the north. It sucked up the seas and made of them mountains. A place once lush with trees was now covered by rivers of ice.

Rain and hail fell without stopping, layer upon layer, freezing all they touched. For this was a greedy land, its long ice fingers reaching out and clutching fertile things. Over that high country a cold wind roared. From that hard place a dense fog drifted. Earthmaker, whose body this was, the rain Her tears, shivered and cried out, 'Sky, what do you want with my humans, that you make war on Earth?'

'It was not I,' Sky answered, 'but the dead stars. They will not stay in one place. I have nowhere to bury them. They are drawn toward Sun.'

'But my humans are dead,' She cried, 'their bodies crushed and thrown.' And all around was desolation.

Eda stopped, looking around at the stunned faces, a wildness in her eyes. She even frightens herself, I thought, as I got to my feet. "Thank you, Grandmother," I said, grabbing the old woman's wrists. "Let me take the story from here. Let me tell the best part." I moved my hands to her shoulders and pushed downward. "Sit and rest," I said. "Lugo, help your mother."

I looked at their upturned faces. If Tenja's premonitions were true, then Eda's story could be right, as far as it went. But Tenja had known more than fear. And so would they. "All was desolation," I said. "But Sky sent a messenger. Wind came sighing to Earthmaker. 'It is true the people suffer and all life with them. But never believe that this is the end. Do their souls not live on? Do they not return to the Source when bodies die? Their fears may loom like clouds, their grief burn like unshed tears. Do these not disappear? Life here is but a dream of exile. Do the people not come home?' And Earthmaker answered, 'Yes.' "

The People stood and stretched and wandered off to sleep, having had enough of stories. Eda twisted away from Lugo and marched toward her house alone. It was time to get Gokihar. I turned to walk toward Birch when a strong hand grabbed my arm. Lugo. Even in the dark, he stood so close I could see the urgency in his eyes. Was he angry? I tried to pull away, but he held more tightly. "Thistle," he muttered, so low that no one else could hear, "good words." He let me go. I watched as he disappeared into the night, standing motionless.

"Thistle, are you coming?" Birch called.

I hurried over to her, taking my sleeping boy. "Have you noticed that all the West people are strange?" I asked.

405

It was not long after, still early in the summer following Gokihar's birth, that I gazed into Sky's black distance one night and first saw the new stars.

The Changing

IN THE YEARS THAT FOLLOWED, we watched the dusty cluster of lights overhead. The fledgling stars grew so slowly they hardly seemed to change. Four years had passed since I'd first noticed them. They'd become a part of our lives, no more remarkable than a new tree in the forest. Change continued all around us, though there seemed little cause for fear. The woods were blessed with warmth, our bodies browned by Sun's sweetness. We never returned to the high summer cave. Ochre and Rube tried taking the old path to the mountains during our second summer at the beach. They came back dismayed, saying that the marshland now stretched to the foothills. And when they slogged their way through it and climbed to the high meadows, the reindeer were gone. Had so many died or had they found a new home, perhaps a way around the mountains and north? We never knew.

But the heat brought new life to the woodlands. Red deer roamed freely. Aurochs lumbered between the trees. Antelope, elk, and boar abounded. Our lives were slowly turning. We were becoming a people of the forest.

Lugo had managed to make the bows and shooting spears he'd described. And Ochre, loving the hunt more than habit or pride, had quickly claimed the new tool for his own. The red-haired man had gone to work changing Lugo's design. Like a child again, he happily chipped little flint points into different sizes and shapes. He'd tried different kinds of wood for the shafts as well, testing several before he was satisfied. Pine had become his favorite for bows, elm for arrows. He'd even made an arrow all of wood, carving a blunt-tipped point from the shaft. It stunned small game and left the fur undamaged.

It was fun to see the two of them together, the practical hunter and the sullen newcomer, laughing over each other's mistakes. Zalec made most of the arrow heads, since he had a gift for stone. But before long Ochre and Lugo were teaching all the men how to make shafts. Once a stick was smooth and straight, they notched one end at an angle, filed a stone point to fit snugly, and bound it with sinew and pitch. After it dried, they wrapped feathers on the other end for balance. It was Magla who designed our first quiver, making a long pouch and decorating it with fox teeth and fur. Soon all the men wanted one.

The hunters brought in squirrel and beaver and marten as well as the large grazers we'd always eaten. The small animals we used for both their flesh and fur. As Lugo had promised, the new weapon was so fast we could even hunt birds, which were plentiful. With the warm weather, the flying creatures came earlier and stayed longer. Cormorant, heron, swan, and stork flocked to our shore, as well as bittern and black-headed gulls. The woods were noisy with grouse. All of them made their way to our fire.

Losing themselves in their work, the People seemed to leave their sadness behind. Nor was there talk of the future. We butchered the mother deer our first winter near the sea, roasting the flesh in the time called When the Babies Cry from Hunger. Her meat turned that desolate month into a time of satisfaction, keeping us plumper than in winters past.

Birch and Leu had managed to keep the young deer alive. They took them to pasture in the warm months, watched for wolves, brought in grass and moss for the winter, hauled water, raked their droppings, and penned them up each night. The deer had bred in their third year. We now had a herd of four stout animals. The long days alone in the meadow had brought the two young people closer as well. The quick girl beamed at the plodding boy, seeing in him some secret not visible to other eyes.

Thur was with me once again, though I'd feared for her safety that first winter before we butchered the deer. She never hunted with anyone else and sometimes snarled at the others. They knew when to leave her alone. Two years ago, she'd returned to the woods to give birth to a litter of wolf pups, coming back to us lean and haggard and alone a few months later. Those pups were wild. They never approached the camp but ran in a pack of four wolf-dogs, barking at our deer until Leu pelted them with stones.

I'd seen Wolf only a few times since the People returned, and Raven not at all. But Thur had found the big grey animal. Sometimes I glimpsed the two of them bounding across the meadow. I'd figured out that it was Wolf's eyes following me whenever I walked in the forest. Surely it was Wolf who'd fathered the pups. Now, two years after her first litter, Thur's sides were bulging again. Things would be different this time, I'd decided. I kept her leashed day and night. I'd see to it that these pups were born in camp and taught to hunt with all of us. Maybe they'd even watch the deer.

The newcomers, especially the West people, had taken longer to settle into their new lives. Lugo and Vasto had left us twice, hoping to cross the mountains and find the people they'd left behind. Once they were gone for half a year, both times coming back dismayed. The path they'd originally taken was flooded and they could find no way around. They'd stared bitterly at the West Sea for months after their return, the same sea that lapped at their old shore, blaming the water for their loss. I'd heard of ocean-faring people who crossed open water, but we had no such boats. Not even the Fish People sailed that far. Still discouraged, the two men seemed resigned to staying.

Eda continued to confuse me. She never tired of telling us about the West people's superiority, but she had no intention of leaving. She'd begged her sons not to go, said their lives were here now. We had no place for her as a Story Teller since everyone hated her stories. But she'd found a new role for herself. Taking pity on our ignorance, she'd decided to instruct us in the ways of her people, showing us how to carve cups and bowls from wood, combs from flat bones. I'd come to realize that she wasn't really cruel, just frightened. Now, with her hands busy making things and her mouth busy teaching, she'd left behind her ugly ways and made a new home. In time, perhaps her sons would settle in as well. Vasto was as sullen as ever. But Lugo didn't seem so bad, once he'd found his place among the men.

My life had changed since that long winter alone, becoming simple and peaceful, but busy. Gokihar and the People filled the days. My ideas filled the nights. Sometimes I watched the night sky, but I was too occupied with my son to think about things as distant as falling stars. He'd grown into a robust boy. By his second year, he was toddling through the campsite, following the older boys with his own small bow. In his third year, he sat with Lugo and Ochre, watching the men and their carving. Sometimes his presence spilled over into the nights as well, entering my dreaming. Once again I'd see the little boat and the seven mountains. Only now the boat carried a rider. Some mornings, when I watched Eda making her wooden cups, I'd be reminded of that dream. I'd wonder if we could hollow out an entire log and make a boat that way. But I didn't have time to find out yet.

In Gokihar's fourth year, we encountered another change. Like all the others, it was both a blessing and a loss. The Fish People came to join us. It was on a bright afternoon in late summer that we first saw them. We'd been picking raspberries for three days, eating our fill and preparing the rest for winter, mashing them and mixing the paste with slivers of meat. The fruit kept the meat from spoiling and softened it. Gokihar had been helping, his face and hands stained red.

From along the shore to the south came a high, familiar cry. Looking up, I saw a small figure scurrying along the beach, waving her arms. Everyone dropped their work.

"Ziva!" I called. "It's Ziva!" I hurried toward her, Magla and Yarrow following.

Behind the Fish Woman plodded a band of silent people, still bright with feathers and pelts, but without their lovely smiles. They stopped when we reached their leader, stopped and huddled around her, the older ones staring at the ground, the children looking up with solemn eyes. Ziva burst into tears.

"It's gone, it's gone!" she said. "Fish Island is gone!"

"What do you mean, gone?" I asked. "How . . . ?"

"The Island is gone, our home is gone. The water took it," she sobbed, her shoulders shaking.

I thought of their fine beach, laying gentle as an open hand, golden sand-fingers stretching to the sea. Then I glanced at our own rocky shore, higher and harsher than theirs. Had the water risen here?

"Come sit," said Magla, taking Ziva's hand and putting an arm around the shoulders of the Fish Woman's lovely daughter. "Come to the camp and rest. Eat something. Save your story for when the men return. You'll stay with us for now." We spread mats for the newcomers. They dropped wearily around our circle. We brought them water and apples, sorry for their trouble, but excited they were there. All except Eda. She hovered at the edge of the group and glared at the strangers through narrowed eyes.

The men returned at dusk with a red deer and six rabbits. Ochre stopped short when he saw the large group huddled there, waiting to eat. I'd counted close to fifty of us in all. He glanced at Magla, the line between his eyes deepening. But the eyes of the other hunters lit up at the sight of the beautiful visitors. The brown faces of the young Fish People, men and women alike, were framed by intricate braids and dangling cowry shells, their glowing cheeks decorated with delicately painted lines. Yet these people weren't really so different from us, I thought. They had the same dark eyes and wavy, black hair. They simply lived more aware of pleasure. And wore fewer clothes. Whatever it was, our hunters stood taller that night and the Mothers laughed more often as they piled food on the visitors' plates.

Magla brought out dried turnips, apples, and salmon once the fresh meat was gone. Eda continued to glower at the edge of the circle. When I brought her a slice of dried salmon, she grabbed it and muttered, "These newcomers will have to start fishing tomorrow or move on." She was right, of course, but we were in no danger of starving.

Once their bellies were full the Fish People began to relax. Like a mother lion with her cubs, Ziva sat at the center of the group. Next to her were her daughter, Luba, and Belov, her yellow-eyed son, both full-grown. Eager to tell their tale, she began speaking soon after dark. Her story continued until the first birds of morning, the children falling asleep where they lay.

It seemed that the disaster had come quickly, without warning. Fish Island had disappeared overnight, the little broken boats set free and bobbing near shore the next morning. "We awoke and saw them, the boats. There was nothing else, nothing left," she said. "Only water. And then the sea began to lap about our feet. It edged upward, devouring our shore. We gathered everything we could, our pelts and food, crammed it into packs. The beach grew damp and the sand

route home from the Fish People

began to fall away. We ran, then watched the water from the cliff, watched the sea take everything." She recounted all their losses. "That island was my heart. The shore my people's memory. And now they're gone." She sat quietly, looking out to sea.

The People who were still awake looked uneasily at one another, not knowing what to say. I'd noticed them throughout the night, seen them frown and shake their heads. Ochre's head had jerked sleepily as the tale went on. Once Ziva finished and he had a chance to speak, he bolted awake and turned to her. "This Fish Island of yours, how high was it?"

Ziva looked at him in dismay, her eyes welling up again with tears. Magla jabbed an elbow in his side. "Fish Island was not so tall. That was not why we loved it," Ziva said, sniffing.

Magla spoke in her most soothing voice. "What my man means to say is that this is a terrible sadness, losing your home in this strange way. He's sorry. He wants to know how high the water rose so he can better understand your suffering."

"How high did it get?" Ochre persisted.

"Perhaps to my chest at its deepest," she whimpered, pulling her tunic tighter. Ochre nodded.

"Everyone, go to sleep now," Magla said to the few of us still left. "The sun is soon rising."

"That's about half a man's length," Ochre mused, speaking to no one in particular. "The sea rose half a man's length."

"Why?" I asked. "Where would the water come from?" We'd had plenty of rain, but hardly enough to change the sea.

"Ice melting?" Ochre replied, shrugging his shoulders.

"Oh." That was possible. I snuggled down next to my slumbering boy, falling asleep to the slosh of the waves.

I was awakened early by the sound of Ziva's voice. "See how the Reindeer People take us in," she was saying, loud enough that even Eda could hear. "We'll stay here for a short time. They will tell us when it's time to move on. Never let it be said the Fish People don't do their work!" Soon they were all scurrying around, some clearing stones for their shelters, others weaving fish traps of grass and sticks. I rubbed my eyes, remembering the industry of these people. It would be a long morning.

The shore was noisier, but it was exciting too. Our lives blended peacefully. However, as the summer days slipped by, with the bone piles growing and the fat flies buzzing, one problem came to light. "This place stinks," Eda muttered one afternoon, not long after the Fish People's arrival. She was right. So Magla and Ziva devised a plan. They asked the men to dig two long trenches, one for fish bones, one for our waste. Each day the Mothers threw a layer of dirt over the furrow and the smell soon disappeared.

Eda was still unhappy. I noticed that she came to me with her grievances, rather than bother the older women. Maybe she thought they'd tire of her complaining. She had no such qualms with me. Several days after the Fish People arrived, I was on the beach with Gokihar and Narta when Eda sought me out. Though Narta was five and big enough to play with the older children, she preferred Gokihar. The girl had her mother's large eyes and delicate hands, her father's muscular body. On this day the two of them were gathering stones to build a little wall. I was sitting cross-legged, watching them, when I heard footsteps. I looked behind me. Eda, probably with some new complaint.

I'd made it clear that when she talked to me, she was never to speak cruelly of Gokihar, never call him "the wolf child," or tell stories of wolves devouring the earth. She was no longer as rude as she'd once been, but I still watched her carefully.

"What's the boy doing?" she asked. I said nothing. She spoke again, a little louder, "How are you and Gokihar?"

"We're fine, Grandmother. And you?"

"The noise of this place bothers me. It's like living with sea lions. My people did not live like this," she said, spitting out her words, "naked as young rats. You should have seen us, proud and smart. No one here can understand." She shook her head. I waited, knowing there was more to come. She soon continued. "You like these people, don't you? I see how your eyes light up at these young men and their soft ways."

"They're our friends, Eda. The Fish People helped us in the past. They've always helped us. Ziva saved my life."

"Oh, her and her yellow-eyed boy. So. I suppose you'll join with one of them, then?" Perhaps this was the heart of her question.

"I have no plan to join . . ."

"I see now, with their coming, that there's not much time."

"Not much time for what?"

The old woman paused, wiping a hand across her face. She mumbled, "Not much time for you to have another child."

"Another child?" Eda had asked me last winter if I ever thought about another baby, but I'd ignored her then. Why should she care?

"Magla says you're in your twentieth year. Already your boy is four. Soon he'll need less of you." Her voice changed as she spoke. She sounded like a kindly grandmother. "Surely it's time for a joining, if you're ever to have another child, someone to be with you if, when, you grow old. My sons . . ."

"Eda, I have Gokihar. His father may still return. I don't need . . ."

"Don't be hasty. Before you look at these other young men, these new people, I ask just one thing." She sounded breathless.

"Yes, go on," I said.

"Consider joining with my Lugo."

"Ma, look!" Gokihar cried, pulling on my arm. "Look at the wall!" I smiled down at him, his dark eyes peering up at me through hair like autumn grass.

"Good work," I said. "Try putting mud between the stones. They'll stay even better." I turned back to Eda. "Should I ever think of joining, which I may never do, I'll consider Lugo first. That's all I have to say." I leaned over to help Gokihar mix water into the dirt.

Oddly enough, I'd been thinking about that very thing, that perhaps some day I'd join with Lugo. He wasn't so bad when he was away from his mother. Ochre spoke highly of the long-faced man, said Lugo was a good hunter when he wasn't brooding. I especially liked his arms. It would be good to have another child. Besides, Lugo was strong and

I needed help on a few things. He had a special way with animals, being both more patient and less tender-hearted than I. I wanted him to be the one who helped me train the pups. He still pretended to laugh at my ideas, but I could tell he was beginning to understand. Except for Gokihar's father, Lugo was the only man with whom I'd ever thought of joining. But I wouldn't give Eda the satisfaction of thinking it was her idea.

The old woman was still standing behind us. I turned and squinted up at her, shielding my eyes. "You're in our light," I said. She sighed and walked away.

Ziva's daughter, Luba, walked by just then with two of her friends, her smooth hips swaying, a cowry-shell belt dangling at her waist. Whenever she crossed the grounds, the men found a reason to pause, even if they were eating. I'd noticed Lugo's eyes following her from time to time. Maybe he had his own thoughts about a joining. I wondered if Eda had ever told her son about her plans for him. It was odd that she was so concerned about a grown man who seemed to need no help from her. Luba's brown legs disappeared as she ducked into her mother's little shelter and the men went back to work.

It seemed that the Fish People had come to stay. In less than a month, they'd set up five shelters. Their chimes, made of shell and bone, several to each house, clacked in the wind all along the beach. Despite what Eda had to say, they got on well with everyone and did their share of work. Besides, their habits and skills were different from ours and I looked forward to all we could learn from each other. Even Eda enjoyed showing off her knowledge. The Fish People marveled at her cups and the wooden mallets she made for cracking nuts. When Ziva begged her for a cup of her own, Eda snorted but went right to work, showing her how to lay a hot coal on a piece of wood to burn out the center.

I enjoyed the Fish People's fancy tunics, finely-stitched garments decorated with fish bones and delicate shells. Silka made one for herself, beautiful, but more trouble than I cared for. Lugo and Vasto showed the newcomers how to clear brush and fell trees with a stone ax, while the Fish Men taught them about underwater traps and grass nets.

Once again we settled into a new life, fifty of us living close together. It was hard at times, but at night, when we all sat at the fire, I felt safe and warm, part of something. Even when winter came, we managed to store enough food so that no one died or even lost their teeth. And so another season passed.

One bright day, just after the Fish People's first winter on our shore, just before Gokihar's fifth year, Ziva summoned us all to the beach. We'd had little snow that winter, but it had been raining for days. Now the sun was finally shining, but the ground was still too muddy for the men to hunt. Everyone was home, basking in the sun, restless. I, for one, was bored and eager for something new. Ziva must have sensed our mood. We gathered around her, hopeful.

"Belov, come here!" she called to her handsome son. Unlike most of the men from his group, Belov rarely fished, spending his days making things with his hands. Now the young man strode past us and stood before his mother, his slender legs graceful and even darker than the others, his black hair falling smoothly over his narrow shoulders. With a quick motion of his hand and a toss of his head, he brushed back one long strand. "Belov, you must show them the reed boat!"

"Very well," he answered softly.

He turned and walked down the beach toward their shelter, his body seeming to glide over the rough ground. As I watched his dark back retreating, I felt other eyes on me. I turned to see Lugo, who scowled and quickly looked away. I'd hardly spoken with him all winter. He had nothing to say when his mother was around and that was the only time I saw him. There was no reason for him to be cranky with me now.

Ziva's lilting voice caught my attention again. "What Belov will show you, you have never seen before," she said proudly. "From far to the south it comes, brought north by his father and taught to our people before my son's birth. There are humans to the south who make wonderful things and do many wonders. My Thistle has seen some of their beauty. Remember?" She gestured toward me and smiled broadly.

Ever since she'd come to join us, Ziva and I had shared a special bond. Sometimes she even called me 'daughter.' Of course I remembered. Their beach, the steep cliff, the rock inlaid with blue stones, the stones themselves, set in a substance that gleamed like the sun. The image was as bright as the day. I smiled back at her. Maybe I should tell Lugo about that exquisite wall. He liked learning new things. Maybe then he wouldn't be so cranky. I did need to speak with him. I'd asked him last fall if he'd help me teach the pups. He'd said he'd think about it. Now they were six months old. I needed an answer. I glanced his way and saw him staring at the ground. He looked ill.

"Stay close by," Ziva continued. "Belov is preparing something to show you. He'll return soon. Just a little while." Maybe Lugo had been sick. I'd seen little of him lately. The men left early each morning to hunt and didn't return until dark. Unlike the times when they'd followed the reindeer, they were rarely gone more than a day or two at a time now. But they'd taken so many red deer that they had to cover more ground, walking for hours before they found tracks. If I didn't speak now, it could be awhile before I got another chance. I made my way through the expectant crowd, the wet ground sucking at my feet.

"You are a stranger in the springtime," I said, smiling and glancing up at his rough chin. The West People scraped off their face hair with a sharpened rock. It always surprised me to see his uncovered jaw.

"You are a stranger all the time," he replied gruffly, talking to the sea.

I was accustomed to his surly manner. Hoping to see him smile, I bantered, "If you'd try my idea with the pups, you wouldn't have to spend your days walking the hills. You'd stay close by. Your mother could visit."

I knew right away I'd said the wrong thing. An angry redness flooded his face. "It is not my mother's company that I seek," he replied.

What had I said that offended him? Perhaps he was seeking Luba. Confused by his displeasure, I tried to explain myself. "It's just that I know she has a plan . . ."

"Nor are her plans a concern to me." He shook his head, glaring down at me. Then he muttered, "I have stayed away from you so that you could come to see me as separate from Eda. She has reasons of her own for wanting us together. Those reasons are not mine." He looked away.

Once again I'd said something wrong. I hadn't even had a chance to ask him about the dogs. They'd be grown before I got my answer. Still hoping to make things better, I reached for his arm. Off to the side I noticed Eda, watching us. I dropped my hand and whispered, "I'm sorry."

Belov was returning, clutching something in each hand. I watched curiously as he approached. One hand held a tiny boat, the size of a child's toy, narrow in the middle, curving upward at the ends, woven from hollow reeds. In the other, he carried a bundle of tightly rolled reeds, bound by long fronds. Belov walked past us and toward the fast-running, snow-swollen river. Everyone followed. Then he knelt on the bank and placed the little boat in the swift stream. It wobbled briefly, righted itself, and floated away, riding high in the water toward the sea. The Fish People were great swimmers. Belov could have easily retrieved the boat by himself. Instead, he held the reed bundle in both hands and jumped into the frigid water, letting the current carry him as he floated after the tiny craft.

reed boat from the south

"See, see!" Ziva exclaimed, clapping her hands. "He floats!"

"Does it ever sink?" asked Eda, her eyes growing large as she watched the reed bundle.

"Only when it gets soaked through. We can cross any river with this, any river. Or make rafts to carry things, at least long enough to get across a river or move downstream." Rafts made of grass? I'd never heard of such a thing.

Just before the little boat headed into the open sea, Belov grabbed it and paddled back to shore, one hand still around the bundle of reeds. The image of the little boat reminded me of something else, another idea I'd been thinking about almost as much as the dogs. But I'd really need help for that. I looked again for Lugo. He was sitting nearby, arms resting on his knees, watching the little boat and the young man swimming back to shore. I walked over to him and bent down to speak, choosing my words carefully.

"Lugo?" I whispered.

"What?" he said, as if it pained him to talk.

"I'm sorry I made you angry." He shrugged. "I always say the wrong thing. I don't know why. I want us to be friends."

His face softened.

"Will you help me with a plan?" I continued.

He looked at me and rolled his eyes. "What plan is this?"

"If you laugh, it will be the last plan I ever tell you," I replied. "Will you help? I'll hardly talk."

He smiled slightly and I knew the answer. Finally, I had a helper.

Strange Harvest

THAT DAY ON THE SHORE, WHEN I ASKED FOR HIS HELP, marked the beginning of my friendship with Lugo. Not long after, he started working with the pups, three solid black ones and one fuzzy grey. He took them on short trips to the woods when it was too wet to hunt. Before long, he was bringing them along with the men for the day. The hunters didn't mind, once they saw how the dogs obeyed him. All four of them were good trackers. But it was when Lugo and I started working on the boat that I came to know him better. We began that task early in the spring. It soon became an undertaking that seemed to have no end.

Ever since I'd seen Eda's hollow wooden cups, buoyant and sturdy, I'd thought of making a boat from a hollowed log. Like most of my ideas, it turned out to have some promise and be far more diffficult than I'd imagined. It was because of Lugo's patience that we stayed with it at all. Not really patience. He cursed and flung down the tools many times, stalking off into the woods to think, coming back eventually. But come back he did, shaking his head and starting again. We hollowed out small logs for practice, laying hot coals on top of the wood to burn out part of it, then cutting and scraping with an ax he'd made especially for the job. By summer, we'd found a shape that didn't capsize or take on water.

Then we looked for the stoutest tree we could find, settling on a big pine north of camp. Lugo worked for four days to chop it down, hacking the soft wood with a stone-headed ax. It took us another three days to cut off the limbs. Gokihar and Fire helped us lop off the short branches using little knives Lugo had made for them. Excited by the thought of our own boat, Gokihar began following the man around the camp, hanging on to his every word.

One wet day, after we'd trimmed the branches, Lugo persuaded the men to pull the massive log to the sea and float it the short distance home. Finally, amid grunts and curses, they'd rolled it back out of the

moving a log downstream

water and onto a level stretch of beach near the cave. That part was easy, compared to the scraping, burning, and smoothing we did for the next two months. Even when Lugo was gone with the men all day, he came back to the boat at night. Ochre and the others took pity on him and helped him chisel out the log.

The outer work we did afterwards, shaping both ends into narrow points extending from the broad base. Eda and Ziva often stood on the beach, watching the slow progress and sharing their observations. It was Eda who showed us how to cover the porous wood with pitch to keep it from swelling. When the day finally came to pull it into the water, the vessel floated. Two people could easily fit inside and maneuver it with short paddles. The boat still needed improvements, being

too heavy to carry and too tedious to build. And it capsized the second time out. Ochre immediately thought he saw the flaw in our design and went to work on a boat of his own. But I was proud of our accomplishment.

The two older women had become friends of sorts, ever since Eda had seen Belov's small reed boat. Admiring great skill of any kind, she'd been impressed. She'd warmed to Ziva, seeing her as an equal. They'd shown up to watch the day the men hauled the boat into the water. I'd heard Eda say triumphantly to the little Fish Woman, "Ah, the work of the West People. My sons learned from my brothers, who learned from my uncles, masters of wood, all of them. Fortunate for you that we're here."

Ziva had only smiled and nodded, willing to accept almost anything Eda said. Later she confided to me that the dug-out boat would be nothing but trouble and could never match the reed vessels from the south. Maybe, but I had to see for myself.

I was glad for the two women's friendship. Before Ziva came along, I'd been Eda's closest acquaintance, a role I was glad to share. Perhaps there was a deeper reason that Ziva had befriended the older woman, letting her have her small pleasures. Ziva was far wiser than I in matters of the heart. She may have sensed long before the rest of us that, beneath the surface, all was not right with Eda.

All that winter, Eda had seemed content, claiming her place as Elder and Teacher, beaming as she told of the wonderful people she'd left behind. I welcomed her new predictability, forgetting the wildness I'd once seen in her. And why shouldn't Eda have been happy? The winter had been mild, the easiest we'd ever known. Spring had come early, the snow melting quickly, the damp ground greening promptly. Birdsong had filled the forest while the nights were still long. Even the

snowgeese had returned early, their fuzzy broods hatching in the month of Waiting, wobbling behind their mothers when there should have been ice on the river. All that spring, I'd relished the clean simplicity of the dogs and the boat, work and sleep, the order of our days. It should have been enough for anyone. We had no reason to complain.

But while winter may have rested and spring come tenderly, Eda was changing like an unknown plant beneath the snow, turning to some bitter season of her own, some chilling in her soul. There were parts of every day when she wasn't with us. Her body was there, but not her mind. She'd gaze at some unknown danger which only she could see, gaze and moan. Looking back, I think I sensed the change earlier and ignored it. It reminded me too much of my last days with Tenja. Perhaps I'd given her over to Ziva to still my own uneasiness. If so, I was not alone. As the days grew longer and Eda became more anxious, everyone began avoiding her. Lugo kept an eye on her and made sure she ate. Though the old woman still crept up on me from time to time, Ziva was the only one who sought her out.

While I wished Eda no harm, I was relieved she had someone to talk with besides me. I tried to be polite, but I disliked this side of her. And I felt sorry for Lugo. He'd worked so hard on the boat, it seemed unfair that he had this new worry, with no time in between to rest. It was my concern for Lugo, rather than for his mother, that kept me aware of her fear.

"She'll be better when summer comes," Lugo would assure me, sounding uncertain of his own words.

I looked forward to the greening of the forest, hoping Eda would find some solace there. And for a while she did. She began spending her days in the woods, walking toward the trees as soon as she awakened. Lugo would soon follow, bringing her food. Sometimes I'd go

along. We'd find her wandering peacefully. "The trees bring her joy," he said one day. "She says they speak to her." I'd glanced at him and back to the old woman lumbering between the saplings. I hoped he was right.

But if the forest comforted her days, some inner darkness haunted her nights. Some nights she refused to sleep at all. She'd wander along the shore, moaning, the wind sweeping her tunic behind her like vulture wings until her sons found her and brought her home. Then she'd pat their arms and whimper, "My boys, my boys." Everyone would look away, uncertain what to say.

"Summer will save her," Lugo repeated. And so we waited and went on with our lives.

It was good the geese had come early. We needed the hefty eggs and the fat birds, since the fish catches were light. The adult trout still glided, orange and brown, in the gleaming streams. But where were their young? The salmon had all but disappeared. Perhaps they'd found new routes and other spawns more to their liking. "So," the Fish People joked, avoiding each other's eyes, "we fish for eggs this year." We made do and altered our ways, still finding enough to eat.

We tried not to talk about the fish when Eda was near. She saw the worst in any change, sure that a sea bird's shifting flight or the death of a tree portended trouble. One day, as I stood on the shore with Gokihar, waiting for the Fish People to pull up their nets, I heard her labored breathing behind me. She'd followed me again. I turned to say hello, surprised by the gauntness of her face.

"Lugo made you a fine boat, eh?" she said before I could even greet her. "Whatever you want, he can make. Do you not see the way the Fish Women look at him? One of them will take him soon. A grown man can't wait forever."

This was a conversation I avoided. I quickly turned my back and watched the men drawing in the catch. Once again, the nets were almost empty, holding nothing but a few squirming shiners. When Eda saw the flaccid webbing, she grabbed my arm. "See, it's as I told you," she said. "You can't save the fish!" I shook my head and motioned for Ziva to join us.

If Lugo had thought that the greening of the forest would soothe her, that was not to be. Fish changing their routes? We'd seen stranger things than that. But into the lush forest came a greater oddness still, marring the gentle spring and destroying summer's sweetness. A new life began to ripen in the trees, disgusting to all of us, but horrifying to Eda.

OCHRE SAW IT FIRST, coming home early one day after setting out rabbit snares, just as we were finishing our morning meal. "Something strange in the forest," he said to Magla. Eda jumped like a duck near a ferret.

"What?" Magla asked, irritated by anything outside of our routine.

"Come see."

We followed him down the beach and into the woods. Eda shuffled along at the back of the group, her hands to her face. Ziva fell in step with her while the children ran ahead. A few paces into the brush, Ochre pointed upward to a pine branch. A ball of grey worms hung from the bough. Ziva rushed to the tree and knocked the mass off with a stick, bending down to study the writhing creatures.

"I've seen these. To the south. They come with the heat. But they die with frost. They don't stay long."

We weren't likely to see frost for months. "Do they usually come in spring or fall?" I asked.

"Fall," she replied. "These are early."

"Oh."

We walked through the woods that day and the next, seeing a clump of worms here and there, knocking them off before they ate the new growth. It would be impossible to get them all, but we'd get rid of some. At least the birds liked them.

And then, with the first real warming, several days after we'd shoved the boat into the water, great balls of grey worms began appearing on more trees. All through the time called Gathering of Medicine, they were spreading from limb to limb, blooming like squirming flowers. The worms were ravenous. As the warm days continued, they came to drape entire stands of evergreen, devouring each needle, eating the green back to bark. Little clumps of them fell like ripe apples where we walked, leaving a greasy layer on the ground. Ochre took Lugo and two other men south to see how many trees were infected, traveling on the beach to avoid the slime. They returned in three days, having seen no healthy pine or spruce.

The worm eggs continued to hatch. The infestation was spreading northward. By the month of The Great Tree, the evergreens all the way to the timber line had been stripped bare. As if ravaged by fire, the forest stood black and naked as far as we could see. Only the birches showed a bit of green.

A fire was exactly what Eda wanted. Now, when she looked at the forest she'd loved so, she cringed and shuddered, shook a fist at the worms and muttered, "Burn them, burn them! They must be destroyed!" Lugo followed her when he could and gently turned her away from the trees, bringing her back to our circle. Then she'd sit quietly for a while, looking out to sea.

Sometimes Ziva sat with her, talking of the old days and combing

Eda's hair. "The Old Ones," Ziva tried to explain to the rest of us, "those such as Eda, are tied to Earth, their bodies having followed Her for so long. Eda is wild because she feels Earth's aching as her own."

Perhaps that was true. The change in the forest made us more sympathetic, but no one really knew how to act around Eda. Perhaps that didn't matter. She wasn't easily swayed by kindness or diversion. The worms tormented her as if the tree bark were her flesh. She wanted them dead. And she watched for her moment. One windy night, when we were listening to one of Ochre's stories, she slipped away from the fire. No one but Lugo saw her go. But I was watching him. Smooth as a cat, he stole after her. I followed. Up the shore and northward we

went, to the stand of ancient trees, their bare branches rising starkly in the twilight. I saw a glow just ahead and rushed toward it. It was Eda, carrying a torch.

Lugo came upon her just as she was rearing back to fling it into the dead wood. He grabbed her arm. The enraged woman clawed at him, screaming, "We must destroy them!" But Lugo quickly overpowered her and tossed the burning stick on the beach. He laid an arm around her quivering shoulders while Eda sobbed.

Perhaps she was right. Perhaps we should have destroyed them. But all we had was a narrow strip of rocky shore between the timber and the sea. None of us knew how far or fast a fire might burn. Lugo led the old woman home. For days, my dreams were haunted by a vision of the forest engulfed in flames.

◙ ◙ ◙

PERHAPS BECAUSE OF THE BLIGHT in the woods, Yarrow proposed that
we return to the Solstice Gathering that summer, or at least try to
make the trip. We'd continued our own observances here, but there'd
been no journeys north, no reunions, no steaming pools, no huge feasts.
Nor had we heard anything from the other Reindeer People. Perhaps,
if they'd survived the terrible winter five years ago, they still returned
to the Great Tree. Even now, the northerners who'd joined us looked
longingly toward the mountains from time to time.

When Yarrow first mentioned the trip, the People were wary, perhaps afraid of what they'd find or reluctant to leave the safety of home.
But if we were ever to have answers about the others, we'd have to go
see for ourselves. There was little chance of a messenger seeking us
here, at the edge of the land, where no paths crossed. Anyway, the only
traveler I'd met who moved from camp to camp was Ephus. For all I
knew, he was far to the south. Who could tell where he might be, he or
the Arn? Or if Ephus was even alive? He'd be at least forty by now.

But it was the worms that decided things for us. Even Eda would
be going, climbing the mountains on her old legs. Of course, she'd
never been to this Gathering before but Lugo had insisted, saying she
needed the change. Though no one said it, we hoped the creatures
would be dead by the time we returned.

And so, once again, the day for our departure arrived. The old
excitement returned. The nervous crowd talked, waited, and ran back
for what they'd forgotten. Lugo, Ochre, Vasto, and Rube had pulled
the boat back onto the beach the previous day, panting as they'd rolled
it over several logs, drawing it high on the land. We couldn't risk having it taken by a storm.

My eyes sought Lugo in the crowd. He was with the men, laughing at some story. For the first time in weeks, he looked relaxed. Eda's

strangeness had been hard on him. But even Eda seemed happy that morning, smiling while Ziva chattered about the wonders of the hot springs and how the two of them would soak their bones. Maybe I'd finally have a chance to talk to Lugo without the distraction of Eda. I'd never really thanked him for his work on the boat.

This would be Gokihar's first distant adventure. He hopped about on long, skinny legs and listened to Fire and Zale. For days they'd been telling him about the Great Tree and the gathering cave. Though the two of them had been little more than babies when we'd made the last journey, they'd forgotten nothing. My brother was a handsome boy. Though only ten, he brought laughter to everyone. Already the giggling Fish Girls followed him everywhere he went. Zale followed him, too. Now in his eighth year, Zale was a hearty youth who had his father's way with tools but he was reckless and acted without thinking. Most of us had rescued him at one time or another. Fire had kept an eye on the younger boy ever since the summer he'd pulled him from the river. Gokihar looked up to both older boys almost as much as he did Lugo, but I watched him closely around Zale.

Birch and Leu stood hand in hand, her belly slightly swollen. They'd had their joining earlier in the month, an odd celebration, here on the harsh beach with the bare worm trees behind us. Always before, our joinings had taken place in the high valley, the mountains rising behind us, the meadows flung open below. But Change took us down new paths. And now there'd be a new child, the first since Gokihar. How we longed for the promise of a baby!

"It's late! Let's go," Yarrow said. The sun was high and she was ready. Yarrow would have an assistant on this trip. We'd never traveled to the Solstice Gathering from the south before, only from our summer mountain. But the Fish People knew the way. It was the same path they'd always taken. Ziva would assist her with directions, Ziva and her son Belov, who seemed to be her choice for helper and heir.

Yarrow's man, Zalec, was staying behind, keeping watch over the camp. Two elders from the Fish People would remain as well. This would be the first time Zalec hadn't traveled with us, but his bad leg had grown weaker, the flesh shriveling like a dried eel. He'd insisted he didn't mind staying, that Yarrow was to take her place at the front of the group as she always did. I'm sure neither wanted to draw out their farewells.

I myself was glad Zalec was staying. I needed someone to look after the dogs. While he had no real fondness for them, he respected them like he did weapons or tools. No harm would come their way. The pups were almost full-grown and could have made the trip, but I didn't know how they'd behave with strangers. I'd promised Zalec he could choose a dog for his own when we returned.

"Let's go!" Yarrow called again. She began walking.

Everyone fell in line or ran to catch up. Fire and Zale dashed to the front, ahead of the Fish Girls. The three girls rarely took their eyes off Fire, giggling when he looked their way. Fire and Zale would likely join with the Fish Girls some day since we had no girls of our own, except Narta. I remembered my last walk to the Gathering, prancing along with Silka and Birch, reciting the months of the year.

Gokihar was tugging on my hand, eager to join the other children. "Go ahead then," I said. The moment I let go, he rushed off to be with Narta. He'd tire soon, being only five. Narta, now in her sixth year, was the loveliest child I'd ever seen. More amazing than her beauty was her goodness. Unlike her mother at a younger age, Narta never expected special treatment. She needed little from any of us, glowing from some secret source. Silka must have learned from her daughter's example, for even she had become more generous since Narta's birth. Narta was walking with the Fish Girls, as elegant as a deer. She dropped back to be with Gokihar and the two of them walked together, the pale-haired boy towering over the older girl.

I fell into step with the others. We began moving along the shore. Ahead of us, the barren pine and spruce extended halfway up the mountains, where they were replaced by shrub and stone. At least the worms hadn't taken the high brush. How wonderful to leave this place behind, I thought, welcoming the wind in my face. We'd follow the beach northward until the shoreline curved, then continue straight north toward the mountains. The first night, we'd sleep in the foothills. The second day we'd begin our climb.

We were skirting the ancient forest on our right, just before we left the beach, when a movement at the edge of the infested timber caught my eye. I glanced over in time to see a creature peering out from behind a naked pine. He turned and bounded away. Wolf! He must be very old, I thought, a familiar sadness settling over me.

From the beach, we followed a rock-lined stream which made a narrow passage though the wormy trees and to a ridge beyond. Ziva had told us there was a little valley over that ridge and above the tree line. Our plan was to push on for that and leave the trees behind.

I heard footsteps behind me and Lugo sidled next to me. The wind was blowing his hair across his forehead. He stood close enough that I could see the smile lines around his eyes. What a pleasant face, I thought, my sadness lifting. He nodded and smiled.

The Awakening Ice

AT LAST I HAD A CHANCE TO TALK TO LUGO with no interruptions. Eda was with Ziva at the back of the group, her face already flushed. Gokihar was walking contentedly at Narta's side. Lugo slowed his long legs, matching his stride to mine. We walked along quietly. It was good to have him near.

After several moments, he spoke. "Tell me again of your Star Watcher, the one who died."

Tenja? Why Tenja? The simple questions I'd wanted to ask vanished with his request. I felt a tinge of guilt whenever I remembered her. Though I still watched the sky from time to time and recalled much of what she'd taught me, I lacked her single-mindedness. If she were still alive, she'd be disappointed in me. But if she'd lived, I wouldn't have to watch the sky at all. "Well, I don't know what you want to know," I finally replied.

"Just what she taught you. Why the two of you left your people, what she learned when you were on the shore alone."

"How is it you've heard any of this?" I asked.

"From Eda. Some things Ziva told her."

"Oh."

What would I tell him? Should I talk about the hazy balls of light that grew a little larger each year? Why frighten good people with tales of horror, like Eda used to do? Wasn't it better to follow Ochre's example? He just dismissed the lights impatiently as distractions from his work.

"Well?" he said.

"I'm thinking. It's been so long."

It would have been easier to be ignorant of the stars altogether than to understand so little. My knowledge was a net I'd flung about myself, big enough to separate me from the others, but too small to help anyone. I'd kept my thoughts to myself the last four years, swallowed my fear like a bitter medicine, and repeated Tenja's words, "What matters is our love."

My uneasiness had not disappeared. I still felt its weight. Ziva was the only person I talked to about the stars. Tiny Ziva, larger than life. She could take her fear and transform it into something better. I just worried if I thought too much about the future. Better to think about the task at hand.

Now Lugo wanted to hear it all again. It would be different, talking to him. He was just a person, like me. What would I tell him, what would I omit? Could I just say whatever came into my mind, like I'd done with the boat? He hadn't laughed at me then or argued. Lugo was a practical man, but one who considered new ideas. Maybe he'd understand about the lights. A spark of hope flickered. Maybe I didn't have to carry this burden alone.

"Lugo," I said, hearing the tremor in my voice, "there's something you may not know, something your mother knows." I looked around at the happy walkers, their faces bright in the sun. "But if I tell you, your life will change. You may not want that change." I waited.

"And this knowledge—is that what holds you apart?" he asked.

"I don't know what you're talking about. Anyway, it's complicated. I'll tell you tonight, after we stop. I'll tell you about the new stars." I looked up into his dark face and pressed his hand. "I'm going to check on Gokihar."

We cleared the ridge early that evening, soon reaching the valley Ziva had described. A gentle meadow stretched northward, ending below two mountains. The abutting slopes were joined by an ice-filled wedge, from which a tiny waterfall trickled. We hurried across the meadow and dropped our packs, splashing our faces and cupping our hands under the chilly water.

"It's even better now," said Ziva, letting the drizzle fall on her hair. The dripping water had gathered into a tiny stream at our feet, disappearing underground less than a man-length away. "Always before we had to walk to the river. Now a stream comes to us." The water had yet to dig a channel or form a pool, though the ground beneath our feet was damp. It must be a new stream, I thought, born of summer.

We were happy with ourselves, as well as tired. While the women built a fire, the men went for food. We'd eaten oysters earlier in the day, before our climb. But we were famished now.

Ochre, Lugo, and Vasto headed upward to the snowline, no doubt hoping to find some tracks. The others went to find the creek Ziva had described. We heard Ochre's call just before dark and ran to see what he'd found. The three men were moving slowly down the slope. I could make out a dark outline behind them, like a large hump being dragged. Not until they were just in front of us did I figure out what it was. A musk ox, probably an old male. It was hard to tell, since the animal was covered with mud. I'd never eaten their meat before.

I took a step closer, rubbing my hands along the creature's curving horns. "How'd you get it?" I asked. "What'd you use?"

"Patience," Ochre replied. "We used patience." He dragged the carcass closer. "Oxen tire quickly in deep snow," he said. "That much I knew. But they also tire in mud."

It seemed that the high snow had melted, stranding the ox in a patch of boulders and slush. The men had roused the creature from the rocks and into the mud, where it soon floundered.

Magla stepped over, wiping some of the muck from the shaggy coat. "Good hide," she said, pulling the long hairs straight. "We'll come back for the coat when we return."

The men dragged the carcass to a grassy knoll and the women went to work butchering it. Silka and I made a small fire of old grass, there being no wood, and slowly roasted thin strips of the lean flesh. The others waited with growling bellies. By the time we finished eating, the new moon was high. One by one, everyone settled under their robes and dozed under the clear night sky, everyone except Lugo and me.

I covered Gokihar and stood, motioning for Lugo to join me. All afternoon I'd been considering what to tell him about the stars. But first we had to get away from camp so our voices didn't carry. "Follow me," I whispered, laying my sleeping robe across my shoulders. Night was chillier there than on the shore. He moved silently behind me.

The fire had gone out long ago, but we made our way easily across the meadow, our path lit by a sliver of moonlight. I stopped where the earth swelled slightly, patting the ground to be sure it was dry. "Let's talk here," I said. I dropped the robe on the grass and smoothed it. We sat facing each other, Lugo's face shining palely. For a moment, I was so aware of his body next to mine that I forgot the reason for our journey. But once I looked past his face and upward, I remembered.

"See," I said quickly, swallowing hard and pointing. I felt his eyes on me. "The new stars. You can tell they're stars and not planets. Or something like stars. Parts of stars. The stars move all together, the old stars anyway. And the planets move in their own way." I was talking too fast, but my words rushed on. Perhaps my thoughts had been held in too long. Or maybe I didn't want them turning back, toward the man who sat so close his body warmed the air before me. "I won't tell you all of that now, all that about the planets. Just this one thing. That red planet, see, above us, how it shines with an orange light? Tenja called it the Warrior—for its color—the new stars keep moving closer to it . . ."

I looked at Lugo to see if he understood. In that moment, he grabbed me, pushing his face down on mine and stopping my words. I shoved him back, gasping. "Wait. There's something I have to tell you, about the new stars . . . !" His arms tightened around me. "Lugo," I said, grabbing his hands, "I have to tell you something first." He jerked away and I sat silently, forgetting what I'd wanted to say.

And in that silence, he began to speak. His words were bitter. "Do you think I know nothing about the new stars, about the changes that are upon us, about the fear of which the people never speak? You are not the only one with visions of the future, not the only one who dreams and fears and wonders. But you are the only one of us who has chosen to stop living now because of what might happen tomorrow." I glared at him, my mouth hanging open. Still he continued. "You are the reason Eda dragged us here four years ago, although I didn't know it then."

"What are you talking about?" I demanded, ignoring for a moment the stinging unfairness of his words.

"We were never lost in a blizzard. Eda told us a vision had come to her. We were to bring her to some new place, some cave along the shore, where a woman lived alone, a woman with a name like thorns. That we were to find this woman, because the future lay with her. That was all she said. And so we found your people and then we found you. Meanwhile our people moved on. Our old world went on without us. And soon I no longer wanted it back. I only wanted you."

"Because of Eda . . . ?"

"Not because of Eda. For myself," he said. He sighed sharply, as if speaking to a difficult child. "Eda had revealed only part of her vision, not the real reason we were here. Two winters ago, she finally told me. It is that which has made her strange. And kept me distant from you."

I was baffled. What vision would possibly bring them to me, to a lonesome camp on a rocky shore far from the crossroads? "What? What did she say?" I asked.

He took a deep breath and looked away, as if trying to remember the exact words. "She said, 'When Sky makes war on Earth, none will survive but a son of one named Thistle and the woman with whom he joins.' "

He said no more. But the silence crashed around me like thunder. "No, that can't be. She's wrong. No."

"A son of one named Thistle, not necessarily her first son," he continued bitterly. "Eda hoped that you and I would join, that it would be my son, her blood, her people, that survived. I don't think she would hurt Gokihar, for fear of your Earthmaker's wrath. But if another son could be conceived, if there could be another choice, she'd want her line to carry on."

It was as I'd first thought. These West People were strange, with their stories and signs, their wild eyes. I'd heard of madness, had seen the madness that came when babies died. Maybe these people had that madness all the time. That was it! Eda was afraid of her children dying and that fear had made her crazy. So, that was the explanation, the reason for Eda's odd wanderings, why she glared at my son as if the tender boy were an enemy . . .

The silence of the night swelled around me and other moments of madness rose up in my memory. Tenja's torment on the beach, her battle with the visions given to her there. And Grandma Sela's burning eyes. Thought Holder's desolate stare. Had they seen the same future? No, surely it was just that strange old woman, the mother of the deluded fool who sat before me now. For a moment, my old rage toward Eda began to rise. I glanced into Lugo's eyes. There was no madness there, only sorrow, a sorrow far beyond the weariness of the day. My anger fell away. All Eda wanted was to save her son, at least a part of him, in the only way she knew. My love for my own child swelled within me. I'd do anything to keep him alive. Still, the story made no sense.

And what of my Gokihar, Born Among Wolves? Why would my child be the one to endure and survive Sky's attack? Why would Sky want to hurt us at all? And how? How could Sky bring such desolation? The new stars? Surely Earthmaker would never allow such a thing. Surely this was one of those delusions that live at night, fading in the bright sense of day. Yet it had gnawed at me for almost six years. Like a beast that knew its freedom was near. That's how Eda had described it.

Suddenly, all was darkness and the world a bottomless hole into which I'd tumbled. Everything that stood for knowledge vanished —Ora's stories, Tenja's markings, Eda's warnings, my own vision—all of them disappeared, unable to withstand the awful image in my mind. In their wake they left a great dark tunnel and me in an endless fall.

Would I too become mad?

I'd been staring at Lugo's hands as my thoughts raged through me—strong hands, laying across his thighs, reflecting the light of the moon. Solid hands, real. Was their realness more powerful than the terror? With a trembling born of hope and fear, I reached for one of the spectral hands. The flesh was warm in my grasp.

"And you?" I asked haltingly, grasping for something solid. "What do you want?"

"I need no legacy but to live out the life I have. My longing is for a woman, not a child."

"All right," I said. I had been too long alone. I tightened my grasp.

We sat closely but motionless, having come upon a darkness far blacker than night. Death it was, brought quickly forward from the shadows where it had quietly waited. Seeing it, I felt small. At least I no longer had to watch for it alone.

We waited until the first light tinged the horizon, then returned to camp. Everyone was still asleep. I lay down between Gokihar and Narta, hiding in their innocence, awakening when the first beam of sunlight streamed into my eyes. The children slept on, their soft faces mindless of the sky. Everyone else was quiet as well, except for Silka. She sat nearby, stretching her arms, black hair tumbling over her shoulders.

She smiled as she looked my way. "A beautiful day," she said between yawns. "Sun loves us." She seemed amused by something.

It was gloriously warm. I threw off my cover. Strange to be sweating at sunrise at the foot of a mountain. The trickling waterfall threw off little glints of light. The water sounded louder today. Perhaps I'd been too weary to notice the noise last night. I felt odd. Not enough sleep, probably, or my strange time with Lugo. Whatever it was, I was restless. I needed to move.

I pulled on my boots. "Silka, will you watch Goki? I'm going for a walk."

"Another walk?" she said, raising her eyebrows. Her smile grew broader.

I crawled carefully between the dozing children and stood. Now was no time to visit with Silka. The morning was so warm I wouldn't need a cloak. I looked around for Fire, wanting his simple presence. He was sprawled near Zale, his mouth hanging open as he slept. Stepping carefully between the bodies, I leaned down to touch his shoulder. "Fire, get up," I whispered. "Come with me." He rubbed his eyes and followed, too weary to protest. Before we'd traveled far, he turned his back to me and relieved himself.

"Where are we going?" he mumbled, pushing the red hair from his face.

"I feel like climbing a hill," I said, gesturing to the two peaks. "I don't want to go alone."

He shrugged. I'd asked for stranger things. We started upward, taking the most direct way, scrabbling over rocks and grabbing at brush. Fire quickly moved ahead. It would be a lovely day, hot but breezy. A few wispy clouds skidded across the brilliant sky. A hawk careened past us, claws outstretched, swooping down for his breakfast. I started to sweat.

On we went. I watched Fire's brown legs digging into the dirt ahead of me. Above us and to the right, I saw the notch of dirty ice from which the waterfall trickled. Summer was turning the ice to slush. The wind coming over the mountain picked up as we neared the top. It whipped around us from time to time, cooling the sweat on my face. I felt the need to hurry. "Fire, wait for me!"

"Come on, then," he yelled, his voice muffled by the wind.

I glanced back, amazed at the distance we'd come. Far below us the People were beginning to stir. Everyone was probably awake by now. They'd wonder about us, but they were accustomed to my walks.

Fire slowed down and we cleared the summit together. The mountains opened into a clear vista before us. Below us lay a high alpine lake, long and narrow, as bright as the sky. The lake basin was totally rimmed by mountains, the lowest point being the little notch of ice just below us. The water was high, I thought, the shoreline more than halfway up the slopes. It was easy to figure out why. The snow had disappeared from all the peaks, melting in the sun, draining to the lake. Chunks of ice bobbed in the azure water, like angular clouds whipped by the wind. Below us white waves curled, breaking near the ice plug.

glacial plug before the melting

"It's like another sky!" Fire cried, thrusting his arm out over the water while the wind blew back his hair.

Something was wrong. I felt it like a sickness, like awakening ill and trying to remember where you were. Something about the surge of the water against the slushy wedge below. I couldn't think in the roaring wind. But as I lifted my face to the brisk air, some dormant part of me awakened, some animal terror from a distant time. And then I understood.

"Fire!" I screamed. "Get back. Go back! The People! Get them out of there. Run!" He looked at me, confused. I grabbed his arm and pulled him with me, back down the mountain. "Get down there! To the People. Tell them to move!"

Trusting my terror, he scrambled down the slope. I tried to keep up, but halfway down I tripped over a stone and flew to the ground. Standing again, I wondered at the red liquid rising on my hands. All I could think of was my son. Waving my arms, I yelled to the unsuspecting people below. "Get away, go!" Alerted by the rocks we'd dislodged, they saw us before they heard us, their upturned faces seeking me out. Again I yelled, "Climb, hurry. The water!"

Still they stood motionless, unable to hear. I continued downward, stumbling near the bottom, quickly covering my head with my arms and rolling the rest of the way. Lugo was standing over me when I looked up. "Get Gokihar!" I screamed. He hurried away. Fire was there already, telling the skeptical crowd to leave. "Get out of here now!" I yelled. "Before the ice breaks! Follow me." They stood like stones.

Lugo ran back to us, carrying Gokihar. The next thing I heard was his booming voice. "Do what she says!" he ordered. They began scrambling after me. First I followed the edge of the meadow, hurrying along where the mountain met the level ground, away from the waterfall. Then I veered upward at an angle, clambering away from the wedge of slush.

"Where are we going?" they asked behind me. "Why?" "What is it?" My heart pounded above their confused questions. I had neither the breath nor the time to answer. I pointed ahead, showing them our direction. Lugo hurtled up the slope with Gokihar. The others grumbled but kept moving. Finally, halfway up the side of the mountain, well to the west of the falls, I threw myself down, panting. Lugo stopped beside me, setting Gokihar on the ground. The boy ran to me. One by one, the others gathered, sighing and shaking their heads. Eda was the last to arrive, all but carried by Vasto. Wiping the sweat from their faces, they lowered themselves to the ground and looked back to where we'd been. Nothing had changed. They turned to me, glaring.

Yarrow was the first to speak. "What are you doing?" she demanded.

"Wait," I gasped. "Just wait."

By now the sun was high. I could hear the moaning of the wind and the people's panting. No birds. Only silence beyond us. We waited without words. I looked to the distance, avoiding the furtive glances. And then, beneath the wind, another sound, a low grinding as if stone rubbed against stone. Their hot eyes turned away from me and back toward the notch in the mountain. I stared as well, grasping Gokihar's hand so tightly he pulled away. And then we saw it.

The wedge of slush bulged slightly, then gave way, not bit by bit, but all at once, as a great rush of grey water poured through the broken dam and gushed to the meadow below. The place where we'd slept was gone. Still the water surged. Boulders and logs hurtled through the notch as well, tumbling down the mountain. In an instant, beneath our shocked eyes, a wave of dirty foam, faster than the tide at sea, spilled across the land and rushed into each crevice, the hungry water lapping at the meadow's farthest edge. It no longer reflected the blue of the sky. The flood swirled grey and brown, like some dark secret the mountains had released. The gentle valley was gone, swallowed by a great glacial wave.

We sat motionless, gaping at the torrent, hovering, trembling, rats from a storm, our old world swirling away. The waves continued to rise, gouging out great chunks of earth as though water was born to climb. No memories opened to help us understand. This was new. By midday it was over, the land transformed, the water eddying peacefully, satisfied, resting after a feast. The high lake had claimed a new home.

Holding Gokihar, smoothing back his hair, I watched the water settle. By late afternoon, it had receded slightly. A curved ridge of stone and gravel at the south edge of the meadow marked its farthest reaches. A few of the older people were sobbing. Zale and Fire were tossing stones down the mountainside, trying to hit the water. Some of the others, the Mothers and the hunters, were looking at me strangely. Did they think I'd caused it? I avoided their eyes.

Hearing the shuffle of feet beside me, I looked up to see Lugo. Once again, his voice rang out. "Your Earthmaker told this woman about a great danger," he said, gesturing toward me, "and this woman told us. This is a time to give praise and thanks for our safety." As if a great mystery had been solved, the others stopped their trembling and began to smile. Of course that was what had happened. Of course. Earthmaker had spoken to me and saved us. That was it. They nodded and sighed and stepped over to grasp my hand. Once again Earthmaker had saved us. "Good work, good work. Well done." Even Yarrow patted my knee and thanked me, friendly once again. Lugo dropped down beside me.

Once more, all was calm. The innocent water sloshed below us, as if it had simply awakened from a slumber, stretched and turned, and then devoured everything in its path before it sighed and slept again. In its wake, it left no doubt who was master.

The voices around us were soft and tentative, seeking to understand. I remembered something Ida had said years ago, about the People needing many habits and few changes. Glancing uneasily at their faces, I leaned toward Lugo. "Even the mountains are strangers now," I whispered. Who knew what other mysteries lay hidden between us and the Great Tree? Could we push ahead through still more secrets, more melted ice ready to cover us? Did we have the heart to try? Or should we return south to the worm slime? Where would we go from here?

Ochre and Magla stood at the edge of the group, his low voice followed by her higher one, like birds of different kinds answering each other. It would soon be dark. Yarrow went to join them and came back with a plan.

"Build a fire," she said. "We'll sleep here tonight, since this ledge is the only level place."

We burnt more grass, which smoldered in the damp. Some of the roasted oxen flesh was still with us, though we'd lost the heavy hide. We gnawed the cold meat and waited for a leader to speak, any leader. Finally, Ochre took our thoughts and wove a cloak of answers, strong enough to cover us for a while. "We'll climb the hill in the morning," he said, glancing to Yarrow. She nodded. "We'll see the empty lake bed. Thistle says the mountain snow is gone. There'll be no danger of more flooding. We'll find the animals the water left behind. Their carcasses may still be fresh. We'll go no farther, but wait there for Sun's Promise, give thanks, and rest."

That would be all right, I thought, a good plan. Some nodded or murmured. Others shrugged. And so the next morning, I again climbed to the top of the mountain, this time with everyone else. I looked down at the lake bed Fire and I had seen the previous day. All that was left of it were shallow pools and scattered stones surrounded by black muck. Hawks and crows perched on the stones and dived at the mud, feasting. We made our camp high above that valley, to avoid the smell. Then we waited.

Without seeing the morning light burst through its special place near the Great Tree, we couldn't know for sure just when Sun turned south. For four days we watched and rested, thinking private thoughts. Sky seemed the same as ever. All seemed well. By the fifth day, I was sure we'd passed the day of the summer solstice. We headed home warily. As I'd feared, the worms still clung to the trees. But something else had happened in our absence, something so amazing that we forgot the blight in the forest, at least for a while.

448

The Light on the Water

I'D FELT CLOSE TO LUGO THE NIGHT HE TOLD ME ABOUT EDA'S VISION. I appreciated his loyalty and his help with Gokihar the next day. But the flood had driven me back into myself. I was relieved in a way. He made me nervous, unable to concentrate. Life was simpler with just me and my son. I was friendly enough when Lugo came around, though I think he sensed my reserve. If it bothered him, he didn't let it show. He'd accept my change of mind eventually, I hoped.

The trip back home was uneventful. Zalec must have been watching for us. Soon after the camp came into sight, he was on the beach, limping toward us and waving his arms. The wind swallowed his words until we were almost upon him. "A traveler, a traveler!" he was yelling, gesturing for us to follow. Could it be Ephus? Even Anish? My heart raced. Perhaps there were other travelers, as well, wild people for whom the world was home. I started to run. The dogs came to meet me, barking wildly and jumping until I knocked them away.

A strange creature stood in front of our cave, skin dark as currants, black hair wrapped in coils. A close-fitting tunic covered the traveler's

449

chest. At first, I thought the sinewy body was that of a man, until I noticed the small swell of breasts. Dark legs as spare as young trees protruded from a short garment wrapped around her waist. From her neck hung a bone carving, a delicate span of horns the width of my palm. But it was her eyes that caught me. They were like dark suns that had seen all things and loved them.

The traveler gestured slowly toward herself, repeating one word. "Konya, Konya." I took that to be her name.

"She came two days ago," Zalec said. "From the southeast. I think she's waiting for someone. I don't know her words."

Yarrow tried several phrases, but Konya shook her head. Eda spoke the language of the West People to her, our words said differently. Again the stranger looked puzzled. Finally, Ziva whispered something to her son and he ran toward their thatched house. Belov returned with the little replica of the reed boat and held it up to the dark stranger. The woman smiled and nodded.

"Just as I thought," said Ziva. "She's from the Bull People. Belov's father crossed their land, a broad, treeless place cut by rivers. It's south of here, with barren mountains to the east and desert on the west. She's come a long way. I know none of their words."

"Who are the Bull People?" I asked. Ziva knew a little about almost everything.

"A slow, strong tribe," she said. "Lovers of beauty. They make fine things with their hands. Like bulls, they live mostly from grasses. These they cut and grind and cook. They leave grass offerings for their bulls, which they butcher as well."

"That's why they're called Bull People? Because of their strength?"

"That and their stubborness. They can't be pushed or driven by anyone. I've never heard of any of them coming this far north."

Ziva spoke a few unfamiliar words, but the visitor showed no sign of recognition. I stepped closer to the strange woman, gesturing to her pendant and smiling. She smiled back. Then she made a sound like 'sss,' which meant nothing to any of us. Who she was and why she'd come was a mystery.

By evening, everyone had settled in, the beach again alive with drying racks, noisy children, and busy women. Gokihar was exhausted. He hadn't rested well since the flood and I'd sent him inside to sleep. The rest of us were also moving slowly. After a cold supper of dried cod and cherries, we stretched out by the fire. Konya sat quietly at the edge of the group, eating little. From time to time I gazed at her. It was exciting to see a stranger in our midst, especially one from so far away, but frustrating to share so little. An image began to form in my mind.

Perhaps there was a way we could understand each other. Maybe I could bring out my hide, the one with Earthmaker's symbols. I'd rarely looked at it the last five years. At one time, I'd thought of showing it to Eda but I'd decided she was too strange. Yarrow might have been interested, but she had other concerns. Ziva had seen it once. She'd smiled and said it was beautiful. But I could tell she didn't really appreciate it. "I need no marks on hides," she'd explained. "I know your thoughts from your eyes." That was the old way of knowing, I realized. She didn't seem to care that not everyone could do that now. Perhaps there was something in those marks the foreigner could understand. I decided to take it out in the morning, since it was already dark.

I awoke early. From the beach came the sound of male voices, probably Lugo and Vasto at the boat. Lugo wanted to work on it, he'd said, before they dragged it back to sea. He was a hard worker. I admired that. He'd leave with the others when they went to hunt, I was sure, but return to the boat in the evening.

Gokihar ran off to find Fire and Zale, though I wanted to wait in the cave until the men were gone. I brought down the rolled hide with the painted shapes, eager to study it again before I showed it to the traveler. By the time I carried the bundle outside, the women were tending the drying racks and the hunters were gone. I found a quiet spot under a tree and unrolled it. As I ran my hands over the marks, they came to life, each with a story of its own. I thought about the shapes for a while, then went to find the dark woman.

She was where she'd been the previous day, sitting on the shore staring out to sea. Perhaps Zalec was right. Maybe she was waiting for someone. I knelt down by her. "Konya," I began, trying to get the sound right, "Konya?" She nodded. "I'm called Thistle," I continued.

She raised her eyebrows. "Sss, Sss?" she asked.

"Thistle," I repeated.

"Sssle!" She smiled brightly and started to get up.

"No, wait!" I said, grabbing her arm. She sat back down and I spread the hide at her feet. She stared at it, her eyes gleaming. Then she reached for the tree-like **Y**, the symbol of Earthmaker, our shelter, root, and support, and began tracing that mark with a thin finger.

"Ah," she said, nodding and drawing out the sound. She tapped her fists over her heart, then opened them out to the world. Did they have the same symbol for Earthmaker?

I watched as she pointed at the **V**s, **Λ**s, and **W**s. Holding up her hand to let me know she'd be back, Konya crawled to her pack and pulled out a hide of her own. She moved as quickly as a girl, I thought, though I knew from her face she was much older. Her weathered hands unrolled a goat skin. Strewn across it were tiny markings, drawn neatly with a dye and some sharp instrument, the same zigzag shapes I'd used. I had no idea if her marks also meant male and female,

452

like our **V** and **∧** . But surely most people used them as signs for mountain and water.

A long, jagged line stretched from the top to the lower half of the goat skin, veering to the right near the bottom. I pointed to it. "What's this?" I asked, to myself as much as anyone. To the left of that line were the **W**s for water; to the right, a scattering of **∧**s, the sign for mountain. "Is this a map?" I asked, incredulous. Sometimes Yarrow scratched quick maps in the dirt, to help her choose a route. Ephus did that too, but I'd never seen a permanent map. "You're a mapmaker!" I said. Konya looked at me blankly.

Then she pointed to the wavy lines and gestured toward the sea. Those lines did mean water! She'd drawn many **∧**s to the north of us and made smaller ones angling south along the coast, past the Fish People's old home. To the east, she'd drawn no mountains. That would be correct. Everyone knew that country was a rolling plain. A dotted line snaked up from the southeast. Maybe it showed the way she'd come. Maybe this wasn't only a map, but a picture of her route as well. Except that at the bottom of the hide, the dotted lines went straight across the open sea. Was there no land route to her home?

Along the broken lines, she'd drawn open circles, the symbol we used to mark the days. Touching each one, I counted. Fifty-seven small circles, ten of them on the south side of the water. She'd traveled ten days just to leave her own land? Could Earth be that huge? I looked at her again.

For the rest of the morning, we spoke with our hands, even making a few new marks we both understood. Ziva was right. These people were grass eaters. The stranger showed me how they picked long stems of grass, pulled off the seeds, and ground them between stones. Then she drew more pictures in the sand, amazing pictures. Had she really seen such things? And if she knew of such wonderful things, why would she travel so far just to make a picture of our simple land? When I could think of no other way for us to communicate, I left her on the shore and went to bring Gokihar some food.

The men were already back from the woods, disgusted by the worms. Apparently, the meat animals had all fled. We were lucky to have fish. I found Gokihar with Lugo, who was teaching him to carve a fish hook from wood. When the boy saw me, he jumped up and hurried to show me his work. "Thank you, Lugo. For teaching him," I said.

Lugo shrugged, keeping his eyes on his work. "He learns quickly. The traveler, did you find out more about her?"

"Some. I think she crossed the open sea," I said. At that, he looked up and raised his eyebrows. "I'll probably tell everyone about her to-night, as much as I know."

"Good," said Lugo. "Good. Well, I'll look forward to that then." He stood, picked up his tools, and walked away.

I handed Gokihar his food—walnuts, dried apples, salted cod, and water. He wrinkled his nose. "Lugo's strange today," I said.

"Not to me," Gokihar replied.

I sat with him to make sure he ate. After a few bites he ran off to find Lugo. Finishing off his lunch, I went to help Ziva at the fish racks, eager to talk to her about Konya. Yarrow soon joined us. As I'd anticipated, she wanted me to tell the group what I'd learned from the newcomer. Probably because of Gokihar, the People expected me to understand the ways of strangers. I didn't mind, since I loved learning new things. And it would give me a reason to talk about the symbols on the hide.

Just as we were gathering for supper, Gokihar ran up with a string of fish. He and Lugo must have been trying out the new fish hooks.

The catch was too small to cook, but the boy liked feeding them to the dogs. I caught him by the arm before he disappeared again. He'd slept all the previous evening and had yet to meet our visitor. "Come, son," I said. "We have a guest." While I pulled him toward Konya, he looked over his shoulder for the pups.

Konya still waited in the same place, looking out to sea. She must have heard us coming, since she turned and nodded. Then her mouth dropped open. "Konya," I said, "this is my son."

Since my words meant nothing, it must have been his appearance that caught her attention.

"Ah, ah, Sissle," she exclaimed, clapping her hands as if she just remembered something.

"Food," I said, pointing toward the fire circle. "Come with us and eat." She followed willingly. All eyes were on Konya as we joined the group. For once I was glad they were staring at someone besides Gokihar.

Yarrow was already seated, ready for supper. She stood again. "Everyone, listen," she said. It was rude to stare at strangers, no matter how unusual they were. Yarrow wouldn't want the woman to return home and report that we were a crude people. "We will eat now and learn more of our visitor later," she said curtly, scanning the group until everyone looked down. "Eat."

Though the trout and salmon catches had been light all summer, we still had plenty of burbot, a fat fish we roasted on sticks. Konya seemed to enjoy the fish, though she wasn't much of an eater. I was too excited to feel hungry. After everyone had licked the last of the grease from their fingers, I looked to Yarrow. She nodded. I picked up my deer skin and stepped to the front of the group.

"When I was alone," I began, "and Gokihar was inside me, Earthmaker came to me on the shore." Everyone stared at me. Now

455

that their bellies were full, I hoped they had a deeper hunger. I spoke slowly. "Earthmaker showed me a way to keep our thoughts alive, outside of ourselves. In this same way, we can sometimes speak to strangers." I held up the hide, glancing over at Ochre. His face often told me what the group was thinking. The lines on his forehead had deepened, his eyes narrowed. At least he was still listening.

"First are the marks all people know." I pointed to the hills and waves and arrows at the top of the hide. "Other marks have meanings beyond just being pictures. Those are the shapes Earthmaker showed me," I said, gesturing to the twelve other shapes. "One day, we'll talk about them. Some of these shapes, the Bull People also know. Like this one." I pointed to the Y. "Earthmaker's sign. Other marks are similar for both peoples. For us, U is the sign for bowl or food. For the Bull People, it is a bowl as well. But its also the horns of their mother animal."

I glanced again at their faces. A few seemed interested. Some looked confused. Lugo's eyes bore into me like coals on wood. I quickly looked back at the hide.

"Today, I'll give you a new mark, one the visitor showed me. It will help us know her story. Come close so you can see."

Drawing in the dirt, I made a flat line and added a curve to both ends. "This is their boat, made of reeds, like the one Belov showed us. With it she crossed a sea." A murmur rose up from the crowd. People glanced again at the visitor. Lugo crept over and knelt by the drawing. He was surprising, I thought, a reindeer hunter who longed to be a sailor. As well as I could, I explained a little of Konya's journey.

"This one has come from far away, from the southeast, as Ziva says, on a journey of two months time." I paused to let the words sink in. "Yarrow makes maps on the ground. You know what those look like. Konya makes maps on hides. Some of her marks show the route she traveled. It may be that she'll show that hide to others when she goes home. Perhaps some of them will travel here. I don't know why she's here. But I think she's a mapmaker who goes many places."

A mapmaker? People looked at each other. Ochre snorted. "Why would people bother to make a picture of a place, unless they planned to hunt there?" he said.

"To understand the world? To find their way? I don't know." I knelt beside Konya and pointed to her map. She handed it to me. "Here's the picture of her journey," I said as I held up the little goat hide. "This is the sea she crossed." I pointed to the bottom of the hide. Again I heard their "oohs" and "aahs."

"How?" Ochre bellowed. "If that's a sea, how would she cross it?"

I turned to Konya, pointing to her map and then to the boat I'd drawn on the sand. Maybe Ochre would understand that she'd used such a boat. Konya nodded. Then she jumped up, grabbed a stick, and began drawing more boats on the ground, one after another. So many vessels? Their seas must be filled with them. Now I was amazed as well. Who were such people, who could ride about on the water as easily as walk on shore? Could these be the great ones Ephus had sought? The ones who built mountains of stone so they could watch the sky?

As if answering my unspoken question, Konya reached into her bag and pulled out a small, red object. The hairs on my neck prickled at its familiarity. Again calling me "Sissle", she handed the thing to me. I gasped. Just as I'd thought, it was a carving of the Arn's mother beast, done on the same dark stone the Giant had used. Konya traced a line on her map from north to south, then pointed to Gokihar and back to the stone. She must have seen the Arn! She was bringing me their message. Of course, she'd have no way of knowing they'd left a child behind. But once she'd seen Gokihar it would be obvious that she had the right person.

457

Surely the stone was from Anish, though his father could have carved it. They'd made it to the south then! They were safe! I pointed to her home again, then toward the little statue. Were the Arn still there? She shook her head and gestured further south. Perhaps they'd been there and moved on. My heart sank. For a moment, they'd seemed so close. Then they'd disappeared again.

Unmindful of the people still watching me, I stroked the smooth red stone, my memories rising like the sun. Then I turned to Gokihar, holding the carving for him to see. "From your father, or your grand-father," I whispered. "From far away." He smiled and reached up to touch the rock. From the corner of my eye I saw Lugo, kneeling by the boat pictures and staring at the ground.

Where had the Arn met up with this traveler, I wondered? It could have been long ago. Maybe Konya had been carrying the carving for months, even years. Maybe she brought gifts to all the far-flung places she visited. I hoped she could rest here awhile, until I learned more of her words. There was so much I wanted to ask.

I leaned down to show Lugo the little carving. "See the beautiful things the Arn make?" I said, opening my hand.

"Is that what you want from a man, then," he said in a low voice, "a gift every five years?"

He stood quickly and walked away. I watched him for a moment, but I was too astounded by the carving to wonder about Lugo's mood. I held up the stone for the group. "See." I said. "From the Arn. They passed through Konya's land." One by one, the others wandered over to look at the gift. All of our people remembered the Arn's carvings. And the Fish People loved fine things whatever their origin. I passed it around and answered their questions as best I could. This was good for Gokihar, I thought, knowing that those who looked like him made such fine things, and that they hadn't forgotten our people. I had nothing else to say about Konya, so we drifted off to our own places once everyone had held the little statue.

Gokihar fell asleep with the carving in his hand, though I took it back after a while to be sure it didn't break. I lay in the dark, feeling the smooth, cool stone. Long after everyone around me was quiet, I was still restless. Anish remembered us, well, me, anyway. He'd made it to the south. Only he would have sent a gift. Andor had probably made it, but only Anish would have sent it. It must have been meant for me. Konya had seemed to recognize my name from the first, but she knew I was the one when she saw my son.

All of my senses, so long dormant, had come alive with that carving—Anish, his arms, his face, his smell. I was more awake now, in the middle of the night, than I ever was by day.

And now he was beyond the land of the Bull People, months away from me, if he still lived at all. I'd probably never see him again. Perhaps Lugo was right. Perhaps some traveler from another distant land would bring a gift every few years. Maybe that's how Gokihar would come to know his father. More likely, I'd never hear from Anish again.

My body would give me no peace. It was remembering an intensity, an aliveness that even now caused my limbs to shake. I turned from my back to my side to my stomach. Gokihar's little body jerked. Someone near me moaned. There'd be no sleep for me this night. Soon I'd be awakening the others as well. What I needed to calm me was the silver light on the silent sea. Sometimes that helped. I crept out of the cave and to the shore, then sat on the sand and hugged my knees. My skin still prickled. Something wasn't right. Something in me? No, something else. I scanned the quiet beach. Then I realized what it was. The boat was gone!

The Gift

What had become of the boat? Lugo must have taken it out. It was possible that one man could have pulled it downhill and into the sea, if he were really determined. But why would he go at night? It was a foolish thing to do. We'd had trouble with it capsizing. I stood and scanned the shoreline, hoping he hadn't gone too far. The current was deceptive here, swirling over hidden rocks when the tide was high. Lugo didn't know the coast like the rest of us.

My days would be so much easier without that man, I thought, walking toward the shoreline. Upset by a gift from a stranger, he'd decided to take my boat. I stared at the sea, the silver glints on the water unmarred by the outline of man or boat. I felt a shiver of fear. What if something had happened to him? Gokihar would be devastated. He'd taken to following the frustrating man every time Lugo checked the nets, sitting with him by the fire each night.

And then I heard a familiar sound, Lugo's angry curse as he struggled with the boat. The voice came from the south. I squinted until I saw him wading in neck-high water, dragging the capsized vessel. Thank

Earthmaker he hadn't lost the boat. He was about to cross the submerged spine of stone that crawled along the shore. Would he remember the rocks? The least I could do was help him bring in the boat and tell him to hush before he woke the entire camp. Then I'd find out why he'd taken such a risk.

I dropped my tunic and stepped into the black water, my skin tingling at the chill. I swam toward him. "Quiet, you fool," I muttered across the water. "It's not the fault of the boat that it tipped." Lugo stopped short when he heard me and glared. He was breathing hard, as if he'd already dragged the boat a long way. "Give me the rope," I said. It would be best if I guided it over the rocks. As soon as my feet sought the bottom, I realized I'd spoken too soon. The water was too deep for me to stand. I grabbed the rope anyway and swam toward shore, while Lugo pushed the heavy vessel from behind. Once we found a shallow place where both of us could stand, we righted the boat. It moved faster after that.

The current drove us sideways, carrying the boat north of where I'd entered the water, allowing us to clear the rocks. Together we pushed and pulled it to a mooring, nudging the vessel from behind until it sat sideways on the shore. The wind on my flesh was cold. I glanced south toward the place I remembered leaving my tunic. I was too chilly to run that far. As soon as the boat was secure, I hurried back to the sea. Lugo stayed on shore, shaking water from his clothing and his hair. He'd worked so hard he didn't seem to notice the breeze. It would be easy enough for him to bring my clothing. Besides, it was his fault I was here at all. "Lugo," I called, pointing to the south, "would you mind getting my tunic?"

He looked up, frowned, and stepped into the water. "Quiet, you fool," he said, untying the knot at his chest. "It's not my fault that you're naked." His garment slid down his arms and he tossed it to shore. He took a step closer, the water covering his knees, his tall body standing in dark relief against the pale beach. I hugged my shoulders and crept backward until the water was at my neck. I'd have to swim for my clothes. Or take his, if he were going to act like this. I tried to think of something to say, but before I could answer, he plunged into the water and disappeared. A moment later he emerged at my side, knocking me off balance, but not before I felt his warm flesh against my cold skin. I thrust out an arm, ready to swim. As I turned to push off, I felt his hands on my back. Even as I kicked at his knee, his arms tightened around me.

"Stop!" I said. He was a good head taller than me. I'd forgotten his strength. I could have easily swum to shore, but in his grip, I could barely get my head above water. He took another step, forcing me farther out. "It's too deep!" I sputtered as salt water gushed into my mouth. "Stop!"

Was he trying to drown me? I threw my arms around his neck, pulling myself higher on his chest until my head was above water. He took another step. I wrapped my legs around him as well, aware of his hard belly between my thighs. He'd have to go in over his head and submerge us both before he could peel me away. Leaning back, I looked up into his eyes, expecting anger.

Instead of a scowl, I saw a great hunger. His gaze pierced me as if I held some secret of his being. "It's too deep," I said again, breathlessly, slower now so that he could understand. He didn't seem to hear. Beneath the black water, a creature leaped against me, urgent and hard. Lugo. "What are you . . . ?" Bewildered, my question unfinished, I clung to his neck. I gaped, open-mouthed, at his raw face. And then his mouth was against mine, his lips searching hungrily, heating the flesh they touched. With a sweetness I'd almost forgotten, he pushed against me, found his place, and slipped inside. His eyes, so hard and guarded, softened. Then I understood. My life didn't have to be one of waiting. I could live now, every inch of my flesh breathing, aching, thriving. Tightening my legs around his back, I pulled him deeper inside, feeling his warmth and fullness, closing out the world. Once again I felt a tingling in my skin and the tingling became a fire burning in the sea. And then all I knew was the dark ocean surge; the sting of salt water; the rise and fall of the tide between us, like waves that swell before a storm; the sleek warmth of his body as it ground against me; and my own cries, lost in the wind.

We lay near the shoreline long after we were silent, letting the waves wash over us. I watched his eyes, glowing like lights from a forgotten fire. When the first grey line traced the horizon, we wandered along the beach as if we were both too weak to walk alone. I fumbled for my tunic and turned to Lugo, passing my hand over his prickly face. This would be a happy day.

I'd hardly slept at all when the shore came back to life. Hearing the barking of the dogs, I opened my eyes dreamily, then pulled my sleeping robe over my head. Not yet. I ran my hands down the length of my body and back to my breasts, remembering Lugo. I rolled over. Gokihar was already gone. Before long, I staggered out into the sunlight as well. The men were eating, talking about the day. No one glanced up, for which I was thankful. I filled a wooden cup with water and sipped it, gazing at the back of Lugo's head. Gokihar was with him.

Ochre was the first to stand, stretching and yawning. The others soon followed. Lugo strode over to me, the hunger again in his eyes, as well as a tenderness I hadn't seen before. "I'll take the boy fishing today," he said, "if you want."

"Good, yes," I stuttered, feeling the hot color rising on my cheeks. "Good." I looked down.

The two of them picked up their gear and headed toward the river. Gokihar glanced back once and waved. I heard myself sigh. I glanced around the fire circle, not yet ready to meet any curious eyes. Perhaps I'd spend the morning with Konya. Who knew how long she'd be with us? Besides, I wanted to learn what I could about the Bull People. And avoid any questions in my own language. As my eyes followed Lugo's lean body, I realized that Anish was now a part of my past. Still, it would be good to tell Gokihar all I could about his father. And if Konya came upon the Arn again, I wanted her to tell Anish about his son. Perhaps one day Gokihar would seek his father.

I decided to bring Konya another scraped hide so she could keep making pictures. Magla didn't mind, once I explained we could still use it for a tunic. Grabbing a handful of dried apples, I went to look for the traveler. I found her kneeling near a bush, grinding currants between two stones. Soon she lifted the bottom stone and poured the thick, purple liquid into a wooden cup. Several sharpened sticks lay nearby.

"Good morning, Konya," I said, stiffling a yawn. A memory of the night with Lugo flashed by and my body suddenly heated. I melted down next to the skinny woman. "We can draw on this," I said, laying the hides in front of her.

"Sissle," she greeted me, smiling. She was missing several teeth.

I stretched and rubbed the back of my neck. Where should we start? I picked up a stick, dipped it in the ink, and began marking. First I made fifty-seven little lines, pointing to myself and the other people on the beach. "This is how many we are," I explained. I handed her the stick. "How many Bull People are there? How many of you?"

Konya just shook her head and smiled. Then she began etching mark after mark, hundreds of little lines. Perhaps she didn't understand my question.

We made little progress. But for the next several days I stayed close to Konya, even learning a few of her words. At night, I'd slip out to look for Lugo, finding him by the boat. Then we'd wander along the shore or wade into the sea, some nights making love, other nights quiet in the glow of one another's company. I'd found a gentleness about him that he'd kept hidden behind his gruff ways. Sometimes I'd tell him small pieces of Konya's life and travels.

"These Bull People," I explained one night, "they don't really eat grass, just the seeds from grass. They grind them like acorns, mix the powder with water and bake it. I think the grass must be yellow first, because Konya won't grind any now. Every spring their rivers flood and every summer their land fills with plants." Lugo just nodded, taking it all in. He liked to think about things before he talked, while I liked to think and talk at the same time.

One afternoon, Konya gestured for me to follow her toward the river. Lugo was on the bank when we passed, helping Gokihar and Zale with their fishing lines. The three of them dropped what they were doing and joined us. Konya led us upstream to a place where the soil was damp and free of stones. Footprints on the wet ground told me she'd been there before. She dug up a heap of the sticky mud, mixed it with dried grass, and cut it into squares the length of her hand. These she lined up to dry in the sun.

Then she took us a little farther upriver, to a stack of mud blocks already dry. Daubing a coat of mud between each one, she laid out a row and added a second layer. Fire and Zale jumped in to help her, building a small structure as high as my knee. I knew from our discussions that the wall could go much higher. This was the way they built their houses. It was an odd idea, though once the wall dried, it seemed fairly strong. Maybe it didn't rain much where she lived.

Though I could never figure out how many Bull People there were,

Konya did draw me a picture of her countryside, separating the land from the sea with a heavy line. To the north of her land was water, which I already knew. But the Bull People were surrounded by seas on the west and south as well. To the east, they were held in by low moun-

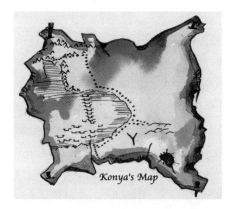

Konya's Map

tains. No one lived beyond those hills, or at least none she knew. Konya had pointed to rocks and sand when she drew that area, making me think it was a barren place. When I asked what lay across the seas, pointing to the south and west on her map, she could only shake her head and shrug. The land beyond the water was a mystery.

But the strangest story of all had nothing to do with Konya's land. It was a story of the sea. In the water which lapped against her country, she drew ships, dozens of ships. These were not the same boats she'd given her people, but even larger vessels. On each one, she made twenty lines. Twenty humans riding on a boat? Judging by her arrows, the ships were coming from both the west and south. Coming, stopping, and staying. There were no marks indicating that they left again. Surely these were the boats of a mighty people, more powerful than even the Bull People. Where had they come from? And why had they left their exalted land for a lesser place? Perhaps they were explorers like Konya, looking for something beyond their shores. But what? Adventure? Food? I had no way to ask. Maybe Konya didn't even know.

Maybe she'd been looking for those same ships here, during those days she'd spent gazing out to sea. It must have been clear to her by now that we knew of no such boats. The water no longer interested her. She did seem to understand that she'd traveled the limits of her

466

current route. Other than a few days of passable mountains to the north, her path could go no farther. Now it was the coast to the south that she wanted to explore. Her map showed it only as a straight line, but I knew there were islands, hot springs, caves, and harbors there that she had yet to see. I tried to tell her about them, even asked Ziva to fill her in about that shoreline. Konya seemed to have little interest in such things.

Gradually, it became clear to me that what Konya most wanted to know was the location of our highest mountains. This seemed like an odd ambition, since these were places no one could get to anyway. Still, that was what she desired. There was little we could tell her. None of us, not even Ziva, knew much about the coast beyond the now-vanished Fish Island. That shoreline was too rough to travel, the stone-covered hills dropping sharply into the churning sea.

Konya was becoming frustrated that we could offer her so little. One day, she made yet another picture on the crowded hide and thrust it down before me. Did I know of such a place? I picked up her drawing. It was a chain of seven mountains, the tallest, the center one, arching to one side like a breaking wave. It was the mountain of my dream!

How would I tell her that? I shook my head and shrugged. Her lips turned downward. Then I laid my head on my hands, as if I were asleep, and closed my eyes, pointing to my head and then her drawing of the mountains. Would she realize I'd never seen such peaks, except when I was dreaming? Several years ago, when I'd first had that dream, I'd asked the others about it. No one could recall such mountains.

Maybe Konya had only dreamed the peaks as well. Maybe no one had ever seen them. Still, couldn't they be real, if they'd come to both of us? Sorry that I couldn't be more helpful, I folded up her drawing. I'd store it away, hiding it on the high ledge with the black rock from the stars.

Before long, the meadow grass turned yellow and summer began to slip away. I wasn't surprised when Konya let us know it was time for her to leave. I'm sure she wanted to be at her own shore before winter. Still, I was sad when the day for her departure came. I hoped she'd find what she was looking for one day. We gathered on the beach to see her off. Belov would walk with her as far as the deserted Fish People's camp, to see what remained of his old home. Magla gave her plenty of food and some new boots. Eda offered her two wooden cups, small things to be sure, but useful. I wished there was some gift I could send with her, something to remember us by, something for the Arn. If she ever saw them again.

And then it came to me. "Gokihar," I called, "come here!" The boy came running over. His golden hair hung in thin feathers below his shoulders. I gathered a handful at the nape of his neck and drew my blade across it, then wrapped the little yellow bundle in a strip of hide. It was the first time I'd ever cut his hair. "Here," I said, handing the packet to Konya, "give this to his father if you see him." She didn't understand my words, but I think she knew my meaning.

Children of the Twilight

I MISSED KONYA'S WARM EYES AND HER MYSTERIES. For months after her departure, I busied myself with the details of each day and tried to forget the hunger in my mind. I longed to see the great lands and wonderful things she'd seen, the vessels, the people, the strangeness. Meanwhile, on our rocky strand, our own small lives unfolded peacefully. I tried to be thankful for that and find contentment in the world around me.

Life on the shore was changing. The worms disappeared with the coming of the winter, as Ziva had said they would. But not before all the evergreens were dead, their grey branches stripped bare so that new vistas opened between us and the eastern hills. Beneath the skeleton trees, where nothing had grown before, scrub and thorn took root, followed by raspberries and juneberries. A few seasons more and there'd be no limit to the fruit we could pick. Still, I missed the old forest and the animals it had sheltered. As the hot, dry years continued, we watched anxiously for lightning and lived in fear of fire roaring through the tinder. So far we'd been lucky.

The deer herd grew slowly. Wolves took an old one and a fawn one spring. Lugo offered to build a pen in front of the cave we'd dug in the rock. That was where we kept them for the night and the winter. In three years we had twelve strong animals. Birch and Leu still took them to graze most days. When their own boy was born, they brought him along to the meadow. Leu had trained two of Thur's pups to help with the deer. A third one he'd had to kill, spearing the dog after she jumped a doe. Ochre said it was the right thing to do, but I hated it.

The fourth pup had gone to Zalec, as I'd promised. The shy creature was good company for the wounded hunter, fiercely protecting him and the camp when the rest of us were gone. As I'd hoped, the People were coming to accept Thur and her tame offspring. Thur herself, now in her eighth year, had started to tire. She slept in the sun most days, near Lugo's slant house. We never saw any of the wolf dogs from her first litter, which was good for us and them.

I finally convinced Magla and Ochre that it was possible to raise geese. The winter after Konya left, I'd trapped both a male and a female and managed to keep them alive through the lean months by clipping their wings. Five eggs hatched that spring and three goslings survived. By the second summer, seven large birds claimed the beach for their own and wandered, squawking, along the shore, chasing children and dogs, lunging at those who came empty-handed, and dodging the rocks we threw. Lugo built another shelter for them, to protect us as well as the birds. The long, narrow pen extended into the sea so that the birds could go after fish. Zale and Fire brought them scraps and water every day. In the winter, the birds stayed in the little cave with the deer, their eggs and flesh a welcomed change.

The biggest change for me had to do with Lugo. Since our first night together at the boat, he'd wanted us to have a joining. I loved our time together and saw how much Gokihar wanted a father, how the man was a kind and steady friend to the boy. But I was in no hurry to live with another person's thoughts all day. Besides, I didn't want to stay in Lugo's shelter with Eda and his

West People's dwelling

brother, and the cave was too crowded for him to move there. But Lugo wasn't so easily dissuaded. The summer after Konya left, he built himself a separate place at the far north end of the encampment, another house with a slanted roof. He moved his belongings in the middle of the day, walking slowly past the busy women, appearing as defeated as a wolf driven from the pack. There he lived alone, looking miserable. Everyone pitied him, looked at me, and shook their heads. How could I be so cruel? To make the poor man sleep alone? And with winter coming on? At last I agreed to the ceremony.

However, before I moved our things, I made one small request. The slant house had no hiding place, nowhere to store my hides with the marks and my sky stone. So I asked Lugo to build a wooden box for them, which we buried under the dirt floor where fire could never take it. Then Gokihar carried our few possessions across the beach and into our new home. The place was fresh and clean, spacious even, though I never got used to the sound of the wind.

Gokihar was thrilled to have a father, though he still liked to sleep in the cave with his friends. As it turned out, I was pleased with the arrangement, happy to have a strong companion and, more importantly, someone who would listen to my ideas. Then, too, Lugo was a

471

beautiful man. He smiled more now. Sometimes it seemed that he smiled all the time. He was more patient than before. His body was a joy.

Thur, who'd always been fond of Lugo, quickly claimed the new house as her own and began sleeping outside that doorway. From time to time, when I noticed her there, I'd think of Wolf and Raven and the strange winter we'd shared on the lonely beach. I'd seen nothing of them for years and my memory of our time together seemed like a dream, an enchantment, magic which disappeared with the People's return. Still, I was happy. Seeing Gokihar grow into a fine, strong youth; watching Lugo's lean, brown hands as he worked; caring for the animals—all these filled me with a warmth I'd never known. Gradually, Konya's face and the adventure of far places faded. I came to live contentedly in the quiet pleasures of the day.

But if my world was serene, it wasn't so for everyone. Newcomers continued to travel to our shore, each with a sad tale to tell. Other reindeer hunters from the northwest, who'd finally given up the hunt and hoped to fish, salmon fisherwomen and their families—sullen people who'd lived along the mouths of southern rivers until the salmon disappeared—a few straggling hunters, alone, with that darkness that comes over men who don't have enough to love. Even a few West People stumbled into camp one day, distant relatives of Eda. They told of a sickness at home, tiny worms that infected sea lions and spread to the humans who ate them, quickly killing the children.

We had many mouths to feed, but plenty of hands to work. In the two years following Konya's departure, our group grew from fifty to seventy. Each season we managed to bring in fish and nuts and fruit enough for all, though we knew some of us would eventually leave. The shore was noisy and dirty, but it was exciting to be part of such a large group.

Still, there were disagreements and feuds, everyone insisting their way was the best. Lugo was surprisingly good at working with the men, valuing what each one brought to us, giving them a sense of belonging and pride. By his third winter with us, he'd emerged as a natural leader. No one seemed to mind. Even Ochre listened to the judgments of the younger man.

Magla continued to watch over the homefront. More interested in detail than I, but lacking Lugo's diplomacy, she managed to see that everything was harvested, stored, cooked, and shared satisfactorily, and that no one went without. It seemed likely that Silka would take her place one day. She and Rube now had another baby. The once-haughty girl thrived on caring for her children and helping Magla manage the People's needs. Like Magla, she knew years in advance whom in our group would be joining and whom should be kept far apart. Silka had become the oracle whom the new people followed as they learned our ways. It was her job to inspire us and she did it well. She was born to inspire, I realized, and that was enough. As our numbers increased, so did Silka's influence.

Half of our newcomers were children. For the first time since my own childhood, we had a group of young ones in need of teaching. No one had taken that role for years, Yarrow having been our last teacher after Idra's death. But Yarrow, tired from caring for her man and troubled by some inner bitterness, no longer shared her wisdom. Of course, her son knew the stories of all the plants within a day's walk, just from being with her. In this same way, we all instructed our children, sharing what we knew best and forgetting anything else. I'd told Gokihar all I remembered of our stories and the stars. Soon I'd show him the hides with Earthmaker's marks.

The children watched the world around them eagerly, quickly learning the People's ways, becoming more like us than their parents.

Even though the daily habits of our growing group were taking hold, something else was missing. Everyone knew where to set up camp, how to clean up after themselves, how to treat the animals and each other. The children were healthy and well fed. But some days, when I watched them playing on the shore, I sensed a different hunger. The deeper things, our stories, longings, and ceremonies, had been pushed aside. They needed a teacher.

It seemed to me that it was time for Yarrow to instruct them again, to tell them of the larger things which made us all the People. I was reluctant to approach her, afraid it would be difficult to convince her that their hearts were empty, though their bellies were full. But my hunch was strong enough that I knew I had to try. So it was that in Gokihar's tenth year, I went to Yarrow to ask if she'd resume her lessons.

She was hunched over her herb bag, laying mint leaves out to dry, her greying hair hiding her face. I sat down and cleared my throat. "Yarrow, the children have grown wild inside." I paused. "They need a teacher."

"I know," she replied.

"You do?" Her answer caught me off-guard and I searched for something to say. "Ah, I was thinking you could teach them, like you did Silka and Birch and me. Tell them the old stories, the ways of plants, the spirits of animals, the things we need . . ."

"No."

"No? You won't be their teacher?" This made no sense, to admit we needed a teacher then refuse to teach, and she the only teacher we had. "You won't do it?"

Yarrow glanced up at me, then lowered her head, which seemed as grey and heavy as stone. "No, Thistle. My time for teaching is done.

Oh, I can speak from time to time, about plants and medicine and such. But that's not what they need. You know that, though you pretend to forget."

"What are you talking about? No one knows our past better than you, no one who's still living. I haven't forgotten your knowledge. Surely you haven't either."

"It's not the past that brings the wildness to these children." Her eyes were hard as she stared back at me. "Not the past, but the future. You know that best of all. That's what you try to forget. The stories of Earth I can tell, but only you can tell them the story of Sky. The time has come for the People to hear that."

"The sky? You mean the things that Tenja told me?"

"Tenja, Ziva, Eda, Earthmaker, all of them. You've learned many things."

"But I've forgotten so much!"

"Then remember it. You live on the beach now. Leave your new man alone for a few nights and watch the sky."

She was right, of course. I'd wanted to forget. And sometimes I'd been successful. I thought of all those months I'd put off Lugo, refusing to move to the shore, refusing to live in the slant house where the night sky loomed between the cracks in the branches, where the hazy lights continued to grow above us, where I longed for winter's arrival so we could cover the thatch with hides. I'd wanted to forget. Some nights, when I lay in our little wooden place, I'd cover my face with the sleeping robe and tell Lugo the brightness kept me awake. I slept better on cloudy nights when I didn't see the lights at all. Of course, a person would have to be blind not to realize that the beams had become clearer the last few months, one as bright as a tiny sun, one like a little moon, both pursued by trails of gleaming followers. But I tried to forget. And now Yarrow was telling me to watch them closely.

"But Yarrow, even if I did remember, even if everyone's words come back to me, what difference would it make? What could I tell the People? What would you have me say?"

"Just prepare them," she answered. "See your duty. The words will come."

Now it was my heart that turned to stone. I turned and walked slowly to the shore, angry at myself for bringing up the matter. Just ahead I saw Lugo and Gokihar. They'd pulled the boat from the water and were rubbing pitch into a small crack. A cold heaviness was settling in my belly.

"Lugo," I called, waving him toward me. With a word to Gokihar, he left the boat and ambled in my direction, smiling. "Lugo," I repeated, my voice trembling.

"What is it? What's wrong?"

I told him what Yarrow had said. He looked away, rubbing his long hand across his chin.

"So," he said at last, "the time has come."

Thus it was that later that summer I began my teaching. Zale, Fire, Gokihar, Narta, and three young ones from the new people were my first students. Some nights, the men and the Mothers sat with us too, making it like old times. Lugo and I had talked about what we'd say, how much and how soon. Everyone already knew the names of the star groups, so we discussed the paths of stars and how to use them to find direction, something I'd already taught Gokihar years ago. We'd decided not to tell the People too much at once, but to talk first about how the sky used to be and later about the new stars, or whatever they were.

It was easy to remember exactly when we'd first seen those unusual lights—just after Gokihar's birth, ten years before. Nor had I forgotten Eda's vision for Gokihar and my duty to teach him well. I'm sure that was the reason I pushed him more than the rest, hoping to prepare him for the future and preserve our remembrance if Chaos did come. Fortunately for both of us, Gokihar learned quickly and didn't mind my demands. While the others struggled with counting and knowing the difference between planets and stars, the boy was taking the boat out at night and finding his way home by the heavens.

So once again I found myself back with the mystery stars, the lights that had first lured me to Tenja and her lonesome vigil, and to nights of gazing, counting, dreaming, and dreading. Only now, instead of Tenja, Lugo was with me. He learned quickly and my watching was not alone. My life had come full circle.

IN HIS ELEVENTH YEAR, Gokihar came to me with an announcement that sent a shiver down my spine. The three of us, Gokihar, Lugo, and myself, were finishing our morning meal. Most of the others had already gone about their work, but we'd slept late, having been awake until Gokihar returned with the boat. "I think I'm ready for a longer trip," the boy said as he heaped more berries into a bowl.

"Nonsense," I replied. "You go too far out and a storm will take you. The boat's too small for the sea."

Gokihar was as tall as most of the men and he had a quiet steady way about him. Most of the People treated him as if he were already grown. He was a capable boy, but a boy nevertheless. And I had doubts about the boat. We'd finally given up on the dugout, at least for a while. He and Lugo had made another vessel, a much lighter boat made of stretched hides coated with resin. This one rarely tipped and could be quickly set right. But I worried about him running to sharp rocks or submerged rocks.

"I'm not going to the sea," he said.

"What are you planning to do, float up river?"

"No. Follow the coast to the south, past where the Fish People lived."

"Why?" I asked. What was to be gained by following that jagged shore? Cliffs meandered near the water, except for the beach that had once been Ziva's home. That was still underwater, for all I knew.

"I've never seen it before. Besides, I'll stay close to land. I can stop anywhere, if there's a storm or something."

"There's hardly a place to put up a boat. You'd never get it out of that current . . ."

"I want to see what's there."

"Then take Lugo with you."

"The boat rides too low with two. We'd rip out the bottom."

"Where will you sleep?"

"I can find some place to put in. I'll stop each night before the tide."

"How far will you go?"

"Down the coast for three days, beyond the place where the Fish People lived, then back."

Each of my questions had an answer. He'd make the trip whatever I said, if not now, then as soon as he could slip away. I looked at Lugo helplessly. He shrugged.

"Seems like he's planning to go," he said.

I looked from one stolid face to the other and then out to sea. Grey clouds were gathering angrily, the wind whipping up little ridges of foam. "Then see that you don't leave until the weather clears," I said. The flaxen-haired boy grinned, jumped up, and ran off down the beach. Black-haired Narta was sauntering toward the drying racks. He quickly caught up with her.

A voice beside me made me jump. "I see trouble for those two," Silka said. She was carrying her son, a robust boy of three, probably heading for the drying racks herself. Silka was one of the few people who were not impressed with Gokihar. Ever since the night that Narta slipped away to join him in the boat, returning at dawn, she'd watched them nervously. She'd forbidden her daughter to go near the boat at all, calling it a flimsy bowl.

"Good morning, Silka," I said. Tight-lipped, she continued walking toward her daughter. Keeping my voice low, I spoke to Lugo. "Go after him when he leaves. Follow him from the shore."

"I plan to."

The sky cleared that afternoon. By nightfall both Gokihar and Lugo were gone, returning seven days later. Lugo slipped into camp soon after Gokihar's arrival, carrying three rabbits on his belt. The boy seemed even more sure of himself, more self-possessed. What other announcements would the future hold, I wondered? It was exasperating to have a son so like me.

That night, the boy basked in the warmth of the fire and the People's attention. He'd made such good time that he continued on south aways beyond the Fish People's old home. We listened to stories of the giant sea creatures he'd seen, creatures never fished by humans. The animals seemed to grow in size as the night wore on, the telling lengthening his memories.

"Did you notice anything else?" I asked, having never been beyond the Fish People's old home, "Any signs of boats or travelers? Any unusual mountains?"

"No, nothing else, Mother," he answered amiably, "nothing but the glow of Lugo's fire from where he hid each night to watch me."

479

Gokihar's Story

"YOU SHOULD HAVE SEEN THEM, MOTHER, like no people I've ever seen. Shorter than you, darker. One took off his tunic to wash and the skin on his belly was dark as a bear's."

Gokihar had just returned from the woods to the southeast. He'd left six days before with Fire and Zale. The older two had come home the second night, bringing a red deer and a wild story about Gokihar meeting up with strangers. He'd told them he'd be back soon and not to worry. They hadn't, but I had. I tried to keep the concern from my voice. "How many were there?" I asked. "Was it a large group?"

"Four. All men."

"What are they doing here?" That question was Lugo's. He'd been anxious about Gokihar, too, ready to go looking for him the next day.

We didn't worry about the boy when he was with Fire and Zale. Those two had been going off to the woods for years. To hunt, they said. I figured it was to feel their own freedom and find travelers with daughters their age, since the young women here were like sisters. They were much older than Gokihar, both more than twenty, but they liked having the boy around. He was strong and quick and a good story-teller. In fact, Gokihar could remember more than anyone I'd ever known. Names, places, explanations—nothing escaped his attention. I was accustomed to being the one people turned to for information, but I suspected he was far more capable than I. The two young men had been asking Gokihar to accompany them on their journeys since last year. This was the first time he'd come home alone.

He'd shown up just before dark, as everyone was drifting toward the fire circle. After his first remarks, he dropped down next to us and grabbed a meaty rib bone. "Let me eat first," he said to Lugo, "then I'll answer your questions." He tore at the meat with his teeth.

Eda was shuffling toward us. She was stooped and thin now, but as cranky as ever. Steadying herself against Lugo's shoulder, she low-ered her body to the ground. "Leave some of that food for the others, boy," she said. "Got lost, huh?"

"Greetings, Grandmother!" He grinned at her with a full mouth. "I knew you'd miss me."

She snorted and grabbed a rib of her own. The two of them had their own way of talking. She treated him like a disagreeable intruder and he acted like an adored child. Gokihar was too good-natured to be bothered by her harsh ways. With each passing year, Eda had begrudg-ingly softened toward him.

Others joined us, greeting Gokihar as they took their food. It was late in the month of Ripening Fruit and the evening air was cool. I wrapped my tunic tighter. The meat was disappearing fast. Magla brought out a basket of apples. Above the chatter I could hear the sound of the river frogs. I glanced at Gokihar, shook my head, and sighed. Thank Earthmaker he was safe.

"Those strangers must have had nothing to feed you," I said after a while, as Gokihar stuffed more venison into his mouth.

Eda scowled at him and reached for an apple. "Couldn't hunt for yourself, huh? Lucky you still have a mother. Even if you do nothing, you get to eat."

"How alike we are, Grandmother," he replied.

"Well, Gokihar, welcome back." Now it was Yarrow's turn to greet him. She'd brought Zalec his food and was coming back for her own. Yarrow was fond of the boy, I knew, and had been angry at her son for leaving him behind. "Zale told me a little of your adventure," she said.

Gokihar nodded and smiled. He'd overcome his boyhood shyness. Though he wasn't usually talkative, he never minded telling us about his journeys. It was rare that we heard about travelers, except for the stragglers who made their way here after some disaster took their home. When he'd finally had enough to eat, he placed his hands on his thighs and took a deep breath. Those who wanted to listen pressed closer, their eyes on the yellow-haired boy.

"We were in the oak woods, our second day out, early in the morning," he said. "We'd come upon the path that goes south through the forest. It had rained the night before, so the trail was still muddy."

How well I remembered that path, the one I'd followed years ago, after Tenja's death. The one that led to the clearing where Anish had found me. The boys said it was well-worn now, what with small bands of northern people seeking new homes in the south and strangers exploring the hinterland.

"It was near there we found the travelers," Gokihar continued. "We saw fresh prints in the mud—sandal prints— woven shoes like the southern people wear." I recalled Konya's tough sandals, made of twisted, fibrous plants. "The prints were fresh, so we followed them. They pointed north. We didn't have to go far before we came upon the camp, right at the edge of the woods." He paused. The People waited.

"Go on, go on," said Eda. "Who were they?"

He pretended not to hear. "When they saw us, they stood and took their spears. They moved slowly . . . like they were tired or sick. We put our weapons down and they did the same. They didn't offer us any food. I figured they didn't have any, since they were so skinny. They didn't have any females, either," he said, glancing at Zale and grinning, "so Zale wanted to keep going." The young man growled a reply that I couldn't understand. "But I decided to stay," Gokihar said, "see what kind of people they were." He glanced my way. "The way home is simple enough. Anyway, I gave them a couple of rabbits and they were thankful."

"Did they know your words?" I asked.

"A few. They're like that man you talk about . . . Ephus. Wherever they go, they learn new words. One of them, I think he's the oldest, he knows the most. They call him Aksara. He was the one I talked to. He'd tell the others what I said and they'd ask him questions. They've seen people like me before."

"Arn?" I asked in amazement.

"I guess they were Arn. Aksara said they live to the south, across the water. They're new to the region. More come to join them all the time."

I'd heard nothing of the Arn for six years, not since the summer Konya brought the carving of their Mother Animal. I still thought of Anish from time to time, seeing his generous smile in Gokihar's face and his gestures in the boy's movements. Now an image of that ragged band flitted across my mind. I remembered the first time we'd seen them, a small group straggling through the meadow below our summer mountain, their wolf dogs carrying packs. And Ephus telling us that with their Mother Animal gone, they believed in nothing and had no place. When they lost their homes, they lost their souls, he'd said. Had they been able to make a new life? "How do they live, these ones like you?"

"I'm getting to that. The South People keep cattle, large creatures with wide flanks and curved horns. The Arn tend the cows and prepare the bulls for ceremonies."

So they'd made a new home. Perhaps they were at peace.

"Anyway, that's all the strangers knew about them," Gokihar said, stopping me before I bothered him with more questions. "But Aksara and the others, I learned a lot about them." He paused and looked around the group. Everyone was watching him.

"The people from the south know many things and do all sorts of marvels. Aksara says so many live in his area that their sounds rise up like the bellowing of bulls. Nor are they all one people. Many groups are spread around over an area so large you could walk for years and never see them all. Farther south is a land ruled by a giant lion, where the men dig their own rivers and make the water flow as they choose. Aksara has seen them. He and his people are mapmakers, like that woman who once came here."

"Konya?" I asked.

"Yeah, Konya. Only their maps are bigger, better than hers. They map the ground and the sea. Aksara says they go on boats to find new places and even figure out the distance to them."

I watched the frowns forming on several faces. Gokihar was clearly impressed with the strangers but, like many young ones, he believed things too easily. I nudged Lugo, hoping he'd stop this nonsense before Gokihar embarrassed himself.

"How?" asked Lugo. He'd either missed my meaning or was too

curious to let his question go unanswered. "How can they measure such distances?"

"I don't know. Aksara said he could teach me. All they need are tall posts and their eyes. They know things we can't imagine." The words tumbled from his mouth like water over bright stones. He raised his chin and looked at me. "But that's not the reason they're here."

"What brings them here, then?" I asked.

"The same thing you always talk about. The new stars."

I sat up straighter. "They're here because of the stars?"

"I think so. They watch the sky and map the movements of the lights. Aksara says humans everywhere can see the traveling stars. Some people have given them names."

Named them? I hadn't thought of that. "If they have the same stars at home, why come here?" I asked. I felt my hands curling into fists. Who were these strangers, to come to our land and lure our children with marvelous stories? We could teach our people anything they needed.

"They're here to learn," he replied steadily, "like us."

"Humpf." I'd heard enough. What if Gokihar was so impressed by these braggarts that he decided to go with them? Yarrow must have sensed my tension.

"The night grows late," she said suddenly. "We'll stop for now and hear more tomorrow."

"Not tomorrow," Gokihar said. "Aksara said I could join them. They'll only be here a few more days. I want to find out more about the stars." He stretched and looked around the fire circle, ready for a change. I watched him as he stood slowly and walked into the shadows. Narta slipped away a few moments later. Now I was angry. Lugo and I walked home in silence, while I listened to the jumble of words in my head.

All along, I'd been carefully preparing Gokihar for the future, for the time I'd tell him Eda's words, Tenja's words, Earthmaker's words, and what I was coming to believe in my own heart. But it wasn't something to explain in haste. I didn't want to overwhelm him. If Eda's premonitions were true, if Gokihar were to be the one who kept our blood flowing and our memory alive, he'd need wisdom and skill far beyond his fourteen years. What if these strangers blurted out too much and confused him with their exaggerations?

Yarrow was at our entrance when we got home.

"Your son is growing up," she said. "He'll be a fine man."

"I'm tired, Yarrow. But I'm sure you're right." I bent over and stepped inside.

"Thistle," Yarrow said, speaking to my back, "these travelers may have something to teach us. What if it were Earthmaker Herself who brought Gokihar to them? The time approaches. Hear him out. You may need this knowledge."

Yarrow looked to me to warn the People. That much I knew. I dreaded the task. How I longed to just study the stars, know the thrill of new ideas, and keep my thoughts to myself. But Gokihar had made that impossible. To run from the future would be to abandon him. Earthmaker had given me no easy path, but it was my path, all my life leading to this end. What was it Idra said the year before her death? "A Changer, to lead, must love the People as much as she loves her dreams." The People and my dreams were now one. I knew my duty. But I didn't want to be rushed. "Of course," I replied, "I'll hear him out."

Gokihar didn't come back that night, but early in the morning he was on the beach with Narta, helping her with the drying racks. A little later he disappeared with Fire and Zale, taking the boat to drag the nets. It rode low with three of them in it and I worried they'd scrape the rocks. They made it home safely late that morning, weighted down with haddock, but light of heart. Gokihar stopped briefly before he left to tell us Fire was going with him to the woods. They returned four days later, both more somber than when they'd left. I was anxious to hear what they'd learned.

"So, Gokihar," Yarrow said, that night at the fire, "these map-making strangers, they've come here to learn. What is it they want to know?"

"The nature of the new stars," he replied.

"And these new stars, what do they take them to be?" she asked.

"I don't think they know. But they're afraid."

"The lights frighten the Southern People?" she asked.

"Well, the people who've come here. Not everyone is afraid. Aksara says some don't care. Some just think they're beautiful . . . like new moons. But the ones who watch the stars and chart their movements are afraid. You can hear it in the names they give them."

"What names?" I asked, trying to keep my voice even.

"Different names. Everyone has different names. Aksara and his people—the ones just beyond the water to the south—they call the large light *Marduk* for 'warrior.' Those to the east of them call it *Enlil* for 'demon.' The people from the west—across the sea from Aksara's home—they call it *Phaeton.* And far to the south, where the lion rules, they call the large light *Set* for 'devil.'"

"What is devil?" I asked.

Gokihar shrugged. "Same as demon. Some spirit that does evil."

"So . . . these travelers think the lights are evil?"

"I guess. But so do we, don't we? Eda says they're wolves about to swallow Earth." I glared at the old woman. She'd promised to stop saying that. "Aksara's stories are not so different," Gokihar continued.

"He thinks *Marduk* comes to make war on Earth."

"And the others?"

"Well, those farther south say that the devil star, the one called *Set*, was once a god himself. He served the great Sky God, who rules all the heavens. But *Set* defied the Sky God and the Sky God cast him down, hurling him toward the sun." Gokihar looked upward and we followed his gaze into the cool, clear night. Above us the two bright orbs glowed like the children of Sun himself. "See their followers?" he said, pointing to the winding trail of lights behind the larger two, their gleam not nearly so bright. "The Lion People say the smaller light is *Set*'s helper devil and the tiny lights are other demons. The Sky God rid the sky of all of them. But now Earth is in their path and could be overcome."

A Sky God, outside of Earthmaker? There were many spirits, I knew, but surely there couldn't be more than one Source. A vague memory was tugging at me, something Ziva had said years ago, when Tenja and I visited the Fish People. Something about a Father God, partner to Earthmaker, but sterner. One who cast humans from their innocence and made them learn by suffering. Could these lights be His work? What a cruel thought. "And your Aksara? What does he believe?" I asked.

"He says the lights are parts of distant stars, tumbling to Earth like dirt clods kicked from a hill. The large one hit another world, Aksara thinks, and knocked off parts of it. The followers are remnants of that broken world. Earth is next in its path."

This story sounded more likely, but no safer. "He's sure Earth is next?"

"Yes, unless the lights go too close to the Warrior planet and hit there first. That's why Aksara and his men are looking for a hiding place in the mountains."

"The mountains? Why there?" I asked. The people around me were moving uneasily, but I had no time now to think about their fear. They'd have to hear this sometime.

"Aksara says those in the mountains might be safe. I don't know why. Just that if Sky makes war on Earth, most life will die, except for life in the mountains. One day, those who've fled upward will return and feed any humans still huddling below."

So that was the reason the strangers were here, to find a safe place. That was the missing piece which explained their presence. Perhaps Konya had come seeking the same thing. I thought of the drawing she'd carried, exactly like the seven peaks in my dream years ago. "And have they found these mountains?" I asked.

"No, but Aksara knows what the safe place looks like. He's looking for a range with seven peaks, maybe to the north."

"Well, he's looking in the wrong place," I replied.

Now it was Gokihar's turn to look surprised. "What do you mean?" he asked, looking doubtful. How could I know something the marvelous travelers didn't know?

"I know the mountains to the north. The seven peaks are not there." The time had come to tell the People what I suspected about Sky's encounter with Earth. "Wait here," I said.

I hurried back to our little house to unearth the dream picture. Fortunately, I'd wrapped the drawing in a second hide before I'd buried the box, so it was still dry. Then I returned across the dark beach and spread the drawing before them. The fire illuminated the charcoal lines. "This is the safe place," I said, tapping my finger on the tall, central peak. "This is what they're looking for." Shadowed heads nodded. Those in the back pushed forward so they could see. Gokihar looked at me with a puzzled expression.

Slowly I began to tell them what I remembered. How the dream of the bobbing boat and the mountains first came to me. Tenja's visions on the beach. Eda's wild tales of Sky attacking Earth. And my own calculations that showed the lights growing faster. I held back only two things—the words of the ancient trees when I first learned I'd have a child, and Eda's premonition that Gokihar would be the one who carried the People's memory. I'd tell him these things alone.

A clamor of questions arose. I answered as best I could, Lugo helping me. When would the battle come? Where would the fire balls hit? What if they came close but didn't touch us? Could they overcome Earth if they didn't actually strike? Would we be safe in caves? Or safer on the sea? What if the World Tree was wrenched and the world tumbled from its place? Why was this happening? Where was Earthmaker?

It hurt to see the fear on their faces. But I felt my belly grow cold when I saw their bitter glances. They acted as if I myself had cast down the stars. I held my arms to stop their shivering. I'd been wise to say nothing about Gokihar. These people might destroy him if they heard he'd be the one to survive. I looked from face to face, willing calmness in the agitated crowd. Maybe if I told them what Tenja had said, that morning before she died, maybe they'd find some comfort there. I swallowed hard.

"There's danger here," I said. "That much seems true. We have more to learn. But why? How? When? These things we may never know. Does anyone know for sure the time of his own passing? We will figure out what we can. But never forget—beyond danger, beyond even death—is Earthmaker and Her love."

"They would rather live," muttered Eda. I hoped no one else heard her.

Gokihar had nothing else to say. He returned to the house with us, quieter than usual. He's just a boy, I thought, a boy with a few blond hairs on his face and arms no wider than Lugo's wrists. Our words around the fire had changed the stars from a distant adventure to an impending danger. For that I was sorry. But I'd had no choice. And I still had to tell him the final part of the story, his role in it. At least that could wait until tomorrow.

"What is it you haven't told me?" he asked suddenly. His voice was sharp.

"Anything else can wait until morning. It's been a long day."

"Tell me now. Or I won't sleep."

I looked at Lugo. He frowned, but nodded. "Go ahead and tell him," he said.

I sat on my sleeping robe and spoke softly, all the while watching the ground. "It is possible, if Sky makes war on Earth, that only one of us will survive."

"What are you talking about?"

I explained about Eda and Earthmaker, telling him every detail I could remember except the one I saved for last. I waited, letting the words sink in. Finally I said it. "Gokihar, the one who carries on our memory may be you."

"Me? That's crazy." I saw the fear on his face, the disbelief. He frowned and raised his eyebrows, clearly not convinced. Of course, I thought, he'd rather die with the rest of us than go on alone. That I could understand. "Why me? Why would I be the one?"

"That I can't tell you. It's Earthmaker's decision, not mine. Maybe because you carry the legacy of two great lines, the People and the Arn. I'm only guessing."

"No! I have other plans for my life. I won't do it. I'll go with Aksara.

I'll follow them. Go south when they leave . . . see their marvels . . ."

I was so weary. I wanted my part in this to be done. "Gokihar, my boy, only a fool thinks he has chosen his life. Life chooses us. It moves through us and lifts us for a while on its power. My life has been to bring forth my abilities so my ancestors' story can live on. That is the purpose of your life as well."

His frown deepened. He looked again at the picture of the seven mountains. Lugo added a log to our small fire. At last the boy spoke. "Have you ever seen such mountains?"

"Only when I sleep," I answered. "Keep the hide. It's yours now. When you find the mountains, go there. Go to the tallest peak. Don't leave until the trouble has passed."

"How will . . .?"

"There will be time for questions and wonderings," I said. "You must promise to find this mountain, make it your home, and stay there as long as Earthmaker commands. Will you do this?"

He glanced at me. His eyes said yes.

Departure

ONCE AGAIN THE BIRCH TREES WERE DAPPLED GOLD and the geese flew overhead. In the crisp and shortening days, I told Gokihar all he'd need to remember. No one knew how much time we had, moments, months, or years, before we met the lights. So, once again, I recounted the stories of the People and the Arn. Lugo talked of the West People as well. We spoke of animals and stars. "In the new world," I explained to Gokihar, "you will be our voice. Tell those to come, whoever they are, that we were once a People. Tell them of our longing and our joy. Then, in the years that follow, when crows circle here and cry, 'ahh, ahh, there is nothing,' others will know we have lived."

Some days my words seemed hardly real. At other times, they swept through me like fire through grass, the memories rising up and calling, "hear me, hear me . . . don't forget!" And then, as the thoughts rushed at me, another voice, a deeper voice, began to whisper:

Don't worry about the words. Don't worry about the words.
Your ancestors live in your own flesh. Listen to their stories in the

493

wind, in the night by the fire, in the day near the sea. Their eyes twinkle in the sunlight on streams.

When Gokihar tired of my stories, or needed time to himself, he took out the boat or walked in the woods alone. A crease had begun to form between his dark eyes. Whether it was from worrying or squinting at the sun, I didn't know. He seemed more serious now and had little time for Fire or Zale. They shrugged and left him alone. Narta was the only one he saw, but less often than before.

One day, as we sat alone on the shore, I told him again of the power that runs in animals and how humans carry that power in themselves. "So, Bird Mother," he asked, smiling, "what is the spirit that runs in me?"

"You pretend not to know," I replied. "But I named you well. You will be the first to enter the new world. Your kind pushes on hardest, listens only to himself, and never quits. Earthmaker surely knew that the power of Wolf would run in you."

Gokihar nodded. Then he was gone again, walking toward the trees, driven by a restlessness that gave him little peace. I went home. Lugo was there, straightening elm wood for arrows. He smiled up at me. "The time approaches," I said. He nodded, his smile fading.

Just then Narta came strolling down the beach, slowing her pace as she neared our house. I still thought of her as a child, although she was a year older than Gokihar and had a woman's form. She'd been turning people's heads since her twelfth year. Now she stopped and looked around, as if waiting for someone. Her high breasts and slim hips pushed against her snug tunic. Lugo shook his head and said, "It's time Silka made that one new clothes."

"Hush," I whispered. "Narta, greetings!"

494

"Have you seen Gokihar?" she asked. She raised a hand and swept her dark hair from her face. Usually direct and confident, Narta was shy when it came to my son. "Zale said he was back."

"He was, but he's gone again. To the woods. Perhaps we'll see him tomorrow."

"Oh," she said. She sighed and walked away.

It was late afternoon. A watery sun tried vainly to warm the beach. A breeze from the sea began blowing, whipping the entry flaps. Perhaps it would rain. The women were hurrying to bring in the drying racks. I noticed a hunched figure scurrying toward us. Eda. She often stopped on her way home from the fish, usually with some complaint; the Fish girls were too lazy, Ziva too bossy, the day too hot. This day she dropped down without speaking and began rubbing her cold arms. The gruff old woman could still irritate me, especially when she glanced at my belly for signs of a grandchild. But I'd grown fond of her. I knew she worried about Gokihar when he was away. I handed her my sleeping robe, which she wrapped around her shoulders.

"Where is he?" she asked.

"Gone again," Lugo replied. "Let's eat." We walked to the cave to join the others.

Gokihar returned two days later. I was coming from the river when I saw him, on the ridge above the cave, his form outlined against the pale morning sky. He was carrying a bundle over his shoulder which bounced as he walked. Lugo had left with the men at dawn, gone to trap geese at a sandbar. It would be good to have some time alone with my boy, I thought, hurrying to the house to wait.

A few moments later I jumped up to greet him. "What have you there?" I asked.

He dropped a wolf pelt at my feet. "It was dead when I found it," he said. "Must have just died. The flesh wasn't touched. Strange that a dead wolf would lie untouched in the forest."

"Where was it?" Recognition began to flood me.

"Just beyond the ridge," he said, pointing behind us. "I wouldn't have seen the carcass at all, but a raven kept swooping at my head." He pushed a strand of yellow hair behind his ear and added, "I'll need a coat when I leave." Now I felt a wrenching in my heart. I'd known he'd be going some day, but it was always some day in the future. Now the future was here.

I leaned down to look at the pelt before Gokihar could see my face. I ran my hand across the bristly fur. There were tufts of orange hair on the paws, the long scar that ran down the front right leg. I turned the animal's head toward me, caught my breath and swallowed hard, seeing a familiar wide forehead and the torn ear. Wolf. My wolf. You, who had befriended me in my life's hardest year. Grief overtook me and I dropped to my knees, clutching the pelt in my arms. "Wolf, Wolf," I cried. "My old wolf, my good wolf. You're gone."

I thought the creature had been dead for years. All this time he'd lived! Had he sat at the edge of the forest, watching, while I went about my days? Had his yellow eyes followed when I tramped through the brush? How coarse I'd grown, how heedless, that this life could have existed next to mine, all this time, without my knowing. My ignorance seemed like betrayal. I sobbed against the coarse fur until my tears were spent. Gokihar stood over me, shifting his weight from one foot to the other.

"Oh, Gokihar," I said at last, wiping my wrist across my nose, "this is not any wolf. He was the one who cared for us when we were alone. It was he who saved us from the snow the night of your birth. He's walked in the forest alone ever since the People's return. Now he's come to us once again."

Gokihar crouched next to me and laid a hand on my arm, waiting, as the sorrow left my body. "It was for him I named you," I said, sniffing. And I told him the story of my winter with no humans, just Wolf and Raven and Thur, the long, white days, and the life that grew inside me. "Earthmaker came to me that winter . . . the trees spoke to me . . . all the world opened its heart . . . and I fell into it. At the heart of the world, Gokihar, is pure joy. There is no separation. That's what I learned that winter."

"Didn't you get lonely?" he asked, touching Wolf's leg.

"Loneliness is just another door, Gokihar, just another entrance."

"An entrance to what?"

How much could he understand? My words would just confuse him. But maybe he'd remember them later, when they made more sense. I tried to explain. "An entrance to the Source, to what abides behind our living and binds all life together. Loneliness comes from believing that we're set apart. All our sorrow comes from thinking the separation is real. But it's not."

"Then why do we believe it?"

"Because we think that we're our bodies and we know that bodies die."

He frowned, deepening the crease between his eyes. "So what are we then? Thoughts?"

"More than bodies and thoughts. We are one with the Source." Usually we spoke of practical things. To talk to him this way was like breathing underwater.

"I don't understand this 'Source,' " he said, frowning again.

"No one does. But, even now, if we walk with a still mind, we can glimpse it . . . the place where a vastness within us is touched by a vastness beyond us."

Gokihar let my words settle in. Then he shrugged. "I have one more thing to tell you," he added, glancing toward the cave and the cooking fire.

"Go get yourself something to eat first," I said. "Then tell me." I needed to wash my face and quiet my thoughts.

In a little while, he ambled back, carrying a stack of Magla's flat bread. It was one of his favorite foods, a mixture of ground acorns and honey baked on a stone. Sometimes she made it just for him. He handed one to me, chewed for a while, and washed it down with water. Lugo joined us. The men had returned early from the river, having come upon a flock of snow geese.

"What was it you wanted to tell me?" I asked the boy.

"I saw those men again, the ones from the south. I showed them the dream picture . . . told them they were looking in the wrong place."

"You did? What did they say?"

"They're going to keep going north."

"Oh." I waited. "Ah . . . are you going with them?"

"Of course not," he replied, smiling his old smile. "You said they'd never find the mountains there." He mumbled something I couldn't hear.

"What did you say?"

"I said I'd look somewhere else."

Again we sat in silence. I'd almost forgotten Lugo was with us. Now I was aware of the rub of his flint against a wooden shaft and a sinking in my belly. Gokihar was going. "I'll make you a coat then," I said, with a heartiness I didn't feel. "From the wolf pelt. I'll need to use a deer skin for the sleeves."

Gokihar nodded. "How long will that take?"

"Three days."

"All right." He took another drink of water and was gone.

Four days later, Gokihar returned, bringing Magla three fat rabbits for the spit. I motioned him toward the lean-to before he headed to the beach to look for Narta. "Try this," I said, standing and holding up the wolf tunic.

"It's done?" He draped the coat over his shoulders. It fell to the top of his thighs and bunched nicely around his neck.

"For cold nights," I said, smoothing the fur. "You look very handsome."

"Good. This will be good." He rubbed a hand over the coarse pelt. "Ah, Mother, I saw that mountain in my dream, the tall one in a row of seven peaks."

"You did?" I caught my breath. "Do you know where it is?"

"Somewhere to the south, I think, along the sea. Maybe a person can only reach it by boat. Maybe that's why no one's seen it. I think I can find it."

"You do? So . . . you'll be leaving soon?"

"Tomorrow."

Thoughts of all the terrible things that could happen flooded over me. "Gokihar . . . !" I wanted to tell him not to go, to forget everything I'd said, go back to how it used to be. But I knew that was impossible.

"What?"

"Don't go alone! Take someone with you . . . promise me. Take Zale or Fire. Do you promise?"

"All right, all right," he muttered, shaking his head, "I'll take someone." He moved a step away. "I'll go before dawn, get as far as I can the first day," he said gruffly.

"Very well. I'll tell the others. We'll say you're going to find your father." I saw no reason to tell them more than that. Everyone knew how restless he'd been these last few months. His departure would come as no surprise. At least he was familiar with the first part of the journey.

We ate well that night, to send him off. I had little to say. For a moment, I wished it were me who was going, Lugo and me. What an adventure! To look for new places, new dreams. How long since I'd done that? But my work was here now. This shore was my place. Maybe Gokihar would return, after he found the mountain, and bring us all to safety! Maybe that was really Earthmaker's plan! But no, unlike the others who crowded around him that night, I doubted that he'd ever be back.

Long after dark, we trudged home, Gokihar, Lugo, and I. Gokihar set his bundle by the door and pulled his wolf coat around him. It was really too warm for it, but I was proud to see him in it.

"I'll rest awhile before I go," he said.

"Son . . ." I'd told him everything many times over, so I hesitated. But I had to be sure, in the rawness of the future, that there was one thing he'd never forget.

"Yes, mother?"

"When the darkness is greatest, when we most feel our separation, a light within us will flare up and show us the way home. Bodies die. Souls return to the Source. The Source is forever."

I lay down by Lugo, pulled my robe around me, and listened to the wind. The night would be too short. "Gokihar! I almost forgot. One more thing!"

"What now?"

"Something you have to take." How had I overlooked it, I thought, remembering that clear night long ago when Grandmother Sela had given me her trust and her gift? Kneeling on the ground, I scraped aside a layer of dirt and pulled out the wooden box I'd buried when I'd made this place my home. "Here," I said, lifting an object that fit easily in my hand, "a stone thrown down from the stars. See how heavy it is, how it shines?" Moonlight flooded through the entrance and glinted off the black rock. I placed the rock in his hand. "Keep it with you always, Gokihar. This stone has been with the People longer than the memories of grandfathers. It tells a mystery we've forgotten." He turned the gleaming object in his hand, thanked me, and placed it with his bundle. How I loved him.

That night, while I slept, Earthmaker walked along the shore. Her mouth never moved, but I heard her clearly:

I am with you in small seasons and large cycles, encompassing ages, embracing the tender and the harsh.

Those to come will separate my powers, name my parts, and honor each one. Each part will go into the world, first to claim its power, then to be despised.

But they will return, as will you, as new earth comes up from below. I am of the Earth and beyond the Earth.

Chaos shatters me, but can't destroy me. My roots are stronger, my vision wiser. My potency grows in darkness as well as light. Held down hardest, it grows deepest, unleashing new life.

I awoke early, the sky grey with first light, and reached over to touch Gokihar's pallet. It was cold. I reached for Lugo's arm and lay silently, sobbing as the beach came to life. Before long Lugo slipped away to join the men. Sunlight poured through the entryway at his leaving. I sat up, dreading the day, in no hurry to move. From the shore came the sounds of laughter and the voices of two men. I crawled to the entrance and glanced out. Fire and Zale were heading to the water with fishing spears. Both of them? That was odd. Hadn't anyone gone with my son?

Suddenly a figure loomed in the entryway, a black shape outlined against the morning light. I heard a frantic voice. Silka's. Higher than usual, as if invisible hands grasped her neck. Had she been running? "Have you seen Narta?" she gasped. "I've looked everywhere!"

I stood and stepped out, the light hitting my face full-force. "No, she's not here."

"Then she's gone, she's gone!" Silka moaned. "She left with him!"

It took me a moment to understand. Then Silka lashed out at me, hurling words like stones. "You did it. You and that wolf child. Took her into danger, took her away. How could you? When will she be back?"

"She won't." The voice was Yarrow's. Silka spun around. Yarrow continued steadily. "It is not for your daughter you should fear, Silka. She has been saved. Fear for the rest of us."

Silka stared at Yarrow. I saw the fear in her eyes. "What do you mean, she won't be back?" she said.

Yarrow answered as if speaking to a child. "The things Earthmaker foretold are coming to pass. Narta has gone with Gokihar. They'll keep our memory alive."

"No!" she cried, looking for a moment like a wounded animal. But her anger was not yet spent. She turned toward me. "You did this, Thistle, you! You, with your strangeness and your so-called knowledge. You always thought you were so much better . . ."

"I never . . ."

"It was you who called this upon us!" she cried.

"Hush, Silka!" said Yarrow. "Your fear makes a fool of you. Go to the circle, both of you. When the men return, we'll talk."

"And will this talking bring back my daughter?" Silka's voice was bitter. She turned and hurried away.

Yarrow and I stood in the rising heat of the day, watching her departure. "So they're gone then," Yarrow said wearily. "Gokihar and Narta . . ."

"Early this morning. I didn't see them leave. I didn't know about Narta."

"Probably just as well." Knowledge weighed heavily on Yarrow, I thought, as I looked at her lined face. She sighed. "Today we'll tell the others and make a plan," she said.

"Whatever you say. Then what?"

"Then we wait. Wait and pray the lights turn."

And so it was, in the Age of the Lion, when the sun at the vernal equinox still rose in the constellation of the Great Cat, that we came to know Chaos.

The Shining Ones

I FOLLOWED YARROW TO THE FIRE CIRCLE AND TOOK MY PLACE. Silka was already there, her rage ebbing, her grief gathering into unshed tears. She must have said something. The other women glanced at me, their questions hanging like dust in the air. It seemed odd to sit in the morning and do no work.

Not even Magla was busy. She stood by the fire, her greying hair coiled about her head, a strip of willow bark between her teeth. When she saw me, she nodded, filled a horn with hot tea, and handed it to me. "Be strong," she whispered. The day was too warm for tea, but I sipped it anyway for something to do.

Only Yarrow went about as usual, bringing Zalec his tea and flint. She told the group we'd talk soon, then went to the shore, her back to us, and looked out to sea.

Eda sat to my right, rocking back and forth, her robe pulled tightly about her despite the heat. Grey hair floated like smoke around her shoulders. Ziva was on her other side. "There, there," the little Fish Woman whispered, patting Eda's arm. The other Fish Women and the newcomers waited at the outside of the circle, whispering among themselves. A few of their children stared at me. One carried a rawhide doll with eyes of red currants. I took an apple from the basket and bit into it. The flesh was soft and I tossed it.

Morning seemed endless. But well before midday, the fishermen returned with their nets. The hunters, who'd been waiting on the sandbars for birds, soon joined them. Ochre strode in at the head of the group and dropped three geese at Magla's feet. For once, no one jumped up to clean them.

He frowned, looked around the circle, and back to Magla. "What's this?" he asked. "Are you ill?"

"Quiet, old man," she said. "We have more to think about than filling your belly."

He lowered himself to the ground. "Well, what?"

"Hush," Magla answered. "Wait for the others."

Lugo took his place beside me and reached for my hand. "Narta went with him," I whispered. "Yarrow says it's time to tell them everything."

Lugo nodded. He'd been ready to tell them for months. "So, he took Narta?" Lugo said, shaking his head. "Smart boy."

A few more men joined us. Finally, Yarrow stood and walked toward us. Her words were tender. "Today a boy has gone to find his father. No big story, that. With him has gone a beloved daughter." The men looked around in surprise. Who? Why? Silka's stricken face told them what they needed to know. "We grieve for her absence," Yarrow said. "But that, too, is a story told many times. No, there is more to this tale than the adventures of the young. For now comes the unfolding of a larger truth."

Lugo's grip tightened. I moved closer to him. Why was there no breeze?

Yarrow resumed. "If we keep silent in times of Change, we can sometimes hear Earth Herself speaking. The crumbling of stones, the warmth of the sea, the glance of a fox. All of these are Her words. And many of us have listened. But when the way of the world continues to baffle us, it is time to come together and speak of strange things."

She looked from face to face. "Some of our old ones are gone. And there are new faces among us. But many of you still remember when Thought Holder walked the land. Think back to that time. It was in those days that the first rumble of discord entered our minds. Some of you were there." Her eyes sought Magla, then Ochre, then me. "It was then that Earthmaker came to us to warn of things to come. First to Thought Holder, then Tenja, then Thistle. Even Eda, still far away." She nodded at the older woman. "We know now that Earthmaker spoke to the southern people. Those who go out on ships. And those who watch the stars. To some among each tribe, it seems, She gave a message. 'Sky will make war on Earth,' She said. And She asked that the message be told when the people were ready. So, with Thistle, we sat and watched the stars, waited and watched the lights."

Yarrow continued. "And then to Thistle, and perhaps to others, Earthmaker came a second time. This time She said, 'Your child has been chosen to keep the people's memory alive.' Now, as the lights approach, Gokihar has gone to find a safe place. He has taken Narta as well. Our memory will survive."

A rumbling went up from the group. Then their questions erupted, one after another, questions they'd asked before, questions I'd tried to answer, questions which had no answer.

"Why is this happening?"

"Where is the safe place?"

"How will they find it?"

"They'll come back for us, won't they?"

"How much time do we have?"

"Who told them to leave now?"

"Who caused this?"

"Wait!" said Yarrow.

"Why Gokihar? Why was he chosen?"

"Wait!" she repeated. "Would you rather none of us survived? No one can answer all your questions. We must do the best we can with our ignorance. And no one is to blame." She looked at me. "One among us may answer some of your questions. Thistle, will you try?"

"No, not Thistle!" Silka jumped up. "Not her. She caused . . ."

"Silence!" Yarrow commanded.

I stood, my head reeling from too little sleep. I'd never wanted this kind of trouble. I'd only wanted to follow Earthmaker where she led, do Her bidding, and perhaps tell the tale. The tale of the joy at the heart of the world. And now, one I loved as a sister was turning against me. Surely Silka only said what the others were thinking. This was a dangerous moment, I knew, the most dangerous of all. The moment when love could be overcome by fear.

"I, too, grieve for the child I'll never see again," I said. "I wish I could tell Silka that the pain becomes easier once the shock subsides. But that may not be true." My eyes stung. I sniffed as I met Silka's glance. "I can only speak to you from the pictures in my mind and the fullness of my heart. More than that, I don't know."

Silka bowed her head. I searched for words.

"You want to know who caused this? In my fourteenth year, I dreamed of a boat, a boat we'd never seen before. That boat has come to pass. Do we have such a boat because I dreamed it? Or did I dream it because it was coming? These lights have not entered our world

507

because of me or any person. They come from a power outside of us. Our thoughts may anticipate them, but they do not control them. I know nothing of the power behind them, except that it is not of the earth. Maybe I can answer a few of your questions, one at a time. Where would you begin?"

"Do the lights mean to kill us?" The question came from Bren, a thin, trembling woman from the east. Her man had frozen in a mountain storm two years ago. She and her babies joined us soon after.

"I think no good will come of the lights," I answered. "It's not hard to see them as demons cast down from the sky. But does the avalanche mean to bury us, or the snow to freeze our flesh? Do we call floods attackers and fires enemies? A power beyond us has been unleashed. I think the lights know nothing of us and that falling is their fate."

The People were quiet for a moment. Ochre's gruff voice interrupted the silence. "You don't call them devils then?"

"No."

"We should call them something, give 'em a name, like those South People did."

"All right." How like Ochre to turn confusion into simplicity. "We could call them the Shining Ones," I said.

"Good name," he replied. "Easy to remember."

"Thistle?" The voice was Magla's. Her thoughts rarely took her beyond the needs of the day. Everyone looked her way. "These lights, are they planets or stars?"

I'd once wondered if the larger light was some rogue planet, but its path was too erratic. And it was too small to be a star. "Not planets, of that I'm sure. Perhaps Eda was right. Perhaps the lights are the stuff of dead stars."

"Maybe the Shining Ones won't come this way at all," said Ziva. "Couldn't they change course and pass us by?"

"That's possible." I tried to remember what Tenja had said about the force of large objects. "There is a power in large bodies that draws small bodies to them. I always thought the lights were heading to the sun. But something has changed. Now the lights are careless. Maybe something has pulled them off course."

"Like what?" asked Zalec. Zalec's mind was always busy. Left behind by the hunters each day, alone with his pain at night, he had time to think. He'd probably been considering his question for days.

"There could be something out there, too far away or too dark to see. Something big enough to draw the lights. Maybe large planets have that power."

"Is Earth a large planet?" he asked

"I don't know."

"How long do you think we have?" he persisted.

I shook my head. The lights were much smaller than the moon, but growing. "Once I would have said they grew from year to year, then month to month. Now it seems they change each day. They're close. Maybe they move faster as they approach the sun. Or look faster because they're nearer . . . not long."

"What if they don't hit us directly, but just come close?" Zalec asked again.

I studied his face. What was he getting at? Perhaps I knew. Two nights ago, while sitting with Lugo on the shore, waiting for Gokihar to return with the boat, I'd noticed something different. I'd wondered then if the lights themselves were changing. Or just getting close enough to reveal something new. "Could it be we've seen the same thing, Zalec? The lightning that sometimes flashes from the Shining Ones?"

509

Zalec nodded.

"It's possible the Shining Ones spew fire," I said. "So yes, I think they may hurt us, even if they don't hit us."

"Enough questions for now," said Yarrow, standing. "Eat something. Keep your strength. Tonight we begin a vigil. We'll sleep on the shore until this thing comes to pass."

"Yarrow's right," I said. "Watch and wait. That's the best thing."

Some of the people stayed to eat. Others wandered away. I walked with Lugo to the sea. The sky was a cloudless blue.

"Good day to be on the water," he said, sitting and stretching his long legs.

"By now he must be near the place where the cliffs drop to the sea. The water's rough there."

Lugo shrugged. "He's done it before, on windier days."

"Do you think we'll know . . . if he makes it?"

"Could be."

Everyone gathered at dusk, carrying their mats to the shore. The night was warm enough without a fire. And we needed darkness, so we could study the sky. I squeezed in between Lugo and Fire. We lay down, folding our hands under our heads and fixing our eyes on the stars. Even the children were quiet, gazing solemnly at the Shining Ones gliding in from the heart of the deep. The cluster of lights hovered beyond the Warrior. What things of beauty they were! Now everyone could see the tiny tendrils of lightning flickering around them like silver fingers.

It was good to hear the People's queries in the dark. In the daylight, I could never be sure of what I'd seen and what I'd only imag-

ined. We spoke hurriedly at first, as if time might
run out before our questions. As night grew
darker, the lightning became brighter. The
orange streaks seemed to crackle like oil
in a flame. "Look how they hurl their
heat!" said Fire. Unlike their parents,

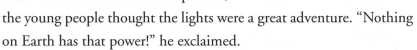

the young people thought the lights were a great adventure. "Nothing
on Earth has that power!" he exclaimed.

"Earth has powers of its own," I said. "Have you no gratitude?"

"I mean no slight to Earthmaker, sister. But maybe the time has
come to honor the lights as well."

"What do you mean to do?" I asked. "Set fire to the trees?"

"Of course not. But Sky wants its honor. What could it hurt, if we
praised the power there?"

I didn't know what to say. I looked at the uplifted faces glowing
with an awesome paleness. Had the Shining Ones won some raw allegiance? A new fear pulsed through me. Something strange was happening to the People, I thought, some shift within them, some new
season in their souls. Was it possible for terror to turn to veneration?
We continued gazing upward, drifting into our private vigils.

We tracked the Shining Ones again the next night. "They look
close," said Zalec. "Like beautiful women, come to dance." He was
right. The largest light seemed almost as close as a neighbor's cooking fire.

A hazy glow surrounded the lights, luminous like the inside of a
clam shell, shimmering in pale silver, red, and green. Something was
different. Now the luster around the Shining Ones seemed to pulsate,
almost to breathe.

"Look at that!" cried Fire. "It's like a jellyfish, shrinking and bil-
lowing. What causes that?"

I'd never seen anything like it. "Maybe wind. I don't know," I replied, watching the delicate changing hues. I remembered how the color of flames shifted sometimes when we tossed new wood or strange rock into a cooking fire. Perhaps different fuels now burned above us.

All that night, the hazy circle grew. Not fast. Slowly. Gently. And then, just after the first light rimmed the east, all of that changed. The sky around the lights suddenly ignited, as when one spills fat into a flame.

"Look!" screamed Eda. "The sky explodes!"

My hands flew to my face. She was right. The glowing circle of light, once delicate gold and blue, now flamed a hot orange. Before our startled eyes, the gentle halo flared larger than the moon. No longer could I see the individual lights, all of the Shining Ones having been devoured in the massive orange blaze.

I held my breath. The blaze continued burning brightly. Was Eda right? Had the sky exploded? Were the Shining Ones gone? No, there was something else. As I watched, the flaming ball seemed to sort itself out, spewing out the cinders it hadn't consumed. The largest light re-emerged with its smaller companion light and their familiar band of followers. As if proud of their survival, the stream of lights continued their triumphant journey. But now, driven by some cosmic wind, new remnants flew among the followers. Something had exploded, that seemed clear. But I didn't think it was the sky.

"No, Eda . . . probably not," I said at last. "I think the lights struck something and broke it. The new followers are the parts that survived."

"What would they hit?" asked Fire. "There's nothing there."

A dark planet too distant for a name? A giant stone whirling quietly through space? I had no idea. "I don't know, but something shattered."

Whatever they'd hit, it must have been huge. The fire in the sky died out, but the glow around the lights returned larger than before. It shone like some pale sun. Dawn came early, though whether the milky light was from Sun itself or the Shining Ones' haze we couldn't say.

The children slept all that dusky morning, while the Old Ones prayed and moaned. I rested my chin on my knees, wondering what the next night would bring. Finally I fell asleep. It felt like I slept a long time, though I couldn't be sure. It was still daylight when I awoke. Lugo was beside me, his body shielding me from the sun. I was hungry. "Where is everyone?" I asked, blinking in the light.

"Gone to the sea to cool off," Lugo replied.

The sounds of children caught my attention. I looked toward the water. Even the Old Ones were there, lined up like terns, the foam sloshing around their thin legs. All except Eda. I looked around.

"Where's your mother?"

Lugo jerked his head. I glanced behind us. Eda sat in the shade at the entrance to the cave.

"Oh. Praise Earthmaker, it's hot," I said, wiping at the line of sweat above my mouth.

"Do you want to join the others?" he asked.

"Not yet." It was good to have some time to ourselves. We'd rarely had a chance to talk since everyone began clustering along the shore. "I had such a strange dream," I said, pushing my hair behind my ears and rubbing my eyes.

"Good or bad?"

"Maybe both. About the people who come after us. Good because that means someone survives. But bad because those who follow forget us." I shook my head. This was one dream I wanted to forget. "Let's swim, then eat something," I said, grabbing Lugo's shoulder as I stood. We walked to the sea.

That night was overcast. I was glad for the clouds. Another day dawned hot and dry. Though it was autumn now, it felt like summer. Hotter than summer. The shore was silent. The sun climbed higher and the grass on the river bank wilted. A panting fox made for his den, mindless that his path took him through our camp. Like dogs on a summer afternoon, we languished near the water. But even the sea was warm. The hot breeze didn't cool us. It was good we'd stored our winter food. At least there was something to eat, should we want it.

"We'll go to the woods for a while," said Yarrow on the sixth day of the heat. Mothers hoisted up their babies. The rest of us took water bags and trudged into the forest, stopping by the apple trees. But the shade brought little relief.

"What's this?" said Ochre, picking a withered apple. The fruit on the tree had shriveled.

"Now Earthmaker cooks for us as well," said Fire, forcing a smile. No one laughed.

The Old Ones rested and we brought them water. "Where's Eda?" Ziva asked. Had she been with us when we left? I couldn't remember.

"Still at the cave, I suppose," said Magla. She was probably right. Eda had been keeping to herself for days, retreating deeper into the cavern in the heat. Even at night, she stayed alone, no longer joining our vigil under the stars.

"Do you think she has water?" I asked Lugo.

"I should see," he said.

"I'll go with you." We left the others in the silent forest. Even the birds were quiet. Or perhaps they were gone.

Eda wasn't at the entryway. We peered in, seeing a grey shape at the back. Lugo took a step. "Mother, are you all right?" There was no answer. He moved closer. "Mother?"

"Don't bother me!" she said.

"What are you doing in here? Have you eaten anything? Had anything to drink?"

"Go away," she answered.

"You need to keep up your strength," he said.

"Why?" she replied. Lugo was silent. "Oh, all right," Eda said. "Get me some water. I'll talk to your woman for a while." Lugo glanced at me, shrugged, and was gone.

I sat on a stone and wrapped my arms around my knees. The cave was cooler than the shore, but clammy. A fetid stench arose from the crevices. "We miss you, Eda. Why is it you never join us?"

"I'd only be in the way."

"Why do you say that?" I asked.

"You want to offer these people solace. I prefer the comfort of my own thoughts."

"Sometimes it's good to talk, Mother, to find comfort in each other."

"Your words, have they brought anyone peace? Has knowledge helped them accept their fate? Has it helped you?"

I tried to keep the irritation from my voice. "I take some comfort in knowing Gokihar will keep our memory alive. That those to come will still know Earthmaker . . ."

"Huh. Who will believe them? Who will care?"

"Eda, what are you talking about?" I glanced toward the entrance. Where was Lugo?

She shook her head. "You've done the best you could, girl. I don't fault you for that. But in the years to come, when humans crawl from caves like rats into the sun, who will remember your fine thoughts?"

The hairs at the back of my neck prickled. She continued.

"When they rebuild their homes and say, 'See what I've done with my own hands,' they'll want nothing that reminds them how easily life is crushed. They will vilify our memory, say we never existed, say life sprung full-blown with them. The past will seem but a feeble preparation for their fine glory. Sky fall and crush the earth? Such thoughts will be blasphemy."

Surely she was mistaken. I leaned closer. "Have you so little faith in Earthmaker and the bond She forged with us?"

The old woman did not give up so easily. "It is not Earthmaker I doubt, but humans," she said. "If Sky makes war on Earth, humans will seek new gods, throw their allegiance to the sky. Our ways will change forever. When humans remember Earthmaker, they will be reminded of death and its sting. Fear will lodge in their hearts like ice."

"They won't!" I insisted. Gokihar would see to that.

"But they will. The legacy of Chaos is too strong. All talk of what has gone before will be forbidden. Those who come will demand order at any cost and shun all reminders of weakness. Fear will be the victor here, make no mistake. Earthmaker will mourn. Her grief will sound like the cracking of old trees. The day will come when She will be forgotten."

I heard footsteps and stood quickly. Lugo was back. He handed the old woman one of her wooden cups and she took a sip. "You've been alone too long," he said. "Come with us."

She drank again. "Oh, very well, my boy," she sighed. "Very well." Reaching for Lugo's arm, she rose unsteadily. We stepped out into the heat and walked toward the shore. It was late. The sun glowed like a blood-red disk ready to dip into the sea.

What New God Has Come to Claim Us?

"Eda thinks our hearts will change, if Chaos comes," I whispered to Lugo. He was laying out a hide for his mother on the rocky shore. The old woman made herself comfortable.

"I'm not deaf, you know," she said as she pulled off her short boots. "Think about my words. If Sky makes war on Earth, Earth will be no comfort. Those to come will shun the Earth and turn to Sky. They will hope to placate the heavens with their offerings. Monuments will rise, each taller than the last. Those to come will climb them and pray to new gods."

Lugo shrugged. "They'll forget all thoughts of Chaos after a while," he reassured her. He scanned the dark beach. We'd decided to wait for the others on the shore, rather than return to the forest. It was cooler now that night had come. "I wonder what's keeping everyone," he said, changing the subject.

Eda was not easily deterred. "The memory of fear will fester like a thorn in the foot, the wound so long forgotten a man believes he's always limped."

I'd heard enough of her worry. "I think I hear Fire's voice," I said. "They'll be here soon. Are you hungry, Eda?"

"Fear will haunt the dreams of the survivors," she continued. "Fear will be a constant companion, a stranger come to stay."

"Magla!" I called into the darkness. "Are you there?"

"Coming." Grey shapes took form around us as the group emerged from the darkness.

"What took you so long? The sun's already set." The irritation in my voice was not meant for her.

"Didn't you see our fire?" she asked.

"No." I'd been too busy with Eda to wonder much about the others.

"Well, your brother wanted a bonfire. He got the young ones to drag some timber to the top of that chalk hill. They piled up the wood and waited for dark to light it."

What a lot of work for nothing. I turned to Fire. "Why? Why would you make a fire on such a hot night?"

The red-haired man shrugged and looked at the ground. Then he lifted his head and met my gaze. His eyes seemed to look through me. "To hail the Shining Ones," he said. "You should have seen our blaze."

"I see you found Eda," Magla said quickly, nodding to the older woman.

"In the cave. We were just talking." I caught Eda's sullen gaze. "She was just saying how hungry she is."

Eda nodded. "Yes," she replied. "I'm starving."

THE NIGHT WAS CLEAR, except for a band of clouds settling at the rim where Earth met Sky. We ate a meal of walnuts and currants, and again turned our eyes to the Shining Ones. It had been several nights since the huge explosion, when the lights had smashed against some object and thrown up debris like a foot kicking sand. Since then the Shining Ones had been obscured, as if surrounded by a cloud. But the dust from the onslaught subsided a little each day. On this night the sky looked almost like it had before the blast. The lights were at their brightest since the impact, the familiar glowing circle restored.

Gazing upward, I saw that more than their clarity had changed. The band of followers still accompanied the larger two Shining Ones, streaming along in an orderly fashion. But the gathering had grown. I'd noticed a handful of new followers right after the impact. Clusters of smaller lights now appeared as well. Could these be stones orphaned by the blast, I wondered, come to take their places with their brother and sister lights? Whatever the new lights' origin, the Shining Ones' growing family continued to advance proudly across the sky. A stream of light unfurled behind each one, like long strands of golden hair.

"They're beautiful!" sighed Ziva. And so they were.

Perhaps it was the beauty of the night. Or something else. I felt a coolness on my cheeks and brushed my hand across my face. Tears.

"What is it?' asked Lugo.

"I was thinking about Gokihar—him looking for his father—remembering my own father. He drowned so long ago, I can't recall his face." Lugo nodded. He'd never spoken of the man who'd fathered him. Perhaps he'd never seen him. I went on, hearing the tremble in my voice. "Gokihar rides on water none of us have ever known. Perhaps he sails to a new god. Even if he never finds Anish, he'll have gone to find his father. That's what Ziva told us long ago . . . the future is the world of the father."

Zalec's shout interrupted my thoughts. "Look! They've changed direction!" He pointed skyward, though we needed no guide. All heads jerked upward. One of the newcomer children, daughter to Bren, began to whimper in her mother's arms.

Was Zalec correct? Had the direction of the lights shifted? I laid a hand on Lugo's arm and craned my neck. There was no way to assess a change from a quick glance. One had to remember the lights' exact path on previous nights. The night was hot. My back ached. I recalled noticing a few nights ago that the tails turned slightly to the right. I'd been comforted by that observation, since it seemed we weren't directly in their path.

"What do you think?" whispered Lugo. Only when he pried my hand away did I realize how tightly I'd been clutching his arm.

Something was a little different, something no one would have noticed except by watching the sky each night. The Shining Ones' long hair now streamed slightly to the left, as if the lights yearned ever so gently for the blood-red planet we called Warrior. I swallowed hard. "Zalec's right. Their path has changed."

It was true then. The demon stars were drawn to planets.

Night after night, all through the hot darkness of that strange autumn, we tracked the demon lights. The children no longer ran. Dogs panted in the shade. Fish were scarce, perhaps gone to colder water. Plants turned brown and sea birds left our shore. It wasn't just the season that killed the plants and sent the geese on their random ways. That much we knew. It was the heat from the Shining ones. Summers had been lengthened since we had first seen these cursed lights. We went about our tasks, carrying water, burying waste. None of the old ways mattered. Our lives were backward now. We slept by day, sweat clinging to our bodies. By night we waited.

There were fewer questions. We knew enough. Some nights we told stories. What I longed for was the sound of laughter. Time and again I remembered the Shining Ones' onslaught, the lightning bolts they'd hurled at their dark victim. Eda said again that the lights were monsters, fiends who spewed fire when they attacked. I'd seen a monster once, washed from the sea, her rotting rib cage large enough for a house. Ochre thought the lights might be like the Arn creature, their mother animal with a snout as long as her legs. But the Shining Ones weren't monsters. Not the kind we knew.

I'd begun to see the sky not as empty space, but as a pulsing world cut by rivers of invisible power. I tried to imagine those rivers while I waited in the dark, those braids of power quivering across great distances, embracing the emptiness, the planets, and the stars. Maybe the power became visible when one large body approached another. Maybe that's what we'd seen before the explosion. The Warrior would soon show us if my suspicions were true.

It was in the month called Return to the Sea that the Shining Ones hailed that sad body. For several nights, we watched the flickering of light between the Shining Ones and the red planet. And then one evening, as we huddled on the shore, the larger demon star poised itself, gathered its power, and attacked.

"See. It comes, it comes!" screamed Eda. "A monster, a serpent . . . see how it uncurls!" Lugo reached for the old woman and turned her face toward him, pressing her head against his shoulder.

The battle had begun. We watched in horror as fingers of demon lightning lashed the Warrior. Once again, a patch of sky ignited. Once again the Shining Ones changed shape, writhing like glowing serpents, diving like golden-plumed birds, striking and coiling and striking again. Surely the planet was hit, its surface scoured. Suddenly the red planet struck back, hurling lightning blasts of its own! As if enraged by this resistance, a plume of light shaped like a thrashing serpent struck again.

The onslaught lasted all night. "See! It's as I told you," Eda whimpered. "Sky makes war on planets." She was right, though no one cared to listen. We longed to see the Warrior, to know if he was wounded, but the radiance of the stellar battlefield obscured anything else. We waited for the haze to clear.

And then, as the first stars of morning twinkled on the horizon, we saw him, the Warrior, emerging from the dust. His red body was intact. Cheers went up along the shore. The Serpent had made war and the planet had prevailed! Resigned to Warrior's resistance, the demon lights forgot him and moved on. Then, in a slow pivot that lasted until dawn, they seemed to discover the moon.

The days that followed burnt us. Would there ever be more rain? For twelve nights we watched as the Shining Ones approached the moon. The lights were now so bright they shone like a second sun. We no longer had darkness, only midday and dusk. Nor could we distinguish between the two larger lights. They'd become the Shining One. Behind them came the followers, unfurling like whips and tails and beards, swept along in tight position.

Midday was the worst. We'd crouch beneath a stand of wilted trees and wait out the heat. Everyone but my brother. Heat didn't bother him. What he hated was the waiting. While the others trembled and fainted, Fire paced the countryside, a penned-up animal seeking his escape. He was a bold man, confident but untested. Eager for a challenge. While the lights frightened most of us, they fascinated him. To him, the Shining One was no enemy, but a chance to prove himself, to awaken the hero who slept within. Sometimes I wished Gokihar had taken Fire along instead of Narta. To help him push on when he got tired. And to spare me the young man's restlessness.

One afternoon, Yarrow and I sat talking quietly, as we'd come to do. Her steadiness kept me calm. Some of the others dozed around us. At the crackle of dry grass, we looked up. Fire was back from his wanderings. He dropped down beside us and wiped his face. He was lighter-skinned than the rest of us, with Ochre's broad jaw and large teeth. The sun had turned his face and his powerful arms the same color as his hair. "What happens now?" he asked.

Yarrow shrugged. The resting ones looked toward him and away. They'd heard his questions before.

"What if we're spared like the Warrior? What if the demon stars singe us and move on? Thistle, what do you think will happen then?" He thrust his chin forward as he spoke.

"I don't know," I said. It was a good question, though. What if we did survive? Our lives had been shaken. Our trust was gone. Could Earthmaker bind us to Her again? Or would we become wanderers, roaming the wilderness, trusting nothing but our own thoughts, accustomed to fear?

He rubbed a square hand across his chin. "I'm thinking of leaving for a while," he said.

Magla sat up, wide awake. "But the heat . . ." she said. My brother had everyone's attention now.

"I'll stay by the sea."

I was surprised he'd made up his mind so quickly. But not surprised he was going. Magla soon ran out of reasons for him to stay. When he slipped into the cave to put some things in a bag, I followed him, hoping for a moment alone.

"What's your hurry?" I asked. "At least stay until tomorrow, sleep here tonight . . ."

"No. I'm tired of sitting around like a rabbit under a stump, waiting for the moment of my death. You have a reason to be here. They look to you for answers. So far I don't like the answers this place gives us. It's time to make my own."

"Where will you go?"

"I have no idea. But if I'm to die, it will be in a place and time of my own choosing."

I followed him back to the shore, where he embraced Magla and Ochre, held my shoulders for a moment, and nodded to the rest of us. "I'll tell you what I find," he said, resuming his jovial way. Then he waved and left. I avoided Magla's eyes, keeping my gaze on Fire as he walked toward the shoreline.

The water had changed in recent days, become more turbulent. Sometimes the waves leaped from the sea. I wondered if the tide was now pulled by the Shining One as well as the moon. The churning water didn't seem to bother Fire. He stepped into the spray, turned to wave again, and headed north. "The man's a fool," Ochre said at last, shaking his head as his son disappeared down the beach.

I tried not to think of Fire's departure. But I found myself wishing all that night that our days could be as they'd been. Golden, peaceful, endless, separated by nights of dreamless sleep. Awakening to the dew and the morning birds and the laughter of children. All of that was gone. I glanced at the sky, watching the Shining One hover over us. That light had become our life. It had taken my son and my brother. What else would it get from me? I wondered if this would be the night the demon lights met the moon.

When the sun went down, everyone returned to the dusky beach, looking for their own small group. I noticed Zale close by. A month ago, I would have expected him to leave with Fire. The two of them had been best friends for years. But he was with Ziva's family now, his arm around the Fish Woman's radiant daughter. The two of them had been inseparable since the night of the last full moon, the night Luba followed Zale into the forest. They were gone for three days.

Bren and her three children sat with our family. Vasto, Lugo's young brother, had moved the sunken-eyed woman into his house in early summer, caring for her young ones as his own. Poor Eda. Nothing had gone as she'd planned. The old woman's days were filled with the noise of the white-haired children. It was unlikely her sons would ever bring her babies that they'd fathered. Bren's two boys began coughing. We'd found it hard to keep everyone well. No one wanted to eat. Most of the fruit was rotten. Fat flies buzzed everywhere. At least the water was good.

The sky was now so bright at night that we rarely saw real stars. I watched the moon as it trembled on the horizon, unsure of itself in the milky sky. Slowly it began to rise. The Shining One waited, as a lion for a fawn. After a while I dozed.

A shriek pierced the air. Eda.

"What . . . what?" I mumbled, jumping up.

"The moon!" she cried.

The moon and the monster lights were now directly above us. Tongues of fire leaped from the Shining One, licking our silver companion. All along the shore, people stood transfixed by the spectacle. Would moon lash back with a blaze of her own?

Before we had an answer, I felt the earth beneath me tremble. My body pitched forward. I reached out my arms to catch myself, staggering to my feet. What was happening? Just as I found my balance, a sudden wind rose up. The sky opened. Sand and gravel rained down on us as if clouds were made of stone. I grabbed Lugo's arm. Together we held Eda, who continued to scream. Earth lurched again. This time a long ripple of ground arose beneath our feet, the crest running along the shore like a wave of dirt.

"Run!" I cried, spitting out sand. The young ones rushed for the cave and the old ones covered their heads. "Run!" I yelled again. "Get out of here!" I heard hollow thuds on the hill above us. Boulders were being knocked about and shaken. "Get off the beach!"

Everyone seemed of one mind as they streamed toward the cave. Lugo took Eda's arm. I reached for Magla. We hurried forward in a tangle of legs and squeezed through the crowded opening. The crowd pressed around us, spilling into every corner. Lugo stood over the older women. I remained in the front with Bren, making sure her children weren't trampled. Had everyone made it inside? Another scream came from the shore. But before I could see who it was, the ground shifted again. A river of stones poured from the hill and tumbled across the entrance, jumping as they hit the ground, then rolling toward the sea. Other stones fell behind the first ones until they covered the shore. I looked out on the silent world. The one who'd screamed was gone, buried by dust and rock. Who had it been?

Lugo let go of Eda, pushed his way to the front, and clambered over the stones, following the memory of the scream. I hurried behind him. The gravel wind still ripped across the shore.

"Zalec!" Lugo called. "Zalec! Where are you?" We'd left Zalec behind? A sick feeling spread through my belly. Why hadn't Yarrow brought him? I couldn't think of everything.

"Zalec!" I shouted as well. From beneath a pile a stones came a deep voice. He was alive! We moved in that direction. A foot bound in worn leather protruded from the rubble.

"We're here! Hold on," Lugo cried above the wind. He heaved a boulder aside. We dug as fast as we could, hearing another moan as we lifted the last of the stones. We came upon a human shape, face down, limp as a pelt. Too small to be Zalec. The moans persisted. Lugo pulled the body away and gently turned it over. Yarrow! She was covered by a shroud of dust and gravel. Blood trickled from her mouth to her ear, cutting a red path across her face. Shielding my eyes from the blowing gravel, I knelt beside her and placed my fingers on her neck. Silence.

Zalec tried to sit up, coughing and brushing sand from his face. "Agh," he gasped. "What happened?"

Lugo crouched beside him. "Landslide."

"I was just sitting here and everything went black,' said Zalec, shaking his head. He put a hand on Lugo's shoulder and pulled himself to his knees. Only then did he see Yarrow's broken form. His face turned white. He pushed Lugo aside and crawled to her, grabbing her limp arm. Then he dropped his hand and moaned.

The others shuffled from the cave and stood over Yarrow's crushed body, covering their faces as the storm howled around us. I stood and laid a hand on Zalec's shoulder, glancing at our forlorn group. The wind whipped our tunics so that we seemed to sway. I shuddered. Who would be our leader now?

Before I could think of an answer, there came a wrenching sound, not of Earth, but far away, some great rumble from the sky. Only then did I remember the battle above us. Making a tunnel with my hands, I looked up. The blowing dirt hid all of Sky's secrets except for a ghostly white glow. Surely that wasn't the moon I saw. It was in the wrong place. Then the roar of the wind again, but a wind like none I'd ever heard, a wind not of Earth. It howled above us from the middle of the heavens, gathering force. The sky turned brown and yellow like an old bruise. Earth lurched and I heard new sounds. Much nearer. The mountains had begun to shake.

"Bring Yarrow!" I called. "Get to the cave!"

And then a small sound, close by, hooves on wood, the reindeer kicking open the slats of their pen. They hurtled past us, all of our hard-won herd, heading for the trees, nostrils flaring. The dogs tore after them. But this was no pursuit. No longer were the animals hunters and hunted. All were prey, driven by fear. We made no move to stop them.

"Hurry!" I called again. "Move."

This time I stayed on the shore to make sure we left no one behind. Then I scrambled after the others. The cries of the children reached me over the howl of the wind. Why was this happening? When would it end? Just as I cleared the beach, the ground gave way behind me. I jumped forward and twisted around. The ground I'd just crossed cracked open like a dry pod. Stones rolled into the trench and it quickly filled with water.

"Thistle, get in here!" Lugo grabbed me by the arm.

He pulled me to the entrance and I pressed against him, my face on his shoulder.

"Is it another landslide?" I asked.

Lugo shook his head. Then a great, wrenching shudder, as if the ground gave birth to mountains. The roof of the cave cracked, but the stone held. Vasto fell against me, pushing Lugo into the wall. Lugo stood and rubbed his arm.

"Are you all right?" I asked.

"Yes, I'm fine."

He was staring through the entryway, looking puzzled. I turned and glanced outside. The mountains to the north were bleeding. Red liquid poured from the closest peak, moving fast, flowing toward the sea. Had my brother made it past that place? Had he climbed or stayed low? Would it have made a difference? In that moment, a second mountain split open, like an egg too long in coals. Then another behind it. I looked up again at Lugo. Did mountains give birth to themselves? Those in the back of the cave pressed forward, asking questions to no one in particular. "'What is it?" "What can you see?" "What's happening?" I moved closer to Lugo, torn between hiding my face and watching the hills explode.

We weren't the only creatures to tremble at the storm. From the shore came the scream of horses. A stallion thundered by with his herd. They leaped the crevasse and raced for the trees as the wind whipped their manes and drove gravel into their flesh.

"See, see!" whimpered Eda. "Sky makes war on Earth! What new god has come to claim us?"

"Quiet!" Lugo bellowed above the wind.

The gale was whipping the sea to a yellow froth. High waves crashed near the entryway. For a moment I forgot about the mountains. "Lugo, the water," I said, tugging at his arm. Seawater sloshed at our ankles and pooled on the uneven floor. He looked down and back at me. "We need to get out of here," I whispered. "This place is a trap."

He glanced back at the shore. Branches flew past as if they were leaves. "I don't know if we can," he said.

"We have to." The water was now over our ankles. He nodded. I turned to face the People. I'd have to yell to be heard over the wind. "Listen. Everyone! The cave is flooding. We'll drown if we stay."

"If we leave, we die as well," Eda muttered. "What difference does it make?"

The People huddled behind her in the grey light, children pressed against their fathers' knees, mothers cradling babies, Old Ones cower-

529

ing in the familiar recesses of the cave. This had been our home since Earthmaker brought us here a hundred grandfathers ago. The bones of our past lay beneath this wet ground. Could our future be elsewhere? Their faces, the ones close enough to see, looked from me to Eda and back to me again. I needed Yarrow. Eda glared at me. I wished we'd left her on the beach.

I took a step outside. The wind roared harder than ever, hurling branches and sand. The grey sea was climbing, claiming the beach for its own. Now the churning water sloshed halfway up my knees. Perhaps it was already too late. I stepped back in, my eyes tight with hot tears. What words of hope could I give these people? "I can promise none of you safety," I said. "I can promise no easy way. The path is uncharted, the future unknown. Those who come with me will have nothing to trust but your thoughts. But those who stay here will die."

The Old Ones looked away. Some of the newcomers lined up behind Lugo, ready to leave. Leu and Birch joined him, their children at their sides. Silka glanced at Rube and took their son's hand. Those with little ones would be joining us.

Frightened Eyes crouched by the wall. A skinny, grey-haired woman, she was like a shadow, always present, rarely noticed. Her frantic eyes no longer seemed so strange. Fear shone in all our faces now. She moved deeper into the cave.

Where was Ziva? I found the tiny woman standing behind Eda, her hand on the old woman's back, her sleek children beside her. "Ziva, are you coming?"

She smiled up at me and shook her head. "We are Fish People. you know." she said in her lilting voice. "We have no place in this new world."

I turned to Zalec. He was leaning against the wall near the

entrance. Zale knelt beside him, keeping Yarrow from the water. Had Zalec been able to climb, he'd have gone with us, I was sure. "Zale will go," the older man said.

The young man looked startled. "I'm staying," he said.

"Go on, boy," his father growled. "Go with them. You have a chance without me." The older man lowered himself to the ground and took Yarrow's head in his arms. Zale looked around, grabbed Luba's hand, and dragged her from the cave. Belov looked after them. "Go on, boy," Zalec ordered the youth. "Get out of here. They'll need help with the young ones."

The water now covered my knees. "Mother, Ochre . . . are you coming?" I asked.

"Your mother wants to stay. This is her home," my second father said. He stepped forward and lifted Yarrow's body, carrying her toward the back of the cave. I turned away from them one last time, wrapped my tunic around my face, and stepped into the wind and rising sea. A gust slammed against me, slapping gravel against my legs, knocking me back inside.

"Go now!" Magla shouted. "Get away! Take the young ones and go!"

Behold a New Earth

THE CREVASSE THAT CUT ACROSS THE SHORE WAS UNDERWATER, the sea lapping a few man-lengths from the cave. "Stay by the hill!" I yelled to those behind me. "Stay off the beach!"

We'd make our way uphill. Take our chances on higher ground. More than the flooding or the landslide, our greatest problem now was the wind. But the storm had to end sometime. Maybe we could find a safe place until then. I began the climb, grasping bushes, moving at an angle. The blowing dirt was blinding, though if I shielded my face and kept my eyes down, I could see the ground, make a path. Lugo was behind me. I felt his hand on my ankle each time I slipped. I turned to call to the others, warn them to stay close. My mouth filled with dirt before I got the words out. I soon gave up walking and sprawled against the hillside. We'd have to slither toward the crest. At least we didn't have to go far. The hill wasn't more than four man-lengths high.

As I neared the top, the wind roared still louder, no longer blocked by the slope. The blast could have sent the children crashing back down the hill if they'd stood. Maybe us as well. I clung to a clump of tough gorse and waited for Lugo. In a moment, I felt his hand on my back.

"What should we do?" I asked through clenched teeth, covering my eyes as I turned to look at him. Lugo squinted at the ground ahead, his hair blown back from his face. Then he motioned behind him. Zale crawled next to him. "What's ahead of us?" he asked the younger man. "Any kind of shelter?"

Lugo knew the countryside well enough, but Zale had roamed these hills as a boy. The younger man held a hand across his mouth as he answered. "Three large boulders. Just ahead. If they didn't roll down."

Lugo nodded. Did he have a plan? He turned back to the others crouched behind him on the hill. "Leu!" he called. "Come with us. Thistle, you stay here."

Leu crept up beside us, dragging his son under one arm. He left the boy with me and crawled over the crest with the men.

Birch took his place, lying next to me with an arm around her son. "What are they doing?" she asked, her mouth near the ground.

"I don't know."

We waited. I was worried about the group behind us. At least they were better off on the hillside than at the crest. Each time I glanced ahead for some sign of Lugo, the storm drove dirt into my face. Soon all I could think about was the howl of the wind. How I wanted silence! When would this end? At last I heard Lugo's voice. I glanced ahead and saw him lying on his belly at the crest just above me.

"Take my hand," he ordered, extending his arm. "Birch, hold your boy and stay down."

I moved like a lizard toward that hand and grasped it as Lugo pulled me over the ledge. Our bellies flat on the ground, we crawled toward the boulders. Somehow the three men had managed to push the large stones together, making a small shelter between them. No wonder Lugo had called upon broad-shouldered Leu for help. I dragged myself inside and leaned against the stone, finally safe from the driving dirt. The men pulled the others to safety one by one. We all crouched within the rock circle, exhausted from our brief journey. Nothing could touch us here. We had no food, no water. But we had time. A little time. And a blessed release from the wind.

Lugo dropped down beside me. "That's everyone," he said, wiping the dirt from his eyes. There were maybe twenty of us. Most of the children were there, though only Belov and Luba had come from the Fish People. All of the newcomers. Except for their Old Ones. All of the People close to my age. "Sea's rising," he added in a low voice.

"How high?"

"Taller than me."

"That much?"

I tried to push away the image that came to my mind. Anyway, the ceiling of the cave was high, uneven, riddled with tunnels and niches. There were probably pockets of air halfway up the hill beneath us. If the water trapped the people inside, they could float up there, tread water, maybe find a ledge, breathe for a while. A few people could do that. Until the air was gone. I reached for Lugo's hand.

A child's whimper came from behind. "I'm hungry," said a soft voice, one of Bren's girls, a pale child who rarely spoke.

"Later," her mother whispered.

I settled back against Lugo's arm ready to wait out the wind before we made a plan. My moment of rest was interrupted by a tugging on my sleeve. Silka. "What is it?" I asked.

Silka's proud face was smudged with dirt. Her eyes had lost the hardness they'd held since Narta's departure. "I'm sorry, " she said, coughing on dust. "Sorry for what I said. I'm glad she's gone. She's safe now, isn't she?"

"Yes. She's safe."

"You're sure?"

"They're safe. I'm sure." I turned away from her pleading eyes. The sky beyond the boulders was a dirty haze. How long had it been since we'd seen the sun? Nothing outside was visible beyond the flying dirt. Nor had the light altered since the wind began. It could have been dawn or evening. Maybe midday. I'd lost track. Maybe it was night, our pale world lit by the Shining One beyond the storm. I glanced at the shadowy forms sitting near me. "When the wind dies down," I said, "we'll find something to eat." I tried to smile. "It may rain soon." No one spoke.

After a while, the gale seemed to spend itself, giving way to a brisk wind. "There," I said to the upturned faces looking my way, "the worst is over. Lugo will take Leu and Zale and look for food."

I crawled out with the three of them, eager to stretch my legs. Now that the wind had died down, we could see again, though the sight held no appeal. The crest of the hill was littered with branches. The pine trees behind us, killed by the worms years ago, had all been leveled. A tall larch lay across our little shelter, its roots torn from the ground. I moved toward the edge of the hill, Lugo at my side. Zale and Leu followed. How deep was the seawater now?

Lugo was right. The sea had risen a man-length or so, not much more. Maybe the lull in the wind had put an end to the flood as well. That would put the water almost at the top of the cave entrance. I wouldn't think about the others now, those trapped below. We'd been wise to leave. I looked again at the water. There was something different about the sea, something floating on the grey surface, something lapping against the hillside. Not the People. No. My heart raced. It was something else. Large forms, pale and dead. Sea calves. Dozens of them. Their plump bodies rose with the motion of the sea, knocked together with each lifting wave.

I grabbed Lugo's arm. "Look," I said, pointing. "Look at them. Look at all of them. I thought it was the People, but it's not." The words kept pouring from my mouth. "The People are still in the cave. Right here below us. Aren't they? They're all still in there. But why are the sea calves dead?" I had to understand.

Lugo shook his head. Leu glanced away, turning his gaze to the sky. Zale tried to answer. "Maybe the heat," he said. "From the melted rocks."

Was that it? Could the molten rock do that to animals?

"Look," said Leu. "There's the moon." He pointed calmly upward.

I glanced at the sickly little glow above us. "No, it's not. It's too far away. Too small."

"No, it's the moon," he insisted.

I stared at his bland face. Were we going to argue about this now, with the sea creatures lying dead below us? "Leu, the angle is wrong. Forget about it." I shook my head, hiding my irritation. Leu couldn't help his mistake. No one could see clearly in that gloom. The light from the Shining One and the haze from the blowing dirt had given the sky a smoky green luster, as when one swims underwater and gazes at the sun. "We better find something to eat," I said.

Seeing the floating carcasses had taken my appetite. It was not just the sea calves that had died. Other small, white bodies lay belly-up as well. But the children needed food. I glanced at Lugo to see if he had any ideas. Suddenly, his face was awash in a dusty, golden haze. Blazing high overhead and behind him was a great light, brighter than the sun at midday. Its radiance flooded the hillside.

Leu pointed to the sky again. "Look," he said, as calmly as if he'd found a misplaced boot, "the demon star is between us and the moon."

That close! So it was. The Shining One hovered to the north, still far away but nearer to the earth than was the moon. The light appeared as an orb of fire with no defining features, its radiance emblazoning the sky with a ghostly orange sheen. Suddenly, against that luminous backdrop, something new emerged which seemed to come from nowhere. Like beetles floating in still water, a silent army of black stones now sailed across the sky. We watched with wide eyes as the stones came closer. As they approached the earth, they burst above us like dry pods thrown into a fire. The rocks became gravel and plummeted to the ground in a deafening, stinging rain.

Terror clutched me like a blast of winter, freezing my words before they were spoken. Now we were to be attacked by stones? Once again the wind mounted up. But this was no earthly storm. The wind came downward as if it whirled from the mouth of the Shining One. I ran back to the shelter and crawled between the boulders, Lugo, Zale and Leu close behind. Pressing between Lugo and Zale, I stared outside. The whimpering of the childrem rose above the clatter of the gravel.

I looked north, toward the mountain range that curled along the bay. Clouds of black smoke rose from four of the peaks. Four red rivers rolled down. Three of them rushed to the sea, swallowing dead trees and steaming when they hit the water. The fourth headed inland. I stared at that red line, trying to imagine where it would end. The country just north of us was rough, a range of tan hills crossed by three gullies. Between the hill we were on and the mountains lay a forest of saplings and dead pines. Surely the gullies were deep enough to stop the molten stone.

Birch crawled in behind me, straining for a view. "What is it?" she asked. "What do you see?"

I turned and looked at her pinched face and large eyes. Before I could answer, the ground beneath us quivered and began to sway. I felt a sudden wrenching. A mad thought crossed my mind—the Shining One was pulling us to it! Then I heard it. A deep, liquid sound beneath the dirt, a sloshing, churning restlessness, as if Earth were a boiling soup. I grabbed Lugo's arm. "What's that?" I cried. I looked outside again, my fingers digging into his flesh. Something was wrong with the land. The nearest hillside rippled like a tan sea. The ground beneath us jerked and I pitched forward, knocking my head against his knee. Someone behind me screamed. It sounded like Silka. I sat up in time to see the ridge in front of us crumble and fall into the sea.

Lugo's voice was fierce. "Everyone. Get out. Move back. Before the hill gives way."

We crawled from the stone shelter and ran uphill, pushing the children before us, grabbing each other's arms as the earth rocked beneath our feet. Another lurch and a ravine opened where our refuge had been. The three boulders jerked, hesitated, and toppled in a cloud of dust.

Silka cried out again and I turned. Before us, farther up the slope, perhaps six man-lengths away, the smooth ground tilted. A ridge of stone suddenly jutted up from the ground like the spine of an angry beast. Beyond the first outcropping the earth again gave way, thrusting more rock to the surface. The new stones toppled and slid sideways, grinding against each other before they lodged into place.

We were blocked on two sides now, by the sea on the west and the stones on the east. I looked into Lugo's stern face, saw the fear in his eyes. He nodded at me and turned to the south, gesturing for the others to follow. We stumbled after him, following the narrow ridge above the sea as a hot wind blasted our backs. Though not as powerful as it had been, the wind now carried the acrid smoke from the mountains. My eyes burned. Once again I covered my face and looked down. A large hare bounded across my path. A family of foxes raced by.

I took a few more steps. The earth trembled again, pitching me forward. I threw out my arms to catch myself. What was that? The dirt felt warm beneath my hands. Then came a soft noise. A noise I'd never heard before. I glanced down. The ground was covered with beetles, hundreds of black beetles, disgorged from their tunnels by the hot earth, shells clacking against each other as they scuttled into the orange light. A grass snake slithered across my arm, pushing the insects from its path. Lugo pulled me up and we hurried after the others, beetle shells crunching underfoot.

My heart pounded. My throat burned. We were coughing. At last we stopped. The children could go no farther. Neither could I. I slid to the ground and looked back, my breathing so loud I no longer heard the wind. Another mountain had given way. More scalding liquid poured down another slope. Was this Earthmaker's blood? Was She dying?

Lugo tried to pull me up, but I resisted. I needed more time. Turning away from him, I continued looking northward. The molten rock from the closest peak was almost at the woods. As fast as a mountain stream, it rushed over the remaining distance and licked at the first of the dry branches, liking them. Another moment and the forest burst into flame. The fire quickly devoured the dry trees and climbed a mountainside, jumping to a high meadow. Clouds of black smoke rose up and were carried inland by the wind. Even at that distance, it seemed I could hear crackling timber.

Thank Earthmaker Lugo had taken us this way and not north. We were safe for now, surely, separated from the woods by a deep chasm lined with stones and by two smaller gullies. Still, the smoke burnt our eyes and nostrils, parched our throats. The children were silent because it hurt to cry. Then I remembered something else. The river lay to the south! I looked back at Lugo. He had a plan. That's where we were heading. Maybe the river would save us!

"Lugo," I said, when I finally caught my breath, "can we make it to the river?"

"Maybe."

Once again we stood. I spoke as loudly as possible, my hands protecting my mouth. "Lugo's taking us to the river."

Silka waved us on. "We'll meet you there," she said.

"No. Come now." The ground lurched again. I grabbed her arm. Bren, the newcomer woman, couldn't stop coughing. Zale grabbed her girls and Lugo took the boy. We moved south, pulling the stragglers along. "We'll be safe at the water. You'll see!" I called to the others behind me. It was foolish to talk in the smoke, but they needed some hope.

We could almost see the river, just beyond the next ridge and down. I ran ahead, weaving through a stand of dead pines, motioning to the others. "Hurry! This way. You can make it!" Suddenly the ground gave way beneath me and my feet were running in the air. I had a moment to glimpse the ripped earth before I plunged into it and tumbled downward. Then came a shock of pain and the taste of dirt. All was black.

WHEN I OPENED MY EYES, it was quiet, dark where I was, but with the orange glimmer still above me. My face felt wet. I tried to lift a hand to touch it. How could it be that my arms were tied? I twisted and heard a cracking sound. I knew that sound. Branches. Breaking. Then I understood. I was caught in the roots of one of those old pines. It must have been torn from the ground as I fell. I could make out the trunk above me, tipped, probably resting on the surface. "Lugo?" I whispered. "Silka?"

No answer. Just the wind. My legs dangled below me. I moved them slowly. No foothold. It was impossible to tell how deep the chasm was. I was hanging maybe a man-length from the top, not much more. Would the roots hold?

They'd scratched me when I fell. That explained my wet face. The blood on my arms made my skin slippery. I began to twist my wrists carefully, working them out of the ropy tendrils. Then all that was left was to pull myself up, slowly pull, feel the sway of the trunk, slow down, pull gently. I edged my way to the surface and over the top, crawling along the side of the trunk to shield myself from the wind.

The black crack in the earth ran like a jagged cut across the ridge, two man-lengths wide in places. There was no one else there. Blood began to ooze into my eyes. I yelled louder, spitting blood and dirt. "Lugo! Silka!" Still no answer. I remembered another time long ago, another time like this, when life still pushed through me like petals in the spring. Another time when I cried out and there was no answer, only the sound of the wind and my echo. There would be no answer now.

Rivers of fire still gushed from the distant hills. Even through the dust I could make out their red flow. I no longer knew the terrain. Our home was underwater. Ridges of stone rose up on what had been a gentle land. Hills crowded upon hills, mountains toppled mountains, fire pouring from below.

Wait! Was that why we'd never found the mountains of my dreams?

They hadn't yet been born? Perhaps at this moment Gokihar and Narta looked from their small boat to seven new peaks, the center one tipped like the crest of a wave. And surely there'd be other survivors, farther inland, climbing and waiting, struggling to survive, longing to begin again. I had done my work, done all that Earthmaker had asked, made Gokihar strong and sent him on his way. My time was finished, but the People would go on.

the mountains of her dreaming

My time was done. How I'd loved it. This brief moment, this single breath from Earthmaker's lungs. Reen and the summer mountains. Tenja and the stars. Anish and the heat of summer. Wolf and Thur. The trees that spoke of Gokihar. And the boy himself, the best of all who'd come before. He would go on and I would return to the Source, to that undivided world where the feeble actions of bodies are remembered as dreams.

A fiery blast summoned me back to the present. High above me the Shining One still glowed, unfurling fingers of lightning from time to time. Lonely Moon shimmered in the distance. Sun cowered on the horizon, hovering at a point it had never been before. How strange. I'd seen the sun in that same place the last time I'd looked, well before we'd run along the ridge. Had the Shining One slowed our turning?

Fear came over me like a cold hand on my neck. I held onto the broken trunk to steady myself, glad for the familiar roughness of wood. The shattered pine recalled an image from the past. An image of the beach and Tenja and the mighty pole that held Earth on its course. Had the Great Tree collapsed, tipping Earth on its side?

And then another blinding flare. I looked upward and to the north. The Shining One was changing! Its tiny followers still danced around it. Stones still exploded above me and plummeted to Earth as gravel. But the companion light, the smaller shape we called the monster child, was pulling away from the larger one. The Shining One, perhaps four times the size of its companion, kept to its northerly place. But the small one began to move downward as if some power were pulling it to Earth. Once the distance widened between the two orbs, the lightning ceased. Then ever so slowly, as if it had lost all interest in Earth, the larger body began to move away, striking out for other destinations. We were done with it!

But the smaller body was not finished with us. That mass seemed to be growing, though I knew it was the distance and not the size that was changing. I had no idea how long I stood in that place. It didn't matter. There was no place else to go. My sore neck became numb. As the monster child came closer, I saw in its glow the outline of a jagged black rock. It was easy to think of it as a burning mountain which dragged a plume of fire behind. I watched it approach for the rest of that endless day, saw it careen toward the northern horizon, knew the moment it rammed into the earth far beyond my vision. The land didn't tremble where I stood, but the impact of the object threw up a dark cloud which blackened half of the sky. A huge dust cloud gathered and began to spread, though there was still ample light to see what lay around me.

I beheld a new Sky and a new Earth. Far more than the ground had changed. The world above was no longer familiar. Sun and Moon hung crookedly. Sky seemed to have fallen, so that dark clouds hovered above my head, close enough to touch. And then, in that waning light, I looked down and saw the strangest thing of all. The sea was being sucked back. It tumbled away from shore as if commanded to move in a new direction. Our stone beach opened up again, but the departing tide didn't stop there. It retreated farther, the sea bed opening like a prairie, a great grey prairie, writhing with wet creatures and lank weeds. Everywhere the sea had been, there now was land.

All that dusky night, as a few odd stars twinkled behind a roof of clouds, I listened to the wind and watched the ocean floor, hoping that I was sleeping and would soon awaken. At last a grey dawn opened to show me one more thing. Along the sea bed, stretching in a line from north to south as far as I could see, perhaps a morning's walk from where I sat, the water had mounted up. It stood like one long cliff, one great precipice. Higher than any peaks to the north, higher by far than I, the water cliff hung there. No bird called. The creatures of the ocean floor were still. I had only a few moments to stare at the horror before me. Then as if responding to some silent command, the wall of water fell with a roar that shook the earth. A leaping crest of foam slammed against the ocean floor, followed by the crash of another liquid mountain. I had wondered how my body would die. Now I knew. I was a grain of sand to this new sea. All that still lived had one long moment in which to scream.

Before the water reached me, I grasped at one final image, one last hope. The image of a towering mountain, its summit thrust above the massing waves, above the carnage of the old world. And two humans, making their way up its side, clutching each other, trembling, praying, waiting for their day. Would there be such a mountain?

Then all was light.

Dear Reader,

The work you've just read is fiction. But it is not fantasy. Many of the events depicted within have been described by reputable scientists. Incidents not documented have been at least hypothesized by respected researchers. While I hope you found the story itself satisfactory, you may be one of those diligent readers curious to know the facts behind the fiction. The following pages are for you. I offer this paragraph as a bridge between a work of the imagination and a more academic exposition. Read no further if you are put off by such things. But read on if you are intrigued by the research that shaped the foundations of this work. I welcome your comments. All my best to you.

Lorraine Dopson, Ph.D.
ldopson@hotmail.com

Epilog

Cataclysmic shifts in the environment, within human history, have not been a rarity. We are a species born of chaos, says neurobiologist William Calvin. Calvin underscores the relationship between mind and environment in *The Ascent of Mind: Ice Age Climates and the Evolution of Intelligence.* He notes that the 2.5 million year Pleistocene or Ice Age was a time of widely fluctuating climate, which included abrupt shifts from melting to freezing periods, and retreating to advancing ice sheets. But it was also a time which spawned major enlargement and development of the human brain (231).

GEOLOGIC PERIODS	Pliocene / Pleistocene / Holocene (to present)
	(2.5 mil. to 10,000 B.C.)
CULTURAL PERIODS	Paleolithic / Mesolithic / Neolithic

The tenth millennium B.C. appears to have been a watershed period in our past, marking the end of a way of life for many humans and the end of life itself for many animal species. What does the scientific record tell us of that time and its people? The following discussion looks at current research regarding human and environmental realities at the end of the last ice age. The review is necessarily brief. But for the general reader who wants to delve deeper into prehistory, the authors mentioned here will be helpful. To this list, I'd like to add another name, that of Mary Settegast. Her comprehensive, scholarly, and fascinating work, *Plato Prehistorian*, recounts European and North African myth and archaeology from 10,000 to 5,000 B.C. in light of Plato's *Timaeus and Critias*. It came to my attention shortly after I'd finished my manuscript. I recommend it heartily.

Comments on Consciousness

We'll begin with a look at several approaches to the study of prehistoric "psychology," realizing that any conclusions one makes in such an esoteric field are highly speculative. (Readers more interested in catastrophe than consciousness may prefer to go directly to the final section, Climate and Cataclysm).

Only a few decades ago we viewed prehistory as a time when churlish men killed big game, communicated by grunts, and sculpted small statues of nude women. But the prehistoric (pre-writing) era has gained our respect in recent years, as evidenced by a number of well-researched works of fiction set in that period. Riveting sagas depict a time of panoramic vistas, beautiful people, big animals, well-crafted tools, great sex, and flexible hours. A possible shortcoming of some of these works is the assumption that our ancestors lived from the same psychological paradigm as contemporary Westerners. Except for a possible increase in inhibition, human consciousness appears unchanged for millennia.

But the mind of a person living in the Late Paleolithic, the thoughts, beliefs, and fears may have differed qualitatively from our own contemporary minds. Consciousness itself may be a product of human history and culture (Jaynes). In fact, there is growing evidence that the facet of mind we call "ego" may actually be a capricious newcomer.

Several factors account for the re-evaluation of our psychological past. The work of Mircea Eliade and Joseph Campbell, on ritual and myth, has contributed to a renewed respect for our origins. The field of depth psychology has provided a helpful paradigm for understanding the evolution of consciousness. The rise of feminist scholarship also has sensitized us to the risk of gender bias in research and the tendency to allow personal assumptions to color the most "objective" data. As a result of these and other considerations, researchers are reconsidering their interpretation of prehistory. Most relevant to this work is the speculation by some researchers that the primordial world was the world of the Great Mother. In Ashley Montague's words, "For Paleolithic man, every day was Mother's Day." The psychological theories of Carl Jung are particularly valuable here.

Depth Psychology and the "Unconscious" Mind

The work of Carl Jung and his associates earlier last century awakened an interest in seeking our "source." In the 1950s, Jungian psychoanalyst Erich Neumann published his classic work on matriarchal culture and psychology, *The Great Mother*. Here he traces the possible psychological evolution of our species, beginning with our early existence in a primal, undifferentiated, feminine realm to our current abode in the masculine world of the ego. This massive work resists feeble attempts at summarization, but amply rewards the dedicated reader. We can only touch on some of the highlights here.

Neumann describes the early psychological experience of both individual and group as "matriarchal" in nature, a period in which we exist in oneness with our surroundings, aware of ourselves only as part of something much greater, not as separate individuals. Our original psychic state, as individuals and as a species, Neumann maintains, is the experience of the *uroborus*, that circle of wholeness represented by the yin/yang symbol. Ego, in an infant or a primordial people, is undifferentiated from the unconscious. This primary uroboric experience is reflected in universal rituals, symbols, dreams, and myths, similar for all people throughout history. This experience of nurturing containment is reborn with each generation and is the resting place of children, the inspiration of artists, and the ecstasy of mystics.

Neumann maintains that the Archetypal Feminine was worshipped in its uroboric state for thousands of years before it was even named. Symbols belonging to this still-unformed image arose spontaneously from the psyche, in the form of nature symbols, pools, trees, or animals. Throughout the Paleolithic Era, human life may have been lived entirely in an uroboric state.

Following this period of embryonic containment, consciousness begins to differentiate. The mind of the individual gradually separates itself from the uroboric whole and the idea of the Great Mother emerges. The Great Mother is a paradoxical archetype, formed of opposites like good and evil that coexist within one transcendent entity. Neumann notes that the idea of a differentiated Great Mother, separate from the uroboric state, is actually a fairly late development in the evolution of consciousness. Not until the Late Paleolithic (c.15,000-10,000 B.C.) is Her numinous power refined and reflected symbolically. At that time She appears in numerous representations of the all-encompassing realms of birth, death, sexuality, and abundance. Humanity is totally dependent upon Her in this stage of development.

The Great Mother was venerated throughout the world well into

Neolithic times, eventually disappearing from our outer lives, but not from our memory. In Jung's terms, the Great Mother archetype is now part of our "collective unconscious." Exploring consciousness at this level is a sort of archaeology of the soul.

Jung suggests that below our conscious, waking mind, there exists a "collective unconscious [which] contains the whole spiritual heritage of mankind's evolution, born anew in the brain structure of every individual. [The] conscious mind is an ephemeral phenomenon that accomplishes all provisional adaptations and orientations....The unconscious, on the other hand, is the source of the instinctual forces of the psyche..." (Campbell, *The Portable Jung*).

Jung describes the relationship between the conscious and unconscious mind in his work, *Civilization in Transition*:

> [D]espite our individual consciousness, [the psyche] continues to exist as the collective unconscious—the sea upon which the ego rides like a ship...nothing of the primordial world has ever been lost. Just as the sea stretches its broad tongue between the continents and laps around them like islands, so our original consciousness presses around our individual consciousness. In the catastrophe of mental illness, the storm-tide of the sea surges over the island and swallows it back into the depths. In neurotic disturbances there is at least a bursting of the dikes, and the fruitful lowlands are laid waste by the flood. Neurotics are all shore-dwellers—they are the most exposed to the dangers of the sea. So-called normal people live inland, on higher, drier ground, near placid lakes and streams. No flood, however high, reaches them, and the circumambient sea is so far away that they even deny its existence. Indeed, a person can be so identified with his ego that he loses the common bond of humanity and cuts himself off from all others (138).

There is a dialectical tension inherent in consciousness, one polarity leading to the danger of being engulfed and swept away by the unconscious, the other leading to an empty "arrogance born of an atrophy of the instincts" (146).

According to Jung and Neumann, the "primitive" person perceives no separation between the subjective and objective world, living a life bathed in the glow of the present. The impetus to separate from the collective is a developmental imperative that causes fear and shame. Even a necessary separation, such as birth, feels like a rejection. Each time one experiences oneself alone and forlorn, the original perceived rejection by the mother is reactivated; she becomes the source of blame. The feeble ego then emerges to cover and move beyond the pain of this separation. In the process, the hero archetype is constellated as an attempt to hide a wound; it creates a defense for the ego, a wall between the objective and subjective world, sheltering us from immediacy. The creation and expression of the hero archetype is, of course, the underlying dynamic in Western culture.

A short comment on aggression and its role in psychological development is relevant here. Human aggression as a "problem" does not seem to arise in the history of consciousness until fairly recently, probably as a result of ego differentiation. Upper Paleolithic European skeletons found in burial sites are unmarked by any but accidental trauma (Settegast 37).

The "Bicameral" Mind

Psychologist Julian Jaynes, in his brilliant work, *The Origin of Consciousness in the Breakdown of the Bicameral Mind*, 1976, reviews laboratory studies of brain lateralization—the organization of the brain into two halves joined by the corpus callosum—as well as a wealth of archaeological and cultural research, and concludes that subjective consciousness, in which we experience ourselves as an "I" capable of volition and thought, did not arise until around 3000 B.C.

Prior to that time, a "bicameral" brain—an instinctual intelligence dependent largely on right brain function and resembling the unconscious mind—commanded our actions. Early humans, lacking a sense of subjective self and thus unable to be self-reflective, heard the commands of the bicameral brain as the voices of gods and acted upon them accordingly. The impetus for subjective consciousness, Jaynes maintains, was the invention of writing, after which time the written word functioned essentially as an externalized authority.

To illustrate, Jaynes cites the *Iliad,* the earliest work to be written down in a language still familiar to us today. In the *Iliad,* humans do not make decisions. The gods command them.

> The characters of the *Iliad* do not sit down and think out what to do. They have no conscious minds such as we have, and certainly no introspections....When Agamemnon, king of men, robs Achilles of his mistress, it is a god that grasps Achilles by his yellow hair and warns him not to strike Agamemnon....It is a god who then rises out of the gray sea and consoles him...a god who whispers to Helen...a god who hides Paris...a god who tells Glaucus to take bronze for gold...a god who leads armies into battle, who speaks to each soldier at the turning points, who debates and teaches Hector what he must do....In fact, the gods take the place of consciousness (72).

Jaynes fleshes out one aspect of our understanding of human behavior, deceit. He observes that "to deceive...is one of the hallmarks of consciousness. The serpent promises that 'you shall be like the elohim themselves, knowing good and evil' (Genesis 3:5), qualities that only subjective conscious man is capable of" (299).

A relevant aspect of brain function, related to cerebral lateralization, is Jaynes' observation that

> women are biologically somewhat less lateralized in brain function than men. This means simply that psychological functions in women are not localized into one or the other hemisphere of the brain to the same degree as in men. Mental abilities in women are spread over both hemispheres...elderly men with a stroke or hemorrhage in the left hemisphere are more speechless than elderly women with a similar diagnosis. Accordingly we might expect more residual language function in the right hemisphere of women, making it easier for women to learn to be oracles (344).

With the development of rational mind following the advent of writing, according to Jaynes, the spontaneous authority of the bicameral mind ebbed. It left behind nostalgic reminders of its passing, such as the power of music or poetry to move us outside our rational selves. But these remnants, he maintains, whether they are oracles or astrology, angels or prophets, are only feeble attempts to clutch at an authority outside of our egos. Like a mirage in a desert, the more we approach, the further the authority of the bicameral mind recedes, disappearing into the horizon. We are left to depend on the developing authority of our rational mind, with its left-hemisphere tenants of reason, order, analysis, and planning.

Jaynes' work is fascinating, informative, and original. The 3000 B.C. date may not apply universally. Several cultures developed sophisticated astronomical and mathematical systems prior to that time, perhaps too daunting a task to accomplish in a "bicameral" state.

While there is some overlap between observations made by Jungians and by Jaynes, their conclusions differ significantly. Jaynes follows a linear model based on neurophysiology and behavioral psychology, and suggests that the primordial "bicameral" mind is superseded by the superior rational mind. Jung and Neumann present the development of consciousness in a more spiral fashion, respecting the unconscious mind as the vital and powerful wellspring of our lives, to which we return repeatedly for sustenance or risk psychic death.

The Mytho-Archaeological Mind

Crucial to any discussion of archaeology and the feminine is the contribution of archaeologist Marija Gimbutas. Her works, which include *Goddesses and Gods of Old Europe* and *The Language of the Goddess*, span several decades and analyze thousands of artifacts from Eastern Europe. The cultural record she uncovers mirrors the evolution of the Great Mother from an undifferentiated, all-encompassing deity of 30,000 years ago to the multifaceted Goddess of the Neolithic era.

Gimbutas assigns ancient Goddess images into one of three categories of efficacy: Life Giving, Death Wielding, and Regenerative. Images of bears or does, for example, are seen to represent the Life Giving or Primeval Mother aspects of the Feminine. Her Death-Wielding images include such epiphanies as vulture, owl, raven, and boar. The Goddess's Regenerative aspects, represented by breasts and vulvas, are often depicted abstractly in ovals, triangles, and concentric circles. While Gimbutas has been criticized for over-interpreting the archaeological record, her vision brings new life to ancient artifacts. Gimbutas sees in these evocative images a powerful female energy which revered creation, life, and Earth itself, and thrived for thousands of years before being overshadowed by a more patriarchal paradigm. She summarizes the impact of this Archetypal Feminine in her work *The Language of the Goddess*:

There is no question that Old European sacred images and symbols remain a vital part of the cultural heritage of Europe....In some nooks of Europe, as in my own motherland, Lithuania, there still flow sacred and miraculous rivers and springs, there flourish holy forests and groves, reservoirs of blossoming life, there grow gnarled trees brimming with vitality holding the power to heal: along waters there still stand menhirs, called "Goddesses," full of mysterious power....The Old European culture was the matrix of much later beliefs and practices. Memories of a long-lasting gynocentric past could not be erased.....To an archaeologist it is an extensively documented historical reality (320).

Metaphysical Notes

Archetypes

According to Jung, the outward traditions of any culture mirror inner psychic elements that are cross-cultural and timeless. These primordial energies or "maps of the genetic code" (Jacobi, *Complex*, 36), expressed in myths, stories, art, and dreams, Jung refers to as archetypes. Like water surging through an underground cavern, archetypal energy carves out the patterns of our inner life. Jungians have identified numerous archetypes that shape our psyches, such as the Great Mother, the enchanted prince, the *puer aeternus*, the Mage, the Wise Man, the number three (spirit), and the quaternity (spirit embodied and represented in the number four).

Our Paleolithic ancestors embodied all the archetypal energy of Original Mind that continues to shape us today. Archetypal references included in this work are derived from material developed by Dr. Charles Bebeau, Director of the Avalon Institute, Boulder, Colorado. The Avalon understanding of archetypal energy corresponds with astrology, an ancient system for understanding the psyche based, of course, on the movement of the planet through the twelve houses of the zodiac. Different astrological designations correspond to different archetypes and all archetypal energy can be expressed through combinations of these twelve signs.

To illustrate, the universe and all it contains is made of energy. Energy assumes one of four forms: earth, air, fire, water. These forms manifest in one of three ways: coming into being, maintaining, or dissolving, (creation, preservation, and change). Four different types of energy manifesting in three ways yield twelve different kinds of archetypal energy. This understanding is the basis of astrology and a number of metaphysical traditions.

The archetype of the Great Mother is based on three smaller archetypes, the Nourishing Mother (sign of Cancer), the Dark Mother (Scorpio), and the Soul Mother (Virgo). This work highlights about half of the twelve archetype/signs. The other archetypes are Mystic (Pisces), Lover (Libra), Artist-Priestess (Taurus), Golden Child (Leo), Elder Leader (Capricorn),Communicator (Gemini), Teacher/Traveler (Saggitarius), Idealist (Aquarius), and the Warrior (Aries).

In the middle of the last century, Jung maintained that modern physics would soon discover that, in fact, there are twelve different types of energy underlying all of creation. In 1995, scientists at the Fermi National Accelerator Lab near Chicago successfully generated a "top Quark," calling it "the last of the twelve building blocks of matter that make up subatomic particles.[1]

Achaeoastronomy

Students of history have long been intrigued by the ingenuity of ancient astronomers. How could so much be learned from observa-

---

[1] Liss,"The Discovery of the Top Quark," *Scientific American*, Sept. 1997.

tion alone, without a mathematical base? Yet evidence suggests that sites as geographically diverse as Machu Picchu and the Great Pyramid at Giza may have served as celestial observatories. Obscure circles of scattered stones and toppled menhirs, notched in such a way that a beam of sunlight bursts through only at the solstice, still keep their secrets throughout Europe and the Americas. Tracking Earth's slow, steady journey through the dark mystery of space must have provided not only knowledge but tremendous reassurance for these early scientists. An aberration in the cosmic order, however, would have been a source of terror.

Hundreds of legends survive to attest to the reality of just such aberrations. Allan and Delair tracked more than 500 deluge myths from around the world, finding that bands of people as diverse as Druids, Greeks, Laplanders (Sami), Welsh, Afghani, Chinese, and Pacific Islanders all recount the legend of a universal flood which almost destroyed the world. All of us are familiar with the story in which water "covered the face of the earth." The survivors, whether they were named Noah (Hebrew), Utnapishtim (Sumerian), or Coxcoxtli (Aztec), were washed out to sea and kept afloat while the rest of the world perished.

Other world myths contain stories of astronomical as well as earthbound events. Some scholars propose that these celestial sagas describe not only imaginary adventures, but the records of actual events, observable data couched in the symbolic language of mathematics and metaphor.[2] Of interest to the work at hand is the story of the world

---

[2] One of the most detailed analyses of myth as metaphor for scientific observation was written by the late Giorgio de Santillana, history of science professor at MIT, in collaboration with Hertha von Dechend at Frankfurt University. See *Hamlet's Mill*, published by David R. Godine, Boston, 1992. See also Hancock, and Allan, Delair.

pillar or pole, a pivotal tale, literally and figuratively, which suggests that ancient humans were aware of the earth's orbit around a central imaginary shaft.[3] So often does the "world tree" figure in mythology that Jung considered the motif to be archetypal in nature. Called variously the World Tree (Norse *Yggdrasil*), Sampo the Great Mill in Iceland and Finland (from the Sanskrit *skambha* for pole), or *Skamba* in India, this pillar was entrusted with the steady turning and grinding of the earth about her axis (Hancock). All myths or metaphors of the World Tree end violently, warning of a wrenching in the world axis that results in widespread disturbances.

Climate and Cataclysm

The last "Ice Age," and thus the Pleistocene Epoch, ended twelve thousand years ago with a rapid increase in global temperature. Emiliani, in a classic work on temperature fluctuation, deduced an abrupt warming around 9645 B.C. in which the average global temperature rose 14 degrees Farenheit in fifteen years, elevating sea levels 400 feet and causing a rapid influx of fresh water over salt water, ("Ancient Temperatures," Emiliani, *Scientific American*, Feb. 1958). His results have never been refuted. The geologic record of this period includes massive earthquakes, numerous volcanic eruptions, catastrophic flooding, and major shifts in land masses. What accounted for such events?

The geological aberrations of that time have been the focus of scientific scrutiny for centuries. Early nineteenth-century investiga-

---

[3] The length of time it takes this slanted pole to make one complete circle of the heavens, turning through the entire zodiac, is 26,000 years. This period, known now as the precession of the equinoxes, was familiar to the ancient Greeks, who derived their information from India. Hindu tradition considered this 26,000 year period a *Yuga* or Great Year.

tors, often stalwart adventurers schooled in biblical history, discovered massive caches of bones and carcasses, as well as evidence of previous worldwide geological turmoil. They knew of no earthly agent that could account for such destruction and took it to be the work of God. Divine "catastrophism" came to be viewed as the mechanism for geological change. The discoveries seemed to offer evidence of a flood of biblical proportions, bolstering support for divine causation. Biblical creation accounts had long suggested that the world came into being between 6000 and 4000 B.C. and that the devastating Deluge followed soon after. Now scholars and the educated public had a way of dating geological and historical events. The terms "predeluvian" or "antedeluvian" became accepted scientific parlance.

But by the middle of the nineteenth century, as the science of geology grew more systematic and the immense age of the planet became apparent, biblical interpretations were discredited. The "catastrophism" baby was thrown out with the flood water (Eigles). Earth changes came to be viewed as the unfolding of gradual, methodical, predictable, and currently existing processes operating in a uniform fashion for millions of years. It was not the hand of God, but the uniform tenets of nature, that accounted for most geological change. "Uniformitarianism" was born. But what natural force could account for such massive, albeit gradual, change?

Swiss naturalist Louis Aggassiz suggested that the agent was ice. As a young man living at the foothills of the Alps, Agassiz knew the Swiss lore of glaciers and had observed for himself the tremendous power of ice on the move. He postulated that it was glacial action, those fluctuating cycles of freezing and melting, that accounted for different geologic eras. Agassiz first employed the term *Eiszeit* or Ice Age in 1837. Shifting Ice Ages became the scenario of Earth's past and glacial action became the accepted mechanism for uniformitarian change.

This paradigm inspired a century of prodigious research and publication. The notion of "Ice Ages" as intrinsic stages in Earth's geology became accepted public knowledge, almost archetypal in nature. Research indicated that, indeed, the Pleistocene had been a time of immense glacial waxing and waning over much of the planet's surface. Glacial change, and the concomitant temperature fluctuations, seemed to occur fairly rapidly in response to predictable cycles of global warming. Speculation centered on several possible causes for such cycles.

Hadington (*Secrets of the Ice Age*, 22) explains that "the fluctuations of climate do not appear to be entirely random...the cycle of cold and warm appears to repeat itself approximately once every 100,000 years and the cold part is by far the longer part of the cycle." Behind such changes are several shifting variables: slight irregularities in the earth's orbit around the sun; changes in the amount of solar radiation reaching earth; unequal distribution of ice mass at the poles; volcanic activity that spews heat-reflecting dust into the atmosphere; the obliquity of the elliptic (the angle or tilt of the polar axis in relation to the sun); geological events which alter ocean currents, especially the North Atlantic Current; the gravitational pull of other planets; and the build-up of carbon dioxide from human or other causes, with the resulting "greenhouse effect."

Definitive research by the CLIMAP project, based on the study of deep-sea and ice core fluctuations, identifies a 110,000-year cycle and concludes that, "Changes in the earth's orbital geometry are the fundamental cause of the succession of Quarternary ice ages, (Hays, Imbrie, and Shackleton).

The uniformitarian paradigm answered many questions about Earth's past but not all. For example, a recent article by geologist Michael

Rampino, New York University, describes a singular event in Sumatra which had major implications for our ancestors. The largest volcanic eruption in 400 million years occurred there 71,000 years ago, overwhelming that island, spewing 4,000 times as much ash into the air as Mt. St. Helens and burying most of India. The sky was probably darkened for weeks, ushering in a six-year global winter and precipitating a thousand-year ice age (caused by accumulated snow mass that reflected sunlight away from Earth's surface). Much of the world population was devastated, leaving perhaps only a few thousand survivors worldwide in isolated pockets of Africa, Europe, and Asia. Penn State geneticist Henry Harpending considers this catastrophe a "bottle neck" event and thinks today's races are all descendants of survivors of the Mount Toba explosion (*Discover*).

Perhaps the distinction between gradual and cataclysmic explanations was too tightly drawn in the past. Indeed, some of the most visionary scientists of the nineteenth century didn't find the two incompatible. As biologist Sir Thomas Huxley suggested:

> To my mind there appears to be no sort of theoretical antagonism between Catastrophism and Uniformitarianism; on the contrary, it is very conceivable that catastrophes may be part and parcel of uniformity. Let me illustrate my case by analogy. The working of a clock is a model of uniform action. Good timekeeping means uniformity of action. But the striking of a clock is essentially a catastrophe. The hammer might be made to blow up a barrel of gunpowder, or turn on a deluge of water and, by proper arrangement, the clock, instead of marking the hours, might strike at all sorts of irregular intervals, never twice alike in the force or number of its blows. Nevertheless, all these irregular and apparently lawless catastrophes may be the result of an absolutely uniformitarian action, and we might have two schools of clock

theorists, one studying the hammer and the other the pendulum (cited by Hapgood, 294).

Describing the final seven thousands years of the Pleistocene in his prodigious work, *The Fingerprints of the Gods*, 1995, Graham Hancock examines numerous studies from both glacial and catastrophic viewpoints and concludes that:

> By 8000 B.C. the great Wisconsin and Wurm ice caps had retreated. The Ice Age was over. However, the seven thousand years prior to that date had witnessed climatic and geological turbulence on a scale that was almost unimaginable. Lurching from cataclysm to disaster and from misfortune to calamity, the few scattered tribes of surviving humans must have led lives of constant terror and confusion...episodes of tranquility would have been punctuated again and again by violent floods ...sections of the earth's crust hitherto pressed down (by) billions of tons of ice would have been liberated by the thaw and begun to rise again, sometimes rapidly, causing devastating earthquakes and filling the air with terrible noise (218).

Neurobiologist William Calvin notes the interplay between the two paradigms when he describes the human contribution to global warming, a relatively new instrument in the discordant symphony of climate change:

> The abrupt climate change in the relatively recent past, merely 11,500 years ago, leads one to ask how often these things normally occur, even without a greenhouse warming. My count of the published records from the Greenland ice cores is roughly 20 cold spikes in the last 120,000 years for the North Atlantic region. And that is 40 sudden changes, either sudden cooling or sudden warming, every 3,000 years

on the average. It seems urgent that we use (computer) simulation to help figure out whether we might accelerate mode-switching behavior with our rapid forcing of the climate (via greenhouse gases), whether we might...trip one of those abrupt climate changes (236).

The emerging paradigm in geological thought seems to be a combination of both catastrophism and uniformitarianism, something which Boston University geologist Robert Schoch calls "punctuated equilibrium" (*Voices of the Rocks*, 1999). Schoch states he simply followed the evidence to his conclusion that the planet's chronology is "a sequence of steady states interrupted by periods of radical change" (interview with William P. Eigles, "In Defense of Catastrophes," *Atlantis Rising*, No. 19, 37).

What mechanisms account for catastrophic change? Natural events, such as random earthquakes, floods, and tornadoes, have some impact. But Schorch maintains that the most powerful impetus for these occurrences is extraterrestrial. That is, asteroids, meteorites, and comets (or bolides) may have significantly and abruptly altered the course of human civilization many times in the past. Some of these cosmic events are predictable. (Schoch estimates that the next predictable swarm of bolides will strike Earth around 2200 A.D.). What possible extraterrestrial agent exerted a traumatic influence on Earth in 10,000 B.C.?

Regardless of a scientist's theoretical bent, there is a widespread consensus that Earth underwent a very significant climate "event" twelve thousand years ago that ended the Paleolithic Era, eliminated dozens of animal and plant species, and severely impacted human culture for several centuries. Zoological, geophysical, and mythological evidence of such destruction abounds. Several new works present compelling research for catastrophic casualty of a non-terrestrial nature. Two principal ones will be noted here.

Physicist and systems scientist, Dr. Paul LaViolette, concludes that the trauma around 9500 B.C. resulted from a volley of cosmic waves emanating from an explosion at the galactic core. In *Earth Under Fire*, LaViolette explains that such explosions occur in 26,000 year cycles. Twenty-six thousand years is the length of one full precession of the equinoxes, or the period it takes for the wobbling North Pole to "draw" a complete circle and return to its original orientation.

Scientific data for the work at hand was drawn primarily from the prolific and very readable research of two British scientists, D. S. Allan of Cambridge, and J. B. Delair of Oxford. Their monumental book, *Cataclysm: Compelling Evidence of A Cosmic Catastrophe in 9500 B.C.*, published in the United States in 1997, chronicles numerous examples of zoological, geophysical, astronomical, and mythological evidence indicating major earth anomalies within a few hundred years of that date. Disturbances they cite include an initial heating of seas and earth surfaces, bombardment by astral debris, uplifting of major mountain ranges, massive crustal ruptures, collapse of sea beds, redepositing of marine sediments at alpine sites, widespread volcanism and lava flow, submersion of old land masses such as Beringia, deposit of erratic boulders, and hurricane-force winds. Other changes include aberrations in the earth's orbit, reversal of earth's polarity (the "Gothenberg flip"), interruption of the magma tides, the annihilation of millions of animals, and a precipitous drop in world temperatures.

Though the event was so traumatic it nearly annihilated Earth, it was not cyclical in nature and thus is unlikely to be repeated soon.

The source of such destruction? After reviewing all the known astronomical possibilities for an event of this magnitude, Allan and Delair conclude that the most likely agent was the violent and relatively close explosion of the Vela Supernova in 11,000 B.C. Debris from this explosion, they state, careened across interstellar space on a mad path toward the electromagnetic pull of the sun, acquiring a high electromagnetic potential of its own. The Shining One was a portion of that exploded astral matter. This plummeting remnant became visible from Earth some 1500 years after the explosion, allowing astonished humans to track its awesome journey for almost twenty years and heating the atmosphere as it approached. Its disintegration became the stuff of worldwide legends in which "the sky made war on the earth."

Such legends, in conjunction with painstaking research, may provide a clearer window to our physical past. Relegated to the basement of history for centuries, catalogued as soulful myth or the colorful legends of simple people, ancient stories are re-emerging with messages for today. Allan and Delair have retrieved hundreds of these tales from all reaches of the planet. Again and again, the stories our ancestors told are much the same.

Hesoid's *Theogony*, for example, recounts the memory of a great and fiery conflagration, beginning when a celestial body was cast from the sky and ending when a flood ravaged the earth. North American Indians tell of an archaic time when a rain of fire fell upon Earth so that all that existed burned. Toltec legend concurs. Forty other legends recount the same story.

The myths often share the observation that the blazing celestial visitors to Earth included one major body, a smaller body, and a "host" of attendants. The objects, long tails streaming behind them, were sometimes thought to be gods and hailed as "serpents," "leviathans," and "dragons."

Iceland's *Ragnorak Epic* recounts how:

[A] shining monster...remains in the sky until the last, to fling fire over the whole world, so that the race of man perishes with the gods, and all are finally engulfed in an overwhelming sea (Allan 275).

To the Greeks, the larger astral remnant was *Typhon* or *Phaeton*. To the Egyptians it was known as *Set*, another term for the Hebrew name *Satan*. The visions of John in the Book of Revelations reflect this same legend:

And war broke out in heaven: Michael and his angels fought against the dragon; and the dragon and his angels fought, but they did not prevail, nor was there a place for them in heaven any longer. So the great dragon was cast out, that serpent of old, called the Devil and Satan, who deceives the whole world. He was cast to the earth, and his angels were cast out with him (Revelations 12: 7-9).

Following a fiery attack from heaven, three other commonalities often figure in these catastrophic tales: the shift of Earth on its axis, a flood, and a global winter. Early Native Americans tell of a terrifying celestial event which "turned the world upside down" (Allan 114, quoted from Lockett, *Unwritten Literature of the Hopi*, 1933). Plato, in his work *Timeaus*, which includes a description of the destruction of Atlantis in 9600 B.C., states that Earth moved "forward and backward, and again to the right and left, and upward and downwards, wandering everyway in all six directions" (191). The Andaman Islanders and the Greenland Eskimos say that long ago "the earth capsized" (118). After the fiery attack and the shifting of the poles comes a great flood. Then, finally, a fourth commonality emerges after the floodwaters recedes: an endless winter in which bitter cold covers the earth and the sun forgets to shine.

Do these celestial sagas contain more than imaginary adventures? Might some be the records of actual occurrences, couched in the symbolic language of mathematics and metaphor? If we still our minds and listen, perhaps we will hear the voice of an ancient ancestor calling us from the grave, telling us that life is fragile and unpredictable, and our history far more immense than we have ever dreamed.

Bibliography

Adams, Raymond, M. Victor and A. Roper. *Principles of Neurology: Major Categories of Neurological Disease.* New York: McGraw-Hill, 1997, 568-569.

Alley, Richard B. and Michael L. Bender. "Greenland Ice Cores: Frozen in Time." *Scientific American* February 1998: 80-85.

Asimov, Isaac. *The Space Spotter's Guide.* New York: Dell, 1989.

Bates, Albert. *Climate in Crisis.* Summertown, Tennessee:1990.

Bebeau, Cher and Charles Bebeau. "Archetypes: The Goddesses and Gods Behind the Drama." *The Resurrection of the Dark Mother.* Unpubl. Boulder: Avalon Institute.

Bright, Chris. "Tracking the Ecology of Climate Change." *World Watch: State of the World 1997,* 78-94.

Bryant, Page. *Starwalking: Shamanic Practices for Traveling into the Night Sky.* Sante Fe: Bear, 1997.

Buhner, Stephen Harrod. "Sacred Plant Medicine." *Shaman's Drum* Fall *1994*: 25-31.

Burenhult, Goran, ed. *The First Humans: Human Origins and History to 10,000 BC.* San Francisco: Harper, 1993.

Calvin, William. *The Ascent Of Mind: Ice Age Climates and the Evolution of Intelligence.* New York: Bantam, 1991. "Climate Instability and Hominid Brain Evolution." Abst. *American Geophysical Union,* 18 June 1998. "The Great Climate Flip-Flop." *Atlantic Monthly* January 1998: 47-64.

Campbell, Joseph, ed. *The Portable Jung.* New York: Viking, 1971.

Clarke, G. *The Stone Age Hunters.* New York: McGraw-Hill, 1967.

de Chardin, Teilhard. *Hymn of the Universe.* New York: Harper and Row, 1965.

Delair, J. B. and D.S. Allan. *Cataclysm: Compelling Evidence of a Cosmic Catastrophe in 9500 B.C.* Sante Fe: Bear, 1997.

Ehrenberg, Margaret. *Women in Prehistory.* Norman: Oklahoma UP, 1989.

Eigles, William. "In Defense of Catastrophes: Interview with Robert Schoch." *Atlantis Rising* No. 19: 37, 68.

Eisler, Riane. *The Chalice and the Blade.* San Francisco: Harper, 1987. *Sacred Pleasures.* 1995.

Eisley, Loren. "Man." *The Random House Encyclopedia,* 1983.

Emery, K. O. "Sea Levels 7000-20,000 Years Ago." *Science* 11 August 1967.

Emiliani, Cesare. "Ancient Temperatures." *Scientific American* February 1958.

Gamble, Clive. *Timewalkers: the Prehistory of Global Colonization.* Cambridge: Harvard UP, 1994.

Gardner, John, trans. *Gilgamesh.* New York: Knaupf, 1984.

Gimbutas, Marija. *The Civilization of the Goddess: the World of Old Europe.* London: Thames and Hudson, 1991. *The Goddesses and Gods of Old Europe: 6500-3500 B.C., Myths and Cult Images.* 1982. *The Language of the Goddess: Unearthing the Hidden Symbols of Western Civilization.* 1989.

Goodman, Jeffrey. *The Genesis Mystery.* New York: Times Book P, 1983.

Gore, Rick. "The Dawn of Humans: Neanderthals." *National Geographic* January 1996: 3-23.

Graham, Rex. "Making an Exceptional Impact." *Astronomy* May 1998: 36-41.

Guterl, Fred. "The Panther Mountain Crater." *Discover* August 2000: 52-59.

Hadingham, Evan. *Secrets of the Ice Age.* New York: Walkers, 1979.

Hancock, Graham. *Fingerprints of the Gods: the Evidence of Earth's Lost Civilization.* New York: Crown, 1995.

Hapgood, Charles. *The Path of the Pole.* New York: Chilton, 1970.

Harner, Michael. *The Way of the Shaman.* San Francisco: Harper, 1990.

Hays, J. D., John Imbrie, and N. J Shackleton. "Variations in the Earth's Orbit: Pacemaker of the Ice Ages." *Science* December 1976: 1121-1132.

Heggie, D.C. ed. *Archaeastronomy in the Old World.* Cambridge: Cambridge UP, 1982.

Hopkins, John-Mark and Wilson Sibbett. "Who Were the First Americans?" *Scientific American* September 2000: 79-87.

Jacobi, Jolande. *The Portable Jung.* New Haven: Yale UP, 1973.

Jaynes, Julian. *The Origin of Consciousness in the Breakdown of the Bicameral Mind.* Boston: Houghton Mifflin, 1976.

Jung, Carl. *Memories, Dreams, Reflections.* New York: Vintage, 1989.

Kunzig, Robert. "A Tale of Two Archaeologists." *Discover* May 1999: 84-89.

Kurten, Bjorn. *The Ice Age.* New York: Putnam, 1972.

Krupp, Edwin. *Echoes of the Ancient Skies: the Archaeoastronomy of Lost Civilizations.* New York: Harper and Row, 1983.

LaViolette, Paul. *Earth Under Fire: Humanity's Survival of the Apocalypse.* Schenectady, New York: Starlane P, 1997.

Linden. Eugene. "Lost Tribes, Lost Knowledge." *Time* 23 September 1991: 46-56.

Liss, Tony M. and Paul L. Tipton. "The Discovery of the Top Quark." *Scientific American* September 1997: 54-59.

Lopez, Harry Holstrum. *Of Wolves and Men.* New York: Scribner's,1978.

Loye, David. *The Sphynx and the Rainbow: Brain, Mind, and Future Vision.* New York: Random House, 1983.

Marshack, Alexander. *The Roots of Civilization.* New York: McGraw-Hill, 1972.

Martin, Paul S., et al. "An Ice Age Murder Mystery: What Killed the Mammoths?" *Discovering Archaeology*, September/October 1999: 30-56.

Matthews, Caitlin, et al. "The Goddess." *Gnosis* Fall 1989: 18-67.

McCoy, Ron. *Archaeoastronomy: Skywatching in the Native American Southwest.* Flagstaff: Museum of Northern Arizona P, 1992.

McInnis, Doug. "And the Waters Prevailed: Two Geologists Trace Noah's Flood to the Violent Birth of the Black Sea." *Earth* August 1998: 46-49.

Meaden, Terrance. *Stonehenge: the Secret of the Solstice.* London: Souvenir P, 1997.

Menon, Shanti. "Indus Valley, Inc." *Discover* December 1998: 67-71.

Metzner, Ralph. *The Well of Remembrance: Rediscovering the Earth Wisdom Myths of Northern Europe.* Boston: Shambhala, 1994.

Miles, Hugh. *The Track of the Wild Otter.* New York: St. Martin's Press, 1984.

Milisauskas, Sarunas. *European Prehistory.* New York: Academic P, 1978.

Neumann, Erich. *The Great Mother: an Analysis of the Archetype.* Princeton: Princeton UP, 1974.

Olsen, Melvin. "The Bear." Baiki: the North American Journal of Sami *Living Spring* 1993: 6-7. "The Bear Hunt." *Baiki* Winter 1993: 8-9. "Siedde." Baiki Winter 1993: 6-7.

Phillips, Patricia. *The Prehistory of Europe.* Bloomington: Indiana UP, 1980.

Plato. *Timaeus and Critias.* London: Penguin, 1977.

Ponte, Lowell. *The Cooling.* Englewood Cliffs, New Jersey: Prentice-Hall, 1976.

Pringle, Heather. "New Women of the Ice Age." *Discover* April 1998. 62-69.

Rauber, Paul. "Heat Wave." *Sierra* September/October 1997: 34-41.

Revkin, Andrew. *Global Warming: Understanding the Forecast.* New York: Abbeville, 1992.

Reynolds, Jan. *Far North: Vanishing Cultures.* San Diego: Harcourt Brace, 1992.

Rudgley, Richard. *The Lost Civilizations of the Stone Age.* New York: Simon and Schuster, 1999.

Schick, K.D. and N. Toth. *Making Silent Stones Speak: Human Evolution and the Dawn of Technology.* New York: Touchstone, 1993.

Schneider, David. "The Rising Seas." *Scientific American* March 1997: 112-118.

Schneider, Stephen H. *Global Warming.* San Francisco: Sierra Book Club, 1989.

Schoch, Robert. *Voices of the Rocks: a Scientist Looks at Catastrophes and Ancient Civilizations.* New York: Harmony Books, 1999.

Settegast, Mary. *Plato Prehistorian: 10,000 to 5000 B.C. in Myth and Archaeology.* Cambridge, MA: Rotenberg, 1987.

Stanley, Steven M. *Children of the Ice Age: How Global Catastrophe Allowed Humans to Evolve.* New York: Crown, 1996.

Stern, Philip Van Doren. *Prehistoric Europe: from Stone Age Man to the Early Greeks.* New York: Norton,1969.

Velikovsky, Immanuel. *Earth in Upheaval.* New York: Pocket Books, 1977. *Mankind in Amnesia.* New York: Doubleday, 1982. *Worlds in Collision.* New York: Dell, 1950.

von Franz, Marie-Louise. *Creation Myths.* Boston: Shambhala, 1995.

Ward, Tim. "The Blood of Spring." *Common Boundary* March/April 1977: 32-34.

Watson, Traci. "What Causes Ice Ages?" *U.S. News and World* Report 16 August 1977: 58-60.

Wold, Peter O. *The Call of Distant Mammoths: Why the Ice Age Mammals Disappeared.* New York: Copernicus, Springer, Verlay, 1997.

Book Order Form

Additional copies of
The Light at the End of the World
are available by mail order:

	Qty	Price	Total
The Light at the End of the World		$19.95	
Subtotal			
Discounts **For 5 or more books, subtract 5%** of cover price **For 10 or more, subtract 10%** of cover price			
Sales Tax Residents of ND, add 6%			
Shipping & Handling Add $2.95 for each book			
TOTAL AMOUNT			

Make checks payable to:
ANGEL FIRE PRESS
P. O. Box 7374
Bismarck, ND 58501-7374